Trained as an actress, Barbara Nadel is now a public relations officer for the National Schizophrenia Fellowship's Good Companions Service. Her previous job was a mental health advocate in a psychiatric hospital. She has also worked with sexually abused teenagers and taught psychology in both schools and colleges. Born in the East End of London, she has been a regular visitor to Turkey for over twenty years.

Also by Barbara Nadel

Belshazzar's Daughter
A Chemical Prison

Arabesk

Barbara Nadel

HEADLINE

First published in hardback in 2000
by HEADLINE BOOK PUBLISHING

First published in paperback in 2001
by HEADLINE BOOK PUBLISHING

10 9 8 7 6 5

ISBN 0 7472 6219 5

Typeset by Palimpsest Book Production Limited,
Polmont, Stirlingshire
Printed and bound in Great Britain by
Clays Ltd, St Ives plc

HEADLINE BOOK PUBLISHING
A division of Hodder Headline
338 Euston Road
London NW1 3BH

www.headline.co.uk
www.hodderheadline.com

To my parents

Chapter 1

From the high vantage point of their apartment balcony the two men watched as the routines of the early morning city began to take shape. Men and women, still yawning and stretching from all too quickly curtailed sleep, slopped water across the pavements in front of their shops, cafés and lokantas. Preparation for the thick dust that would later come both from the already choking traffic and on the shoes of passing shoppers, commuters and tourists. And as the gathering pall of cigarette smoke hanging over the ever increasing group of shifty men assembling in Sultan Ahmet Square evidenced, tourists in particular were expected to be numerous. No self-respecting carpet or tour guide tout could or should still be in bed once the sun has risen over the Bosphorus. Some tourists like that sort of romantic nonsense, especially in the summertime when sleep is not that easy to come by. Up they get to watch the light hit the water, and then on their way back to their hotels and pansiyons satisfied, they will find it difficult not to be entranced by a truly beautiful carpet or the promise of a tour up to the legendary Forest of

1

Belgrade. And in truth the tourists usually get what they pay for – whatever that might be. In Istanbul, it is said, a man can very easily satisfy all of his desires both earthly and divine. That the getting of those desirables might lead such a man, or woman, to discontent or even rage has little to do with either the city or its inhabitants. When you have been on the world stage for as long as Istanbul you are expected to deliver a very great deal to those who come to visit you. Çetin İkmen regarded the swelling ranks of touts, dodgy dealers and others who have knowledge of tourists with something between contempt and admiration.

'If only I could look upon the carpet men with new eyes, I might find their predatory nature quite interesting,' he said as he lit what was his third cigarette of the morning.

The man standing beside him was slightly taller and considerably younger. In every other respect, however, (even down to his almost ceaseless cigarette smoking habit) he was almost an identical copy. 'Still bored, then?' the young man said as he turned to face his father.

'I have this unpleasant feeling that when I don't work I actually cease to exist.'

'You're right, in the sense that you've built your entire identity around being an inspector of police,' his son replied. 'Had you involved yourself in other things years ago you'd have more extensive inter-ests now.'

Although his son had spoken without any overt malice, İkmen's interpretation of his words was underpinned by his knowledge of his eldest son's opinions.

'You mean, I suppose,' he said, 'that I should have taken more account of you lot and your mother.'

'Amongst other things, yes. For instance you could have watched the football with the rest of us last night, but you chose to be out here being miserable.'

İkmen followed, with his eyes, the progress of a small, red-haired woman he knew to be a local prostitute. As she stopped at the cigarette kiosk across the road he recalled that she usually smoked Camels. As a sort of exercise in self-flagellation he attempted to recall what brand his son smoked, could not, and so descended into still deeper gloom.

'I don't like football, it precipitates crime,' he said, breathing heavily on the already stifling early morning air. 'Oh, Sınan, what can I possibly do with all this bloody leisure time! How can I go on without even a pathetic watery little beer?'

His son, almost despite himself, smiled. 'Dr Akkale, as you well know, has said that if you rest, eat properly and refrain from alcohol, you could be back at work in a month. Thinking of sick leave as "leisure", which you hate, is only helping to make you more anxious. And that makes your condition worse.'

'You think so? I mean professionally. Not as my son but as a doctor?'

'I'm no expert on stomach ulcers, but I've witnessed

my fair share of patients with a negative attitude towards their condition, whatever that may be, and I know that it really doesn't help.' For just a second he put one hand gently on his father's thin shoulder. 'If you could just relax, watch television – not football, other things – talk about nothing to Mum and the children, read . . . You're a very literate man. You always encouraged us to read.'

'Yes, but at my age I think I might have read most things actually *worth* reading.'

'Oh, what utter nonsense!' And as if to illustrate his point, Sınan reached across to the small table that routinely collected both dust and books from all those members of the İkmen family who liked using the balcony. He picked, at random, one volume from the pile. 'Have you read this?'

İkmen, whose eyesight had in the last year started to deteriorate, leaned back a little the better to see the title. '*The Black Book* by Orhan Pamuk,' he read and then shrugged. 'So?'

'It's very good. Unlike most of the things you have read in the past it has been written by someone who is alive, Turkish and sober. But don't let that put you off.'

Vague mutterings about the benefits of reading the works of Thomas Hardy in the original English accompanied a very cursory perusal by İkmen of this, to him, very new author's work.

'Basically, it's a detective novel,' Sınan explained,

'but it is also a work of philosophy which tackles the problem of who we are, as Turks.'

'Eh?'

'It's like a collage, but of ideas as opposed to pictures. It's clever and witty and it's about—'

Just at that moment Sınan's exposition was drowned out by an extremely loud burst of Arabesk music emanating from the open door of a taxi in the street below. An uneasy blend of traditional Turkish tunes and ornate Egyptian laments, Arabesk is for good reason sometimes dubbed the 'music of the slums'. Most of its performers, many of whom originate from the countryside, possess keen, often painful memories of poverty amongst the shanty districts and cheap tower blocks which even now house many of those peasants who come to the city in search of work. Always mournful and sometimes also critical of the plight of the poor, Arabesk has by turns been patronised by politicians and banned by same on the pretext that it undermines the nation's happiness. Not that the millions of its devotees care about such opinions. To İkmen and his son, however, whose faces only relaxed out of their grimaces when the music had ceased, Arabesk was anathema.

'Miserable, sentimentalised excrement!' İkmen said in a voice loud enough to permit those in the street below access to his opinions.

His son shrugged. 'It's as much a part of our national identity as lokum, or the harem system or this mad belief we all possess that if we copy them closely enough the Europeans might just get to like us one day.'

İkmen smiled. 'So are you now one of those who believe we should turn our eyes eastwards?'

'No. But as Pamuk illustrates again and again in his writings, we are some of the most contradictory of Allah's creatures. The stereotypically cruel Turk who is also the willing butt of arrogant European jokes. The melancholy, lovelorn Turk who is at the same time both faithless and subtle. Our women smoke, drink and work like men and yet they still live lives circumscribed by their fathers and husbands. I could go on and on.'

'Yes,' his father agreed, 'you probably could.' Then moving forward to take the book from his son's hands he said, 'But far better if I read this. If this Pamuk is as good as you say I will discover it rather more eloquently from his words.' He sighed. 'And if it's a detective novel too then so much the better.'

Sınan wiped the first bead of sweat of the day from his brow and then smiled. 'You'll be able to pick holes in his method.'

'I expect I will. And I'll probably become angry in the process and might need to be left alone for a while in order to rage.'

'So if I hear you huffing and swearing as if you're actually in physical pain . . .'

'You will know that I am simply enjoying a good read about murder, Turkish identity and lokum.'

'And not—'

'And not intoxicated in any way, shape or form. Just stimulated and annoyed.' He laughed and then lit another cigarette.

'Right,' Sınan agreed, lighting one of his own.

'OK.'

'OK, Dad, fine.'

Gently, but with some insistence, Sınan reached out and took the book from his father's hands.

Confused by this action, İkmen mumbled, 'Hey! What the—'

'Nice try, Dad,' the younger man said as he clutched the book tightly to his chest. 'But if you think that anyone in this family is going to leave you alone in the apartment for more than a minute, even if it is just supposedly to read a book, then you must think again.'

Uncharacteristically, İkmen was, for a moment, dumbstruck.

'You see, Dad,' his son continued, 'I know all about your bribing Bulent to buy you a bottle of brandy. Which, by the way, he and his friend have now probably consumed.' He held up one small hand in order to silence his blustering, red-faced father. 'I know this because when you tricked Mum into leaving the house this morning, I got up and intercepted my brother before he could see you. Bulent is now at

Sami's apartment and when he returns some time later on today he will, knowing him, have a very sore head. You will have no brandy and I might as well continue to read this book which will not now provide you with a cover for your drinking activities.'

İkmen, livid and desperate, raked his fingers viciously through the strands of his thick, greying hair. 'But I am so bored with this illness! I'm so sick of the pain! I am so humiliated to be so fucking useless!' Then turning to face his son, his eyes just a little wet from tears of frustration, he added, 'And I am so ashamed of what must be the most amateurish attempt at deception in all the history of dishonesty!'

Sınan smiled. 'It was quite dreadful, yes. Were you not unwell I would be afraid that you might have—'

'Lost the plot? Yes,' İkmen said, turning to look out into the sun-flooded street once again, 'yes, I feel very much like that myself. When I'm not feeling nauseous I'm having my guts stabbed from inside by some invisible bastard. It's hell! All I want to do is get back to how I was before – go back to work and, yes, have a *few* drinks just to make the day run more smoothly. Be myself with all my faults and foibles and . . . and, oh, just do what I do!'

'Until you get better you can't.'

'But while I'm idle like this I'm tense!' As if to illustrate the point, İkmen held his slightly shaking fingers up to his son's face. 'What if they decide to force me to accept retirement? They've already made Suleyman up to inspector.'

'At your request, Dad.'

'I can't dispute that. Nor would I change it. I like him. He's a good man and a fine officer. But,' and here he shrugged, a half smile hanging loosely about his lips – hopelessness tinged with just the slightest hint of his usual sharp humour, 'but if I, ulcer or no ulcer, do not get back to my work soon I am going to turn into one of those contradictory men your Mr Pamuk speaks of.'

'Identity confusion is common to all Turks.'

'Oh, is it?' With some difficulty İkmen pulled himself up to his full height. 'I think not. Well, at least it isn't for me, or rather it wasn't until I got this bastard illness.'

'Yes, but Dad—'

'No! I know you think that all this rest nonsense is the answer to my problems, but I know myself better than anyone and I can tell you that it is not. I need to be out there,' he said, sweeping both arms out across the dramatic panorama of the old city, the Blue Mosque, the Hippodrome, Aya Sofya – his city, 'on the street with Suleyman, Cohen, Arto Sarkissian, even bloody Ardiç.'

Sınan, who found his father's fiery eyes and heroic posture just a little amusing, pulled İkmen's arms back down to his sides. 'Sorry, Dad,' he said, 'but the Eva Peron pose was just a little bit too much for me.'

Suddenly deflated and, if the truth be known, also very tired, İkmen sank down heavily onto one of the wooden chairs that ringed the small table. 'Sorry.'

'That's OK. I just wish I could help you, that's all. But until you've something to do that you actually *want* to do, I don't see how any progress can be made.'

'I must await developments,' İkmen said with a shrug.

Sınan sat down beside his father and took one of his hands gently between his fingers. 'Perhaps you should look upon this time in the same light you do when you are waiting for a break in one of your cases.'

'Dead time.'

Sınan laughed. 'Is that what you call it?'

'Yes,' İkmen said, his thin face resolving into the ghost of a grin.

'So what do you normally do during dead time then?' Sınan asked hopefully. Perhaps his father could use some of his dead time activities now.

'Well, first I bend my mind to the problem in as concentrated a fashion as I can,' İkmen explained.

'And then?'

'And then I get horribly drunk, consult a few dubious soothsayers and generally come up with some sort of plan from thereon.'

'Dad!'

'Well, you asked,' İkmen said, his eyes twinkling evilly. 'You asked, I told you, you didn't like my answer . . .'

'Which leaves us precisely where?' Sınan said, letting go of his father's hands and lighting another cigarette.

İkmen, who joined his son in yet another smoke, put his head down into his hands and sighed. 'Awaiting developments, I suppose,' he said. And then through gritted, furious teeth, 'Patiently, fucking waiting!'

When what is now İstiklal Caddesi was called the Grand Rue de Pera, back in Ottoman times when heavily fezzed Sultans routinely appointed food tasters, comical midgets and other such exotica, the apartments that still line this great thoroughfare were predominantly residential. More recently, however, due to a combination of high rents, lack of modern amenities and a certain shabbiness not entirely acceptable to younger Turkish citizens, many of these dwellings are now used as offices or storerooms. Nestling between shops selling Nike, Armani or Hugo Boss, once impressive, heavily stuccoed doorways can easily be found by those with an eye for such things. Lintels bearing legends written in the Roman alphabet proudly proclaim 'Apartments Paris', 'Apartments de Grand Rue de Pera'; examples all of the late nineteenth-century Ottomans' love of and undying admiration for anything and everything Gallic. That most of these once elegant apartment buildings now house either large numbers of fake Lacoste sweatshirts or groups of young men and women working diligently

11

at word-processors and chattering mainly in Turkish is merely a reflection of how quickly and totally times have changed. So common is it for these once elegant, now draughty apartments to be used for commercial purposes that the few that remain as residences are almost ignored.

It was therefore into an İstiklal Caddesi unaccustomed to the tragedies of birth, marriage and death that the young man with the sharp Kurdish features ran when he found the body of the young woman. Out of his home in the Apartments İzzet Paşa and into a street that, early in the morning as it was, remained almost as still as it had been at four and five, the dead hours of the night. Only two old men, peasants in felt caps, smoking cheap cigarettes and clacking rosaries between their fingers, saw the youngster as he passed, weeping and red-faced, like a fallen angel tearing madly away from his wrathful God. Not that the men commented, of course. The young man obviously had problems of some sort, but given his current condition, it would be both difficult and probably prurient for either of the old men to inquire what they might be.

What they did comment upon, however, was his identity.

'Wasn't that, you know,' the shabbier of the two asked his slightly more modish companion, 'that singer, the one who . . .'

'Has relations with that blonde,' the other replied in hushed, scandalised tones. 'Allah will punish such

unnatural behaviour,' and then raising his arms heavenwards in a gesture of supplication, he added, 'if it
please Him.'

His friend sighed heavily as he watched the rapidly
retreating back of the young man and then said softly,
'I think his punishment, by the look of him, has already
come to pass.'

Living with others, however kind and tolerant those
others might be, is never easy. Ever since he'd separated from his wife the previous year, the newly
promoted Inspector Suleyman had been renting a room
from one of his more lowly colleagues, Constable
Cohen. Although completely different in nearly all
respects, including age, religion, class and values,
Suleyman and Cohen had first become friends when
the former was still in uniform. And in spite of
Suleyman's rapid rise to inspector, they had remained
close. Indeed when the younger man had first left his
wife, Cohen had permitted him to stay rent-free to
allow, as he put it, 'the bastard lawyers to screw your
bank account'.

Loud, colourful and kind, Cohen and his wife Estelle
included the elegant and cultured Suleyman in all their
pursuits both familial and religious. As well as being
expertly catered for by them with regard to his own
Muslim calendar, Suleyman had been included in
celebrations to mark Passover and Chanukah. He had
also attended a vast and, as it turned out, ill-fated

meal to mark the return of the Cohens' eldest son, Yusuf, from his tour of conscript duty in the eastern provinces. Wounded in places the eye could never see, this young man's bizarre behaviour at that dinner had been just the start of what turned out to be a very rapid descent into psychiatric instability. When Yusuf was finally admitted to an institution, Suleyman, as well as the Cohens themselves, had felt sad but relieved.

However, to say that Suleyman had experienced a quiet life since Yusuf's departure would be erroneous. As well as having to endure the sound of Estelle's frequent rages at the endless sexual faithlessness of her husband, there were the neighbours to take account of too. Cohen's apartment, though large, was not situated in the best part of Istanbul. Karaköy, which is that district that runs from the eastern end of the Galata Bridge up the hill of the same name to İstiklal Caddesi, is not for the faint-hearted. Though dotted with many fine old buildings, some of Genoese and Armenian origin, plus the now lovingly restored Neve Shalom Synagogue, Karaköy also possesses its share of tatty apartment buildings. The one the Cohens had moved into twenty-six years previously was the one they still lived in now. Not once in all those years had the place been so much as painted, let alone properly decorated. With the notable exceptions of one new television and an even more erratic plumbing system, nothing much had changed in all that time, at least not for the better anyway. The locals had always been dubious but in the last ten years they had become, to use a Cohenism, far more 'serious'. Despite the very best efforts of the city authorities, now run by the traditional Refah party, to flush such elements out, the old ways died hard. Indeed, in this case, they actually prospered. And, although the cheap dancing girls, petty thieves and even the legal brothels had gone away, they had been replaced mainly by full-on, streetwalking prostitutes and drug dealers. The very loud and very young girl who lived in the apartment next door and who routinely woke Suleyman in the middle of the night with her harsh laugh and passion-filled screams was quite openly a cocaine addict. That she knowingly lived next door to two police officers did not restrict her behaviour in any way. It had about as much effect upon her as it did upon her enormous pimp who liked to laugh out loud at Cohen's diminutive figure. That the criminal had access to far more sophisticated and greater numbers of weapons than the law man had much to do with this casual disdain. The effect upon Suleyman of all this was to make him angry and, despite his feelings for Cohen, very anxious to leave as soon as his finances permitted. Sleeplessness of the order he was experiencing now was neither healthy nor good for his new, far more responsible position in life.

Until almost exactly four weeks previously, Mehmet Suleyman had been a sergeant working for the city's leading homicide detective, Çetin İkmen. Although happy in his work, Suleyman was both ambitious and, especially since his separation from his wife Zuleika, extremely needy where money was concerned. So at the end of the previous year, 1998, he had put in for promotion. Supported by İkmen he had, after not too long a wait (given the gargantuan bureaucracy of the Turkish police establishment), achieved the promotion he desired and had hoped to work beside his old boss for quite some time before being let loose on his own initiative. But then İkmen, who had, as far as Suleyman was concerned, always complained of stomach pains, had suddenly become very ill indeed. Initially admitted to hospital, İkmen had been diagnosed with multiple duodenal ulcers. Although he would need surgery at some time in the future, for the moment he was prescribed medication, dietary restrictions and rest. Just thinking about this regime made Suleyman's handsome features resolve into a wry smile. The 'old man' was almost as passionately attached to the notion of eating irregularly (and then only junk) as he was to his beloved brandy and cigarettes, his twin, if second-league, obsessions. His first was his work. According to the inspector's eldest son, Sınan, to whom Suleyman had spoken the previous evening, İkmen was not only plotting to get hold of alcohol at every possible opportunity but was also going a little mad from his enforced idleness.

Suleyman put his tired head in his hands and yawned. Although there were other experienced detectives in the homicide division with whom he could, theoretically, discuss the more troubling aspects of his new position in life, he knew that they saw him as a dangerous rival – people like old Yalçin who openly mocked Suleyman's aristocratic background while at the same time telling others to 'watch out' for the younger man's keen intelligence. You didn't get this sort of thing from İkmen who, better than the lot of them put together, would have gladly backed his protégé in any argument with old guard types – and enjoyed it.

It was in these silent, between-shift moments that Suleyman missed İkmen the most. The old man had always come in early and had always been there when Suleyman arrived, alert and ready for at least a short discussion of any lingering woes the younger man may have carried with him from the previous day. But, sick or well, the relationship between İkmen and himself was due to alter, at least in the working environment. Now Suleyman was responsible not only for his own security and actions but for that of his new sergeant too. İsak Çöktin, at twenty-five, resembled in some ways the youthful enthusiast that Suleyman himself had once been. Although some had seen his assignment to Suleyman's command as a subtle snub to the stylish aristocrat, Suleyman himself did not view it in that light. Whether or not Çöktin was a 'mountain Turk', that bland euphemism for those of Kurdish descent, as some of the older and more conservative elements whispered he was, did not concern Suleyman. Çöktin had been born and brought up in Istanbul, in admittedly one of the more downmarket districts. And though his tousled red hair did point towards blood that was not entirely Turkish, his record as an officer was impeccable. That İkmen personally liked him a lot was also a plus. İkmen, who by his own admission was the son of an Albanian soothsayer, possessed an almost unfailing sixth sense when it came to judging people's characters. And 'Mickey', as he had dubbed Çöktin because of his almost uncanny resemblance to the scruffy American film star Mickey Rourke, was 'all right'. Just how 'all right' Çöktin was, Suleyman wasn't to learn until he picked up the telephone which now buzzed harshly at his tired ears.

'Suleyman,' he drawled by way of introduction.

'Inspector, it's Çöktin,' a voice barely capable of containing its excitement replied.

Suleyman sat up just a little bit straighter. 'Where are you? What's going on?'

'I'm at the İzzet Paşa Apartments on İstiklal Caddesi.' Then pausing briefly to take a large, nerve-calming breath, he added, 'I'm with Erol Urfa, or at least I was until—'

'From your tone,' Suleyman interrupted, 'I take it we are talking about *the* Erol Urfa?'

'The Arabesk star, yes, sir.' With even greater excitement he added, 'Actually in the next room from where I'm standing now, actually, sir.'

'Really? Why?'

Silence greeted Suleyman's inquiry and so he couched his question in rather more overt terms. 'Why are you there with Mr Urfa is what I'm trying to get at, Çöktin.'

'Oh, well, because he says his wife has been murdered, sir.'

Suleyman, as if shocked by a current of electricity, stood up. 'What!'

'Yes, here in his apartment. The body's in the kitchen.'

'Are you sure?'

'Well, without jeopardising the integrity of the site more than I had to, I did check and anyway it was quite obvious—'

'No! No!' Suleyman put his hand up to his head and held what was now a lightly perspiring brow. 'What I mean is, are you sure that the woman is his wife?'

'So he says.'

Suleyman sighed, speaking again on the outgoing breath. 'OK,' he said, 'I'll be with you as soon as I can. Keep Mr Urfa away from the site so that the doctor and forensic don't have to deal with too much conflicting information.'

'OK.'

Then just before Suleyman replaced the receiver, a thought occurred to him which rather graphically made him suddenly aware of just how inexperienced he was. 'Oh, and Çöktin, er . . .'

'Yes, sir?'

'What leads you, apart from Mr Urfa's opinion, to deduce that this lady has been murdered?'

'The smell of bitter almonds,' Çöktin said with the simple clarity of one who knows he need elaborate no further.

Chapter 2

The man who had really rather frightened İsak Çöktin when he first saw him running up to and screaming 'Help me!' at the kiosk where he was buying cigarettes was now sitting as silently as stone on what was probably his bed. Dr Sarkissian, although a pathologist by profession, was always mindful of the pain the living frequently experienced in the presence of the dead and had, in order to alleviate Mr Urfa's hysteria, administered ten milligrams of something Çöktin could not remember to the traumatised man. Known simply as 'Erol' to his millions of dedicated fans, Urfa looked in reality rather older than his reported twenty-five years and, probably unsurprisingly, less handsome than his publicity photographs. Not, of course, that those wolves from the press and television stations would be fazed by Erol's uncharacteristically haggard looks when they did, probably sooner rather than later, set up camp outside the scene of this tragedy. Big stars equalled big headlines, especially when they involved not only murder but also a juicy secret.

Erol Urfa, known to his most passionate devotees

as 'The Sad Nightingale', had shot to fame four years earlier via his rendition of the extremely sentimental song of the same name. Originating as he had from some tiny, obscure village in the east, fame had very quickly overwhelmed Erol who had, according to those who cared about Arabesk, made some very bizarre decisions. The most notable of these was his much publicised affair with the veteran Arabesk star, Tansu Hanım. Although as blonde, if not more so, than Madonna at her sleaziest, and notwithstanding millions of liras' worth of plastic surgery, Tansu had to be, by old Inspector İkmen's reckoning, at least the same age as he was. So even saying she was fifty was being kind.

Of course to someone of Çöktin's age, such a strange course of action had to have reasons that had nothing to do with love. There were numerous possibilities. When he first came to the city, Erol had been fresh and lacking in credibility. The vastly experienced Tansu would have given him that as well as enhancing her own flagging career with his vibrant and youthful presence. What that presence did for her bedtime activities was also quite easy to see as well. And with managers and agents, if the press were to be believed, involved in every aspect of the lives of the rich and famous, who could even begin to guess what influence they were also exerting upon this pair? Not that Erol and Tansu's relationship was in any sense a secret. Pictures of them holding hands, kissing or just shopping appeared almost weekly in most of the newspapers. What was a secret, however, and a big one, was the existence of the girl now lying dead in Urfa's kitchen. If the woman who looked, even in death, like a peasant girl of no more than sixteen was indeed Erol's wife then firstly, why had he kept her a secret and secondly, why had he married her after the beginning of his affair with Tansu?

'Sergeant Çöktin?'

He turned round quickly at the sound of his name and found himself facing a police photographer. 'Yes?'

'Inspector Suleyman wants you.'

With a brief nod of acknowledgement, Çöktin glanced just once more at the motionless Erol Urfa before moving off in the direction of the kitchen.

Although for some the mere appearance of men within a kitchen is incongruous, the two that Çöktin found himself facing as he entered looked far more comfortable in that setting than the dead woman at their feet must have done when she was alive. Although not nearly as elegant as the younger, slimmer Suleyman, Dr Arto Sarkissian possessed the same sort of casual grace and wore similar, if larger, designer suits. Both blended very easily with the clinically beautiful, all-metal German kitchen. The girl, in her multi-coloured, multi-layered, heavily headscarfed ensemble, looked like little more than a bundle of rags.

'Well, Çöktin,' the Armenian said with his customary, almost unfathomable jollity, 'you were right, I believe, about the substance involved.'

'Cyanide?'

'A distinctive bitter almonds smell plus the livid appearance of the hypostasis would seem to suggest death by oxygen starvation. Carbon monoxide can cause the same effect in the skin but not the bitter almond aroma. A most excellent preliminary deduction on your part. Well done.'

'Thank you, sir.'

Then, turning to Suleyman once again, the doctor continued, 'I will of course have to test in order to confirm my findings, but I think it is only a formality. There are some interesting deposits in Mrs Urfa's mouth which suggest she may have ingested the substance in food, but we'll see.'

'Could she have done it herself?' Suleyman asked as he looked down at the dead woman with more, or so Çöktin thought, than a little distaste.

The doctor briefly sucked his bottom lip before answering. 'Mmm. Suicide. Could always be, of course, but with, so far, no note to that effect I can't be certain. There is a pen, as you can see, on the table, but . . . Once the forensics are completed I'll be in more of a position to say. However . . .'

'Yes?'

'I have my own thoughts. Strange as it may seem in a world characterised by the Internet and remote guidance weapons systems, we could have a good old-fashioned poisoning on our hands.'

Suleyman smiled. 'I wasn't aware that that method had gone out of style.'

'Oh, it hasn't. As you and I both know, Inspector, people are regularly despatched via overdoses of drugs both prescribed and illicit. But real, honest-to-God poisons are unusual. With the exception of weedkiller, actual poisons rarely turn up in our line of work – ask Çetin İkmen if you don't believe me.'

Çöktin, who had been listening very attentively to all this, bent down and looked searchingly into the woman's horrified open eyes. When alive, he imagined she must have looked something like his own mother when she married his father. Child brides both, certainly in his mother's case, from some little village so insignificant it barely boasted a name.

'When women are poisoned,' the doctor continued, 'I subconsciously, I must say, see the shadow of the harem.'

Suleyman gave Sarkissian one of his almost obscenely perfect smiles. 'You are, I take it, theorising that a woman may have perpetrated this act?'

'Oh no,' Sarkissian replied, waving his hands dismissively in front of his face. 'I am just a doctor, not a theorist. That is your job, my dear Suleyman.'

'But?'

'But,' he was smiling again now, obviously pleased to give vent to his thoughts however off kilter they might be, 'our Mr Urfa is extremely popular with women. I thought, as I expect you did too, that he was solely involved with the lovely Tansu Hanım. And if I am shocked that he has this little wife then perhaps others were surprised also. Surprised and envious maybe. Not that my silly, florid mind is totally obsessed by old harem tales of women slipping poisons into the sherbet of their rivals, you understand . . .'

'But it is a most unexpected turn of events nevertheless,' Suleyman concluded.

'Talk!'

All three men turned to face the source of the harsh, rather common voice that came from the man now slumped against the doorway of the kitchen.

'While you talk you do nothing about my Merih,' Urfa growled, pushing roughly against the hand of a young constable who was now, too late, attempting to restrain him.

Moving forward in order to protect the gaze of his live patient from the face of his deceased charge, Arto Sarkissian put one friendly hand out towards the famous singer in a gesture of concern. 'Now—'

'Merih,' the man repeated the name, his voice now clearly exhibiting that deliberate but slurred quality of the unhappily sedated.

'No, Ruya,' the doctor corrected, 'or that was what I thought you said your wife's name was.'

'Yes, Ruya, my wife, she was, is . . .' Urfa slumped

26

forward a little, his head dropping towards the doctor's shoulder in a movement of despair. 'And Merih . . .'

Suddenly and for no reason that he could logically fathom, Suleyman was possessed by a shiver of apprehension. The sort of feeling İkmen had always told him he must learn to trust. 'Who is Merih, Mr Urfa?' he asked. 'If Ruya was your wife, then Merih is . . . ?'

Looking past the doctor's shoulder, directly at the body of his wife, Urfa whispered, 'She is our daughter. She is just ten weeks old.'

'But . . .'

Then, his eyes filling and finally overflowing with tears, Urfa choked, 'She was with her mother. She was always with her mother! But now she has gone. I see her nowhere.' And with that his eyes turned up inside his head as he lost consciousness.

In retrospect, a pink, open-necked shirt was not as respectful an ensemble as he would have liked for the occasion, but then when one is in a hurry one does not always think of such things. And İbrahim Aksoy had been in a tearing hurry as soon as he had put the phone down on the luminous Tansu Hanım less than half an hour before. When, so the star had told him, she had earlier that morning attempted to contact Erol Urfa at his İstiklal Caddesi apartment, she had been answered not by her beloved but by a very curt man who had informed her that Mr Urfa was currently 'indisposed'. Quite who this person was, why he was in Erol's apartment and what this 'indisposition' might consist of was not disclosed. But Tansu had been worried enough to contact the only person she knew she could really trust vis-à-vis Erol, his manager İbrahim Aksoy. As, effectively, the owner of the young superstar, Aksoy would either maximise publicity for his charge's indisposition, if that were appropriate, or cover it up in as diplomatic a fashion as possible. Either way he would sort it, just as Tansu's own manager had, over the years, dealt with such indispositions of hers – her jealous lovers, her plastic surgery operations, all those abortions.

Quite what İbrahim Aksoy had been expecting as he made his way to the İzzet Paşa Apartments, he could not now recall. That it included neither clusters of armed policemen nor an earlier, almost surreal encounter with a peculiar man who claimed to be a neighbour of Erol's was pretty certain. If asked, Aksoy would probably have described the peculiar man as retarded. This man had, unbidden, approached the corpulent manager as the latter puffed his way past the old French consulate at the Taksim end of İstiklal Caddesi.

Barrelling out from Zambak Sokak on the right and lumbering rather more closely to Aksoy than the latter found comfortable, the man simply said, 'Mrs Ruya is dead.'

Aksoy knew that Ruya was the name of the contentious country wife his client insisted upon keeping.

'Mrs Ruya who?' he asked, anxious as one in his position would be to clarify matters.

'Mrs Ruya across the hallway.'

'Across the hallway? Across the hallway where?'

'From my apartment.' Spoken through a long, thin strand of drool, the man's words smelt as well as sounded. Aksoy took a handkerchief out of his pocket and placed it delicately across his outraged nose.

'And your apartment is where?' he inquired.

'Mine is İzzet Paşa Apartments 3/10,' he said.

Aksoy's lipid-encrusted heart, aware just like his brain that Erol's address was İzzet Paşa 3/12, did not know whether to jump for joy or sorrow. If this congenital idiot was correct, then the inconvenient child bride was now no more. Just to make certain, however, he asked, 'You do mean Mrs Ruya Urfa, I—'

'Didn't do it myself!'

'Eh?'

Quite suddenly this extraordinary creature had, for some reason, taken fright. Why, Aksoy could not imagine. He had, as far as he was aware, been quite polite to the fool, or at least he thought he had. For a few moments he stopped and watched as the man, the fat on his back wobbling over the creases in his shirt, retreated down the road, muttering things that Aksoy could not catch.

Later, as he approached what turned out to be a knot of policemen standing in front of the entrance to the apartments, Aksoy prepared himself for the fact that what the 'idiot' had just told him might actually be true. He also readied himself to use that information if necessary.

Aksoy was intercepted by a tall, uniformed man. 'Yes, sir,' he said, 'may I help you?'

'I have come to see my client, Mr Urfa,' Aksoy said with a smile. 'I am his manager, İbrahim Aksoy. You may have heard—'

'Nobody is permitted to visit Mr Urfa at the present time, sir.'

'Oh. Is he in trouble then, or unwell?' Aksoy, whose mind was in reality exploring all the possibilities that would now exist for Erol if Ruya really were dead, placed a concerned expression upon his face, hoping it might just belie the loudness of his shirt.

The officer remained coldly impassive. 'I cannot comment, sir.'

'Oh.' With a twirl of his moustache Aksoy feigned moving away and then, thoughtfully, twisted round to speak to the officer again. 'It isn't anything to do with his wife, is it?' He watched the policeman's eyes narrow. 'Little Ruya?'

'Why would you think that?' The 'sir' bit had quite gone from the officer's speech now.

'Oh, just a passing comment somebody made to me.'

'What do you mean? Who?' Both the policeman and his gun leaned down menacingly towards Aksoy who felt himself go just a little bit pale.

'Well, it was a man.' Then looking quickly from side to side to ensure that no one else was listening, Aksoy added, 'An idiot type actually. Said he lived here at the apartments.'

'Yes.'

'Just mentioned that Mrs Urfa, Ruya, may have, well, er, may have sort of died and—'

'This man was a neighbour?'

'So he said.'

The expression on the policeman's face was, for just a moment, almost indecipherable. A mixture of what could have been suspicion coupled with stone-faced gravity. İbrahim Aksoy found it, whatever its composition, really rather frightening. He quickly changed the subject back to one that directly impacted upon himself.

'So,' he said, 'can I see Mr Urfa now? Offer him comfort, the loving shoulder of a true friend . . .'

Although it seemed like so much more, probably only a second or two elapsed before the policeman replied.

'No,' he said, and grabbed hold of the manager's shirtsleeve, pinching just a little of the plump man's skin between his fingers. 'But you can come and see the inspector. He'll be very interested in your idiot.' Then turning to one of his colleagues he suddenly smiled and said, 'Did you see the match last night?'

Leaving Çöktin to sit with the now conscious Urfa,

Suleyman quietly took hold of Dr Sarkissian's elbow and led him out into the opulently mirrored hall.

'What I don't understand,' he said as he tried, but failed, to avoid observing his own figure in the glass, 'is why Erol Urfa didn't tell us his daughter was missing in the first instance. I mean, surely as soon as he could see that his wife was dead his first thought must have been for his child.'

The doctor, who had managed to position himself so that he could not see any part of his own body in the numerous mirrors, sighed heavily. 'In theory you are right. However, shock can do very peculiar things to people. Finding one's wife dead, although I cannot speak from my own experience, could I believe temporarily rob a man of his everyday wits.'

'Yes, but even so, with a child involved . . .'

'More of a baby than a child. Ten weeks old. It's very new and Urfa does not even live here in the accepted sense.' He paused briefly and shook his head. 'But then perhaps we are not the best of men to be considering whether or not a man may easily forget his newborn infant. Although, as you lot say, Inşallah you will know the joy of parenthood one day, my dear Suleyman, even if I may not.'

Not a little embarrassed by what the much older and rather regretful man had said, Suleyman smiled briefly before changing the subject. 'So what we have then is a possibly murdered woman and a missing child.'

'Who may,' Sarkissian said, raising one finger to

make his point, 'be the key to the mother's death. Somebody may have killed Mrs Urfa not out of desire for the woman's husband but in order to possess the child.' Then clapping one hand affectionately across Suleyman's back, he added, 'Could be awfully melo-dramatic this, you know.'

'Not a little like the music Mr Urfa makes.'

Sarkissian indulged in a muted laugh. 'Quite so! Çetin İkmen, as I know you must appreciate, will be thrilled.'

Although Suleyman, for whom the subject of İkmen was delicate on all sorts of levels, did not immediately answer the doctor, it was not his silence that caused the latter to suddenly wrinkle his brow into a frown. Some-thing which seemed to be behind Suleyman's shoulder appeared to be the culprit. As soon as Suleyman turned and followed the line of Sarkissian's gaze, he knew exactly what had given the medic pause.

He revealed his amusement via the tiniest of smiles. 'It really is a very awful shirt.'

'Awful doesn't express fully what I feel about it,' the doctor replied with some vehemence. Then thrusting one hand forward in order to indicate the figure now lurking alone in Urfa's dining room, he inquired, 'Who is that man anyway?'

'He's Urfa's manager, İbrahim Aksoy.'

'What's he doing here?'

'He came here wanting to see Urfa. He also reckons that somebody he describes as a "retard" told him Ruya

Urfa was dead even before he reached these apartments. This "idiot" told Aksoy he was a neighbour.'

'But nobody knows that Ruya Urfa is dead except ourselves, Urfa himself and—'

'And, the person who committed the act, if this is indeed murder. Yes, Doctor. The men are in the process of visiting all the other apartments in the block now.'

'And Aksoy? What of this grotesque in pink?'

Suleyman smiled. 'Disarmed and alone, he is, I think, frightened enough to be telling us something approximating to the truth.'

The doctor, his eyes wide with surprise, inquired, 'You mean he came in here carrying a weapon?'

'No,' Suleyman said. He slipped his hand into his jacket pocket and pulled out a very small mobile telephone. 'Only this.'

Sarkissian's face rearranged itself into a picture of recognition. 'Which, had he used it to call the press corps—'

'Would have been like placing a bomb under this investigation before it has even begun,' Suleyman concluded.

As both the doctor and the policeman stood looking at Aksoy as if he were an exhibit in one of the glass cases at the Topkapı Museum, the manager turned slowly to return their gaze. His eyes reflected a deep, almost hysterical fear.

* * *

Unlike İbrahim Aksoy, Kenan and Semahat Temiz were, as they always had been, very calm around policemen. Secure in their habitual law-abiding innocence and cushioned by their not inconsiderable fortune, Mr and Mrs Temiz were not even mildly fazed when a young and to them rather abrupt policeman came to the door of their apartment. They had of course overheard all the commotion from that strange young woman's apartment across the hall for some time and had even spoken briefly about it between themselves. Their son Cengiz was wont to say from time to time that the young man who sometimes came to visit the girl was some sort of popular music star, but then Cengiz did make things up. It was therefore fortuitous, or so the old couple thought at the time, that Cengiz was out when the policeman called.

'Good morning, officer,' Kenan said as he opened the door, as was his wont, just a crack first and then the whole way once he had identified the caller. 'Is there a problem? Can we help you at all?'

'You might, yes.'

Semahat, who had now joined her husband at the door, smiled at the officer through a haze of her beloved Angora cat's fur. This animal, whose name was Rosebud, went everywhere with her mistress except outside the apartment.

'Well, show the officer in then, Kenan,' she said to her husband as she turned to go back into her drawing room.

'Oh, yes, but of course. Please come inside.' Kenan, his old, lined face just touched by the thinnest blush of red, ushered the officer into the hall and then, following his wife, into the drawing room.

Without even pretending to the usual niceties that normally predate any sort of Turkish conversation, the officer launched into his reason for being in the Temiz family apartment. The quantity of lovingly tended high-quality Ottoman copper artefacts it contained was quite lost on him.

'I understand from other residents that you have a son,' he said, addressing his remarks only to Kenan.

'Yes,' the old man replied. 'Cengiz.'

'Is he in?'

'No. He went out some time ago.'

'It is his custom,' Semahat expanded, 'to take food to the cats of Karaköy and other locally deprived areas.' Tucking Rosebud's tail underneath the cat's behind, Semahat lowered herself gently down onto a silk-covered divan. 'We are, officer, as you can see, great lovers of our beloved Prophet's most faithful animal friends.'

Taking a notebook and pen out of the pocket of his shirt, the policeman continued, 'Large, is he, your son?'

'He's a big man, yes,' Kenan said and then, stuttering a little as a slight unease overtook him, he added, 'Er, just, um, what is this about, officer?'

'A bit simple too.'

Semahat, her cat still in her hands, sprang from her seat like a panther. 'I beg your pardon!'

Looking at her properly for the first time and seeing, for his pains, the face of an elegant but outraged elderly lady, the policeman cleared his throat and then mumbled a very brief and barely audible apology.

'If,' Semahat declaimed, her eyes most definitely, if metaphorically, looking down upon the officer, 'you mean that my son suffers from Down's syndrome then that is indeed true. Though chronologically our son is now forty-five years old, his mind is that of a child.'

'Not an easy thing to bear,' her husband added, his face now slightly turned away from the hub of the conversation. 'Even if he is a good boy.'

'At what time did your son leave this morning?'

'At about seven, as is his custom,' Semahat replied.

'Mmm.' The officer paused to look around the room for a moment. 'Do you know which exit he used?'

'Which exit?'

'It would be helpful,' Semahat enunciated with not a little acid in her voice, 'if you could, officer, tell us what all this is about. My husband and I are accustomed to rather more consideration from the police than you are currently exhibiting. Not that we have had that many dealings with you fellows before, of course.'

'If you could just answer the question, madam.'

A moment of impasse hung briefly between the old woman and the young policeman. Neither was accustomed to being talked down to by others. Kenan in his own, faltering fashion eventually broke the spell.

'My son always uses the, er, the fire escape,' he said. 'It saves taking the food for the cats from the kitchen and into the living areas. It also,' and here he briefly lowered his eyes, 'um, means that not so many, ah, people, um, see him go, if you know what . . .'

'I see.' The policeman wrote something down on his notepad. Details, the couple assumed, about their son.

As he finished his small paper exposition, Semahat cleared her throat. 'Before we go any further, officer,' she said, 'I think I would like to speak to your superior. In fact I think I will insist upon that, if you don't mind.'

The officer looked up sharply. 'You want me to go and get Inspector Suleyman?'

'If he is your superior, yes.'

'Oh, right.' Slowly and, Semahat observed, rather thoughtfully, the officer put his notebook back in the pocket of his shirt and then rubbed his face somewhat nervously with his hand.

'Now would be best,' she pressed.

'Oh, right.' As he walked out of the room, Semahat got the impression that the policeman was leaving with his tail, metaphorically, tucked between his legs. This Inspector Suleyman was obviously a person who frightened the young man quite a lot. Not, of course, that she, even despite her white-faced nervousness, had any intention of being over-awed by this character.

Kenan, his legs now giving way to the shaking that had afflicted other parts of his body much earlier, sat down. 'I wonder what he's done,' he said to his wife without looking at her.

'Cengiz? He's done nothing,' she stated simply. 'He is a child.'

'Not in every way,' her husband said softly. 'Not with girls . . .'

'Yes, he is!' She followed this with some furious stroking of Rosebud. Then cooing into the animal's delicate ear she whispered, 'He doesn't like naughty girlies, does he, Rosa? Not Daddy Cengiz. No.'

'Semahat—'

'No!'

'Mr and Mrs Temiz?'

The man who now stood in the doorway to their drawing room was, obviously, older than the young policeman they had spoken to earlier. He was also, by his gravely appropriate smile, his good clothes and handsomely confident demeanour, of quite a different order socially. For a moment Semahat found herself wondering what this charming stranger could possibly want with them.

'I am Inspector Suleyman,' he said and moved forward to take Kenan's hand in his own and then gently bow respectfully across the old man's wrist. 'My officer thinks it more appropriate that I speak to you.'

'He was most rude,' a still angry but nevertheless slightly mollified Semahat said from behind Rosebud's not inconsiderable fur.

Inspector Suleyman's chiselled features became grave. 'I am very sorry if he caused offence to you, madam,' he said. 'Please be assured that I will personally reprimand my man for—'

'Yes, yes, thank you.' Kenan, who was now on his feet again, agitatedly paced across the floor. 'But what of Cengiz, Inspector? What of my son?'

Suleyman placed both his hands together in front of his mouth before removing them and speaking. 'The situation is this, Mr Temiz,' he began, and then suddenly changing tack completely he said, 'Could we all sit down?'

'Oh, yes! Yes, where are my manners!' the old woman said, giggling slightly and nervously at the back of her throat, like a girl.

They all sat down. The elderly couple watched and waited expectantly for what words would drop from the lips of a man who was at least their equal.

'My officer tells me that your son left this apartment at seven o'clock this morning via the fire escape exit. Is that correct?'

'Yes,' Kenan said, 'it is what we told the boy. True.'

'So when my men arrived at these apartments at seven forty-five, your son was out?'

'Yes.'

Suleyman looked down briefly, thinking, before he continued, 'You must know by now that my men and I have been across the hallway in the apartment of the family opposite.'

'Yes.' Semahat, almost in spite of herself, frowned. The young woman and the baby. The people Cengiz talked of sometimes, at moments when he felt . . .

'One party from that apartment has this morning been found dead,' Suleyman said.

'Oh!'

'Allah,' Kenan exclaimed. 'What, er . . .'

'Whether the circumstances surrounding this person's death are suspicious or not we do not yet know for certain,' Suleyman continued smoothly. 'However, what we do know, from the testimony of a friend who came to visit the family this morning, is that a man answering the description of your son and claiming, further, to originate from these apartments knew about this event and talked to him of it before we did.'

'What time did this man say he met our son?'

'At around eight.'

Semahat smiled. 'Ah, but Inspector, you and your men were already here by then.'

'Yes,' Suleyman smiled, 'but if Mr Aksoy is correct then he met your son before he arrived here. Your son, or whoever it was Mr Aksoy spoke to, talked of a death, claimed his own innocence and then, for some reason, ran quickly northwards, back on İstiklal Caddesi towards Taksim Square.'

'But,' Kenan was frowning as if finding the conversation difficult to follow, 'but Cengiz never goes to Taksim Square, at least not alone.

'Well, according to Mr Aksoy,' Suleyman said, 'he came shooting out of Zambak Sokak which, as you know, is already at Taksim.'

'But that's nowhere near to Karaköy, where he should have been, it's . . .'

'Do you have any idea where your son is now, Mr Temiz?' Suleyman asked.

Kenan looked distractedly at his watch. 'Well, he's late . . .'

'Somebody must have told him about this death!' Semahat said as she stood up and with uncharacteristic lack of care let Rosebud drop heavily to the floor. 'That must be the explanation. Someone told him and now he's frightened to come home because of all the policemen.'

'That is indeed possible,' Suleyman replied, watching closely as the old woman wrung her hands hard one against the other. 'But until I can speak to Cengiz about these matters I will not know.'

'You mean you want to question my son? About death?'

'I am afraid I will have to, Mrs Temiz. If only to eliminate him from my inquiries.'

Kenan, his mouth now dry with cold fear, coughed. 'But Cengiz is—'

'Our son is as a little child,' his wife interjected, her

face suddenly small, caved in upon itself in its desire to hide from what seemed to her all this awfulness.

'I understand that your son has Down's syndrome, Mrs Temiz,' Suleyman replied kindly, but then injecting just a little more hardness into his voice he said, 'However, if I am to move towards the truth of this situation, and that after all is my job, then I must question everybody who may know something about it. And that, Mrs Temiz, includes your son.'

Chapter 3

Even without ever clapping eyes upon the actual person of Tansu Hanım one could, if one were observant and knowledgeable, roughly gauge her seniority by looking at her home. Occupying a large swathe of land along the shores of the Bosphorus at Yeniköy, its magnificent nineteenth-century gates did not in any way prepare one for the 1970s concrete horror that arrogantly fronted the great waterway. Constructed prior to legislation designed to preserve old Ottoman buildings, the erection of Tansu's house had deprived the world of something, although now barely remembered, far more graceful.

Bought, so it was said, with the proceeds of her third album, Tansu's house had been originally designed to emulate the German Bauhaus style. And indeed as an installationesque, artily functional type of building it would have worked. But with big pink painted roses adorning every door plus gaudy posters of now rather old European film stars on every wall, the house looked violated. The fact that the young architect who had drawn up the original plans in 1972 had, co-incidentally, shot himself seven years later was the subject of some mirth amongst those people possessed of taste. It was these same people, usually educated folk, who also liked to laugh at the lady herself.

The woman who was now teetering noisily across her brilliantly polished parquet flooring was, in spite of her young lover's universally acknowledged obsession with her, something of an old joke. Tansu's official line on her own life was that she had come to Istanbul from her home city of Adana in 1970 at the tender age of sixteen. That she left a child who was already ten years old behind her was something Tansu never mentioned. And when the child, now a man of nearly forty, had spoken to a reporter from *Hürriyet* back in Tansu's darkest days, in the late 1980s, it had caused her to disown her son completely and nearly ruined her career to boot. Had Erol Urfa not come into her life three years previously and helped her rebuild both her career and her self-esteem she would now, she knew, be as wrinkled and as unemployable as the numerous fifties European film stars upon whom she had once modelled herself.

Struggling both with shoes that were too high for her and with barely contained anxiety, Tansu reached for the bottle of pills on the coffee table.

'If only he would phone me himself I could rest,' she said as she attempted to take the lid off the bottle.

Her companion, a woman who looked like a slightly younger, more relaxed and considerably more sensibly shod version of Tansu, calmly reached out and took the bottle from the latter's shaking hands. 'Erol will call as soon as he is able,' she said. 'You will be the first to know if it is anything serious.'

With a petulant flick of her long platinum hair, Tansu threw herself down onto one of her chintz sofas and then let her hands fall heavily between her thin, brown knees. 'That man I spoke to could have been something to do with the bitch,' she growled, her eyes suddenly hard and full of spite.

The other woman, taking Tansu's hand in hers, placed two pills in her palm. 'Here, take these, they'll make you feel better.'

'Could even be her brother.'

'Except that you said his voice was posh,' the other replied, her tone slightly amused. 'Ruya is a village girl, remember, about as posh as your Erol.'

'My Erol is perfect and don't you forget it!'

'That is not quite what you were saying last night, dear,' the other replied as she pawed a little obviously at the small book at her side.

'Why you—'

'Oh, for the love of Allah,' the other woman cried, her patience snapping, 'take your tranquillisers, Tansu, and shut up!'

For a moment Tansu looked as if she might object to what had been said, but then she took the pills and when they had gone placed her hand across her large, heaving breast in a gesture of relief.

The other woman raised an eyebrow. 'Better?' she inquired.

Tansu sighed heavily and then flicked her sunglasses down from her head to cover her eyes. 'You know that the bitch is also a witch, don't you?' she said as she moved her attention from pills to cigarettes.

'No, she isn't,' the other woman said, expressing just enough obvious 'patience' in her voice to give it an edge. 'She is, as I have said before, just an ordinary girl from Erol's village. He married her because he was long ago betrothed. It's village stuff, Tansu. You know the score.'

'No, I don't! I come from a city!'

'Yes, you do, as do I and our brothers. But Mum and Dad came from Peri which, as we all know, is not shown on all maps.'

'Oh, shut the fuck up, Latife!' As she spoke, Tansu dropped her heavy onyx table lighter onto the floor. Its weight shattered one of the wooden parquet panels.

A veteran of many similar scenes, Latife bowed her platinum head just slightly towards the floor, averting her eyes from those of her sister. 'I'd be careful of the floor, Tansu,' she said calmly.

'Oh, fuck the fucking floor!' shouted Tansu, now up and prowling once again. 'I can always get another fucking floor!' She threw both arms dramatically into the air. 'What I want is my love! I want him to come here to my bed! I want to know that his "indisposition" doesn't mean screwing that flat-chested little bitch!'

'But you have done all you can, Tansu. You telephoned Aksoy Bey—'

'Who has not bothered to return my call! Who has switched his mobile telephone off so he doesn't have to speak to me!'

'Well, if you're that worried, why don't you and I go up to İstiklal—'

Her speech was swiftly and effectively cut short by the smart slap Tansu delivered to the side of her sister's face.

'I have to attend a lunch at the officers' club in less than an hour, you stupid whore!' Then gathering her breath and her composure as comprehensively as Tansu ever could, she continued more calmly, 'I cannot let our soldier boys down. If I let them down then I let Turkey down.'

'And you are all of Turkey's darling.' It was said without irony. But had Tansu turned away from dramatically staring at the ceiling (and at scenes from her own legend depicted thereon) she would have noticed that Latife was smiling just a little.

'Yes, I am,' Tansu said and for a moment she held onto the heroic pose before, with a small whimper, she threw herself back onto the couch. 'But how will I endure it without knowing where my darling is?'

'You'll just have to be strong, won't you?'

'Yes. Yes, I will.' Tansu drew heavily on her cigarette and then sat up. Her face, now heavily stained with tear-sodden make-up, was attempting to resolve itself into a mask of passion. 'For Turkey.'

'Yes. For Turkey,' her sister said as if doing something awfully mundane like reading a shopping list. She picked up her book and rose to leave the room. But as she passed the rapt Tansu, she bent down towards her and said, 'You want me to get your favourite columnists there just before or just after you arrive?'

Without altering her melodramatic pose, Tansu replied, 'Before.'

'And will you be happy brave or choking back the tears brave?'

'I think that military men would prefer real sacrifice,' Tansu said quietly. 'They will want, I feel, to know that I still love them even in the midst of personal crisis. It mirrors their unselfish bravery for the motherland.'

Latife, who was now standing by one of the rose-painted doors, looked down at her sister and suddenly, with almost overwhelming affection, said, 'Whatever you want, my dove.'

By the time the news about Tansu Hanım's emotional breakdown at the officers' club and the subsequent press dash to the supposedly dying Erol Urfa's İstiklal Caddesi apartment had reached the ears of Çetin İkmen, Mehmet Suleyman was already on his way to his former superior's Sultan Ahmet apartment. With Urfa now being looked after by his manager and forensic all over the apartment, he needed a few minutes at least away from the press corps in order to collect his thoughts. Çöktin, who had not as yet come into contact with the press, was out looking for the elusive Cengiz Temiz as well as co-ordinating activities with regard to Urfa's still missing daughter. The man that reporters were already describing as 'the dashing investigating officer' literally fell across the toy-strewn entrance to the İkmen family home.

'If you continue to steal Tansu Hanım's air time she'll pull your face off,' the older man grinned as he warmly embraced his colleague.

Suleyman smiled, if a little weakly. 'I'm absolutely exhausted.'

'Then let's go to my office,' İkmen said, reaching up to put his arm around his friend's shoulders.

'Your office? I didn't know you had an office at home.'

'I mean the balcony actually, Suleyman. Fate has not, as you know, seen fit to enhance my financial status for some time. But if, like me, you don't mind street dust or the odd exchange with the demented old man next door, then it serves.' As they passed by the door of the kitchen, İkmen called out, 'Two teas for the balcony, Fatma, please.'

The female voice that replied was well laced with acid. 'When I'm good and ready, Çetin, and not before.'

'I do have Mehmet with me, my sweet soul,' he added, a look of pure mischief curling across his face.

And his efforts were rewarded.

'I'll do it right away,' the same, slightly sweeter, female voice replied.

'You know,' İkmen said as he led Suleyman out onto the balcony and then slowly sat down in his chair, 'if you could capture that special something you do to women and then sell it, you could give up policing for ever.'

'At the moment that looks quite appealing actually, sir.'

Both men shared a knowing smile. İkmen took his cigarettes out of his pocket and threw one at Suleyman before lighting up himself. Then he settled back in his chair and looked quizzically at his one-time subordinate.

'So Mr-smoking-again-because-now-I'm-a-bigshot, what, apart from the bastard press, the dead woman and the absent child, is on your mind?'

Suleyman sighed before lighting up in what to İkmen was a worryingly enthusiastic fashion. 'So you know about Urfa, Urfa's wife, the missing child . . .'

'Like other mortals, I listen to the radio and I have my sources,' İkmen said with a knowing smile. 'Any ransom demands?'

'No. Not yet.'

'Doesn't mean there won't be. Just because a note

wasn't found in the apartment, if indeed that is so, doesn't mean that the child hasn't been abducted. If the perpetrator gets off on publicity, a hiatus forcing something like an appearance from Urfa on television could be just what he wants.'

'Or her.' Suleyman smiled.

İkmen in response raised his eyes briefly towards the aqua blue sky. 'May Allah strike me down if I forget the women!' Then looking again at Suleyman he asked, 'Is that, seriously, a real possibility?'

'Urfa is, for want of a better term, a sex symbol,' Suleyman said as he drew long and hard upon his cigarette. 'Women want to get near to him, they desire him—'

'Here are your glasses of tea.' Fatma İkmen set the small silver tray down in front of the two men. Suleyman was unaware of such things but Fatma, who had recently lost five kilos of fat since her, never mentioned, 'female' operation, was wearing quite a thick coating of recently applied lipstick.

She stood back to look at Çetin's old partner and sighed. 'Ah, but you look so smart!' she said. 'Your mother must be so proud!'

'I'm glad you approve of the suit, Mrs İkmen,' Suleyman replied, skating over the issue of his mother's opinions. He had not seen her who had given him life since he had left his wife the previous October. 'It's good to see you again.'

'And you, Mehmet,' she said and then, with a sharp

glance at her husband, she added, 'I can't tell you how grateful we all are to have you here—'

'Yes, thank you, Fatma,' İkmen interjected and smiled at her through clenched teeth. 'You just go and enjoy the kitchen again for a bit.'

The two men left off their conversation for a few moments after Fatma retreated. Quietly they enjoyed their tea, their cigarettes and the unrivalled view İkmen's tatty old balcony afforded of the great Sultan Ahmet Mosque, its gardens and its sad royal child-filled tombs.

'Also, Ruya Urfa died by cyanide poisoning,' said Suleyman when the time finally seemed right. 'Forensic are right now exploring the possibility of death by misadventure. But there were no bottles immediately evident that contained such a substance or derivatives thereof and with no suicide note—'

'We are probably looking at a homicide which,' İkmen said with a sharp raising of one finger, 'Dr Sarkissian probably feels is particularly "feminine" in character?'

Suleyman smiled. 'Yes. Have you spoken to him?'

İkmen's failure to reply to this was pointed. 'Which is why my earlier discounting of women was so erroneous,' he said. 'Poison is considered by some, including the dear doctor, to be a particularly feminine mode of despatch. That coupled with copious amounts of envy . . .'

'You are thinking of Tansu Hanım?'

'Along with the rest of the nation probably, yes,' İkmen said. 'Although the missing child adds rather a different dimension, don't you think?'

'Yes.'

'Bitter childless women . . .'

'Obsessed devotees of Erol's music,' Suleyman added.

'Psychopaths.' İkmen drew hard upon his cigarette and then scrunched the butt out in the ashtray. 'Anyone else?'

'We're actually looking for one of the neighbours at the moment,' Suleyman said as he watched two Oriental tourists struggle with their phrase book in the street below. 'Erol's manager claims this man told him about Ruya Urfa's death before he reached the apartment this morning. The neighbour's knowledge could possibly precede both Mr Urfa's discovery of the body and our arrival at the scene. Of course, he could simply have witnessed the aftermath of Erol Urfa's discovery of the body and then drawn certain conclusions from that. But until we interview him we won't know.'

'Is this manager person reliable? In your opinion?'

Suleyman put his cigarette out in the ashtray. 'He's loud, theatrical and given to offensively dreadful shirts. But I don't think he would lie about such a thing. I mean, it wouldn't profit him in any way to do so.'

'Mmm. Unless, of course, he's protecting his human

investment.' İkmen sipped his tea thoughtfully. 'And the neighbour? What of him?'

'According to his parents, Cengiz Temiz is forty-five years old and has Down's syndrome. He has been known to enter the Urfas' apartment from time to time. He is, apparently, rather fond of the baby. When he saw Temiz this morning, Urfa's manager, İbrahim Aksoy, thinks he may have taken fright for some reason. Çöktin is out looking for him now.'

'If he is Down's you do know that you may have some real problems interrogating him, don't you?'

Suleyman sighed. 'It won't be easy, no.'

'In my experience, which is only small,' İkmen said, lighting yet another cigarette and then rubbing his stomach as if experiencing some pain there, 'he's going to be very frightened and very suggestible.'

'Yes.' And then leaning across to look at İkmen more closely, Suleyman said, 'Are you all right, sir? I'm not tiring you, am I?'

İkmen gave him the sort of look that, unchecked, could possibly curdle milk. 'I'm actually better doing this, as well you know, Suleyman,' he said and then rapidly changed the subject back to something that interested him. 'He'll probably, if my experience is anything to go by, confess immediately. However, if you do need help with that there is always Dr Halman.'

'Yes,' Suleyman said as he turned his head just slightly to one side at mention of the psychiatrist's name. Whether this could be interpreted as evidence supporting current station gossip concerning Suleyman and the rather older female psychiatrist, İkmen didn't know. But if his ex-deputy was having an affair with her he was getting rather better at concealing the fact.

'Anyway,' the younger man said as he drained his tea all in one draught, 'I must go now. Thank you, sir, for what has been a very pleasant few minutes.'

'The pleasure is all mine,' İkmen replied and then looking down towards the floor lest Suleyman see the misery in his eyes, he added, 'I miss both the job and you.'

'You'll be back soon enough.' Suleyman placed a hand gently on İkmen's thin shoulder. İkmen patted the hand with dry, skinny fingers.

'Well, whatever happens, you have quite a cast of characters for this one, don't you?'

Suleyman laughed. 'Men in bad shirts, people with low mental ages, superstars . . .'

'The lovely Tansu Hanım . . .'

'Who I hope to see tonight, after we've made an official statement about Urfa's child. Everybody, via the press, will be aware that she's missing by then, but . . . I know it's always a risk but we need to get the whole country looking. Just because the father is both an adulterer and, from my short conversation with him, rather inarticulate, doesn't mean the child should suffer. I just hope that whoever killed her mother doesn't have even odder designs on the baby.' He stood up.

İkmen too, with just a little more difficulty, rose to his feet. 'Will Çöktin go with you to Tansu Hanım's house?'

'He may.'

'I'd take him, if I were you.'

'Oh?' Suleyman took his cigarettes out of his pocket and lit up.

'Yes,' İkmen said, 'for his linguistic skills. Although I happily know nothing about Arabesk music, I can still recall Tansu's early successes. I remember her being described as a "mountain Turk" in those early days. I've heard her speaking voice too, and it's heavily accented. I wouldn't be surprised if Erol's lack of articulation derives from the same source. Just because they both sing in Turkish doesn't mean they necessarily fully understand it.' He moved his hands expressively in front of his chest as if offering Suleyman something very tasty on a large plate. 'Çöktin is a Kurd and so is Tansu at least. Use him, Suleyman. They'll trust him more than they'll ever trust an old Ottoman like you.'

'My promotion has not robbed me of my social status then?'

İkmen laughed. 'No. I'm afraid it hasn't. You look very uncomfortable just discussing all this theatrical Arabesk stuff.'

The younger man looked sadly down at the floor. 'I know. I'm so ignorant about it.'

'Which is why,' İkmen said, reaching forward and embracing his friend once again, 'I think I might do a little research around just who these overpaid people are and exactly what they do. I may even, may Allah protect me, voluntarily listen to some of their music!'

Some things that, at first sight, appear extremely eccentric can turn out to be quite logical in genesis. İstanbul's tiny underground railway, known as Tünel, is one. It is old, it is so cheap as to be totally unviable from a financial point of view and with only two stations on the 'line', one can hardly go far by this method. History, however, as is often true of so many odd phenomena, provides the logic needed to understand the existence of Tünel. Built by French engineers in 1875 it was designed to carry European merchants resident along the Grand Rue de Pera to and from their offices in Karaköy. Whilst under the ground these privileged foreigners would be well-protected from the extreme weather conditions of winter and summer and also from the pimps, prostitutes and other desperate subjects of the Sultan who for all remembered time have haunted this part of the city. So the merchants got their business done in comfort and without distress and the Sultan earned their gratitude if not their precious pounds, francs and Deutschmarks. These days, with the aid of a jeton priced at virtually nothing, one can ride Tünel in order to save oneself the effort of walking either up or down the Galata

Hill. This is particularly useful for those who do not want to experience the excitements of some of the streets round about. However, for a person to continually travel from top to bottom and vice versa for a whole afternoon is odd. Tünel may well be endlessly fascinating for railway enthusiasts but for a fat man who was obviously local and rather 'simple' to boot, it was bizarre. At least that was what the jeton vendor at the Karaköy end of the line thought when he called the police late that afternoon.

To be fair, the police were discreet although the vendor couldn't help thinking that sending plainclothes detectives to deal with the man was a little over the top. The young redhead in charge took two others with him onto the platform to wait for the train. They even bought jetons which was very strange given what some of the local 'uniforms' did with regard to fare paying, which was basically nothing.

When the little two-carriage train sighed to a halt at the bottom of its journey, Sergeant Çöktin scanned those people exiting the carriages for a man of large girth. His two colleagues stood at the barrier in order to look at people as they came past and indicated, as soon as the rush was over, that they had not found the man in question either. The first carriage being obviously empty, Çöktin moved quickly on to the second where his efforts were rewarded by the sight of a large man counting slowly on his fingers. With a brief movement of the head, Cöktin signalled to his colleagues to come and join him. He then sat down opposite the man and, when he had caught his eye, smiled.

'Good match last night I thought,' he said, jauntily pandering to every red-blooded male's obsession, football.

The man just stared glassily ahead of him, his mouth open and dry looking.

'Not enough goals, but still plenty of excitement,' Çöktin persisted, taking great care not to mention either of the teams involved (Galatasaray and Beşiktaş) for fear of causing offence.

'I haven't got enough money to get back up now.' The man may have been exaggeratedly round but his voice was quite unusually flat.

Çöktin felt all the hairs on the back of his neck stand up. 'Oh,' he said, 'that is unfortunate. Do you need to get home?'

'Need to get back up. Keep going.'

Çöktin's two colleagues moved to sit down behind the man.

'Do you have a cigarette?' he asked Çöktin, putting out his hand, hopefully, for what may or may not be given to him.

'You can't smoke in here,' Çöktin replied as the carriage doors swished shut.

'For later,' the man persisted, pushing one stubby finger against Çöktin's knee.

'Well, all right then.' Çöktin casually sorted through

his pockets looking for his cigarettes. 'So what's your name then?'

'It's . . .' His mouth, which had obviously not tasted a cigarette for some time, slavered expectantly as Çöktin slowly took a single cigarette from his packet.

'Mr . . . ?' Holding the cigarette just slightly out of reach, Çöktin lifted one questioning eyebrow.

'Cengiz,' the man said as he leaned forward to snatch the item from Çöktin's grasp. 'Got a light for it, have you? Got a light?'

'We're not supposed to smoke in here, Cengiz, it's not—'

'Cengiz Temiz,' the man said, reasoning, or so Çöktin thought later, that the revelation of his whole name might just make him change his mind with regard to the light.

With a glance at the driver who was patiently waiting outside, Çöktin leaned forward and lit the cigarette which now belonged to Cengiz Temiz.

The doors of the carriage swished open.

By the time most people were sitting down to their evening meal it was common knowledge that, firstly, Erol Urfa had a wife, secondly that the wife and not the star was not so much indisposed as dead, and thirdly that the Urfas' young daughter was missing. That extremely well-spoken police inspector told the nation that based upon the time of the woman's death the baby could have gone missing as early as the previous evening.

One of those who had watched the television broadcast was a grey-faced Erol Urfa. Now ensconced, at least temporarily, in the lounge of İbrahim Aksoy's Şişli apartment, he looked at the plate of chicken and beans that now sat in front of him almost with horror.

'You should eat that,' Aksoy said as he poured himself yet another large rakı. 'It will make you feel better.'

'No, it won't.' His voice, which was as dead as his eyes, bluntly expressed the reality of the situation. With his wife dead and the baby Merih still missing, Erol Urfa was not going to feel better for some considerable time to come.

İbrahim Aksoy sat down on the sofa beside his protégé and sighed.

After a while, Erol Urfa spoke once again, of terrible things, in the distant tones of one who has experienced more than he or she can bear. 'I keep thinking about the word "murder",' he said, 'but when I think it and I see Ruya's face I cannot put the two together. Who would want to kill her? I just don't know.'

'You know that the police are going to interview Tansu, don't you?' Aksoy, although now outwardly recovered from his earlier interrogation by the police, still shook just a little when he spoke directly of the day's grim events.

With some obvious difficulty, Urfa turned his tension-wracked neck to look into his manager's face. 'But Tansu knew all about Ruya. She accepted the situation. She is from a country family, she knows how things are.'

'Perhaps,' Aksoy said as he cut and then lit a very large cigar, 'you should tell the police about how it really is with you and Tansu.'

'What do you mean?'

'Well, I mean how it's basically for publicity. The old sex goddess and the smooth young country boy. All that fantasy stuff that makes those hoards of middle-aged women and their silly teenage daughters buy your music.'

Erol Urfa's long, almond-shaped eyes closed up just a little, indicating that, angry as he now appeared, he was still under some sort of sedation. 'Although I know that publicity was your only intention when you introduced Tansu and me, I thought you knew by now that I love her.'

'You do? Really?'

'If I did not, why would I be with her, sleep in her bed, give myself totally to her?' Then suddenly with a muscular fierceness he took hold of İbrahim Aksoy roughly by the collar. 'What kind of man do you think I am, İbrahim?'

'All right! Calm down!' Aksoy cried as he pulled Urfa's fingers away from his neck. 'I just thought that what with her being so old and you—'

'You thought me the kind of man who would do anything to become famous? Well, I can understand that even if it is not so.' With calm but determined fingers, he took the cigar from Aksoy's mouth and placed it in his own. 'But I am not that man. I love Tansu because she makes me feel things no other woman can. She treats me like a Sultan, she knows everything. And she loves me.'

'So why – forgive me, Erol, but I am confused now – did you bring Ruya here if you felt that way about Tansu?'

Erol Urfa gave Aksoy back his cigar and then put his hands up to his face. He gently rasped his chin with his fingers. 'Because I am a man of honour. Because we were betrothed as children.' Then looking up quickly at Aksoy he added, 'What is written cannot be unwritten. Not even love can do that.'

Inwardly İbrahim Aksoy gave thanks that he, with his well-known propensity towards multiple lovers, was neither from the country nor of 'mountain Turk' extraction. The customs of these people, or so it seemed, were imbued with a rigidity that transcended both wealth and social position.

'That police inspector won't arrest Tansu, will he?' Erol Urfa asked.

'I don't know.'

'She didn't kill Ruya. I know this.'

İbrahim Aksoy frowned. 'How do you know? Were you with Tansu last night?'

'No.'

'So where were you?'

The young man looked down at the large and complicated kilim at his feet. 'I was with a friend. I told the policeman.'

'The inspector with the bad smell under his nose?'

'No. The other one.' He turned away as he spoke as if he did not want Aksoy to see his eyes. 'The one with the red hair. We spoke,' and then turning back, his eyes now full of tears, he added, 'you know?'

'Ah.' He had, Aksoy recalled now, vaguely wondered about the young policeman with the slightly harsh accent. So he had spoken to Erol in what must be their own language, had he? Silently he wondered whether the urbane Inspector Suleyman was aware of this fact. He wondered at a still deeper level just who this friend Erol had been with was and whether he or she or the events that were now crowding around his charge would have any impact upon sales of Erol's latest album. Not that he could air such views to Erol without looking like a heartless dog.

As the images on the television moved from factual news items into that strange land that is inhabited by dubbed Brazilian soap operas, Aksoy leaned forward to switch the set off. As he reached out, a woman who looked not unlike Tansu thrust her heaving breasts towards the face of an elderly man wearing a bad wig.

'Do you think my daughter is dead, İbrahim?'

Aksoy pushed the 'Off' button and then slid back into his seat again. He didn't know. How could he? In so many ways Erol was like a small child with his constant asking of impossible questions. How? What? Why? When? He had come to the city like this and, unlike other migrants who had built a kind of cynical second skin, he had remained childlike in this respect. If he didn't know him better, Aksoy would think that perhaps Erol was using this innocence of his to cover . . . To cover what? To cover the fact that perhaps he was capable and willing to ki—

'I don't know what has happened to Merih any more than you do, Erol.' He spoke quickly, anxious to block out what was developing into a worrying thought. There were whole swathes of Erol's time outside of work and Tansu and his publicity that he knew absolutely nothing about. Time, he imagined, Erol spent with his own kind.

'Yes, but—'

And then the telephone rang. As he went to pick it up, İbrahim Aksoy noticed that Erol Urfa did not take his eyes off his face for a second. He hoped the young man couldn't sense what he was thinking.

Suleyman switched the car radio off as soon as Tansu Hanım's familiar voice floated out of the machine. He'd had quite enough of that for one night. He took a tape at random out of the glove compartment and he pushed it into the machine. He was pleased to discover that the music he had chosen was Dvorak's New World Symphony – civilised and yet, to him, undemanding. The music together with the inky darkness of the night provided some little comfort for his tired mind. He still had to remain alert enough to be able to get home, or rather to Cohen's place which was the nearest thing he had to home now, but it was a whole lot easier without that woman's raucous tones in his ear.

Just over two hours ago he had entered a house that quite frankly beggared belief. Tansu's home combined the worst excesses of progressive architecture with the tastes of a person who would be far more comfortable in what remained of the old gecekondu shanty districts. The woman herself, who had greeted him lying prone across a large pink sofa, had he could see, been beautiful at some point. Small and thin with the exception of her enormous silicone-enhanced breasts, Tansu Hanım did indeed look a lot younger than her years until one went up close. Even the thick make-up couldn't hide either the old acne scars or the quite livid tracks of the plastic surgeon's knife. Magazine photographs could be air-brushed, movie cameras could have any number of filters available for close-ups, but real life was quite different and Tansu the star was not the same as Tansu in the flesh.

He'd been ushered into 'the presence' by a woman who announced herself as Tansu's sister. Although possessed of the same platinum-blonde hair and a fairly extensively renovated face, the similarities between the two stopped there. While Latife went off to make tea with her very own hands, her sister wept copiously for her 'beloved' Erol Urfa and for the tragedy that had so recently overwhelmed him. It had of course been Tansu who had, via a few well-chosen words about her lover's supposed 'indisposition', sent the press corps screaming up to the apartment on İstiklal Caddesi. In a civilised block like the İzzet Apartments, Suleyman had been able to keep the crime scene unusually discreet; since so few people actually knew that Erol had a flat there, it was really quite easy. Until, that is, Tansu's performance at the officers' club. That alone made him dislike her and as he'd struggled to get any sort of sense from her thickly rouged mouth, his feelings had become more and more hostile.

All she could talk of was Erol Urfa. Although she did from time to time, briefly, express her sorrow at his wife's death and the disappearance of his daughter, most of her words alluded to how she was feeling. But then some of these older women who had younger lovers were both obsessed and desperate to retain their affections. But Suleyman quickly turned his mind away from that particular subject and thought about what he had actually learned from the conversation with Tansu.

Erol had not been with her on the night of the murder. According to Çöktin, Urfa had been with some old friend of his from back east. No name had, as yet, been forthcoming but Suleyman had already determined to question Urfa himself at the earliest possible opportunity. Çöktin had spoken to the star in his own language, exhibiting an implicit solidarity that may or may not have been helpful with regard to the extraction of information. Tansu had been at home all that evening, mainly sitting out on her veranda which had become, or so she said, so pleasant since she'd had a nearby wasps' nest destroyed. Her sister said that she had been with her on the veranda too, for all that was worth. Of the woman's two brothers, the eldest, Galip, had been at the İnönü Stadium watching the football match live while apparently the younger one, Yılmaz, had watched the match on television. Both men had been co-operative in a bemused sort of way until, that is, their sister, finally catching on that she could be a suspect in this affair, became quite hysterical during the middle part of the interview. Leaping like a cat, all claws bared, from her sickbed, she had paced the room spitting verbal bile at quite imaginary accusers for some time. Suleyman had been horribly embarrassed at the time. It had been difficult, after that, to have any sympathy for a woman who was, though ageing, still a spoilt, vicious child at heart. Suleyman knew he would have to take care not to condemn her out of hand. She, if anyone, had good reason to want Ruya Urfa dead but there was nothing, as yet, to connect either her or her relatives directly to the scene.

But time would tell. Forensic had lifted several sets

of fingerprints from the apartment, as well as some faint footprints. Soon the process of identifying to whom these belonged would begin, as would the interrogation of Cengiz Temiz who had been discovered finally on a Tünel train. According to Çöktin he would say absolutely nothing beyond denying that he had killed Ruya Urfa. Now down in the cells for the night, he would have ample time, if he were capable of such thoughts, to reconsider his words. His parents had, apparently, already engaged one of the city's top defence lawyers.

The mobile telephone that was sitting on the seat beside him buzzed into life. Suleyman picked it up and put it to his ear.

'Suleyman.'

'Hello, it's Sarkissian. Just thought I'd let you know that the cyanide that killed Mrs Urfa was administered in a sweet.'

'Oh?'

'Yes, almond halva to be precise. Clever, eh?'

An almond sweet to cover the smell of the bitter poison? Yes, it was, and if Çöktin was right about Cengiz Temiz, it was far too clever for him.

'Thank you, Doctor,' Suleyman said at last. 'Will I see you in the morning?'

'You will. Your office. At what time?'

'About nine.'

The doctor laughed. 'You rise too early for me. Make it ten and I'll be there.'

'I look forward to it.' Suleyman smiled as he switched the phone off again.

So Mrs Urfa was seduced to her death by sweet things, was she? No remnants of the sweet had been found outside of Ruya Urfa's body, which suggested that whoever had given her the halva had taken the residue away with them. After, that is, he or she had watched the victim fight for breath and then die. Cyanide, which is a very quick-acting agent, robs the bloodstream of oxygen thereby effectively asphyxiating the victim.

Perhaps it was these grim thoughts that made Suleyman, unconsciously, pull off the long shore road and head for a small wooden house that nestled discreetly behind a row of trendy art shops. But perhaps not. The pretty Bosphorus village of Ortaköy where, hopefully, he could spend a little time before returning to Cohen's unruly apartment had become quite familiar to him in recent months. That he had fetched up here so unconsciously was, however, a worry. If he was driving to Ortaköy without thinking then what else was he letting slip about his visits to the village?

After he had parked his car, he walked up to the salt-stained front door and knocked. For quite some time he heard nothing from inside. The lights were on but even so no one was in, or maybe the old man was at home alone. Suleyman put his hands into the pockets of his jacket and watched as the earth beneath his feet juddered just very slightly. 'Only a tremor,' he muttered softly to himself, his usual mantra to chase away the demons of the earth. And, indeed, the tremor did subside almost as soon as it had begun even if his heart persisted in racing. One never knew when the demons beneath the city might get tired of such paltry spells.

The woman who eventually opened the salt-stained door was short and blonde. The thick black ciga-rette sticking out from between her fingers made her, together with her long, sleepy eyes, look rather like a plump Lauren Bacall.

'Hello, Inspector,' she said in that strange, foreign way of hers. 'This is a nice surprise.'

'Hello, Dr Halman,' he said. 'I was just passing and . . .'

She smiled broadly at a neighbour who was walking by and then said to Suleyman, 'Father is out with some old university friends but if you don't mind having your drink prepared by me . . .'

'That would be very nice.'

He walked into the house. She closed the door behind him. He walked straight up the stairs and into her bedroom. Zelfa Halman, following, discarded her skirt at the doorway.

Chapter 4

Mina rose quickly from her bed and stepped lightly across to the window. As she did so she looked back, briefly, to make sure that Mickey was still sleeping. She could just see his open mouth breathing heavily through the thick mat of his long grey hair. She opened the curtains, revealing the quiet early morning street beyond. She let her eyes rove searchingly across the shuttered old building opposite.

Mina herself couldn't remember when the old İskender Hamam, the public baths, had been open for business. For all of her life the owner, Madame Kleopatra, had been dying up in that top bedroom where Mina's mother had attended to her needs for the last fifteen years. It was said that Madame Kleopatra had once been part of that odd and rare phenomenon, a Graeco-Turkish marriage. But no one could remember her Turkish husband these days and the old Greek herself, now finally drifting senselessly along on the cloud of morphine her doctor gave her every evening, barely knew her own name. Not that Madame Kleopatra or even Mina's mother, Semra, were the objects of Mina's thoughts at that moment. It was the child that had her thoughts now, that little life that Semra guarded just as surely as she had once cared for Mina herself.

Though not ideal, this arrangement was better than if she had the child with her. Semra only had to attend to her barely conscious charge a couple of times a day, times during which she could take the child along too if the little one were restless or wakeful. Mina's work was of quite a different order. The last thing the usually European men whom Mickey pimped to her bed wanted was a child around while they exacted release from her body. Mickey didn't know about the child but then nor did anyone else in Mina's immediate vicinity, apart from her mother and, of course, poor old 'Fat Boy'.

Mina moved her gaze down the face of the building and into the street. A short, skinny figure caught her eye as she scanned for signs of early morning life. It was a policeman, a local, that Jewish cop who had sometimes visited her when she was younger. Though physically unpleasant he was not, she recalled, a bad man. Cohen, that was his name. He had quite amused her by translating dirty Turkish words into his native tongue, Ladino, the language of the Jews. That facility, plus his very obvious distrust of Mickey, had made her like him. She turned back from the window and looked again at the wasted form of the man in her bed. Mickey had first come to Turkey in the year of her birth, 1970, an English boy on the hippy trail to India who had found İstanbul's drug scene to his liking and decided to stay. She didn't know exactly how old he had been then but she imagined it was around twenty. In the years that followed, Mickey had done lots of different things to enable him to pay for his drug habit; pimping for Mina was just the latest of these. The child would not fall in with Mickey's plans, except perhaps as something that could be sold in order to obtain drugs. He would hate it, were he to discover its existence.

But then Mickey knew nothing of what occurred in the İskender Hamam anyway. Though resident in Turkey for nearly thirty years, he still couldn't speak the language and therefore knew nothing about Semra or Madame Kleopatra or, more importantly, Madame Kleopatra's regular doses of morphine. So the child was safe, for now. In the future, however, things would have to alter. The child had changed everything now; for the better, to Mina's mind, although not yet as totally as she would have wanted. In order to be with the child she would, somehow, have to get rid of Mickey. How she might do this she didn't know. But an idea came to her later when she finally managed to slip out to see Semra and the child. Through a crack in Madame Kleopatra's door, Mina saw the smart Phanariote doctor use his big syringe to plunge the dying Madame Kleopatra into yet deeper painless euphoria. Mickey, too, when he was particularly bad, let others, as he put it, 'medicine' him. Sometimes he even let Mina do it.

The child pawed gently at Mina's small, empty breasts while the prostitute cooed lovingly, smiling into the little one's eyes.

Various fingerprints and some faint footprints had been found in Ruya and Erol Urfa's apartment. Some fingerprints no doubt belonged to one or other of the couple. Forensic were not yet able to say to whom each example belonged but they did know that there were four distinct types of print, only one of which represented that of a small child. Cengiz Temiz was, so far, the only person who had been obliged to supply prints for matching – with the exception, of course, of Erol Urfa. Suleyman was, as he told Dr Arto Sarkissian when he met him in his office at ten o'clock that morning, still keeping an open mind on the seemingly innocent Arabesk star.

'But if Urfa did kill his wife that doesn't answer the question about the whereabouts of his child,' Sarkissian pointed out.

Suleyman, whose face, the doctor observed, was rather more tired and drawn than was usual even for him, lit a cigarette before answering. 'He could have taken her to some friends, some of his own sort from the east. Everybody in the country was watching the football that night so nobody would have noticed.'

'But he's a nice-looking boy and although his poor wife was quite a plain little thing, well . . .' He paused in order to rub a hand roughly across his sweating forehead. 'To kill her in order to be able to marry that Tansu creature is—'

'Mad, or the act of a man who is unbelievably ambitious.'

Sarkissian smiled. 'Now if we were talking about his manager I would say that either or both of those things could apply. But Urfa himself?' He shrugged. 'I don't know. He doesn't strike me as either even if there is, oh, I don't know, something about him I cannot quite place.'

'Something not quite right?'

'Yes.'

'I have the same feeling myself.' Suleyman flicked the end of his cigarette into what Arto Sarkissian instantly recognised as one of Çetin İkmen's ashtrays. 'But then there's an awful lot not right with Cengiz Temiz too.'

'The Down's . . .'

Suleyman nodded.

Through the frosted glass in the door of Suleyman's office they both observed the vague smudges that were a senior officer of both their acquaintance and an unknown woman offering her body and her jewellery to him. Suleyman and Sarkissian did what they knew Çetin İkmen would not have done, and ignored it.

'Has he spoken yet or is it still just rote denial?'

'As soon as I walked into the room he flung himself under the table,' Suleyman replied. 'I don't think I've ever seen a person in such a state of terror.

He drools, he gibbers, he stutters that he didn't kill anyone . . . But how he could possibly know that Ruya Urfa was dead before Erol had even arrived at the apartments is a mystery. His parents and one of the other neighbours maintain he was well away from the apartment when they heard Erol scream. The door to the apartment was shut, according to Urfa, and so it wasn't as if Cengiz could have spotted the body from the hall.'

'He usually went out through the fire escape anyway according to his parents,' the doctor pointed out.

'Yes.' Suleyman sat down behind his now rather messy desk and ran his fingers through his hair. 'He denies what he should not know, his parents were absent at the time of the murder and he's terrified beyond belief. Whether he did it or not, I've no idea. But I'm certain he has some knowledge of the events surrounding the death. It's just getting at what they might be. And until forensic come across with something I am temporarily at a loss.' Glancing briefly at his one dust-grimed window he said, 'I just hope that when they do call, it's to my mobile. The switchboard's been jammed since dawn with press calls, Erol's more demented fans and various unhappy individuals who claim to have the child. The latter, of course, require action by uniform and I must get out of here myself in the near future – if I can get around the TRT pack who appear to be constructing gecekondu accommodation in the car park.'

With a smile, Arto Sarkissian rested his considerable behind on the edge of Suleyman's desk. 'You probably need to speak to Zelfa Halman with regard to Cengiz Temiz.'

'I've mentioned him to her,' Suleyman said in the kind of automatic fashion he knew he should avoid. For was it not just one step from talking about mentioning things to stating where that mentioning occurred? 'She advised rather more intervention with the parents at this stage, until forensic come up, or not, with something. I have instructed Çöktin to meet them when they arrive, no doubt accompanied by Mr Avedykian, later this morning.'

'They've already gone to the top for their lawyer then?'

Suleyman shrugged. 'It is their right. And if they are rich enough to buy Avedykian, well . . .'

A pause hung between the two men for a while as they both recalled their previous dealings with Sevan Avedykian. Principal among these was the moment, only ten months before, when İkmen aided by Suleyman had been obliged to tell Avedykian that his son, Avram, had been murdered by his psychopathic lover, Muhammed Ersoy. Suleyman could still vividly recall the stony silence that had accompanied the greying of Sevan Avedykian's face, as well as the hysterical screaming that had signalled Mrs Avedykian's knowledge of the facts. Arto Sarkissian had once been a friend to Avram and as a fellow Armenian had visited frequently, for a while, after that. But not recently. For as Sevan Avedykian's sorrow had grown, so his silences had hardened. Every fibre of his body shouted to Sarkissian that he should have alerted the father to the son's activities many years before. And perhaps Sarkissian should have done just that. He had, after all, known about Avram's obsession with Ersoy for many years. True, he didn't realise quite how dangerous the fabulous Ersoy was until it was too late. Not that Avedykian would have listened then any more than he did now. And so, after just one abortive attempt to explain his involvement in Avram's past, Sarkissian had walked out of the Avedykian house for what he hoped was the last time. That had now been three months ago.

After looking down briefly at his pocket diary, Suleyman broke the silence. 'I've learned who Erol Urfa claims to have been with on the night of the murder. Çöktin told me.'

'Oh?'

'Yes. Ali Mardin; he owns a small pansiyon on Yerebatan Caddesi. Like Urfa he is a . . .'

'He's Kurdish,' the doctor assisted. 'Don't you think you should take Çöktin with you, in that case?'

'No. I think it might be better if I impress upon Mr Mardin the seriousness of what has happened alone. I want to cut through as much clan loyalty as I can. These people need to know that only two things are of importance to me – the safe return of Merih Urfa and the apprehension of Ruya's killer. I don't care what

values these people adhere to or what they consider
their origins to be.'

'How very modern,' Arto Sarkissian said with more
than a hint of irony in his voice. 'I wish you luck
although I do have some anxieties. I mean, you are
dealing with people – Erol, Aksoy, Tansu and now
possibly Mardin – who know how to keep secrets
very effectively. After all, Ruya and Merih were, until
yesterday, nonexistent people.'

'Yes. Strange.' Suleyman's eyes glazed over as
he considered this point. 'I would have thought that
Aksoy would have wanted to exploit the fact that Erol
honoured his village betrothal. Man of principal mar-
ries little country girl. After all, most of his fans are
of a certain class . . .'

Sarkissian laughed. 'Oh, you terrible snob!' he said.
'But yes, I suppose they are mostly peasants. It does
rather depend upon what Aksoy had in mind for Erol
though. And his affair with Tansu was frequently
headline news. That woman is so volatile she ensures
whoever she is with is never out of the public eye.'

'And if the public are fascinated by a person, they
will buy their tapes, CDs or whatever.'

The doctor bowed in agreement. 'Precisely.'

'How horribly cynical.'

'That's business.'

There was a knock at the door. In response to
Suleyman's call to enter, a smart, if rather nondescript
young man, entered the office. Tipped as Suleyman's

replacement, İkmen's new sergeant, Orhan Tepe was one of those men who always looked cheerful, whatever the occasion. And now was no exception.

'What is it, Tepe?' Suleyman said, only briefly looking away from the doctor.

'We've got some people downstairs who claim they killed Ruya Urfa. They say they've got to see you, sir.'

Suleyman groaned. 'Crazies.'

'Well, yes, but, er, not obviously so, sir,' said Tepe. 'Not mad old women in rags or men who think they're Adnan Menderes.'

'Oh,' the doctor said with a smile, 'unusual crazies, eh?'

'Well, if you call two teenage girls wearing chadors unusual then, yes, they are, sir.' Turning back to Suleyman, he said, 'Shall you be coming to see them, Inspector, or shall I just get their parents to collect them?'

I am an addict for the sorrow that you bring
I embrace the knife's edge of your disdain
I am lost
I am gone
I am dead
Until your sweet return into my life happens
  once again.

As he looked at what he had just written, Çetin İkmen

shook his head in disbelief. 'You know,' he said calling out to Fatma over the top of the tape he had been transcribing, 'I think the state should give the Ministry of Culture some sort of award for attempting to get this dross banned back in the eighties.'

'That's Tansu at her best!' his wife answered as she walked over to the stereo and made to turn up the volume. 'She sings of universal emotions, Çetin; of love and loss and—'

'Don't touch that dial!' he shouted. 'In fact, turn it down, will you? Makes me want to jump into a bottle of brandy and stay there. I don't think I can stand any more ungrammatical sorrow-filled insults to my intelligence.'

'All right, all right!' Fatma said as she laid the towel she had been using across the back of a chair and then turned the music down to almost silence.

'No wonder the suicide rate in dumps like Sivas keeps on going up. They listen to this stuff all the time out there. Being in the country is bad enough but with this going on day and night . . . I'd be slitting my throat within hours.'

Fatma, already wearied by the younger children, who were on vacation, and the housework, sat down beside her husband. 'Oh, you've been listening to Arabesk all your life without noticing,' she said. 'People play it everywhere. I play it. I like it.'

'You,' he replied, touching just the end of her nose with stern affection, 'should know better.'

'It's romantic.' She shrugged. 'The stars themselves are romantic. Women like such things. Even Çiçek will sing along to Arabesk at times, when she's not listening to those Western musicians. We are Turks, we like to imagine ourselves involved in grand passions like the singers. And then we like to have a good cry.'

'A rather sweeping generalisation there, Fatma,' her husband said with not a little amusement in his voice, 'confounded, of course, by people like myself who want to vomit when we hear it.'

'Oh, that's just you!'

'And Suleyman and Arto. I can't really even see Commissioner Ardiç getting damp around the eyes just because some spoilt old plastic-surgery victim has been cast aside by a lover who is young enough to be her son. I may be wrong, but . . . It's just all "Oh, I can't live without you", "I think I want to die"; it's so unremittingly morbid! It's helpless too, which I don't like. I mean, have you seen that photograph of Tansu on the front page of *Hürriyet*?'

'No. I haven't really had time for reading.'

He reached over to the table and grabbed hold of one of the newspapers stacked behind a heap of ironing.

'Look at this,' he said as he spread the paper across his wife's knees. A large photograph of an anguished Tansu howling into a white-and-silver lace handkerchief screamed off the page. 'Poor Mrs Urfa lies dead on a slab, her baby, who is described but not shown, is missing and what do we get? A photograph of some adulterous old has-been who reckons that her poor Erol is so badly traumatised their love will never be as it was ever again. It's sick!'

'I agree we should see a photograph of the baby. If members of the public are to look for her they need that.' Fatma's face was set with the seriousness of the subject. 'But people do like this romance thing with Tansu and Erol. I myself find it disgusting because he's so young. I would hate it if one of our sons became involved with an older woman. But bad as they are, Allah has punished them now and it is not for us to judge.'

İkmen, whose opinion of religion of whatever type placed such phenomena somewhere between folk tales and the astrology columns in newspapers, rolled his eyes with impatience.

'And also,' Fatma continued, 'you have to remember that Tansu, anyway, is not always helpless.'

'Oh, I know that,' İkmen blustered on a laugh. 'She's reputed to have the most volcanic temper, be totally selfish—'

'No, I mean in her music,' Fatma said. 'There are some songs where the words are resentful rather than sad. They're often songs about her lover being stolen by another woman. They're really quite, well, I suppose you'd call them sort of tough.'

'A bit masculine, you mean?'

'No, her tone is much the same as in the others. But in songs like "I Want None of You" or "Hate Is My

Only Friend" the words are very strong, very . . .' She thought hard to find the right words, 'very sort of bitter, I suppose you'd say.'

'Expressing the collective frustrations of the lahmacun-eating classes?'

'Those are your words, not mine,' she said as she rose and picked up her towel once again. 'Anyway, I have things to wash. I haven't got time to sit about with you. Oh, and you might have a word with Bulent whenever he decides to come in.'

İkmen looked up and frowned. 'Why?'

'He's lost his job.'

'At the Pudding Shop?' İkmen's face took on a thunderous look. 'Why this time?'

'He turned up drunk,' Fatma said with more than a little edge to her voice. 'I think you should speak to him, don't you?'

'I've never been drunk at work!' he roared as he followed Fatma's retreating figure with his eyes. 'I used to take a drink, but only what I could handle. I was never drunk! What was the boy thinking, I mean—'

'He doesn't care, Çetin,' Fatma called out from the kitchen. 'As long as he's having fun he doesn't care.'

'Well, I'll just have to make him care then, won't I? If he's wobbling around in public he could get arrested even!'

'I think that may be the object of the exercise,

actually.' Fatma put her head round the door of the kitchen and sighed. 'I mean, what better way to get back at you, eh?'

'But why would he want to get back at me? Am I not a good father? Do I not listen to his ghastly adolescent ravings without complaint? Have I not always had a stable job in order to provide for my—'

'I think that's the problem.'

For a moment he just sat and stared at her, his mouth open and a little dry. 'You mean the job?'

'Well, it's a bit sort of with the establishment, isn't it? He's young. It's what they do, Çetin.'

'Is it indeed?'

'Yes, and you're going to have to be very calm when you tell him off or he'll do it all the more. I don't know how you're going to achieve this, Çetin, but you're going to have to be very "modern" indeed.'

And then she was gone, leaving her husband even more desperate for a drink than he had been before.

Although they gave the outward appearance of being devout Muslims, Deniz and Gülsüm Ertürk were in fact obsessed with only one thing – sex. That they didn't realise this was a tribute both to their youth and to the fact that the twins had been raised with only scant education in that area. All they knew was that ever since they had seen Erol Urfa for the first time three years before, they had been in love. They'd been fourteen when Erol's plaintive tones had entered their lives and ever since that moment he had dominated their every waking moment.

As much as they loved Erol, the sisters hated Tansu. One of their favourite games was to ascribe all her successes, both personal and professional, to witchcraft. Deniz had once heard that some people in the far east of the country worshipped Shaitan and she had taken it into her head that Tansu might be one of them. These people, it was said, always avoided blue, a colour that Tansu with her shades of dramatic red, black and white seemed to shun.

The death of Erol's wife had, however, taken the twins to a new dimension. Now, as they sat silently looking at the stern inspector across the table from them, was their finest moment as fans of Erol Urfa.

'We could stand it no longer, you see,' Gülsüm said as she nervously twisted one edge of her chador between her fingers. 'Erol is special, he deserves so much better than just a peasant girl.'

'And so you killed her,' Suleyman said, noting the fine, cultured accent of the two young women. A lot of high-born girls had taken to the veil in recent years. In some cases it was a form of rebellion against Westernised, materialistic parents. But they still, he reflected with grim amusement, retained all of their prejudices against 'peasants'.

'She was no good for him. She didn't love him,' Deniz added as she leaned across her sister's chest.

'So how did you kill her then?' Suleyman asked.

For just a few seconds the sisters exchanged a glance and then Deniz said, 'We poisoned her.'

'With?'

'With the stuff that Reşat uses to kill the rats,' Gülsüm said, enthusiastically adding, 'It contains cyanide.'

Suleyman frowned. Although the press had reported that Mrs Urfa had been poisoned, the substance involved had not been named. This could just be a coincidence, however. 'And who is Reşat?'

'He is our father's servant. He tends the garden. Rats come up from the water sometimes and so he kills them.' Deniz gave her sister a slow, sly smile. 'But we used it for another purpose.'

'And the child.' Suleyman leaned forward the better to see into their sweetly deranged and identical eyes. 'What did you do with Erol Urfa's child?'

Gülsüm looked at Deniz and then stared blankly back at Suleyman. Then she tipped her head just lightly towards her sister and smiled.

'The baby wasn't there,' Deniz said with the kind of direct confidence not popularly associated with the wearing of the veil. It was a confidence Suleyman recognised as one to which a person can only be born.

'So how do you account for the baby going missing?'

'How should we know?' Deniz replied haughtily. 'We only killed the peasant woman, we would never have hurt the baby.'

'Not Erol's,' her sister put in. 'He wrote "The Long Road to Your Heart" which means so much to me. He is a true and great artist and we would not even think of destroying such a genius's child.'

'You do know,' Suleyman said, leaning back in his chair and then lighting a cigarette, 'that Mr Urfa is from peasant stock himself? Unlike you girls he has always had to work rather than spend his time musing upon impossible imaginary romances.'

Gülsüm, outraged, looked across at her sister.

'How dare you speak like that to us!' Deniz blustered at Suleyman. 'We came here in good faith to confess to a crime and not only do we not get to see Erol to apologise to him but we are subjected to your rudeness too.'

'We're not afraid of the police, you know,' Gülsüm added. 'Our father knows three judges—'

'And your father is where right now?'

Gülsüm looked down at the floor and murmured, 'He's with Mummy in New York.'

'Leaving you two alone? I can't believe that,' Suleyman said, knowing that however virtuous a girl might be or however modern her parents, Turkish adults rarely left a woman's honour to chance.

'Our brother Kemal takes care of us,' Deniz said sulkily and then waving her hand in front of her face she added, 'Do you have to smoke!'

Suleyman replied with a face as straight as his back. 'Yes, I do. Now, I think that I should perhaps call Kemal before we go any further.'

Deniz sniffed. 'He's at his work now.'

'And anyway he won't come,' Gülsüm said. 'He finds us tiresome.'

Suleyman could appreciate Kemal's point of view.

'His opinion of you is immaterial.' Suleyman rose from his seat and then motioned forward the female officer who had been standing at the back of the room. 'You have admitted to a very serious crime about which you appear to have some knowledge.'

'That's because we did it, you silly man!' Deniz said haughtily. 'And as soon as we see Erol we will tell him why and make him understand.'

The female officer was now beside Suleyman. They exchanged a brief, knowing glance.

'Well, I'm afraid that seeing Mr Urfa at this stage is out of the question,' Suleyman said gravely. 'Victims do not usually see suspects until the case comes to trial.'

'But—'

'Officer Kavur here will take you down to the cells.'

'The cells?' Deniz shrieked.

'You will have to be detained, Miss Ertürk,' Suleyman said and inclined his head to Gülsüm. 'And your sister too. I must investigate your claims and see if they have substance. In the meantime, I cannot have you on the streets if you are indeed murderers. You must see that.'

'But can't we just see Erol for a little while when we're in the cells?' Gülsüm pleaded. Officer Kavur placed one hand heavily upon her shoulder. 'Don't you dare touch me!'

'Officer Kavur and myself may do what we like,' Suleyman said as he took Deniz gently by the arm. 'We may even use handcuffs if the need arises.'

'But we're just—'

'Young girls, yes,' he said, releasing his grip on Deniz and then smiling. 'And if you go quietly now with Officer Kavur and my constable outside, I will call your brother and perhaps then we will be able to sort this thing out.'

'But Erol, can't we—'

'Just go,' he said, as Kavur waved the two girls forward in front of her. 'Please.'

As the door shut gently behind the policewoman and the girls, Suleyman sat back down. That the girls had named cyanide was spooky, but nothing else in their story fitted the facts. Suleyman put his head in his hands and wondered how many more such scenarios involving Erol's fans he would have to endure.

Even though fully twelve hours had passed since the police had left her home, Semahat Temiz was still shaking with indignation. They had explained why they were removing three large sacks full of Cengiz's belongings but the careless way they had bundled them up was inexcusable. All his shoes had gone, plus his jackets and most of the contents of the washing basket. Some books and magazines had been taken too. Semahat knew nothing about these and said so to the police.

On the plus side, however, was the fact that she trusted Sevan Avedykian implicitly. Kenan had originally protested that the lawyer's rates were extortionate. But as Semahat had told him, after she had engaged Avedykian, if you wanted the best, you had to pay for it. After all, not every lawyer would head straight for a police station as soon as a client was in custody. But Sevan Avedykian had. He'd got very little out of either the sergeant who had apprehended Cengiz or the man Semahat now thought of as 'the big boss', Commissioner Ardiç. Avedykian had however seen Cengiz.

'The main problem is that he won't speak,' he told the parents as the three of them entered the police station. After signing in at the reception desk, he went on, 'He won't either confirm or deny their accusations. It makes them,' he flicked his head at a small knot of uniformed officers, 'very suspicious.'

'But if he's done nothing to be ashamed of then there is no need for speech,' Semahat protested.

'I take it as given that Cengiz is innocent,' Avedykian said with a thin smile, 'but to be honest, madam, we must look at this logically. Both you and your husband were out, on the night of the murder, you sir, at the İnönü Stadium watching the football. Cengiz was home alone and so the only evidence the police may rely upon with regard to his movements are his own testimony and forensic evidence. Nobody else in the apartments saw him that night—'

'Well, precisely! And if that ghastly little impresario or whatever he is had not had that so-called conversation with my son then we would not be here now! You would have thought the ridiculous man would have realised that Cengiz is as he is and discounted his words.'

'Mr Aksoy may well have done, but the police cannot.' Avedykian lit up a large Cuban cigar. 'The calculated use of cyanide in a sweet plus the clever timing of the event does however work in our favour.'

'How?' Kenan, his eyes red from lack of sleep, temporarily rose from his stupor.

'Well, Cengiz couldn't possibly have planned such a thing!' his wife exploded.

'Unless his actions came about by chance,' the lawyer added, 'although what his motive might have been I cannot imagine. But we must wait now for the forensic evidence to be assessed and for the pathologist to finish his work.'

'What do you mean?'

'Well . . .' This was not easy. Avedykian knew that Kenan and Semahat Temiz never spoke of the time, twenty years before, when Cengiz had been arrested for exposing himself to a young girl. 'Although time and mode of death have been established, the pathologist must now look for other evidence – injuries, signs of, er, abuse, er . . .'

Painfully aware of what her lawyer was attempting to say, Semahat changed the subject. 'So who are we seeing now then, Mr Avedykian?'

'Sergeant Çöktin is coming to meet us. He will ask you some questions you are not obliged to answer.'

'Will we be able to see our son?' Kenan asked.

Sevan Avedykian sighed. 'That I don't know,' he said.

'I mean, they could have beaten him or anything,' Kenan went on, tears filling his eyes. 'You know how it can be.'

Avedykian had opened his mouth to tactfully respond when a red-haired man appeared in front of them and said, 'I think you'll find your son is all right, sir.'

'How can you be sure?'

'Your son, Mr Temiz,' Çöktin said, 'is the responsibility of the investigating officer, Inspector Suleyman. If anything were to happen to Cengiz he would personally rip the offender apart.' He smiled.

'He sounds,' Kenan remarked, 'like quite a violent man.'

'He did have lovely manners,' his wife recalled, with just a tinge of affection.

'If violent,' said Kenan drily.

Çöktin smiled. 'The inspector is both the perfect gentleman and a very frightening person too.' With an evil grin he added, 'His kindness frightens me to death.'

Avedykian sniffed a little contemptuously at all of

this Suleyman talk. When Avram had been killed he had seen rather more of the haughty Ottoman than he liked. But he turned his mind away from that now, focusing his attention on the present. Though so much shorter than Çöktin, the lawyer looked down his nose at the officer and asked, 'So I take it we can now see Mr Temiz, Sergeant?'

'Yes, Mr Avedykian.' With a sweeping gesture he pointed to a badly stained door at the end of the corridor. 'Shall we go, madam, sir, Mr Avedykian?'

Chapter 5

Ali Mardin had been very reluctant to discuss his friend Erol Urfa. As various groups of tall Australians either took or replaced their keys on the board behind Mardin's desk he responded to Suleyman's requests in monosyllables.

'So, if you didn't watch the match or any other television, what did you do the night before last, Mr Mardin?'

'Talked.' His accent, like Urfa's, was rough with country tones.

'About?'

Mardin shrugged. 'This and that.'

Mardin was comfortably seated behind his desk but there was nowhere for Suleyman to sit, forcing him to shuffle restlessly from foot to foot. The extreme heat of the summer was debilitating enough without this.

'And were you alone, yourself and Erol Urfa?'

'Yes.'

'Are you sure?'

Ali Mardin lifted his heavily lined, element-worn face to look at the policeman. He could be, Suleyman

99

thought, anything from thirty to fifty-five years old. 'I am sure. I am not a madman.'

Suleyman sighed and then wiped his wet brow with his handkerchief. Middays in August had to be the closet thing to hell. 'At what time did Erol Urfa leave your premises?'

'In the morning when he went home.'

'Did you see him go?'

'No.' And then curling his lip into a sneer he said, 'What you want? That I should sleep with him?' He waved one hand dismissively to the side. 'I don't screw men.'

'I didn't say that you did.'

Mardin first burped and then grunted his grudging agreement. His lack of manners enraged an already unhappy Suleyman.

'Well, Mr Mardin,' he said through now tightly clenched teeth, 'your contribution to this investigation has been so fascinating that I fear I will have to go now before I become totally entranced.'

'Eh?'

'So if you will just allow me to look at your identity card I will be on my way.'

A very strange moment followed during which Mardin appeared to become frozen both mentally and biologically. As the blood raced from his face, rendering his walnut-hued cheeks ashen grey, it was as if this very simple request of Suleyman's had temporarily robbed him of the will to exist.

'Is there a problem?' Suleyman asked as he leaned, fascinated, across the desk towards Mardin. 'I do hope not.'

Inside his jacket pocket, Suleyman's mobile made its presence felt. He took it out and, turning aside from the traumatised Mardin, pressed the receive button.

'Suleyman.'

'Hello, Inspector,' Çöktin said. 'I thought I'd better let you know that Erol Urfa is going to be on television tonight.'

'What?'

'TRT are going to broadcast a plea by him for the safe return of his daughter.'

Suleyman sighed deeply. 'I dislike these things, especially in view of the fact that we don't have any idea who we are dealing with in respect of the child. Have TRT approached the commissioner regarding involvement from ourselves?'

'No. As I understand it they, or perhaps Mr Aksoy, want Erol to be filmed in a domestic setting, soft focus and that sort of thing. They intend to build a programme of sorts around the plea.'

'We'll need to know what he intends to say,' Suleyman replied. 'Is he still at Aksoy's place?'

'No. He's with Tansu Hanım at her house.'

'I'll have to get out there to see him then.' Suleyman wiped his hand across his brow. Blast this interminable heat! 'How are Mr and Mrs Temiz?'

Çöktin groaned. 'Hostile.'

'No word from forensic?'

'Not yet. Although a Mr Ertürk has returned your call. It was a bit garbled but it would seem that he's speaking at some sort of conference. He says, if this means anything to you, that you can keep "them" until he's finished.'

Suleyman raised his eyes up to heaven in despair. 'I don't believe it!' He turned round to face Mardin who, once he became aware that Suleyman was watching him, started frantically to turn out the drawers in his desk.

'So will you go out to see Mr Urfa then, sir?'

'Yes. Perhaps you'd like to contact forensic and inject a little urgency into their investigations.'

'OK.'

'Well, keep in touch then, Çöktin,' Suleyman said. 'I'll see you later.'

'Goodbye, sir.'

Suleyman terminated the call and then turned his attention back to Ali Mardin.

'So has that identity card turned up yet, Mr Mardin?' he asked.

For the first time since the policeman had arrived, Mardin smiled. It was a limp, sheepish sort of thing, but it was a smile nevertheless. 'No, I'm afraid that it hasn't. It—'

'You do know that it is a serious offence not to show your card to an officer when he requests it?'

'Er, yes, er—'

'If I had the time, I would pursue this further now, but . . .' What was important here was the fact that the missing child seemed to be getting somewhat lost in all the activity around the murder. 'I will send one of my men round in the morning to view your card,' and then looking up rather fiercely he added, 'That will give you ample time, will it not?'

'Oh, yes, yes!' Mardin agreed as he bowed down in a way that Suleyman felt was not entirely natural to him. All this obsequiousness had, he thought, come about rather too rapidly. It made Suleyman wonder just what lay behind it all. Was his card simply missing or did he not possess one? Was his card in fact someone else's or was there something on it of which he was ashamed? There were lots of possibilities, none of which he had time to explore now.

'Oh, and if you do think of anything else you would like to tell me about your evening with Mr Urfa, you will contact me, won't you, Mr Mardin?'

A little more guardedly, the man said, 'Yes.'

'So I expect we will meet again.' Suleyman held his hand out to Mardin.

The man shrugged as his dry palm touched Suleyman's hand. 'Maybe. Goodbye.'

'Goodbye.'

As he walked out into the searing midday sunlight, Suleyman took his sunglasses out of his jacket pocket and put them on. Then, as casually as he could, he briefly glanced across at the rather stylish Japanese car that was parked outside the carpet shop opposite Mr Mardin's hotel. So, still there then. Still containing the same amiable-looking married couple. He sighed. Following him to Mardin's place was one thing but now that he was going back to Tansu's ghastly house he did not need this. As it was, he would probably have to fight his way through the gang of press vultures who were, apparently, camped around the singer's property. But how to deal with his tail?

If İkmen had taught his protégé anything it was that meeting certain, usually unimportant but troublesome people head on was much better than ignoring their irritating behaviour. The 'doing it with humour' bit did sometimes elude him, not being a natural like his old boss, but he was prepared to give it a try.

He crossed the road and, with a smile, knocked on the window of the car. With a smooth swooshing sound, the window descended to reveal a widely smiling young man and his equally youthful female passenger.

'I just thought I'd let you know,' Suleyman said, 'that I'm not going to drive like a lunatic in order to get away from you. The late Princess Diana's driver made that mistake when attempting to get away from the French press. I'm certainly not going to die for the sake of their Turkish counterparts.'

'Ah . . .'

'So, by all means follow me if you must. But the drive will be slow and boring and could, quite possibly, involve a hold-up courtesy of my friends in the traffic division. Do I make myself clear?'

The man's over-friendly expression resolved into a scowl.

'I suppose so,' he said, but then brightening just a little he added, 'May I quote you on that then, Inspector?'

She'd just managed to get the child down for an afternoon nap when there was a knock at the door.

'I'll go,' she said to her mother. Madame Kleopatra had been restless for the last few hours and Semra, now seated quietly in the little back yard, was exhausted.

'Oh, it's you,' Mina said as she opened the door to a small, middle-aged policeman with attitude.

Cohen shrugged. 'I heard that Madame is really dying now. I've come to say my goodbyes.'

'I didn't know you knew her that well,' Mina said as she moved aside to let him in. 'I thought maybe you'd come to see me.'

He put his hand gently under her chin and pulled her face close to his. But he didn't kiss her as she thought he might. 'Not this time, my little soul,' he said. 'This time is for Madame alone.'

She took his small dry hand in hers and, with only a quick glance back to ensure that the child's door was shut, she led him up the creaking wooden staircase to the strange eyrie that clung to the side of the old baths' caldarium. The story was that Madame's husband had built this bedroom because he had poor circulation and was therefore always cold. The heat from the caldarium had, so the tale went, made his life much easier. Given the present scorching conditions, Cohen was glad that the baths were no longer in use.

Although it was obvious from the rattling sounds that emanated from the rickety wooden bed that they were in the presence of one who was dying, the pattern of light from the delicate filigreed shutters made Madame Kleopatra, if not lovely, not unpleasant to look upon.

Mina motioned Cohen into one of the chairs beside the bed and then sat down herself. With a smile the policeman took one of the old woman's hands in his and then kissed it.

'You know,' he said looking at Madame but addressing Mina, 'when I was a child Madame used to let me and my brothers bathe here for free.'

'Why did she do that?'

He looked away from Madame just briefly in order to smile at Mina and then he said, 'We were poor, you know. My mother died when we were very small and Dad was just a useless drunk. We moved here from Balat so that the old man didn't have to go so far to get to Çiçek Pasaj.'

'A Karaköy story.'

'You have it,' he sighed. 'Well, Dad didn't exactly have a lot of control over us and so, as young boys will do, we went around pretty filthy most of the time. At

school we were looked down upon, scruffy uniforms.'
He laughed as he looked down at his less than perfect
police uniform. 'Until, that is, Madame happened to
see us one day. "Bring those poor Jewish boys to me,"
she said to that skinny old eunuch with the gold teeth
she'd taken in God alone knows how long before.'

'A eunuch? What—'

'It's a long story,' he said with a dismissive wave
of his hand. 'But anyway she led us in, directed us
to the men's section and we had a bath. Then before
we left she told the eunuch, in front of us, "You are
to let the Jewish boys in whenever they wish and you
are to charge them nothing." She said it very haughtily,
which is what she was like.'

'So when did you last see Madame then?' Mina
asked.

'Oh, it has to be thirty years ago now,' Cohen said. 'I
know that the baths were closed by then and everyone
said Madame was dying.'

'So why are you here now?'

'I was passing and she just stuck her head out of this
window.' His gaze drifted across the filigree shutter. 'I
raised my cap to greet her and she smiled one of her
haughty ones. "So they made you a policeman, did
they, Jew?" she said, and I replied, "They wouldn't
have done if you hadn't cleaned me up, Madame."
Then she scowled. "Oh rubbish," she said, or something like that. "They would have had you anyway.
You're a clever little man, I could see the brightness

in you and your brothers always. And if your police friends should ever say otherwise, you send them to me." And then she slammed the shutter closed and was gone.'

'Did you ever know Madame's husband?'

'No. Why?'

'Well,' Mina said, 'my mum says Madame had no family of her own but her husband's people should probably be told that she's dying.'

'I have no idea who they are,' Cohen said. He turned back to look at Madame just as she opened her eyes. 'God!'

'No,' the old woman rasped, 'not God.' She lifted up one papery hand and patted the side of his face. 'Come close, Jew.'

Her breath was both laboured and rank and although he knew logically that she was just an old, dying woman, Cohen felt repelled. As she began to whisper, he winced. By the end of her little speech his expression was, however, one of shock rather than repulsion. At first Mina thought it was the rapidity with which the old woman sank back into coma that so disturbed him. But as soon as she saw the policeman whisper inaudibly into the old woman's insensible ears and then jump up from his seat as if scalded, she thought that perhaps Madame had said something shocking.

'What did she want?' Mina asked as she followed his rapidly retreating figure out of the room.

'Nothing,' he said shortly, hurrying down the stairs.

'Yes, but . . .'

Just as Cohen drew level with the door to the child's room, the baby began to cry. For a moment, possibly because his head was still full of whatever it was Madame had said, Mina thought that he hadn't noticed.

But she was wrong.

'Is that a baby?' he asked as, uninvited, he pulled the door open.

'Yes,' Mina said, 'it's a friend's. I'm looking after it for her.' Then, pushing past Cohen, she went over to the bed upon which the baby lay wrapped in a pretty gold brocade cover.

'I didn't think you lot often had children,' Cohen observed as he let his eyes drift distractedly around the room. Then, as if to himself alone, he added, 'What a terrible place to house a baby.'

'It's not so bad,' Mina said and held the child protectively against her chest.

Cohen shrugged. Then turning quickly he walked smartly out of the room without another word. As he disappeared, Mina let go of the breath she had been holding and then kissed the baby's head. Whatever Madame had said to Cohen had certainly shocked him. But in the circumstances that was probably a very good thing.

As soon as Suleyman's car disappeared down her drive, Tansu's demeanour changed completely. Whereas her mood had been one of soft conciliation and even at times tearful distress while the inspector was in her house, his departure provoked something far more malevolent.

'I can't believe you agreed to speak that posh boy's words without any discussion,' she snarled at a grey-faced Erol. 'We're stars. We don't just get pushed around!'

'He is a policeman, Tansu,' Latife said as she put a calming hand on her sister's shoulder.

'When I want your opinion, I'll ask for it!' Tansu roared and then hurled herself down at Erol's feet. 'You just say whatever you feel you need to in order to get Merih back, my darling. Don't worry about whether the police are there.'

Had Erol Urfa had any emotional resources left with which to respond he would probably have stroked Tansu's head as was his custom. But he was like stone now. Anxiety and sleeplessness had taken their toll and when he did respond it was with only a very weak smile.

As Tansu covered Erol's leaden legs with tear-stained kisses, Latife felt that the time had come for her to leave. There was no point in talking to either of them in their current moods and besides, if Tansu as she so often did managed to provoke Erol to lovemaking in spite of his own feelings, she did not want to be around. She strode out of the room, her face set and grave. But when she was once again by the swimming pool her mood lightened. She picked up the book she had been reading before the policeman arrived and, with a smile, resumed her studies.

By five o'clock that afternoon the results of the finger-print analyses had come through. They necessitated the reappearance of Cengiz Temiz in Interview Room 3. A very tired-looking Suleyman observed the trembling man sitting opposite him with something between odium and pity. Çöktin, who sat beside his boss, leafed briefly through the documents before looking up again as Suleyman spoke.

'So, Mr Temiz,' Suleyman said, 'I ask you again, where were you on the evening of the eleventh of August nineteen ninety-nine?'

Cengiz Temiz just carried on shaking, his mouth lolling open, soundlessly.

'I do need some sort of answer from you, Cengiz,' Suleyman continued in what he hoped was a rather more conciliatory tone.

Cengiz Temiz's small eyes darted rapidly between the two faces in front of him. Although he did not feel able to admit it, he wanted to go to the toilet quite badly.

'I didn't hurt Mrs Ruya,' he said as he pushed his hands between his legs and leaned forward.

As this was the first thing that Suleyman personally had actually heard Temiz say directly to him, it was quite a breakthrough. It also gave him the opportunity to tackle the man regarding more recently acquired evidence. Before he began he tried to bear in mind what Zelfa Halman had told him about speaking to people like Cengiz. It also briefly passed through his mind what the psychiatrist had said about the chances of someone like Cengiz being able to both plan and execute quite a complex murder. In the face of the evidence, however, he had to put that to one side.

'Cengiz,' he said leaning forward in order to show the man his fingers, 'do you remember when one of the officers downstairs asked you to put your fingers in ink and then press them down onto paper? It made finger marks or prints.'

'Mmm.' It was a grunt without any accompanying movements. Suleyman assumed that it meant Cengiz understood.

'Well,' he said, 'what we do is, we look at your prints and the prints of some other people and we try to match them with finger marks our forensic people collect at the scene of the crime.'

Nothing. Suleyman looked across at Çöktin who, for some reason, was smiling at Cengiz Temiz. When Suleyman cleared his throat, the younger officer changed his expression.

'Now it seems,' Suleyman continued, 'that your fingerprints match some of those at the scene of Mrs Urfa's murder. Not that you are alone in this. We've also found prints from Mr Urfa, baby Merih, and Mrs Urfa's prints on lots of things including kitchen equipment and her pen. The problem we have with you is that only your prints have been found on Mrs Urfa's body. Forensic have found your marks on the lady's spectacles and on a gold bangle round her wrist. Do you know what I'm saying here, Cengiz, or—'

'Didn't hurt Mrs Ruya! Didn't do it!'

'Didn't do what, Cengiz?' Suleyman insisted. 'What didn't you do?'

Once again the silence rolled in across the terrified wastes of Cengiz Temiz's face.

'Look, Cengiz,' Çöktin put in, 'if you didn't hurt Mrs Ruya or if what happened was an accident then you don't have to be frightened, do you?'

'When people die people get hung.'

'Not now. People do go to prison but . . . Look, Cengiz, if you didn't kill Mrs Ruya then just tell us when you touched her and—'

'She was cold after . . .'

'She was cold after what, Cengiz?' Suleyman asked, feeling his heart racing with the anticipation of one who knows he might be on the verge of a breakthrough. 'After . . .'

'Must go to the toilet now.'

'Yes, all right, but first—'

'Now.'

Çöktin, who was much less excited about what Cengiz might be about to say than Suleyman, said, 'I think you ought to let him go now, sir.'

'Yes, in a—'

'Now!' Cengiz's face was really quite contorted. As he grimaced and gummed his way through a succession of expressions, Suleyman, who had not noticed this need in his prisoner before, lost valuable seconds in argument.

'This urgency is really very sudden, Cengiz,' he said, 'in view of what we have been talking about.'

'I think it's all part of his condition, whatever it is,' Çöktin whispered into Suleyman's ear. 'I think you'd better let him go.'

'Yes, but—'

It was then that the sound of running water accompanied by deep, humiliated sobs were heard coming from Cengiz's large sad frame. Although unable to understand the more subtle aspects of life's diversity, he did know that in this horrible, dirty little room with policemen firing questions at him he was once again in trouble that would cause him pain. And this time, he knew, they would not just send him home when they had finished their questions. This time they were going to keep him.

Tansu stood on the very edge of the cliff, her eyes streaming with tears. Then with a flick of her proud head she turned to the man wearing some sort of foreign uniform who stood beside her and spat, 'I would rather die than be your woman!'

And with that she, or rather a stuntwoman, launched herself into the deep blue abyss below.

'Singers should never act,' Çetin İkmen said as he lit a new cigarette from the butt of his last smoke. 'Elvis Presley stands as a warning to us all.'

'Oh, I enjoyed his films,' Fatma said as she passed briefly in front of the screen herding a reluctant child towards the bathroom.

'None of us is perfect,' her husband muttered as he watched a picture of a group of young army conscripts flash up on the screen. Erol Urfa performing his duty for the Republic.

'You know, Fatma,' he called out over both the sound of the television and the running water from the bathroom, 'if I wanted to know when Tansu Hanım was born or where Erol Urfa comes from I wouldn't have the faintest idea from this programme.'

'She's a little shy about her age,' Fatma yelled back. 'It's why she chooses to change what Allah has given her.'

'The plastic surgery?'

'Yes.' With dripping hands she re-entered the living room and stood for a moment, her hands on her hips. 'Have you seen Bulent yet?'

İkmen's face darkened. 'Only from the balcony.'

Fatma raised her eyes towards heaven. Then changing the subject once again she said, 'Did I hear you say that Kleopatra Polycarpou is finally dying?'

'You shouldn't listen when I'm on the telephone,' İkmen said with an expression of what could have been mock sternness on his face.

Fatma, who was accustomed to such looks, simply carried on, 'But is she or—'

'Yes, it would seem so,' İkmen said with a sigh as he watched a piece of film showing Tansu and Erol on the beach at Bodrum. 'Cohen went to say goodbye.'

'And phoned you up to tell you?'

'Yes.'

'Why?'

'Because there is a problem with . . .' Suddenly realising what he was being drawn into, he stopped, looked at Fatma and said, 'And you know Kleopatra Polycarpou how, Fatma?'

'Oh, I've never known her myself, Çetin,' she said with a smile. 'I know of her because I've heard you speak of her and because Mrs Onat kept house for her for a while before she took on that,' she sniffed as if she had a bad smell under her nose, 'that woman.'

İkmen frowned. 'Nothing was ever proven against Semra Arda.'

'Only because that girl was dead by the time she got to hospital!'

'Well, nobody else came forward to say she'd been doing abortions on them too!' İkmen said with some heat in his voice. 'If there's no proof there's no case!'

'Unless it's pol—'

'I don't want to even begin to talk about areas of law enforcement that I do not understand!' he shouted. 'I deal with straight criminal homicide, Fatma, as well you know. I don't do political stuff. I do what happens when some greedy son decides to put rat poison into his father's Ayran. Along the way some of my suspects are actually exonerated, one of those being Semra Arda.' He held up one finger to silence Fatma and then said, 'Who is, by the way, not a subject you or Sibel Onat or anyone else should be discussing in terms of guilt!'

Before Fatma could answer, a child's voice floated in from the bathroom. 'Mummy!'

'I don't know how that child gets so filthy!' Fatma said as she turned to move away, her rising temper now moving in a different direction. 'She's like a boy, that one!'

'Which one?' İkmen asked.

'Gul,' she answered, and then added spitefully, 'You should learn the children's names sometime, Çetin!'

Before she left the room, she stopped briefly to listen to a very mournful song that seemed to be wrenching itself painfully from Tansu's unnaturally white throat.

'So which one is this, then?' İkmen asked, tipping his head towards the television set. 'Seeing as you are some sort of expert on this stuff.'

'"Hate is My Only Friend". One of the bitter ones I told you about,' Fatma replied and then with a toss of her head she added, 'I can sympathise with this sometimes.'

And then she was gone, leaving only her husband's scowl in her wake.

Turning back to the television, İkmen listened with what became, eventually, interest. This was, as Fatma had said before, very bitter stuff indeed.

> *You have taken him from me*
> *My peacock one*
> *Now hate is my only friend*
> *One day I will leave here*
> *I'll come to you then*
> *With a knife as my only love*
> *I will cut out your heart*
> *When you are alone*
> *Because hate is my only friend.*

Although Tansu smiled sadly as she sang, the message within the song was as clear as it was homicidal. It was really very unpleasant. With a frown, İkmen leaned forward and grabbed hold of the stack of tapes underneath the television.

Over in Karaköy somebody else was watching, if with rather less interest, this account of how Erol Urfa had found fame and now tragedy. Not that Cohen was really taking any of it in. His mind had become stuck several hours ago at the house of Madame Kleopatra and, as he looked at his watch for what had to be the tenth time that hour, he wondered if the old woman was dead yet.

Mehmet Suleyman, who was quietly sipping tea in

the chair opposite his friend, was engrossed, however. 'I'd be prepared to wager that this programme is what TRT have prepared should Erol die suddenly,' he said. 'It's so comprehensive. I almost expect to see a photograph of him at the end with his dates of birth and death underneath.'

'Mmm.'

'I just hope that when he does actually make his plea, Erol keeps to the script we agreed. Çöktin met him at the studios so he should be all right.'

'Why didn't you go?' Cohen asked, looking at his watch yet again.

'I had to see a man about his deluded sisters and anyway Urfa asked for him. Why do you keep looking at your watch?'

Cohen shrugged. 'No reason.' Then creasing his brow he said, 'Why would Urfa want Çöktin? I mean, you're the big man in this one, aren't you?'

'Perhaps it's something to do with their similar origins. Perhaps he trusts him more than me. I don't know.'

'Yes, well, you high-born boys can be a bit—'

'Sssh!'

As Erol's devastated face came into focus on the television, Suleyman leaned forward in order to turn up the volume.

'I don't have much to say,' the star, his voice obviously labouring under tranquillising drugs, drawled, 'except that I would like my Merih back now please.

There are certain foods she must not have, chicken and beans – she has allergies. You could, without meaning to, harm her in this way. Whoever you are, understand that this child is my whole life. If you have a soul then please return her to me. I don't care how you do this.'

'Don't mention locations, Erol, there's a good boy,' Suleyman muttered.

'If whoever has my Merih loves my music then please see from my face how dead I am now.' Tears rose unbidden to Erol's eyes. 'And if you hate me, think of Merih. I am her father, her only family now. Please, everyone, look at this photograph of my daughter and if you see her then contact the police. Telephone and fax numbers will appear at the end of this broadcast. Thank you.'

'No "İnşallah she will be returned to me" stuff then?' Cohen said as he turned aside to reach for his coffee.

'No. What you heard is what we agreed.'

'I thought you lot always appealed to God.'

'I thought you lot always made a lot of money until I came to live here,' Suleyman snapped back.

Cohen resumed looking at the now frozen image of a baby on the TV screen with a smile on his face which then rapidly and strangely faded.

Suleyman, thinking that perhaps he had gone too far with his remark, apologised. 'Sorry.'

But Cohen was not listening. With a sharp move

forward he went in close to the screen and peered myopically at the image.

'Mehmet,' he said as his fingers traced the edges of what appeared to be a shawl the baby was wearing. 'I've seen this before.'

'What?'

'This shawl,' he looked up, his face now ashen, 'I've seen it today.'

Suleyman dropped down onto the floor to join his friend. 'Where? Where have you seen it?'

'At Madame Kleopatra's hamam. With Mina.'

Chapter 6

'And Mina is who?' Suleyman asked as he turned round to look at a very winded Cohen behind him. Because his colleague had shot out of his apartment so quickly after the Urfa broadcast, Suleyman was still missing certain vital details.

'She's a prostitute.' Cohen paused briefly in order to take in a bit more oxygen. Living on a hill did not, as Cohen knew, mean that one could necessarily deal with steep slopes. 'Her mother is Semra Arda who works for Madame at the hamam. I saw the baby with the shawl there.'

Suleyman stepped lightly to one side in order to avoid a large pothole in the road. It was full of old Coke bottles and newspaper. 'So Madame Kleopatra's is where we are going now?'

'Yes. And no.'

'Eh?'

'It was Mina who had the baby, Mehmet. I can't go back to Madame's now, she's dying and besides . . .'

'Besides what?'

Cohen shrugged. 'I promised Madame that I . . .

Look, Mehmet, there are some problems around Madame. There are . . . things.'

Suleyman stopped in front of what looked like a tiny, deserted Greek church and then pulled Cohen into the overgrown garden that had once been a graveyard.

'What things?' he hissed, as he unconsciously conformed to his sombre surroundings. 'What do you mean?'

'I promised I'd only tell the inspector.'

'What? İkmen?'

'Yes. Which I've done now.'

'How does she know İkmen if she's been in bed for the last thirty years?'

Cohen smiled. 'The inspector knows everyone.'

Silently wondering whether he would ever attain the heights of simply being known as the inspector, Suleyman simply said, 'Oh.'

They stood in silence for a few moments. Cohen looked up as Suleyman, without thinking, spelt out the name of some long dead Greek which was carved into a fallen tombstone.

'Cohen, are you absolutely certain about this shawl?'

'Well, I was a bit in shock about what Madame had said to me at the time, but . . . I think so. It was very sort of gold, like the one on the television.' He frowned a little as he attempted to recall it in detail. 'It had a fringe like that . . . It . . . When I think about it now I think that Mina was a bit nervous. She grabbed the baby up quickly.'

'And it could not have been her own child?'

'She said she was looking after it for a friend.'

'Mmm.'

Two young green-clad conscripts passed by, arm in arm. They gave the two mature men in the graveyard puzzled looks.

'But Cohen,' Suleyman said on a now rather frustrated sigh, 'if we are to see this baby then we are going to have to go to Madame Kleopatra's.'

'No Mehmet, we need to go to Mina's.'

'So we just go marching into a brothel—'

'No. Mina works independently, like they all do round here now,' he paused to look over his shoulder, 'opposite Madame's. She might have the baby there but if she hasn't then her mother will have it at the hamam. Either way, if we can get Mina on her own then I think she'll probably tell us the truth. But we have to get past Mickey first.'

Suleyman sat down on the small broken wall of the graveyard and put his head in his hands. 'And Mickey is?' he asked patiently.

'He's an English hippy. He's also Mina's pimp. And he takes heroin.'

Without lifting his head, Suleyman murmured, 'Fantastic.'

'It's probably Mickey who took the baby. He's always looking for new ways to make drug money,' Cohen said as his voice rose in the excitement of the moment. 'Perhaps he even killed Mrs Urfa too.'

'Unless Mina did, or Mina's mother or any number of other people up to and including the man forensic evidence has placed at the scene of the crime.' He stood up quickly and put his hand to his head. 'What am I doing here?'

Cohen, suddenly angry at being doubted by his friend, reached up and grasped Suleyman by the shoulders. 'Look, Mehmet,' he said, 'that picture on the television shocked me. I know I've seen that shawl and I know where. Can we afford to ignore that? I mean, you play this however you want to. If we have to go to Madame's, well then I suppose we have to do that. You're the boss, after all. But we need to check it out, don't we?'

Suleyman sighed. 'Yes, we do. I want to see this baby – if, indeed, it's still there.'

'And if it isn't?'

'We will meet that eventuality if and when it arises.' He strode off back towards the road, 'Come on.'

Mickey Anderson threw his arm heavily around the young boy's shoulders and smiled. Behind him, clad only in a thin nylon negligee, his 'property' sneered at the back of his head before going to her room.

'So was that the best lay you've ever had or what?'

'Excuse me?' the boy replied as he attempted and failed to understand Mickey's colloquial English.

'Don't matter, kid,' Mickey said through several layers of food-encrusted beard, 'just give me the five million you owe me and you can get off home to your mum.'

The boy frowned doubtfully. 'Five million?' he said. 'But you say—'

'Ah, but this says seven million and rising,' Mickey said as he quickly pulled a knife out of his belt and held it up to the boy's head. 'Seven, kid,' and then resorting to one of the few Turkish words he knew he whispered, 'Yedi, to you,' into the boy's ear.

As the boy slowly put his hand into his pocket, Mickey smiled. 'There's a good boy.' He took the large wad of notes from the youngster's fingers and without counting it thrust it into his belt. Then with a hard punch to the middle of the boy's back, Mickey said, 'So now fuck off!'

The boy didn't need telling twice and as he ran into the street, Mickey followed at a more leisurely pace, replacing his knife as he went.

It was dark now, nearly midnight. The best time for his kind of business. Mickey grinned. Some of the bars had shut, disgorging back into the city those in search of something a bit more exotic than alcohol. Soldiers, sailors, airmen, old men, impotent Russians – rich and curious boys usually came after the clubs had shut in the early hours. But not always. There were, he noticed, some rather noisy 'suits' gathered beside that shitty old hamam where Mina went sometimes. There'd been a bit of crying from over there earlier in the evening which had sounded weird and unnerved Mina with her first trick. But the place was in darkness now and as quiet as the grave. Mickey shoved a cigarette into his mouth and wandered towards the source of the laughter.

There were three of them. Two were youngish men, in their thirties, the third was probably about fifty. The fifty, who was for some reason wearing sunglasses, and the plainer of the two younger ones appeared to be taunting the tall, good-looking one who was laughing in that wobbly, drunken manner.

'Hello, boys,' Mickey said, putting on his best friendly smile. 'What's happening?'

The older man who could not, seemingly, speak English just shrugged. The young plain one said, 'Hello,' and then putting one hand on his drunken friend's chest he added, 'Tomorrow he is married!'

'Oh, is that so?' Mickey said. 'That's nice.'

'Yes!'

'So where have you been then, boys?'

The tall handsome one stopped laughing just long enough to say, 'To drink and drink and drink!'

'Oh.'

'Yes,' the plain one said, 'it is the last time that my friend is a free man, you know?'

The older man said something in Turkish and they all laughed, including Mickey who said, 'Yes, freedom, right. So what are you doing now then?'

The plain one, who eventually gave his name as

Orhan, said, 'I don't know. Maybe look for some girls or . . . I don't know.' He laughed.

'Oh, some girls, eh? What, for all of you or just . . .'

Orhan laughed. 'I am married and so is Balthazar,' he said, indicating the older man who now stood in the shadows. 'No, for Mehmet only. It is his night.'

'Right.'

Mehmet, who was quite obviously heavily intoxicated, leaned against the side of a large, dark Mercedes and then giggled as his legs started to give way. Balthazar quickly ran to his aid.

Mickey wiped his moist brow against the back of his hand and then looked up at the star-filled sky. 'Well, if you want women,' he said, 'you've come to the right place.'

'You know some? Pretty ones?'

'Yeah,' Mickey shrugged. 'One or two.'

'They must be clean,' Orhan said, his face now quite set and serious. 'My friend cannot get a disease if he is to be married.'

'No. Course not.' Mickey looked over his shoulder at the doorway of his apartment block and then cleared his throat. 'Look, I may be able to help you out. If you can give me a minute . . .'

Orhan looked doubtful but he assented anyway. As Balthazar strained to pick Mehmet up off the ground, Mickey sauntered back to the apartment. As soon as he was inside the hall he took his mobile telephone out of his pocket.

* * *

It was only when she was standing outside Cengiz Temiz's cell that Zelfa Halman realised that she had omitted to put on any underwear. She looked down with horror at her unsupported breasts and groaned. But then this, or events like it, were not uncommon. Forgetting knickers or cigarettes or leaving the front door of the house open for burglars was all part of the being on call at night experience.

Although part of her work, from time to time, necessitated working with the police she did not have to come out to cells on a regular basis. Just being in the building made her shudder. It had never been this squalid in the cells operated by the Garda back in Dublin. The Irish half of her hated this hot, smelly squalor even if the Turkish portion did, on some level, understand it. She had, in the past, had many heated debates regarding treatment of prisoners in custody with the man who worked with this every day, the man whose prisoner she could hear screaming now. Quite where Mehmet Suleyman was at present she did not know and the rather oafish officers at her side either did not have that information or were not prepared to tell her. Perhaps they knew that their superior and this much older woman were lovers and were having a bit of a laugh, as it were, behind her back.

'Open the door,' she said to the heavily scarred individual to her left.

As he moved forward, keys in hand, the other two, a man and a hard-faced woman, removed their batons from their belts and held them up.

'You won't need those,' she said as she surveyed the scene around her with a jaundiced eye.

'He's raving, we might,' the woman replied shortly.

'If any of you do anything over and above restraint I'll make your boss's life hell and then you'll be sorry.'

The man with the keys opened the door and then stepped back smartly. 'Doctor.'

Probably since the dawn of time and certainly since what is known in Europe as the Dark Ages, reports have circulated regarding so-called wolf-men. Whether these creatures are transmogrified people such as in the werewolf legends or simply individuals who have either been raised by wolves or who have gone wild in some way depends in part upon where geographically these individuals have been found. In nineteenth-century Romania, for instance, a demonic or supernatural explanation would have been logical. In a police cell in the middle of İstanbul in the dying days of the twentieth century madness seemed the most likely explanation to those now observing Cengiz Temiz's bizarre, howling behaviour. When not screaming and hurling his now bloodied arms against the walls, Cengiz raised his shaggy head up to the ceiling and howled.

'How long has he been like this?' Zelfa asked

as she attempted to make eye contact with the distressed man.

'Couple of hours.'

'A couple of hours!' She was furious and, although she didn't take her eyes off Cengiz for a second, she made her feelings very clear to the officers at her side. 'Why wasn't I called before? Too busy eating kebab and dribbling over girly magazines?'

'But, Doctor,' the female officer began, 'I am—'

'I include you in that too.' Zelfa's Irish directness was quite unaffected by what this woman obviously felt was a tremendous insult.

Cengiz screamed like a banshee, hurling his considerable bulk pogo-style into the air. Making certain one more time that one of the small syringes she had taken from the drug cabinet before she left the hospital was at the top of her bag, Zelfa turned to the man at her side and said, 'I want you and the others to restrain him while I talk to him.'

As she stepped into the cell, the stink from Cengiz's unwashed, sweaty body nearly knocked Zelfa flat. Babbling and raving, Cengiz had wet himself more than once and had also, she noticed, thrown food and drink up the walls. Somewhere down the corridor the sound of another prisoner joining in with the screaming reached their ears.

Holding one open hand out in greeting, Zelfa moved forward. 'Hello, Cengiz, I am Dr Halman, I've come to help you.'

'Aaaahhh!'

Keeping her eyes on both Cengiz and the two officers who were now closing in on him, Zelfa also took in that the man was shaking. Whether this was from shock, fear or just sheer exhaustion she did not know. What she could see of his wounded arms indicated only superficial grazing.

As the first officer got a lock onto one of Cengiz's arms, the other one pulled him down to the floor. As his face hit the mess beneath him, Cengiz howled. Quickly, lest his breathing should be impaired, Zelfa moved forward and shifted his head to one side.

'It's all right, Cengiz,' she said, 'I only want to talk to you and then try to make you more comfortable.'

'I want my mummy and daddy!'

'Yes, I know, and if you can be quiet for a while perhaps we can do something about that.' Then looking the officer directly in front of her straight in the eyes she said, 'This place is a fucking disgrace!'

'Inspector Suleyman said he should be put here,' a female voice from the other side of the room said caustically.

'In view of what happened to another disordered prisoner down here last year I doubt that Inspector Suleyman wanted you to let him harm himself!' She looked up into the woman's sneering face and added, 'Inspector Suleyman has the wit to know that when someone is bleeding he is usually injured!'

The woman said something which could have been

'Well, you should know' or words to that effect, but Zelfa chose to ignore it. The last thing she needed right now was a dissection of her private life.

Now a little quieter than before, Cengiz's eyes were full of sad tears. Zelfa sighed. Why Cengiz's fingerprints had been on Ruya Urfa's spectacles and jewellery she didn't know. More recently, a pair of his shoes had been found to match dusty footprints in the hall of the apartment as well. But looking at him now it was difficult to credit this man with a coldly calculating poisoning. In order to do something like that one would have to know many things: what cyanide was, that it could be disguised within almond halva, that it would work very quickly, that it was a good idea to do it while everyone was either at or watching on television a passionately anticipated football match. This had to be beyond someone like Cengiz. And for a moment, before she took hold of her emotions once again, Zelfa felt very angry with Mehmet for putting this poor creature through this terrible ordeal. Not that Mehmet, given the evidence, had any choice in the matter.

'You can sit him up,' she said as soon as she could see that Cengiz's breathing was becoming calmer.

The two officers grunted as they raised Cengiz onto his haunches. Their prisoner was a big man and he was also exhausted, quite unfit and therefore a dead weight.

'Now, I can give you some medicine—'

'No! No, not—'

'Ssshh! All right, all right,' she said as she gently placed her hands across his and looked up into his face. 'You don't have to have it. If you are a good, quiet boy and—'

'I hate it here!'

She smiled. 'Yes,' she said, 'so do I. But if I can get you moved to a cleaner place so you can get some sleep then we won't need to give you any medicine, will we?'

'Don't want medicine!'

'No,' she said, 'of course you don't and I will not give it to you provided you try to get some sleep.'

One of the officers holding Cengiz cleared his throat. There was, Zelfa noticed, a look of extreme alarm upon his face. He, at least, had counted upon the medication to give him an easy shift. Well, fuck you! Zelfa thought as she smiled at Cengiz again.

And, almost as if he saw and understood her thoughts for himself, Cengiz started a long, slow grin back at this strange, pale little saviour.

Mickey made the two other men sit in the kitchen as he took their wobbly friend through to the bedroom.

'Help yourselves to rakı if you like.' He pointed to a bottle on top of one of the greasy work surfaces. But the men did not answer, they just stood very straight-faced and quiet. Now inside the apartment they were much more subdued, with the exception of Mehmet.

When Mickey opened the door, Mina was standing in front of the wardrobe mirror, studying her face. She turned, scowling, until she noticed that her client was considerably better looking and cleaner than her regulars.

'This is Mina,' Mickey said, a smirk spreading over his hairy features. 'All right?'

Seemingly drinking in every gram of Mina's considerable figure, Mehmet grunted his assent.

Mickey smiled. 'OK, mate,' he said, 'no violence or weird stuff and we'll all be friends.' Then clapping him firmly on the back he whispered, 'Enjoy yourself.'

As soon as Mickey had closed the door behind him, Mina pulled the straps of her negligee down to reveal her breasts. 'Hello,' she said, 'can I—'

But before Mina could articulate just what she was offering this unusually urbane new client, Mehmet Suleyman had his hand over her mouth and his gun to her head.

Chapter 7

Hell, it is often said, is a state of mind. Sometimes, however, the infernal zone can take on an all too physical manifestation. For Mehmet Suleyman it was a police station full of people yelling their own agendas. Given the conflicting nature of the individual needs of the various groups, the result was chaotic.

Erol Urfa, who had been called in some time before to identify his daughter, was edgily awaiting her reappearance from the room where she was currently being examined by a doctor. Resplendent in a black and red velvet suit, he had come in with his manager, what appeared to be all of Tansu's family and, strangely from Suleyman's point of view, İsak Çöktin. With the exception of Çöktin, the party looked as if they were dressed for cabaret which was what, in a sense, they appeared to be providing with their deafening babble of anger punctuated by occasional forays into tearful relief.

There was one group, however, that Suleyman was anxious to interview. Semra Arda, her daughter Mina and the English pimp all needed to be formally interrogated. The two women wept continually while the man just shook soundlessly within his handcuffs: Suleyman hoped their states were transitory although, logically, he knew it was unlikely. As soon as Cohen had appeared at the hamam and inquired after the baby, Semra had broken down and admitted that the child in her care was Urfa's. When Mina had been arrested she had denied this. There was a lot to sort out, and that was without the problems now being presented to him by both Cohen and an irate Zelfa Halman.

'We can't leave Madame to die alone,' Cohen said as he leaned tiredly against Suleyman's desk.

'Well, you'd better try to find out who her doctor is and get him over there,' and then dragging his hands wearily down his face Suleyman said, 'Why she isn't in hospital is beyond me.'

'But I don't know who her doctor—'

'Well, ask Semra Arda, she should know! Or perhaps even Inspector İkmen! He seems to know everything there is to know about everything!'

'Oh, right.'

'Go!' And then turning to the fuming woman in the corner, Suleyman snapped, 'And? Yes?'

As soon as the door had slammed behind Cohen, Zelfa Halman started. 'What do you think you are doing with Cengiz Temiz?'

'What?' Either through tiredness or genuine forgetfulness Suleyman was suddenly and completely confused.

'Cengiz Temiz?' She moved towards him, her cigarette held before her like a weapon. 'You know, the man with Down's syndrome you put into the care of three characters straight out of a Lovecraft short story.'

'Eh?'

'When I arrived less than an hour ago he was hysterical, swimming around in his own piss and had mutilated himself! God knows how long he'd been like that. I strongly suspect that those cretins you had charged with his care only called me when they smelt his blood!'

'Dr Halman—'

'I'm telling you now that if the Temiz family make a complaint, I will support them.' She rudely pointed her cigarette at his face. 'I expected better of you, Inspector! You and İkmen are usually more compassionate than what generally passes for policemen in this bloody country.'

'Upholding prisoners' complaints is your right, Doctor,' he said.

'In Ireland—'

'Where people are frequently bombed and shot,' he looked up at her face which was now white with fury. 'Yes? You were saying?'

The switch from Turkish to English was sudden and ferocious. 'Don't even begin to tell me about the country of my birth, Mehmet! Don't even breathe about things you don't understand! There is about as much similarity between yourselves and our Garda as there is between a rock and my arse!'

'Then perhaps, Dr Halman,' he said, joining her in the English language, 'you should return to practise in the country of your mother.'

'Don't think I don't want to!'

He turned aside to retrieve a stack of files from the floor. 'If that is what you want, that is what you must do.'

As a thick, resentful silence enveloped the room, Suleyman opened the top file and made some attempt to get beyond the first sentence. Out of the corner of his eye he watched as she paced angrily up and down in front of his desk. Then suddenly and explosively, once again, she said, 'So do you want me to go or—'

'My personal feelings are irrelevant,' he answered, slipping easily back into his native tongue. 'If you are professionally frustrated here . . .'

'So you'll not ask me to stay for any other reason then?'

Anxious that those outside should not be privy to an exchange that had now taken on a personal edge, Suleyman returned to English again. 'If you wait for me to beg, you will wait a long time.' Turning aside to pick up his cigarettes he added, 'If you fail to understand then speak to your father.'

'Oh, I understand all about Turkish male pride all right!' she said as her eyes unbidden began to water. 'It fucking stinks!'

He stood up quickly, towering above what was now the shrunken figure of his opponent. 'I have no more time for this,' he said. 'I have people to interview. If you wish to draft a report on Cengiz Temiz and leave it on my desk I will attend to it as soon as I can.'

'So I'll not be seeing you at the house for a while then?'

'That decision is entirely in your hands,' he said and then, turning sharply, he put his hand on the door handle and turned it.

It may have been an optical illusion but Zelfa Halman did think that she saw just a little wetness around his eyes as he moved away. But as he opened the door onto the babbling hordes outside she flung the word 'Bastard!' at him anyway.

Those beyond the door suddenly became very quiet.

Çetin İkmen switched the telephone off and then flung it carelessly onto the floor.

'What's going on?' Fatma said as she kicked the sheets back over to his side of the bed and turned her sleepy face up to his. 'Is it Bulent?'

'No. Go back to sleep.' He kissed her lightly on the lips and then swung his legs over the side of the bed. As he sat up, he felt his head swim with tiredness.

'Çetin . . .'

'I have to go out,' he said as he shakily placed a cigarette in his mouth and lit up.

Fatma opened her large brown eyes and blinked. 'Why? You're not working.'

He breathed the smoke deeply and then almost instantly clutched at his stomach. 'Someone needs me.'

'But you're not well!' She sat up, suddenly and shatteringly awake. 'Anyway, who needs you so much Çetin? At this hour?'

As he clipped his watch onto his wrist, İkmen sighed. 'Madame Kleopatra. It's a long story, but basically Suleyman has left her in the hamam to die alone.'

'But Mehmet wouldn't—'

'Yes, but Cohen says that he has. Dr Katsoulis is on his way but he's having to come from his home in Anadolu Kavağı. Madame is an institution, she should not die with only her nightmares for company.'

'Why should she have nightmares? She was, I thought, always a good woman.'

İkmen stood up and stretched, cigarette in mouth. 'When Halil and I were little, Mother used to take us to the İskender Hamam. It was a long way for us but Madame even then had something of a reputation. Like most women, Mother would take food, all the clothes and potions we needed for the day and,' he smiled, 'her cards. Madame lay great store by my mother's predictions.'

'So she's a witchcraft friend, is she?' Fatma said with a scowl. Despite having been married to Çetin for nearly thirty years, Fatma still did not approve of her late mother-in-law. That she had been Albanian lent her a strange 'otherness' that was forgivable. Her practice of the so-called black arts was less acceptable.

Her husband, dressing hurriedly now in the half-light from the street lamp outside, ignored Fatma's disdain, as was his custom. 'Then when Mother died, Madame played a different type of card game with my father,' he said. 'Madame, Mimi Sarkissian and Timür would play for hours for just a few kuruş – until Madame took to her deathbed.'

'Was her husband still alive then?'

İkmen knotted his tie and shrugged. 'I don't know. Arto's father had died which was why Mimi used to come.' He sighed. 'I can't believe Mimi died so quickly after Timür. When Madame goes, that whole way of life will have disappeared.'

With a grunt of pain as her back creaked, Fatma hauled herself across the bed and then kneeled up to help her husband with his tie. 'You're a good man, Çetin İkmen,' she said, her lips a little tight around this admission.

When she had finished arranging his tie, İkmen bent down to kiss his wife again. 'I am an old sinner, as well you know,' he said with a smile. And then flinging his jacket across his shoulders he crept quietly towards the bedroom door.

Fatma who had far too many children to be able to help herself said, 'Drive carefully.'

*   *   *

As soon as Mina Arda took her eyes off the female officer across the desk and looked at Suleyman, she started to shake. That moment when she'd first seen what had to be the most attractive customer she'd had for years now seemed very far away. Now, by sharp contrast, she could barely tolerate his voice without wanting to be sick.

'You do have a right to legal representation,' he said.

The female officer cleared her throat in a way that Mina interpreted as disapproval. Not that talk of lawyers made any difference to Mina anyway. With absolutely no assets beyond her meagre 'wages' from Mickey, she knew what type of lawyer she could afford.

'No,' she said, 'I don't want that.'

'I should tell you,' he said as he settled himself next to the female officer and lit up a cigarette, 'that the charges against you are very serious. Your mother claims she did not know the child you appeared with on the night of Mrs Urfa's murder was Erol Urfa's daughter until she saw the broadcast yesterday evening. She says you "needed a child". Can you tell us about that?'

'No. But if you ask my mother, she will.'

'You're being very obstructive for one who is facing charges of both kidnap and murder.'

'I didn't kill Mrs Urfa! I didn't even know her!'

'But you came into possession of her child in order to fulfil some sort of need.' He flicked the ash from his cigarette into an ashtray and then leaned forward across the table. 'Did perhaps Mickey procure the child for you or—'

'Mickey has got nothing to do with it! He may be a crazy violent bastard and I hate him, but—'

'You don't need to protect him, you know,' the female officer said. 'He can't hurt you now.'

'Officer Kaya is right,' Suleyman put in. 'You must look to yourself now, Mina.'

'Look,' Mina said, tears rising in her eyes once again, 'whatever Mickey may or may not be, he's got nothing to do with this!'

'Considerable quantities of hashish have been discovered in your apartment. Mickey, we know, made a call to a known drug dealer just before I entered your apartment. Together with an ampoule of what would seem to—'

'It's morphine,' Mina said and then added quickly, 'which is mine.' She sighed. 'Mickey hates children. He would have gone crazy if he'd found out I had the baby. I stole the amp from the lady my mum looks after.'

'Madame Kleopatra?'

'Yes. I thought that if I could give Mickey a little bit extra every so often it would allow me time to go and see the baby.'

'So he does take opiate drugs then?' Kaya asked.

'What do you think!' Mina then turned back to the hated Suleyman. 'Mickey isn't involved in this, Inspector. Let him go.'

'So, if Mickey isn't involved and you did not kill Mrs Urfa in order to procure her baby, how did this all come about, Mina?'

Mina slumped her chin down onto her hands and murmured, 'Can I have a cigarette?'

Suleyman pushed his packet and lighter across the table to her. Mina lit up and then, on a sigh, she began.

'It was the fat boy who brought her to me,' she said and then, seeing the look of confusion on Suleyman's face, she explained, 'He's a client of mine. He's middle-aged, lonely and . . . he says he loves me and . . . you know. He brought me the baby with some wild story about how her mother had been killed by a devil. He said that with the mother now dead and this demon or whatever on the loose, he had to put the baby somewhere safe and so he came to me. Not that I cared very much where the little one came from, as soon as I saw her, I knew that I wanted her. Just like the fat boy knew I would.'

'So how soon after that did you realise that the child was in fact the missing Merih Urfa?'

'I had a feeling when I heard about it on the radio sometime the following afternoon. Then when I saw the little one on the television . . .' She shrugged.

Officer Kaya frowned. 'How did this fat boy know,

as you put it, that you, a working woman, would want a baby?'

Mina looked from Kaya across to Suleyman and then back at the woman again. 'I'd rather tell you alone or with another lady, if . . .' She put her head down and looked at the floor.

'So do you know the name of this fat boy?' Suleyman said, quickly changing from a subject that he knew he couldn't handle to one that he could.

'Yes.'

'Well?'

Mina looked up into what seemed to her to be his hard eyes. 'He didn't do it, you know. It was as he said, a demon.'

'Well then, if it was a demon, your friend has nothing to fear, does he?'

As soon as he had said it, Suleyman realised that he had spoken in that patronising way the upper orders were wont to do when attempting to communicate with the poor and ignorant. Not that Mina was a member of the latter group, as he soon found out.

'A smart man like you doesn't believe in demons, Inspector,' she said. 'I know you're just trying to get me to deliver my friend and—'

'If you don't, Mina, you will stand trial for kidnap, at the very least, on your own.'

'And given the profile of this case,' Kaya put in, 'you could go to prison for a long time.'

'Besides,' Suleyman said as he ground his cigarette

out in his ashtray, 'perhaps what your friend saw, though not a demon, was a person whose description could be very useful to us. We do need to catch this person before he kills again, you know.'

Mina took a long drag on her cigarette and then tapped some ash out onto the floor. 'The fat boy might be a bit crazy, but I definitely heard him call the demon a her.'

'So he saw a woman somewhere in the vicinity of Mrs Urfa's apartment presumably, and . . .'

'He saw her coming out of the apartment, I think. Then he went in to get the baby.'

Suleyman frowned. 'How?'

'I don't know.'

'Well, I need to know and very quickly, Mina.' Suleyman rose to his feet and walked over to her side of the table. 'And now would be as good a time as any.'

He placed his hands firmly on the table one each side of Mina's body. She cringed. Towering above her, his tall body reeking of expensive aftershave and privilege, she suddenly felt very small and very frightened. People, she had heard, sometimes disappeared in places like this. Hard-faced policemen could and did do awful things, the bazaars were full of such stories. And just because this man and his unnatural-looking woman in uniform hadn't beaten her yet didn't mean anything really. Mina felt her heart begin to pound. Perhaps she should have taken the inspector up on his offer of a lawyer after all. Not that it was too late now, but . . .

'I'm waiting, Mina,' he said gently, wheedling into her ears. 'If this person kills again you will not only be answerable to the law but also to Allah. You will have colluded in another death. Think about it.'

'But if I say,' she said through the tears that were now spilling heavily down her face, 'you will hurt him and I know that he didn't do it. He is gentle and good.'

Pressing home his rising advantage, Suleyman placed his lips almost on Mina's ear as he whispered, 'But if he is innocent I will have no reason to hurt him, will I?'

Officer Kaya, who had been watching what seemed to be almost a seduction enacted before her, shifted nervously in her seat. But neither Suleyman nor Mina paid her any heed.

As he moved Mina's chin upwards so that he could look directly at her face, Suleyman said, 'Please tell me his name now, Mina. Please.'

As his large slanted eyes bore into hers, Mina murmured, 'His name is Cengiz Temiz.' And then, all of a sudden as if a spell or some such had been broken, her revulsion of him returned and Mina put her head down and vomited onto the floor.

When he returned from putting Erol Urfa, the baby and entourage into the vehicles to take them home, İsak

Çöktin was smiling. 'When he comes back tomorrow, Erol's going to fill the station with roses, by way of thanks,' he said gleefully.

'Is that going to happen before or after his interview with your boss?' Cohen asked acidly.

'Don't you think it's wonderful that the baby has been found safe?' Çöktin said as he sat down next to an exhausted and strangely plain-clothed Cohen.

'Well, seeing as how I was there, yes I do,' he said. 'You were with Urfa, weren't you?'

'Yes.' There was something a little guarded in Çöktin's reply which Cohen picked up on immediately. 'He was very distressed after the broadcast. He's getting edgy about when he might be able to collect his wife's body. He wants to take her home to his village.'

'Until Dr Sarkissian's finished taking samples, he'll have to stay edgy. And anyway I find all this concern after death a bit insincere. I mean, it's not like he was that interested in the poor woman during her life. Too busy running around with that old tart.'

'You don't understand,' Çöktin said with some heat in his voice.

'Oh yes I do,' Cohen replied in kind. 'Erol Urfa wanted it all. He wanted to be the dutiful son of his father and marry the little girl he was betrothed to who could and would give him children. He also wanted to further his career and have some real dirty sex with that Tansu. There is nothing you can tell me about men, sex and arranged marriages, so don't even try.'

As they both sat in disgruntled silence, Sergeant Orhan Tepe passed by and smiled. 'The hippy has asked for somebody from the consulate,' he said as he threw his car keys into the air and then caught them again. 'But I'm going home to my wife and family.'

'Lucky you,' Cohen murmured dejectedly.

Tepe laughed. But then just before he reached the door to the car park he turned and said, 'Is your name really Balthazar?'

'Oh, fuck off!'

When the door had closed behind Tepe, Çöktin looked up at Cohen and sighed.

'He's always so happy, isn't he?' he said, looking after Tepe, a slight frown upon his face. 'But then his wife has recently given him a son and I guess that has to be reason enough.'

Cohen, relieved that further discussion of his name did not seem to be on the agenda anymore said, 'So was the Urfa baby all right? No rashes from beans or whatever it was she wasn't supposed to eat?'

'No.'

'You do know that the inspector would have had your balls for staying on with Urfa, don't you?'

Çöktin, missing the point of just who Cohen was talking about, said, 'He seemed OK when he arrived with you and the prisoners.'

'I'm not talking about Suleyman!' Cohen said with

just the hint of a bitter laugh in his voice. 'God, you're young! No, I was talking about *the* inspector, İkmen. He always wants to know where everyone is all the time. Feels personally responsible for us.'

'You're not criticising Inspector Suleyman, are you, Cohen?'

'Not to you,' he said as he stood up and moved towards the front office. He opened the door just as Dr Halman swept majestically out of the building, her face vaguely furious. As he stood amid the general hubbub of police officers coming and going, Cohen wished that, rather than wait for Mehmet, he could just settle himself to going out to see İkmen at Madame's. But then he had a really rather important report to write plus he felt that, in view of Dr Halman's expression, Suleyman might really need him.

Despite the fact that the car, which was taking the most direct route back to Yeniköy, was passing through brightly lit streets, Merih Urfa stayed resolutely asleep in her father's arms. Although exhausted, Erol couldn't take his eyes off her for a second. From time to time he reorganised her shawl in order to make her more comfortable. Tansu, who cooed at the child occasionally when she wasn't staring blankly out of the window, sat on one side of her lover while on the other was Erol's manager, İbrahim Aksoy, who was smoking a large Cuban cigar. Despite their police driver and Tansu's sister Latife, sitting beside the officer, Aksoy was being extremely candid about his protégé's future.

'Of course we'll have lost the George Michael fan base now,' he said as he flicked his ash out of the window.

'What do you mean?' Tansu inquired as she took her cigarettes out of her bag and lit up.

Aksoy sighed. 'Darling, we marketed Erol after what I call the "George Michael model". It's why we kept poor Ruya such a dark secret. Like George Michael, I designed Erol to appeal to the young teenage girls who, I know you will agree, would cry bitterly if they discovered their idol was a married man with a child. With you in tow I knew we could retain the children and fascinate their mothers at the same time. It was perfect. But Erol's fatherly state is now out in the public domain, like Michael's homosexuality. I'll have to find an altogether more mature image for him now.'

Latife, who had until now been sleeping, suddenly found herself awakened by wreathes of acrid smoke.

'I don't think it's a very good idea to smoke around that baby,' she said, winning a smile of agreement from Erol.

Aksoy, who had been genuinely unaware that what he was doing was wrong, quickly put his cigar out in the ashtray in the car door. 'Sorry.'

Tansu, however, was quite another matter. 'Well, she'll have to get used to it if she's going to live in my house,' she said, giving her sister the sort of look that could strip paint. 'I have to smoke.' And then, as if to make the point even more strongly, she took a drag on her cigarette and blew it into Latife's hair.

'I'm sure we can come to some sort of arrangement,' Erol said, taking Tansu's free hand in his and kissing it. 'After all, we won't be with you for that long, Tansu.'

'Oh, but you mustn't go now!' the ageing singer cried, hurling her cigarette out into the night as she clung, limpet-like, to Erol's arm. 'Not now that you're—'

'We can't stay with you for ever, Tansu,' Erol said and nervously looked across at Aksoy.

'No,' his manager agreed, 'it would hardly look right, Tansu darling. Not, at least, until things are finalised with regard to poor Ruya. You must see that.'

'Yes, but well,' she was pouting now, thwarted in her desires, child-like, 'well, we could get a nurse or maybe Latife could—'

'As soon as I can I must set about making a home for Merih and myself.' Erol hugged the child tightly to his chest. 'I must do the right thing.'

'And what about me?' Tansu asked, her long, thin eyebrows arched with arrogance. 'What about the "right thing" for me?'

'In time all will become clear,' Aksoy said with what seemed to Tansu misplaced confidence. 'I have a meeting tomorrow with Ferhat Göktepe.'

'With my agent?' a very agitated Tansu cried. 'Why are you meeting him?'

'To discuss how we may jointly facilitate your careers in the light of this tragedy. How you two plus little Merih here may be—'

'I don't want Merih exploited!' Erol said as he tore his arm away from Tansu and looked angrily at his manager. 'I want things to be quiet now.'

Aksoy laughed. 'Oh, Erol,' he said, 'I don't think there's much chance of that, do you?'

Erol Urfa's features flushed, forcing him to turn back to face the front of the car. But then the truth, he knew, could provoke many emotions, including anger. Of course İbrahim Aksoy was right, there would be no peace until the business of his wife's death was concluded. Her killer, sooner or later and whether or not it turned out to be that odd neighbour, had to be nailed. Until then, suspicion and rumour would abound, not least about himself. If nothing else, his appointment with Inspector Suleyman tomorrow morning was testament to the fact that he was hardly out of the frame yet. After all, with Tansu sitting extravagantly at his side, he didn't exactly fit the traditional model of an ideal husband.

As the car passed in front of the heavily guarded Dolmabahçe Palace, the driver no doubt noticing Erol's sweat-swamped face said, 'Would you like me to turn the air conditioning up, Mr Urfa?'

'Yes,' Erol said as he smiled into the sleeping face of his child, 'that would be nice.'

Chapter 8

At first the thing in front of his face was no more than a vague blur. Given his current assignment plus the rather disordered state of his thoughts, Suleyman thought that it might be a pool of blood, possibly even his own. Well, the thing was red and so a pool of blood was not such a crazy idea. But as he raised his head slowly from the surface of his desk, he began to see certain details he had not focused on before – petals, stems, a vaguely sweet perfume.

'A sprig of bougainvillea,' İkmen said as he picked it up and sniffed at its flowers, 'from the garden of the İskender Hamam.'

Suleyman's eyes which were sore and small from lack of sleep blinked as the harsh light from the rising sun outside assaulted them. 'Sir?' he said huskily. 'What . . .'

'Madame Kleopatra died almost exactly an hour ago,' İkmen said as he slipped down wearily into the chair in front of Suleyman's desk. 'I left Dr Katsoulis to make the arrangements. After all, she was a Greek and so is he. It's fitting. When he's done I'll send

Cohen, if that's all right with you, and a few of the youngsters over to dig up the fig tree.'

Suleyman, who had by this time pulled himself up in his chair, put his hand up to his head and groaned. 'Why a fig tree?'

İkmen smiled. 'Ah, but of course you don't know, do you?'

'Know?'

'Cohen, for all his unsavoury habits, is at centre a good man. Strictly speaking he has broken the law, but . . .' He pushed his cigarettes and lighter across to Suleyman who had been distracting him by searching for his own. 'When he first went to see Madame, she told him something, you see.'

'I knew that,' Suleyman said as he lit up and then relaxed back into his chair. 'But he wouldn't tell me what.'

'She told him,' İkmen said with a strangely inappropriate smile upon his face, 'that the body of her late husband is buried beneath the fig tree in her garden. She also told him that she killed him.'

'So how was Cohen breaking the law?'

'He should have opened an investigation immediately. That garden should have been dug up while the old woman lay dying upstairs. After all, homicide is homicide whatever the condition of the perpetrator. But,' he sighed and then smiled again, 'she wanted him to promise that he wouldn't do anything until after her death, which he agreed to.'

'He told you, sir.'

'Only because she asked him to. Madame Kleopatra is, or was, one of those characters I came to know through my mother. Probably quite insane. But she was always very interested in my brother and myself when we were young, perhaps because she didn't have any children of her own. I believe she was very good to Cohen and his family too although I don't know how or why. When I make my report I will say that Madame confessed to me on her last gasp.'

Suleyman rubbed his head again and then smiled weakly. 'That would seem to be the best course of action.'

'Good.' Standing up quickly, İkmen said, 'And now I'm going to take you to breakfast.'

'Oh, but I've got Erol Urfa at nine and I have to get back to Cengiz Temiz.' With nervous rapidity, Suleyman moved various papers around on his desk as if searching for something. 'I must draft a report for the commissioner and then there is the issue of Dr Halman . . .'

İkmen kindly but firmly placed his hand across Suleyman's, effectively bringing his manic searching to a close. 'If you were to look at yourself from the outside, Suleyman,' he said, 'you would see a man staggering under too many issues. You would see, as I do, confusion and rising anxiety. Now I'm going to take you to that very expensive tourist café across the road and I am going to buy you lots of coffee, some eggs and replenish your cigarette supply. The place has a balcony from which we can view all of our beautiful if polluted waterways. There,' he said as he slipped one arm around Suleyman's shoulders and pulled him to his feet, 'you will offload some of your worries onto me and we will talk.'

'But you're not well, sir,' Suleyman said as he shakily achieved verticality.

'Yes, that's right,' İkmen replied with a smile, 'I'm not well, so I'm not involved, so I'm not interfering in your work. Oh, and by the way, my name is Çetin from now on,' he said with a twinkle in his eye as he proffered his hand to his colleague. 'Hello.'

Suleyman took the hand with a small bow and, smiling, said, 'Mehmet. Mehmet Suleyman.'

Although still early, the streets of the old city were already alive with activity. A horse-drawn cart carrying a huge pile of fruit eased its way down the narrow street, only just avoiding collision with an eccentrically parked BMW. Two little girls resplendent with vast hair ribbons both laughed as the horse appeared to do a last-minute double take. The shaven-headed simitci boy behind them sneered at what he perceived to be the irrationality of such an ancient form of transport. In the shops on the periphery of this scene, the carpet and leather goods men were putting their wares out onto the pavement for display. Occasionally a little competitive, if cheerful, banter would pass between them – stuff about prices and the scandalous degree to which one's rivals over-inflated their charges. From various, and numerous, directions, the sound of Arabesk music floated up towards the two men talking and drinking coffee on the balcony of the Marmara Türist Restaurant.

'Now that you've found the baby and are, therefore, officially heroic, you'll have to deal with the press again,' İkmen said as he drained his coffee cup and then signalled to the waiter that he would like some more.

'Yes,' Suleyman replied with a scowl, 'although I think that the details of the arrest of Mina and company are best left unsaid.'

İkmen laughed. 'I would have paid good money to see you negotiating for a prostitute. Mina Arda must have thought her business had taken a turn for the better when she saw you.'

'You know that her mother performed an abortion on her when she was seventeen,' Suleyman said, lowering his voice as he recounted this scandalous fact. 'She claims she has been unable to conceive since.'

'Semra Arda has been suspected of such practices for years,' İkmen said with a sigh. 'I arrested her on suspicion of just such an offence involving another girl about ten years ago. But there was no proof.'

'But to give your own daughter an abortion!'

İkmen shrugged. 'It's quicker and cheaper than going to a doctor, plus you don't have to explain anything. These are very poor people, Mehmet, ordinary standards do not apply.' He lit another cigarette and leaned back in his chair. 'So the man with Down's syndrome gave the baby to Mina presumably because he knew she either liked or wanted a baby?'

Suleyman waited until the waiter had taken their empty coffee cups away and replaced them with full ones before answering.

'Yes,' he said, 'although until he speaks to us we won't know how he got hold of the child. Mina says that Cengiz Temiz rescued the baby from the Urfas' apartment after seeing what he describes as a female demon in there. At least that is what she claims he told her.'

'This Temiz is, I assume, very frightened.'

'Yes. He speaks, when he does, in sort of harsh monosyllables and wets himself. It doesn't help either that his lawyer is Sevan Avedykian. When he's with him he won't let Cengiz answer any questions anyway.'

İkmen tipped his tiny cup up to his lips and sipped the hot liquid. 'That's his job,' he said, and then pausing for a moment's thought he added, 'Have you thought about engaging Dr Halman to help you?'

'I have.' His face took on a dejected expression here. It was a pose that, İkmen thought, looked particularly miserable. 'But she was called out to Temiz last night while I was in Karaköy. She found him in a terrible state. She went berserk at me when I arrived – lots of stuff about the evils of the Turkish judicial system. She says that if the family make a complaint she will support it. I can expect her report on my desk at any time.'

'Ah.' And then speaking with his eyes turned away from Suleyman, İkmen said, 'That must have been quite hard for you in view of the fact that you and Dr Halman—'

'Our private lives must be walled,' Suleyman said, his eyes suddenly hard as he repeated the old Ottoman adage.

'Yes, but if you will continue to find the women you work with irresistible then those walls are going to contain windows,' İkmen replied with some passion. 'You only just got away with it with Sergeant Farsakoğlu. I suppose with Dr Halman being half foreign it is a little better – not that Zelfa isn't a wonderful lady. She makes me laugh at least. But . . .'

'I think the doctor will probably return to Ireland quite soon,' Suleyman said as he dismally looked into his cup. 'She certainly gave me that impression last night.'

'She probably wanted to shock you,' İkmen said. 'She can't exactly leave that old father of hers, can she? And anyway, she'd never find someone like you back in Dublin.'

'Can we drop this subject now, please, sir, er, Çetin?'

İkmen shrugged and then, leaning forward across

the table, he said, 'So what about Erol Urfa and this secret wife of his? A bit convenient that she's now dead, given his obvious preference for Tansu Hanım.'

Suleyman took a cigarette out of his packet and lit up. 'I'm seeing Urfa this morning.'

'And?'

'And I must confess that I find the whole situation totally confusing. Tansu, Erol's manager and, seemingly, the whole Arabesk community knew about Ruya and the baby. They made no secret of it. Erol's prints as well as those of Cengiz Temiz have been found in the vicinity of the body although, unlike those of Temiz, not on the corpse. But Erol, it would seem, had the most compelling motive to do away with a woman foisted onto him by his relatives. Strangely, he seems to really love Tansu, or so Çöktin feels.'

'Çöktin?'

'He stayed with Urfa after the broadcast last night.' Registering the look of concern on İkmen's face, he added, 'I'm not happy about it. Both Urfa and Tansu are Kurdish, as is Çöktin. There's already talk that the sergeant is taking rather more than just a professional interest.'

'Well, you know what you have to do,' İkmen said.

'Yes.'

As if by some sort of sorcery, the music that one of the waiters put onto the restaurant tape machine was 'May It Pass' sung by Tansu Hanım. It was, İkmen noted to himself, one of her 'pitying' numbers. Melancholy and slow, it was in sharp contrast to the more bitter songs which, he'd noticed from the sleeves of his wife's tapes, were the ones she appeared to have written herself. Not that she put a great deal of vocal venom into these numbers for, like this one now, her interpretation of whoever's work she was singing was uniformly sad.

It seemed apt, at this point, to throw Tansu into the cooking pot of impressions along with everyone else. 'Tansu Hanım had considerable motive too,' he said.

'Yes.'

'Perhaps she is Cengiz Temiz's demon woman. You should show him a photograph of her.' He smiled. 'She doesn't exactly have a reputation for being sweet and kind.'

'No, although she possesses an alibi for that evening. Her sister—'

'A relative's about as reliable as a politician in this context!' İkmen blustered. 'I know you've been preoccupied with the missing child, but – you should ask the servants if you want the truth! Get on to it!'

Suleyman, thoroughly chastised, put his head down. 'Mmm.'

İkmen, wisely, changed tack. 'Are you still waiting for any more forensics?'

'Yes. I should have the results later on today. Some fibres require analysis and Dr Sarkissian still has some samples to take before the body can be released for burial. If we get any more forensic evidence on Cengiz Temiz we won't need him to speak,' Suleyman sand miserably.

'I take it you don't hold with the idea that Mr Temiz killed Ruya Urfa.'

'Not really, no. I do think he is involved in some way. In fact I think that he may be the key to this whole affair. But actually killing? No.' He looked out across the two great sparkling waterways, the Golden Horn and the Bosphorus. 'The cyanide, which let's face it is not easy to come by, was administered in a sweet that the murderer knew would disguise the smell of the poison. It all happened at a time when, I believe, the perpetrator knew most people would be in front of the television. It's all too clever and complex, I believe, for Cengiz.'

'It may be,' İkmen said as he placed a large bundle of banknotes onto the bill that had, somehow, during the course of their conversation, landed on the table. 'But you'll have to ask Zelfa about that, I feel. Only a professional can really make that sort of judgement.'

Suleyman sighed. 'I know.' Then looking down at his watch he said, 'I must go.'

'Yes.'

As he retrieved his jacket from the back of his chair, Suleyman said, 'Thank you for my breakfast, Çetin. I do feel a little better now.'

'Good.' He stood up. 'So can I send Cohen and

some boys out to the İskender Hamam then, Inspector?'

'Yes. Get it done.' Then frowning as he stood, he added, 'I wonder what motive Madame Kleopatra had for killing her husband?'

'We'll never know now,' İkmen replied. 'Perhaps he abused her. Maybe he was unfaithful. The motive could have been monetary, racial, religious, almost anything. But they're both dead now and so . . .'

'You know,' Suleyman said as he walked towards the steps of the balcony and out into the street, 'in a sense I know as little about Ruya Urfa as you do about Madame's husband.'

İkmen, now out in the full sunlight and sweating profusely, said, 'Yes, well, Mr Kleopatra, as some used to refer to him, was a bit of a cipher, I suppose. I am not alone in never having met him. There were even some who believed he didn't exist.'

'Mmm.' Suleyman put his sunglasses on. 'A man of nowhere.'

It was strange to see the large bulk of Commissioner Ardiç doing anything physical for anyone other than himself, much less a very young-looking man. But as Mr Kemal Ertürk left the building, Ardiç held the door open in order to expedite his exit. It was only when he turned away from his guest and looked at what was now cluttering up his station that he scowled.

'What is all this about?' he said to no one in particular, his arms attempting but failing to encompass the sheer scale of the invasion of red roses.

Çöktin, who had observed the arrival of the flowers some minutes before, said, 'They're a gift from Mr Urfa, to say thank you for finding his daughter.'

'Oh,' Ardiç said, suddenly and quite alarmingly, to those who really knew him, becalmed. 'And are they for all of us, Sergeant Çöktin?'

'No, sir, just for Inspector Suleyman.'

'Oh, really.' The large man walked across to one of the bigger displays and helped himself to the card that nestled amongst the blossoms. 'How very thoughtful,' he said, 'but also,' and here his tone resolved into something much more familiar to his colleagues, 'how fucking embarrassing! Get rid of them!'

Officer Kavur, who had been sniffing the plants appreciatively, said, 'Oh, but—'

'Am I,' Ardiç said as he dramatically cast about the reception area like a particularly bad actor, 'invisible to you people?'

'No, sir.'

'Then do as you're told and throw those things into the car park!'

'Yes, sir.'

As he made his way behind the front desk, Ardiç barked, 'Oh, and you can come with me, Kavur, I want to talk to you.'

Kavur's eyes became very large as she signalled

her fear to Çöktin. Briefly he squeezed her hand as she passed.

Erol Urfa arrived at the station just as Suleyman was finishing giving his orders to Sergeant Tepe. The inspector hoped that Erol hadn't heard what he had been discussing with his inferior, namely his friend Ali Mardin.

'So if he can't produce it, bring him in,' Suleyman said as Tepe started to move towards the stairs.

'Yes, sir.'

'Ah, Mr Urfa,' he said as he turned towards his guest, 'shall we go to my office?'

'Yes.' Coming alone like this, Erol Urfa seemed much smaller and shyer than he had appeared before. He was nevertheless as immaculately dressed as ever, in the most expensive and worst of taste. Before they mounted the stairs, Suleyman called for two teas to the old half-asleep çaycı who was drifting soporifically over by the front entrance.

On the way up, Erol asked Suleyman whether he had liked the flowers.

Suleyman frowned. 'Flowers, sir?'

'Yes, I sent them to thank you for getting Merih back for me. Roses.'

'Well,' Suleyman said as he held the door of his office open for his guest, 'that is very kind of you, but I don't know of any flowers arriving.'

'Oh. Oh, then I must contact the florist.'

'Well, yes, but . . .' Suleyman sat down heavily behind his desk, indicating that Erol should sit too. 'If they have not been sent then please, with respect, retrieve your money and do not do this again.'

'Eh?'

'I'm afraid that in the context of my job they may be seen as a bribe, sir. It's very nice of you and I'm very sorry, but I fear that is how it is.'

'Oh.' Erol looked down at the floor, his expression one that Suleyman imagined he must have employed to some effect as a child. 'Oh, I'm sorry, Inspector. I—'

'There is no need to apologise, Mr Urfa,' Suleyman said. He opened up one of his files and took hold of a pen. 'Now, I know that you have already given a statement regarding the discovery of your wife's body and the events leading up to that, but I do have to ask you certain other questions, which is why you are here today.'

'Yes, I understand.' Putting both of his hands onto the edge of Suleyman's desk, again in a childlike gesture, he said, 'Will I be able to take Ruya home soon, Inspector?'

'That is up to our pathologist, Mr Urfa.' He smiled a little sadly. 'I don't think it will be long. I suppose your family are anxious to see her properly buried.'

'Oh, they don't know,' Erol said as he nervously clicked his thumbs one against the other on the edge of the desk.

Suleyman frowned. 'You mean you haven't tele-phoned—'

'They don't have a telephone. Or a television.'

Although Suleyman knew that Erol originated from somewhere 'out east' he had not realised until now just how 'east' that was. Even crazy border towns like Doğubayazit had telephones and televisions. Some of the villages could still be without, although he thought that was doubtful. İkmen, or rather Çetin as he was now, had seen satellite dishes as far east as Kayseri on his quick trip to see some old relative in Cappadocia the previous year. The completely no technology family was becoming an oddity.

'So how,' he asked, 'do you communicate with your relatives? Do you write?'

'My parents, like Ruya, can't write,' was the simple reply.

'So . . .'

'We don't communicate, Inspector.'

Suleyman offered Erol a cigarette and when the latter refused, took one himself and lit up. 'But forgive me, sir, if you do not communicate then how did your wife come to arrive in the city? How did your marriage take place?'

'I married Ruya in my village. We were betrothed.'

'So have you been back since? Did your wife ever visit her family?'

'No and no,' Erol smiled. 'It's complicated.'

It sounded, Suleyman thought, like one of those

feud situations that sometimes occurred. One family or member of one family against another group or tribe. Not that that particular interpretation made any sense in this context. Urfa had gone home in order to marry his betrothed which not only implied an amicable union between two families but also a willingness on the singer's part to participate.

Suleyman leaned back in his chair. 'So do your family follow your career, Mr Urfa? Are they keen?'

'No,' and then before Suleyman could ask any more questions he said, 'Why all the inquiries about my family, Inspector?'

'When a person dies in suspicious circumstances we are obliged to explore every eventuality.'

'I said in my statement that my wife had no enemies I was aware of,' Erol said with just a slight edge to his voice.

'Yes, although I can't help feeling that Tansu—'

'Tansu has always accepted the situation with Ruya.'

'You did, I believe, marry your wife after you met Tansu Hanım. Is that correct?'

Erol moved his hands down into his lap and looked at the floor. 'Yes.'

A brief hiatus followed during which the elderly çaycı came in and placed large glasses of tea on Suleyman's desk.

As he gently plopped two small sugar cubes into his tea, Suleyman began his questioning once again. 'Forgive me if I am wrong,' he said, 'but I cannot imagine that a lady like Tansu Hanım would be happy about the idea of her new young lover, er, sleeping with another woman.'

'Things are different where we come from!' The look on Erol's face now was both bitter and deeply offended. With a dramatic flick of the wrist, he pushed his tea violently to one side. Suleyman, to the singer's obvious annoyance, did not react.

'Indeed,' he said. 'So tell me about that.'

'A man must produce children.'

'Yes.' Unbeknown to Erol, Suleyman was in a not dissimilar position, or at least he had been until Zelfa had stormed out in the wake of her anger over Cengiz Temiz. Not, he imagined, in the same league as this country boy, however. To men from his part of the world, children were utterly crucial, whereas to him, well, he still wasn't quite sure how he felt about babies. His brother had one who was completely charming but then Suleyman himself did not have to get up in the night to attend to her so what did he know? 'So your need for children plus your honourable fulfilment of your betrothal forced you into marriage?'

'No. I did love Ruya.' He turned his head to one side, his eyes now brimming with tears. 'It's . . .'

'A man may love more than one woman?'

Erol nodded. 'Yes.'

Outside in the street the sound of heavy tourist buses bouncing over the tram lines mingled harshly with the cries of street vendors and the heaviness of the thick, summer heat. Suleyman was feeling, if not looking, very soporific. In an attempt to rouse himself, he pulled himself up straight in his chair and then sipped determinedly at his tea.

'Mr Aksoy was not, I take it, too happy about your marriage,' he said as he put his cigarette out in one of the ashtrays.

'No. He said it would be bad for my image,' the singer replied as if reading the words he spoke from a book or autocue. 'But I did it anyway.'

'Was it Mr Aksoy's idea to keep your marriage a secret?'

'İbrahim has always presented me as a star for the young girls, you know?'

Suleyman muttered his agreement to this self-evident fact.

Erol shrugged. 'So marriage would not be good publicity. But then I didn't want a lot of people to know either.'

'Why?'

'Because it is important to keep your private life to yourself.'

'You don't do that with Tansu Hanım though, do you?'

'No.' Like a rather harshly scolded schoolboy, Erol looked down at the floor, his bottom lip quivering slightly with pique. 'But Tansu is different, you know? It started with her to help my career. İbrahim introduced us.' And then looking up sharply, he added, 'But I do love her now, you know. She is a wonderful lady, Tansu. I know that some people laugh and say bad things, especially now. But I will not desert Tansu. I will do right by Ruya, but . . .'

'But you will stay with Tansu, possibly eventually marry.'

'Oh, no.' Erol was adamant. 'I will marry another woman from my village. I must have a son.'

'But you've just said that you will stay with Tansu Hanım.'

'Yes.'

'So it will be as before with . . .'

'Oh yes,' Erol said with what to Suleyman seemed like staggering simplicity. 'Do you have any idea who killed Ruya yet, Inspector?'

But before Suleyman could answer, there was a knock at the door.

'Come in,' he called as he lit another cigarette.

Arın Kavur's face was a flushed as she put her head a little nervously round the side of the door. 'Oh, Inspector, you're with somebody.'

'Yes? And?'

'Ah . . .'

Seeing what amounted to an unaccustomed reticence in her expression, Suleyman got up from his desk and walked over to her.

'What is it?' he asked quietly as he took her elbow in his hand and moved her out into the corridor.

'It's Commissioner Ardiç,' she said. 'He wants to see you.'

'All right, when I've finished.'

'No, now, Inspector,' she said and then turning her head to make sure that nobody else was about to hear what passed between them she added, 'It's about those two Ertürk girls.'

Suleyman smiled. 'Ah, the obsessed fans.'

'Their brother has complained about their being detained.'

Suleyman muttered angrily, 'Oh has he? It was Mr Kemal Ertürk who told me to hold on to them!'

'Yes, well . . .'

'And until you went around to the house and spoke to the gardener, what choice did I have? The stupid children just came out with cyanide . . . And the gardener did indeed have some, didn't he? None was, so far as he could tell, missing but . . .'

Kavur shrugged. 'He wants to see you anyway.'

'Well, when I'm done with Mr Urfa, I'll be along.'

'Mmm.' She looked nervous and unsure – common reactions amongst Ardiç's inferiors.

Suleyman sighed and then smiled weakly. 'I'm expecting the Temiz's lawyer, Mr Avedykian, here at any minute,' he said. 'If you can go and greet him for me, I'll finish with Mr Urfa and then telephone Ardiç.'

'Yes, but—'

'If you are with Avedykian, Ardiç will not bother

you.' He put one hand encouragingly on her shoulder. 'Have courage and keep out of sight. Oh, and when Mr Avedykian does appear, get hold of Sergeant Çöktin. I know he's in this building somewhere; I'll need him for the Temiz interview.'

'Does he know that?'

'Yes.' And then with a small bow Suleyman took his leave of Kavur and re-entered his office.

As he resumed his seat and apologised to the singer for his absence, he made a mental note to ask Erol about the officer he had just been speaking of with Kavur. İsak Çöktin had worked over and above his duty hours after Erol's broadcast and when he and the singer's entourage had entered the station the previous evening, they had looked extremely comfortable in each other's company. Perhaps too much so. There was also the issue of the apparently illiterate Ruya's possession of a pen – covered in her prints. That was strange. Suleyman commenced this new line of questioning in a spirit of inquiry, but also aware it was a way of postponing the evil moment when he would have to talk to Ardiç.

Chapter 9

Like İkmen, Cohen was not overly fond of physical
exertion and so as a group of younger officers began
digging up Madame Kleopatra's fig tree, both the
inspector and the perennial constable sat in comfortable wicker chairs with the old woman's doctor. The
undertaker who had called to collect Madame's body
some hours ago had lingered in order to reminisce
about the glory days of the İskender Hamam, but
now he had gone, leaving only those who needed
to be in the garden for the purposes of what could
be grim work ahead. One of the neighbour women
had occasionally looked out of her window and into
the garden, but a couple of sharp ripostes from İkmen
had, seemingly, brought her inquisitiveness to a halt.

'So did you know Madame's husband, Doctor?'
İkmen asked after he had taken a deep draught from
his water bottle.

'Yes,' Katsoulis replied, 'I did. He was a miserable
bastard.'

'I only ever remember her being alone,' Cohen
observed as through half-closed eyes he watched the
young men dig.

'Well, you're both somewhat younger than myself,' the doctor said, 'although Mr Kleopatra must have taken his leave during your lifetimes.'

İkmen turned and faced the doctor with a frown upon his face. 'Do you remember my mother, Doctor? She used to see a lot of Madame when I was a child. Ayşe İkmen?'

Katsoulis laughed. 'As if I could forget!' Then leaning forward towards İkmen, he said, 'Forgive me, Inspector, but your mother was a most notable woman. Everybody knew that the gift of sorcery was most finely perfected in her. If one wanted to know one's fate in life one had only to go to Ayşe İkmen and it would all become clear. There were many said she was in league with Shaitan, she was so accurate!'

'Perhaps she was,' İkmen said as the cloud that was the manner of his mother's early death passed across his face.

'Oh, don't say that!' Katsoulis cried, crossing himself several times as he spoke.

İkmen laughed. 'I'm only joking. Besides, she was always far too fond of chicken to be a true believer.'

'Oh, that is appalling!' Katsoulis laughed. 'She was Albanian, wasn't she, your mother?'

'Yes.'

The doctor mopped his brow with his handkerchief. 'She'd be in good company now with all these Kosovans in the country.'

Cohen, who had been puzzling over an earlier remark

of İkmen's, said, 'What do you mean, she was far too fond of chicken to be a true believer?'

'The so-called Shaitan worshippers, or Yezidis—'

'A sect from the east somewhere, I believe,' the doctor put in.

'Yes,' İkmen said, 'well, they have some strange habits which accord, apparently, with their beliefs, one of which is not eating chicken.'

'Oh, I see,' Cohen said. 'I didn't know that.'

'Yes, it is one of those—' Suddenly İkmen stopped mid-sentence, as if a thought of some sort had occurred to him. But just at that moment he was unable to articulate it because with a loud whoop of victory, one of the young diggers signalled that the party had indeed found something.

'Is it what we're looking for?' Cohen asked as he rose out of both his stupor and his chair.

'Looks like it,' the young man said as he leaned heavily across the handle of his spade.

'Come on, let's go and have a look,' İkmen said. He took hold of Katsoulis's arm and pulled the elderly man to his feet.

The thing the young officers had exposed was not directly under the tree but just in front of it. As they approached, İkmen, Katsoulis and Cohen could see what appeared to be a very stained and rotted piece of cloth which, as they drew nearer, seemed to be caught under something long and thin. One of the youngsters had jumped down into the hole containing what was, presumably, a skeleton and, as the three men reached the site, he was bending down to examine it more closely.

'This'll have to go to forensics now, I suppose,' he said as İkmen staggered down to join him in the pit.

'If you'll help me down, I should be able to give you a positive identification,' the doctor said as he wavered nervously on the side of the pit.

İkmen frowned. 'Well, I know you knew him, Doctor, but he is a bit, well, desiccated.'

'That's all right,' Katsoulis said with some confidence, 'I will know.'

With İkmen and the young officer pulling from below and Cohen pushing from up top, it was slow work manoeuvring the elderly man into position but after a bit of effort and a lot of sweating they eventually managed to achieve their aim. Once in the hole, Katsoulis looked down at the long, stick-like things before him and then sucked thoughtfully on his lip.

'Now the head is . . .'

'It's there, sir,' the young officer said as he pointed to a round protuberance at the far end of the pit.

'Ah.'

As the doctor made his way shakily towards his goal, some of the tired young men up above shared amused glances. İkmen, who declined to comment on their behaviour, consoled himself with the grim thought that one day these well-muscled young men would be as Katsoulis was now. It made him smile.

The doctor bent down low in order to look at the dirt-caked skull. Had he been younger and fitter he would probably have got down on his haunches to examine the remains, but as it was he could only peer down at something that looked more like a clod of earth than a face.

'Would you be kind enough to clear some of the dirt away from the face, please, Inspector,' he said. 'I would do it myself, but . . .'

'Yes, of course,' İkmen replied. 'You know I'm not practised in this, don't you, Doctor?' he said. 'I wouldn't want to damage anything.'

'If you move the soil out of the mouth that will be sufficient,' Katsoulis said as he placed a pair of half-moon spectacles on his nose.

Quite why the mouth was of such great significance, İkmen didn't know. However, when he saw the first small glints of metal, he realised, or at least he thought he did.

'There are gold teeth here, lots of them,' he said. 'I do believe Madame was playing us for fools.'

'If there's gold teeth, then that's Murad Ağa, the old eunuch,' Cohen, who had been observing proceedings from above, said with a laugh in his voice. 'Well, the old witch!'

Dr Katsoulis, who was now moving various items around on the face with the end of his cigarette holder, frowned. 'What do you mean, Inspector, playing us for fools?' he asked.

'Well, Doctor, it could mean that Madame killed Murad Ağa and not her husband. Or she killed Murad and her husband and then buried her husband somewhere else in this garden. Or she killed nobody and the eunuch just wanted to be put here when he died. Or maybe the morphine had sent her quite mad.' He shrugged helplessly as he stood up in order to relieve the strain on his calves. 'I'm hoping you can enlighten us.'

'Well, I can,' Katsoulis said as he, too, straightened his back for comfort, 'although I find it hard to believe you don't know.'

'Don't know what?' Cohen asked.

Katsoulis sighed. 'That the discovery of this body means that Madame buried both her husband and Murad Ağa beside this tree.'

'Eh?'

'Murad and Madame's husband were one and the same. Kleopatra was joined in matrimony to a eunuch.'

Sevan Avedykian looked across at the heavily sweating heap that was his client and said, 'Mr Temiz would, I believe, appreciate a glass of water.'

Wordlessly, Suleyman signalled to Çöktin that he should comply with this request. As the younger man left the room in order to get the water Suleyman settled back to take a long, hard look at Temiz.

At forty-five, Cengiz Temiz was both more and less well-preserved than the average man of that age. Although grotesquely overweight his face was quite free from lines and wrinkles. But then the thick, open mouth rarely moved and his eyes which were small and markedly slanted gave no emotion back to the world beyond the occasional flashes of fear. When Çöktin returned with his water, Cengiz Temiz gave no indication that he was pleased or relieved by this. He simply, as he had done for nearly half an hour now, sat in a shroud of self-contained silence.

For Suleyman, however, things were different. There was too much going on in his head, some of which had little to do with Cengiz Temiz. Mr Ertürk had, it seemed, been most scathing with regard to the treatment of his little sisters. How, he'd said to Ardiç, this ridiculous inspector could have been taken in by two silly girls who had hit upon the word cyanide because it was, probably, the only poison they knew, and then detained them under suspicion of murder, was beyond him. True, the gardener did use, amongst other poisons, cyanide to kill certain pests, but Reşat hadn't reported any substances missing and besides, even if he had, there were other families he gardened for besides the Ertürks.

All right, Ertürk had told Suleyman to 'hang on' to his sisters until his conference was over, but he had not expected them to be detained in a filthy cell! These were girls of quality! Born and bred in stylish Yeniköy! But Suleyman had treated them no better than common streetwalkers! That the pair were both manipulative and frighteningly obsessive had not been mentioned. So now Suleyman was in disgrace and that was without the report from Dr Halman that he knew was coming. Some days were like this. Some days suspending oneself from a high place looked attractive.

With a sigh, Suleyman started his questioning once again. 'Miss Arda has told us,' he said, yet again, 'that, knowing as you do that she cannot have children, you presented her with the Urfa baby in order to win her affections and to protect the child from an "evil demon". What I want to know, Mr Temiz, is whether this is correct.'

'My client has already told you that he doesn't know this woman,' Avedykian said, 'and so this line of questioning—'

'Is necessary because of the testimony of Miss Arda. And as far as I am concerned, Mr Avedykian, your client has told me nothing as yet. It is you, if you recall, who has said that Mr Temiz has no knowledge of Miss Arda. What he thinks or knows I cannot tell.' Then turning to face Cengiz directly, he said, 'Both Mina and yourself are in a lot of trouble here, Cengiz. It is trouble that I feel you don't need to be in but only the truth can confirm that. Now—'

'Inspector Suleyman, I feel I must—'

'If I tell you, will my mum and dad have to know?'

Both the two policemen and the lawyer gazed, for different reasons, at what had now become a rather more animated interviewee.

Suleyman cleared his throat. 'That does depend on what you have to tell us, Cengiz,' he said.

'You don't have to tell them anything,' Avedykian put in hurriedly, fearing, so Suleyman felt, that his client was on the verge of galloping irrevocably away from him.

Cengiz Temiz, however, after only a brief glance at his lawyer, went his own way. 'It's about dirty things,' he said as he bent his head low in shame.

Suleyman, confused, looked at Çöktin, who said, 'Do you mean sex, Cengiz?'

'Yes.'

'I really do think that I would like some time alone with my client before—'

'It's all right, Mr Avedykian,' Cengiz said and laid one pudgy hand on his lawyer's slim arm. 'It's naughty but it's not killing.'

Avedykian looked hard into what he could see of his client's eyes and then sighed. 'Well, Cengiz, if you must.'

'So what about sex, Cengiz?' Suleyman asked as he lit a cigarette and then leaned forward towards the downcast Temiz. 'Have you done it or did you just want to do it or—'

'I have sex with Mina.' He turned his face round so that none of the other men in the room could see his eyes. 'Mum gives me money for cigarettes and food but I spend it on Mina.'

'She makes you feel good?'

'Yes. Dirty things do that. Good boys shouldn't and Mum will punish me if she knows, but . . .' He turned back to face them, his eyes wet with tears. 'You won't tell them that I'm dirty, will you, sir?'

Suleyman smiled. 'I won't tell anyone you're dirty, Cengiz. But you must tell me where Mrs Ruya and the baby come into all this. I know that you took the baby to give to Mina but I have to know how you did that. You do understand, don't you?'

'Mmm.' Then, rapidly changing tack, Cengiz looked down at the floor, watched a spider bounce on its web underneath the table and laughed.

'Cengiz?'

He rolled his eyes up in the direction of the taller of the policemen and then wiped some wetness away from around his mouth. 'Eh?'

'Cengiz, Mina has told us that you rescued the baby Merih from a,' and here Suleyman once again had to clear his throat in order to enunciate what were, to him, ridiculous words, 'a demon woman who—'

'Oh, no, no, no, no, no!' He was sideways on now, head down, mouth trembling with anxiety.

Sevan Avedykian placed a comforting arm around his client's shoulders and then said, 'I think you've gone as far as you can go now, Inspector.'

'I would disagree,' Suleyman replied haughtily.

'Besides, if Mr Temiz can tell Mina Arda about the demon then he can tell me. Cengiz?'

'No, no, no!'

Avedykian stood up. 'Inspector!'

'Look, Cengiz,' Suleyman said with more than a little pleading in his voice, 'if you tell me about the demon, I can help you. I . . .' and then suddenly a thought struck him which had not occurred before. But it made perfect sense and so he went with it. 'Look, I can and will, I promise, protect you from her. No harm will come to you or Mina or the baby.'

Cengiz looked up. 'Uh?'

'I give you my word!' Suleyman said with what he perceived as rather unnecessary drama in his voice.

'And the inspector is a gentleman,' Çöktin put in earnestly, 'so his word does mean a lot.'

'You don't have to listen to this!' Avedykian said as he took hold of his client's sleeve and tried to pull him to his feet. 'I think we should terminate this interview now, Inspector Suleyman. My client is distressed—'

'She had silver hair and a fluffy coat.'

Once again, all eyes turned towards Cengiz whose face was now quite white, almost grey.

'Her face was all hissy like a snake,' and here he made an approximation with his own features. The result was, even to Suleyman's horror-accustomed eyes, really quite scary.

'Would you know the demon if you saw her again?' Çöktin asked.

Cengiz, whose face had now reverted to its usual expression, said, 'Yes.'

'Are you sure?'

'Mr Temiz has told you so—'

'Will you please sit back down, Mr Avedykian!' Suleyman, suddenly quite out of patience with the lawyer, roared his request which was, surprisingly, complied with immediately.

'So if I put the demon in front of you in a fluffy—'

'White.'

'A fluffy white coat, then . . .'

Çöktin leaned in towards Suleyman and whispered something in his ear.

'Right,' Suleyman said in response to this. 'Good. Perhaps the sergeant here can get us some photographs to look at in a moment. Now, Cengiz—'

'Mrs Ruya was lying on the floor.' He was crying now, full on, choking sobs. 'She, she never, she never moved when I touched her. Merih was crying—'

'Where was Merih, Cengiz?'

'In her little bed. I love Merih, sir! I—'

'All right, all right. Sssh. Now, calm down,' Suleyman smiled. 'You're doing very well, Cengiz. I'm really pleased with you.'

Sevan Avedykian silently passed a very white folded handkerchief to his client and then sat back quietly once again. Cengiz dabbed at his eyes as he attempted to get his sobs under control. He now looked like he

had a bad case of hiccups. 'Sorry! Sorry!' he said
through gulps of air.

'It's all right, you've no need to be sorry. You're
being very, very good.'

'Am I?'

'Yes. Now I just need to know one more thing and
then you can take a rest.'

Cengiz leaned forward as if waiting to catch the
words physically from Suleyman's lips.

'And that is,' Suleyman said, 'how you got into Mrs
Ruya's apartment. Was the demon woman there when
you went in? Did she let you in? Did you arrive with
her for some reason? What, Cengiz? What?'

Orhan Tepe knocked once on Inspector Suleyman's
door and then went straight in. Well, his news, though
not earth-shattering, was required by Suleyman and
besides it wasn't his particular custom to be subser-
vient. This proud Ottoman prince might think himself
somebody but to Tepe he was just as other men. If
nothing else, seeing Suleyman in the act of procuring a
prostitute, albeit in the line of duty, had proved that.

Although Suleyman's desk was occupied when Tepe
entered the room, it was not by the inspector himself.
With a loud bang as her fist hit wood, Zelfa Halman
slammed a cardboard file shut before looking up
sharply.

'Well?' she asked before she realised that she was
quite out of context here.

'Oh, er, I was looking for the inspector,' Tepe said as he watched her hurriedly slip something underneath the cover of the file she had just closed.

'Well, he isn't here,' she said sharply.

'Yes.'

She stood up, smoothing her skirt down as she did so. She was, Tepe thought, a not unattractive woman for her age. Although quite why the inspector should be so taken with her when he could, surely, have almost any woman he wanted was a mystery. Perhaps it had something to do with her being a foreigner.

'Well,' she said as she moved round the desk towards Tepe, 'seeing as he isn't here then perhaps we should leave.'

'Yes.' But he didn't move. Quite why, he didn't really know. But then he always felt a little on edge in the presence of this woman. The word 'psychiatrist' loomed large and menacing in his head.

'Well, come on then, out!' she said as she literally shooed him ahead of her.

He moved quickly now. She was, for some reason, quite agitated and he didn't want to tangle with her in such a mood. To do so, Tepe felt, might invite all sorts of strange interpretations on her part. His grandfather had been, as his mother was accustomed to say in muted tones, 'taken somewhere' when he became, in the family parlance, 'rather vague'. Psychiatrists could do things like that. One didn't need to be exactly insane in order to attract their attentions. As he watched Dr

Halman disappear down the corridor, Orhan Tepe let out a long sigh of relief. There were some who believed that mental confusion could be hereditary and—

'Inspector Suleyman is out, I take it?' The voice was familiar if unexpected.

'Oh, er, yes, sir. He is,' Tepe said as he looked down into the sharp eyes of Çetin İkmen.

'I saw you leaving his office,' İkmen said, 'in the furious wake of Dr Halman.'

'Yes.' And then feeling the need to change the subject he said, 'I wanted to see the inspector about something.'

'Oh?'

'Yes.' There was a strong feeling of curiosity emanating from İkmen that Tepe felt was not quite appropriate. 'I thought that you were sick, sir.'

İkmen smiled. 'Like all of us, Tepe, I am slowly but inexorably dying. What was it you wanted to see Inspector Suleyman about?'

'Oh, it was just an identity card thing. Some man who needed checking up on.'

Almost without his noticing, İkmen took Tepe's elbow in his hand and led him down the corridor. 'Oh? What man?'

'Well . . .'

'I ask only because, as you say, it is just an identity card thing.' He laughed. 'I like to remain in touch, as you know. And if it's not important . . .'

Tepe shrugged. 'Just a friend of Erol Urfa's, as I

193

understand it. The inspector asked him for his card yesterday but he couldn't find it.'

'So did he find it today when you went round?'

'No. He wasn't there.' He looked down at the floor which, just very slightly, moved. İkmen, he felt, subtly increased the pressure on his elbow. But as soon as the faint tremor had ceased, the pressure eased.

İkmen smiled. 'So where had he gone, this man? Do you know?'

'No, no one knew, or would say. That's what I was coming to tell the inspector. I don't know what he might do about it. I mean, it is rather minor in comparison to the investigation into Mrs Urfa's death.'

'Oh, indeed.' İkmen started moving a little faster. 'Not of course that we must forget details like this, Tepe. Men's lives can often be circumscribed within such trivia, in my experience. Things like identity cards, the words of songs, the syndromes people may suffer from . . .' And then suddenly he stopped and turned to face Tepe. 'By the way, the doctor who examined the Urfa baby, was it Akkale, do you know?'

'Yes.' Tepe frowned. 'Why?'

'Oh, no reason,' İkmen said as he reached out to knock on the door of the medical examination room. 'Just a detail for the organic computer,' he whispered as he tapped the side of his head with his finger.

'Oh.'

'Goodbye, Tepe,' İkmen said as the examination

room door opened to reveal the dark figure of Dr Irfan Akkale.

It is better this way, Erol thought as he folded the last of Merih's little dresses into the bag. Were he to give Tansu time to argue she would become hurt and then he would do what he knew he shouldn't. Stay. Not that he wanted to go. To wake up every morning to the sound of one's name on a woman's lips, to then have one's sexual desires fulfilled without even having to say what they are to that woman – that is seductive. And had he been a different man, there would have been nothing wrong with that. But there was also honour to consider and Tansu, for all her wild rages and bizarre behaviour, deserved respect. Besides, if he gave in now it would only make things worse later when, inevitably, he would leave the city for his village for a time or forever or for whatever may come to pass.

What is written cannot be unwritten.

As he passed the dining table, he looked at the book that lay on top of one of the place mats. The woman on the cover was very beautiful, she had short blonde hair and thick red lips. Had her eyes not been downcast, one hand held painfully up to her head, it would have been an image of some sexual power. But this woman appeared devastated, as if she had just looked upon the face of death. He made to slowly, as was his custom, spell out the words on the front cover but then found that he couldn't. The letters were different, not greatly but enough to make him realise that this was a foreign book.

'It's about Marilyn Monroe,' Latife said as she walked over to him and gently took the tome from his hands. She smiled. 'It's in English.'

'Oh.' Until he had registered a heavy footfall Erol had, for a moment, thought it was Tansu. Now, although his heart was still beating very loudly, he felt waves of relief break across him. 'I didn't know . . .'

'Oh, I don't speak it very well,' Latife said with a laugh behind her voice. 'I've never had lessons. I learned only from the radio.' Then looking up sharply she said, 'Do you know of Marilyn Monroe, Erol?'

He shrugged. 'No. She's very beautiful, if that is her on the cover.'

'Yes, she was,' Latife said. 'But that was taken many years ago. She's dead now.'

'Oh.' Quite why Latife hadn't yet said anything about the large bag at Erol's feet or the sleeping form of Merih, dressed for the street and already in her car seat, he didn't know. But he felt, knowing Latife, that she soon would.

Looking, Erol imagined, into a past of which he could not even conceive, Latife said, 'Marilyn was an American film star. She was beautiful, success-ful, every man wanted her, but all she ever wanted was to be taken seriously.' Latife placed the book back down upon the table. 'She was, you know, a very intelligent woman, hungry for knowledge. It was her passion. Are you planning on leaving my sister, Erol?'

It came suddenly, but as no surprise. Latife was, if nothing else, 'observant'.

'Yes,' he said, his head now slightly bowed. 'I have to. It's not right that I stay with my child at the house of a single woman. It is disrespectful to Ruya and not good for Merih.'

'Tansu is going to be very hurt.'

'I know. And I want her to understand that I do still care for her. It's just that, at the moment, we cannot be together.'

Latife sat down on one of the dining chairs and looked across at the sleeping baby. 'So perhaps when you've taken Ruya home . . .'

'I will visit, as always,' he said as he stooped down to pick up his bag. 'But as for anything else, I don't know. If you would tell Tansu I'll telephone her tonight.'

'Of course.'

He heaved the bag up onto his shoulder and then picked up the car seat. Merih was still soundly asleep and as Erol looked down at her he couldn't help smiling. Despite everything, if he had her he still had hope.

Latife walked with Erol out to his car and helped him load the luggage onto the back seat. They kissed each other lightly on the cheek and then Latife, with a wave, walked back into the house. Erol turned the ignition and then began punching a number into his mobile telephone.

Latife watched him with a smile on her face.

'The trouble, you know, with doctors,' İkmen said as he placed his now empty tea glass down on Suleyman's desk, 'is that they never know anything for certain. Oh, they have ideas, theories and thoughts and when one is either almost or completely dead, they can tell you what the problem might be. But as for actually making a judgement on a living being . . .' He paused in order to rap his knuckles on the desk. 'Are you with me, Mehmet?'

'Oh.' Suleyman looked up from the paper he had been reading so intently and smiled. 'What were you saying?'

'I asked Dr Akkale about the possibility of Merih Urfa having an allergy to chicken and beans. If you remember, her father was very forceful on this point in his television broadcast. I mean the child is very young and I wondered how or even if this might be known.'

'And?'

'And Akkale could neither confirm nor deny it. The child possessed no obvious rashes or wheals but then if she hadn't had any chicken or beans she wouldn't have any. But Akkale also said that given the child's age she would in all likelihood be on a milk-only diet anyway. I mean, I take his point that a person may be allergic to almost anything, but in one so young . . .'

Suleyman rubbed the sides of his face with his hands and frowned. 'Um, I know I may be a little slow here,' he said, 'but why are you taking such an interest in this?'

'Oh, it's just something old Kostas Katsoulis happened to say when we were at Madame Kleopatra's, about the dietary mores of one of the eastern sects.'

'Oh?'

'The Yezidis forbid the eating of chicken. I don't know why. I know nothing about them beyond the chicken thing and the fact that they revere Shaitan.'

'You think that Urfa might be one of them?'

İkmen shrugged. 'I don't know.'

Suleyman turned to his computer and spent a few seconds typing in what İkmen imagined was some relevant data. As various pieces of information flashed up onto the screen, Suleyman leaned back and lit a cigarette. Then after some moments' scanning, he sighed and said, 'Well, his identity card quite plainly gives his religion as Muslim.'

'It was just a thought,' İkmen said.

'Mmm.'

They sat in silence for a few moments as İkmen lit up yet again and Suleyman attempted to tear his eyes away from Dr Halman's report which was lying right in front of him on the desk. As far as he could tell; she had not so far been complimentary about his treatment of Cengiz Temiz. But then he had not expected her to be.

'Before I go,' İkmen said, 'and not wishing to interfere with your investigation, may I just ask a question about Tansu Hanım?'

Although Suleyman replied in the affirmative, his brow was wrinkled with doubt. 'You may, though I don't know whether I will be able to answer or even if I should.'

'Can she read?'

'I should imagine so, yes.'

İkmen shook his head as if trying to loosen a more cogent question from his brain. 'No, I mean really read, Turkish that is. With understanding or even enjoyment?'

'I honestly don't know,' Suleyman said. 'When I went to the house, there were no books around the place as far as I could see. Why?'

'Well, I've been listening to her music.'

At this point İkmen and Suleyman exchanged a look.

'Just out of academic interest, you understand,' İkmen continued and then warming to his subject he said, 'And, guided by my dear wife, I have discovered that Tansu specialises in two types of song – the depressed, morbid variety and the venomous, bitter sort.'

'I thought they were all morbid,' Suleyman replied with a shrug. 'But do go on. What is your point?'

'My point is,' İkmen said, 'that she sings the venomous stuff in exactly the same way as the depressed sort. She talks of murder and mayhem with the same sad little smile on her lips and the same downbeat tone as she uses when she speaks of sadness and loss. If you really listen to it, it's totally inappropriate.'

'So?'

'So, my dear Mehmet, if as we are led to believe by the cassette sleeves, those songs of a homicidal nature were actually penned by Tansu, why does she not interpret them correctly? It's almost as if she doesn't really understand the words.'

Suleyman put his cigarette out in the ashtray and then cleared his throat. It was both interesting and opportune that İkmen should bring up the subject of Tansu Hanım now, but not because of anything to do with her songs. What he wanted to know was whether the description Cengiz Temiz had given him of the 'devil woman' was consistent with Tansu's appearance – if indeed the testimony of a frightened and damaged man, who had not, it had to be faced, recognised Tansu as his nemesis from a photograph, could be relied upon. He also needed to discover whether or not Tansu possessed a blonde mink. As Çöktin had whispered to him during his interview with Cengiz Temiz, hairs from just such a fur had been found on both Temiz's clothes and those of Ruya Urfa. What a strange garment, he could not help thinking, to be wearing at the height of the summer. But then they,

the Arabesk people as a group, were given to excessive
and often inappropriate dress, he knew. And Tansu,
undeniably, had very good motive.

At that moment, İsak Çöktin knocked and entered
the room.

'Oh, Inspector İkmen,' he said as he noticed his
superior's guest, 'it's good to see you.'

'Hello, Mickey Çöktin,' İkmen replied with a smile.
'I see the inspector here is keeping you busy.'

'Yes.' He dragged a chair over from underneath the
window and sat down. 'I hear you spent some time over
at the İskender Hamam, sir. Are you well enough?'

'I find that when I work I begin to feel better,' then
turning back to Suleyman he said, 'Oh, and we did find
a body, you know.'

'Oh.' Suleyman was sitting forward now. It was
good to talk to İkmen but he did really need to get
on. There were places he had to go.

'Yes,' İkmen replied as he, heedless of his fellows,
launched into a story. 'Madame's husband, according
to Kostas Katsoulis. He was in fact the man I always
thought was her servant, the eunuch Murad Ağa.'

Caught, despite himself, by the word, Suleyman
said, 'Eunuch? But I thought they all died out years
ago.'

'Oh, no,' İkmen said. 'I knew one in the sixties.
Imran Ağa. He was very black and monstrously fat.'

'Eunuch's still serve their purposes in some Arab
countries,' Çöktin put in.

'Do they?' İkmen said. 'Where?'

For just a moment Çöktin appeared a little flustered. 'Well,' he said, his pale skin turning slightly pink, 'I don't actually know where.'

'Ah.' From the look on İkmen's face none of Çöktin's discomfort had eluded him as it had the obviously distracted Suleyman. 'But to marry one is very queer, is it not?' he continued. 'I mean what can have been the pleasure . . .'

'There is more to marriage than just sex,' Çöktin said, his head bowed now.

'Yes, Mr Urfa said as much when I spoke to him.' Suleyman rose to his feet. 'But for now we must—'

Çöktin's mobile telephone which was currently residing in his pocket bleeped loudly. 'Oh, sorry, sir,' he apologised to Suleyman as he pressed the receive button. 'Hello?'

'Make it quick, Çöktin,' Suleyman said sternly and moved around the side of his desk towards İkmen.

'My cue to leave, I suppose,' İkmen said as he cast half an eye in Çöktin's direction.

Suleyman shrugged. 'Sorry, but now that Çöktin is here, we must progress.'

'Of course.'

After just a brief embrace, Suleyman led his guest towards the door of his office and opened it for him.

'I hope I'll see you very soon,' he said as he placed one slightly shy hand on İkmen's shoulder.

'Oh, you will,' and then leaning in close to Suleyman,

İkmen, still with half an eye on the quietly talking Çöktin, added, 'You do know that he's not speaking Turkish into that phone, don't you?'

Suleyman turned his head to listen and caught the guttural edge of Kurdish tones.

Chapter 10

By the time he reached Haydarpaşa railway station, Ali Mardin had convinced himself that he was simply going home for a social visit. That this was patently not the case had been graphically demonstrated by the action of gently slipping his identity card over the side of the ferry that had taken him to the Asian train station. There was, he knew, nothing usual about the wilful destruction of official documents. But what choice had he had? If the police had seen it they would have hauled him in for sure. Once in their unforgiving clutches he would, he knew, roll out the whole saga, which, although not exactly criminal, was not going to help his friend. When he got home there were many things he would have to tell Erol's parents – and Ruya's.

But for now, in the twenty minutes before the train arrived, Ali Mardin had other concerns. It was unlikely he would be able to get home without being asked to show his identity card. Soldiers or police or gendarmes could demand to see it and grave consequences could follow upon not producing it. What he needed, therefore, was a lot of luck both in procuring a replacement and in not being too closely looked at if subsequently required to produce it. Getting hold of one was not going to be easy, however. The tall, smart businessmen, distracted by their mobile telephones and portable computers, were probably the easiest targets but they bore so little resemblance to a short, rather scruffy peasant that those viewing such a card would have to be insane to detect any resemblance. Another peasant would be better. But peasants were cautious, as was Ali himself; they kept their possessions close. And Ali Mardin, though no saint, was no thief either.

Perhaps in the closer confines of the train he would have more opportunity. Ali bit his bottom lip nervously as a small group of heavily-armed policemen passed by. He would have to do something quickly. He knew that he could not help looking shifty. Very soon someone would stop him and demand to see his documents. Ali wiped the sweat from his brow on the cuff of his sleeve and then looked around him once again. If only someone would leave a bag or a jacket for just a moment . . .

As the departure for Ankara was announced over the tannoy, nothing immediately presented itself. He had a choice. To get onto the train and take his chances there or continue to scan for possible victims here. How could one know which was the right course of action to take? The policemen were getting onto the train, he could see them. What he could also see was that the station was emptying wholesale into the Ankara Express. Opportunities were disappearing by the second. He had to act and fast.

Dodging from foot to indecisive foot, Ali wavered for a few seconds – until he saw some of his fellow passengers were looking at him. Ah, well. He moved, head down, towards the barrier. Someone, somewhere had once said that with movement came freedom. Ali Mardin hoped against hope that this was the case.

Ever since he had received that phone call in Suleyman's office, İsak Çöktin had been unusually preoccupied. He had assured the inspector that the call was of no great import, but Suleyman wasn't convinced. He didn't like secrets and that included telephone calls he couldn't understand and unauthorised appearances at the homes of suspects. This latter, as he had discussed with İkmen earlier, had to be tackled. The few kilometres that separated the car from Tansu Hanım's home would, he felt, give him an opportunity to broach the subject.

'I was quite surprised to see that you were still with Mr Urfa when we found his daughter,' he said as he edged slowly into the appropriate traffic lane.

'He was very distressed after the broadcast,' Çöktin replied, somewhat baldly, Suleyman thought.

'What do you mean?'

Çöktin shrugged. 'He wanted to talk.'

'About?'

'Is there something wrong with my talking to a victim of crime?' His tone was really quite challenging and, though not exactly out of character, it was more confrontational than Suleyman had expected.

'It is when that person could be a suspect himself,' he said. 'What you have to remember, Çöktin, is that if we look at the situation from a romantic, for want of a better word, perspective, Urfa does stand to gain by the death of his wife.'

'What do you mean?'

As the traffic queue came to a grinding halt, Suleyman turned to his sergeant. 'To free him for Tansu Hanım.'

Çöktin, quite unexpectedly, laughed. 'What, you mean marry her?'

'Not necessarily but—'

'She's old enough to be his mother, sir!'

Suleyman bristled. 'So?'

The two men shared a look that informed Çöktin that he should not really continue with this line of argument. He looked down at the floor and cleared his throat. 'Well, I suppose he might marry her, but . . . Did he tell you that, sir? That he might marry Tansu?'

Suleyman opened the window of the car and lit a cigarette before answering. 'No,' he said, 'quite the reverse, in fact. He said it was his intention to marry another girl from his village, though he said he would still carry on seeing Tansu. But people do lie,

Çöktin, and aside from the initial shock that his wife's death gave him I can see very little of the desperately grieving husband in him.'

'Doesn't mean that he killed his wife though, does it? If Cengiz Temiz is to be believed, the assailant was a woman anyway, though I'm not sure we can necessarily believe Cengiz Temiz, can we, sir? I mean, you must admit to being a little wary about his story. There have to be a lot of questions, don't there? I mean, why did he leave his apartment when his parents were out? Why did the "devil woman" only hiss as opposed to attacking him when he saw her standing over the body of Ruya Urfa? Why was the door left open in the first place? It's too fantastic. We can't take it as absolute truth, can we?'

'No,' Suleyman smiled, 'but nor can we necessarily believe Erol Urfa either. The point I'm trying to make, Çöktin,' he said as he gently eased the car forward a few millimetres, 'is that one must always keep an open mind.'

'Well, yes . . .'

'Even when that openness is extended to people of one's own type,' he looked intently at the car in front, 'if you know what I mean.'

He felt, rather than saw, Çöktin's anger.

'Oh, so people have been saying that just because Urfa and myself—'

'People have been saying nothing.' Suleyman flicked the ash from his cigarette out of the window. 'But that issue will arise unless you are very careful. The slightest hint of partisanship will be both noted and commented upon. Staying with Mr Urfa in your own time and turning up at the station with him and his entourage later are just examples of this.' Then turning to look at Çöktin, he added, 'We must all be totally correct in this matter. If Inspector İkmen taught me nothing else, he taught me that that is the only way to arrive at an honest solution to a crime.'

'Yes, but you come from wealthy—'

'I know exactly where I come from, Çöktin,' Suleyman said with a hard edge to his voice, 'and I know you know I have not always been popular because of it.'

'Yes, but—'

'Every time someone of high birth is either arrested or implicated in a criminal act to which I am assigned, people nudge each other knowingly. I know this.' Then leaning towards Çöktin he said, 'But I also know that the only reason I have survived is because I have never given in to partisanship, bribery or the lure of informal little talks with suspects. There are several prominent families in this city who will no longer talk to me because of my attitude. But I don't care. We are here to ensure that the innocent are protected and the guilty are punished. That is our job.'

'Police work is not always like this,' Çöktin said as he lit up a cigarette of his own. He then added bitterly. 'There are people who are completely innocent who—'

'I do not intend to get into a discussion about anything that occurs east of Ankara,' Suleyman snapped. 'Until today I have never even so much as alluded to the differences between you and myself. But you must be careful with regard to Urfa. He is a high-profile person who is watched, followed and regarded by everyone.' With just a quick, sharp look, he added, 'I'm actually looking out for you, you know!'

Çöktin mumbled something that could have been thanks but then he moved miserably down into his seat and stared malevolently at the car in front. 'You must know that things are different for the poor, whether out in the country or here in the city,' he said. 'Where my parents come from people burn working in the intense heat of the summer for just a few lira, virtual slaves to corrupt village headmen.'

Suleyman sighed. Although accustomed to being told that he couldn't possibly empathise with the common man, he always felt that the resentment frequently levelled at him personally was misplaced. After all, the last of his parents' servants had been given notice (due to lack of Suleyman family funds) when he was four. And besides, the way İkmen had always trained him to see things was that if a person were guilty of a crime, that guilt stood regardless of that person's status in life. And the law, if at times only theoretically, agreed. But he knew, sadly, that there was no way of telling this to Çöktin right now. He had things in common with Erol Urfa – nationality, age, possibly philosophy of life too.

Çöktin didn't want Erol to be a murderer and, in truth, Suleyman felt that it was not really likely. However, as the lead officer in this case, he had to be rational. Çöktin, though an excellent policeman, was exhibiting a blind spot with regard to Urfa that was disturbing. It seemed not to extend to Tansu but then that was perhaps to do with her being a woman or, rather more specifically, a very unpleasant woman. In respect of Erol Urfa, however, Çöktin would have to be guided most carefully. Either that or watched.

As Suleyman regarded his deputy's sulky face out of the corner of his eye, he decided that the latter option might just be the best course to follow.

Ferhat Göktepe, though well-accustomed to Tansu's frequent rages, found himself completely at a loss with regard to her grief. Earlier, in his capacity as her caring manager, he had taken her to an audition for a part in a new film. Although the production company involved were in fact French, the casting of Tansu was only a formality. Göktepe had sent them enough publicity material to convince them that Tansu was 'big' in her own country, which is what the French had wanted. Big, Turkish, a peasant – all that was fine. But the producer, one Marcel Saint Denis, wanted Tansu not for the love interest in what was essentially a soft porn movie but as the scheming elderly mother of the depraved Sultan. Göktepe hadn't yet told Tansu this. And with her behaving the way she was, he couldn't imagine he would be breaking the news to her for some time.

Göktepe looked from the screaming mass of Tansu on the sofa towards the large unopened bottle of champagne on the table and back again. Ever patient, Tansu's sister Latife and two brothers, Galıp and Yılmaz, stood silently behind their sibling's writhing form, looking concerned.

'I'm going to have to speak to İbrahim Aksoy about this,' Göktepe said as he took his mobile telephone out of his jacket pocket. 'Erol must be made to see reason.'

'I'll bring him back myself if I have to,' Galıp said darkly and placed a protective hand on Tansu's shoulder. 'No one uses my sister and then just throws her away.'

'Exactly,' Göktepe concurred. He punched a number into his telephone. 'Which is why I am going to sort it out.' He leaned forward to speak directly to Tansu. 'Don't worry, my brightest star, Ferhat will not let you down.'

But before he could press the send button to make the call, a voice of dissent joined the conversation.

'What you're all forgetting,' Latife said as she moved round the sofa to sit with her sister, 'is that Erol has gone from here in order both to honour his wife and to preserve the dignity of his child. Whatever we may think, it does not look right for him to reside at the home of an unmarried woman, known to be his lover. I mean, the police could even still be—'

'Shut up! Shut up!' Tansu screamed and took a hard if hopeless swing at her sister. 'I want Erol here and I want him now!'

'I don't think you should have said that,' Galıp muttered. He pulled Latife roughly up from the sofa.

The considerably younger Yılmaz looked across at his brother and stuttered, 'D-d-don't you think we sh-sh-should get a d-d doctor?'

Ferhat Göktepe smiled as he finally pressed the send button. 'No need for a doctor to get involved,' he said confidently. 'I'll sort it out with Aksoy so that we'll all be happy and well.'

'I want Erol in my arms now!' Tansu hollered as she leaned forward to grab a cigarette from the table. 'Then we will open that champagne!'

Just before Göktepe got through, the distinctive sound of the electronic doorbell floated through from the front of the building. Knowing that the little maid would get it, all those involved in Tansu's latest drama stayed where they were.

As soon as Göktepe started to speak it was evident that he was communicating only with an answering service. Tansu dissolved into more smoke-wreathed tears.

'Hello, İbrahim,' Göktepe said with a smile on his lips if not in his eyes. 'Listen, my brother, I know it will be a trouble but you and I really need to talk urgently. I am right now here with my lady who is, I do not joke, dying for love of your Erol.'

Yılmaz, who was genuinely touched by Göktepe's words, began to join his sister in tears.

'So you see, I must speak to you, İbrahim,' Göktepe continued. 'İnşallah, between us we can find a solution to this problem.' Then he clicked the phone off, muttering 'You prick' under his breath, smiled at the family and sat down.

A knock on the door announced the arrival of the maid.

'Come in, Belkis,' Latife called.

The door opened to admit a girl who looked as if she was only about twelve years old. She wore a very plain grey tunic which only served to accentuate the thinness of her figure, plus a loud floral headscarf.

With halting steps she approached the disarrayed figure on the sofa. 'There are two gentlemen to see you, madam,' she said as she made a movement that might have been a bow.

Rearing dramatically, Tansu swung round to grab Galıp's hand. 'It's him! It's my beloved with İbrahim Aksoy.'

'Now, Tansu, my soul, let us not get too excited.'

The little maid looked down sadly at the floor. 'Actually it is two policemen,' she said. 'An Inspector Suleyman and another man.'

As quickly as she had taken Galıp's hand, Tansu released it with a disdainful flicking motion. 'What?'

she said to the girl violently. 'What did you just say?'

'Your visitors are policemen, madam. An Inspector—'

'Fuck off!' Tansu snarled and waved the little girl away. 'Don't tell me what I don't want to hear! And tell them to fuck off too. I—'

'Tansu!' Latife hissed She moved round in order to attempt to silence her sister. 'You cannot tell the police to go away!'

'I can! I'm a fucking star, I can do whatever I like!'

Göktepe who had, until now, been silent upon this matter, cleared his throat. 'Yes, you are a star, my darling, no one can deny that, but where the police are concerned . . .' He shrugged as if giving in to the inevitable.

Latife was now hunkered down at Tansu's side. She took hold of her sister's hand and kissed it. 'If you don't see them, darling, they will think all sorts of thoughts that are just not true. And besides, as Turkey's only true beloved star, you must lead the way in being a good citizen, mustn't you?'

A strange moment passed during which Tansu's mood, as the rest of the party all knew, could have moved in either direction. But as her breathing began to settle, they started to have hope.

'Mmm.' It was said through sobs and with little enthusiasm, but as Latife gently shifted some stray hairs out of Tansu's eyes, the singer leaned forward and kissed her.

'Now can I ask Belkis to show them in?'

Tansu swung her legs down onto the floor and reached for a tissue from the table. 'Do I look OK?' she asked, much as she must have done when pleading for approval as a child, Ferhat Göktepe thought.

Latife smiled. 'Not even tears can spoil your lovely face,' she soothed as she gently touched that face once again. Turning back to the maid, Latife said, 'Please show the gentlemen in now, Belkis.'

'Yes, madam.'

'And when you've done that,' Tansu said as she ground her cigarette out in the ashtray, 'you can collect your things from your room and go.'

'Tansu!'

Within a split second the eyes had hardened yet again. 'That is my last word on the subject, Latife,' Tansu said imperiously. She surveyed the trembling girl once again with extreme distaste and shouted, 'Go!'

'Now, Tansu,' Göktepe began.

'No!'

The girl began to cry, 'Oh, but beloved lady—'

'With your hateful eyes of blue and the bad news you always seem to bring, you are a devil indeed! Now get out of my sight, bringer of policemen!'

As the girl ran weeping from the room, Tansu took a deep breath and then lit another cigarette. 'I may not be able to control the world,' she said darkly as she surveyed all of those around her, 'but I will rule over my house without question.'

And with that she settled herself against the back of the sofa to await the police.

'Bulent! Bulent!' İkmen shouted as the front door slammed shut behind the retreating back of his son. Then with a sigh he let his upraised arms flop to his sides in despair. Zelfa Halman, who had observed all that had passed between father and son from the door to İkmen's balcony, walked into the hall and took the inspector gently by the arm.

'Come on,' she said forcefully, 'let's get outside.'

'I'm sorry you had to see that,' İkmen said as he allowed himself to be led into the living room and then out into the thick summer air once again, 'but that boy appears so rarely that I feel I must try to make him listen to reason when I do see him.'

'Growing up is never easy,' the doctor said as she flopped down onto the only comfortable chair to be had. 'He's a teenager. What can I say? I mean, we've all done it, haven't we?' She reached across the table for her cigarettes and then lit up.

'Done what?'

Zelfa Halman smiled. 'Rebelled.' She seemed, to İkmen, to revel in the sound of the word. 'When I was your son's age my parents had just split up so I was sent to live with my Uncle Frank. Oh, and I'd just started college too. It was rough but do you know what stands out about that time now? Remembering, of course, that Uncle Frank is a priest and therefore very pious.'

İkmen shrugged. 'No, I can't imagine.'

'What stands out, İkmen, is the way that I and my friends broke both civil and religious laws. Basically, whenever anyone went across to England, he or she would bring back a whole load of condoms for us.' Seeing İkmen, or so she thought, blush a little, Zelfa added, 'Not that we ever used the bastard things, we were much too scared and ignorant to do that. But, for myself, I'd make sure that Uncle Frank got a look at them from time to time and I did once blow one up in front of his housekeeper. What your son is doing is quite normal.'

'Mmm.' İkmen looked unconvinced, but before the doctor could comment upon this he changed the subject. 'So you were brought up a Catholic then, were you?'

'Yes. Mum was religious and Dad didn't care much so she got her way. And anyway it was Ireland in the nineteen fifties, for God's sake. My father might just as well have been from another planet.'

'So although you are Turkish you would, I assume,' İkmen said slowly and with seemingly some difficulty, 'prefer, for the sake of ease, I suppose, to have serious friendships with fellow Roman—'

'Stop digging, İkmen! I'll tell you nothing, as well you know.'

İkmen, thoroughly chastised and thwarted in his attempt to review Halman's intentions vis-à-vis Suleyman, looked down at the floor. 'Sorry. That was both clumsy and prurient of me. I keep on doing such things these days. I must be getting old.'

Zelfa Halman took a long drag on her cigarette and then said, 'So why did you ask me to come? Not, I hope—'

'No, no.' He sighed. 'No, although connected with Inspector Suleyman, my need to see you doesn't pertain to his private life. It is as a professional that I wish to consult you, Doctor.'

'For yourself? Your own problems?'

'No.' İkmen took a cigarette from his packet and lit up. 'Basically something which may or may not be irrational has been bothering me. This thing, which may or may not have a bearing upon Inspector Suleyman's current investigations, could be absolutely irrelevant. But because I feel as I do, I must explore the issue. Do you understand?'

'Yes.'

Down below in the street, some of the shops were beginning to put their lights on, as much a signal to the coming night as the merciful drop in temperature.

'Dr Halman, do you know anything about devil worship? I don't mean your European burning witches type of thing, but the Turkish version of that.'

'Oh, you mean like the concept of the night belonging to Shaitan, women who cast fortunes, sorcery, the djinn . . .'

'No, no,' İkmen said and then almost unconsciously dropping his voice, 'No, I mean *the* devil worshippers, the Yezidis. You as a foreigner, as it were, might have heard . . .'

'Oh, yes,' she said with a smile, 'you're right that people from this sect might be more willing to speak to me than to yourself. Not, of course,' she added with a twinkle in her eye, 'that I am telling you I have ever had a patient who is a Yezidi.'

'No.'

'No. All the identity cards of my patients have categorically stated their owner's religion as Islam, Judaism or Christianity. And that I can tell you with absolute honesty.'

İkmen leaned forward. 'But?'

'But first I need to know why you are interested in this subject,' she said. 'I mean, I know that you're a dreadful old sinner but membership of the Yezidi is only open to Kurds.'

Hearing the front door open and then close behind what sounded like a multitude of feet and voices, İkmen moved to shut the door to the balcony. 'Now, Zelfa,' he said as he walked back towards the table and sat down, 'you know that I can't disclose police business.'

'Yes, all right,' she said with a smile, 'but am I right

in assuming that you won't use anything I tell you for the wrong reasons?'

'If you mean will I use your knowledge to do harm, then the answer is no. I merely wish to understand something that you who I know has studied our culture more extensively than most might be able to tell me.'

The balcony door swung open to admit a younger version of İkmen.

'We're back,' Sınan said with a grin and then seeing Dr Halman sitting beside his father he added, 'Oh, I'm sorry, Dad. I—'

'This is Dr Halman,' his father said as Zelfa rose to take the young man's hand. 'Dr Halman, this is my eldest son Dr Sınan İkmen.'

'Oh,' she said with interest as she took his warm hand in hers. 'A doctor of what, may I ask?'

'He's a dermatologist,' İkmen said with obvious pride in his voice. 'We're very proud of him.' Turning to his son, he said, 'Dr Halman is one of our leading psychiatrists, Sınan.'

Sınan's eyes shone. 'Oh, how interesting.' He moved to sit at the table with his father. 'May I?'

'Perhaps later,' İkmen said. 'Dr Halman and I are discussing—'

'Oh, right, it's work,' Sınan sighed. 'Although not too much work, I hope, Dad. You know what Dr Akkale—'

'Yes, yes, yes,' İkmen said wearily. 'Just give us a few minutes, will you, son?'

'As long as you don't wear yourself out.'

'I promise I will control him,' Zelfa said with a smile, and as the young man moved towards the door she added, 'It was nice to meet you, Dr İkmen.'

'And you.' He shut the door behind him.

'You know that he could be part of your problem in relation to Bulent?' Zelfa said. She put her cigarette out in the ashtray and then lit up another.

İkmen frowned.

'Well, Sınan is bright, caring, obviously approved by yourself and your wife.'

'You mean Bulent might be jealous of Sınan?'

'I mean he might feel that because his brother is so successful, competing is pointless. It would explain at least some of his behaviour. Think about it.'

'Mmm.'

'And I suppose that, what with Orhan being at medical school too, and Çiçek . . .'

'You have another son training to be a doctor also?' Zelfa Halman said, surprised.

'Yes.'

'If you don't mind my saying,' the doctor continued, 'I think that's quite an achievement for a humble police officer.'

İkmen laughed. 'If you mean am I on the take or . . .'

'No! No, no! I didn't mean to imply . . .' Instead of completing her sentence Zelfa Halman shrugged.

'No, I know you didn't mean to cause offence,'

İkmen said with a conciliatory wave of his hand. 'And none is taken. But your point is a good one.' He sighed. 'And if I didn't have the admittedly small amount of money I inherited from my late father plus the considerable support I receive from my brother, well . . . Well, then perhaps I would be looking at, shall we say, other options. But . . .' He smiled, the doctor thought a little sadly and then suddenly and far more cheerfully changed tack. 'So, Zelfa, Yezidis . . .'

She took in a deep lungful of smoke and then let it out slowly as she spoke. 'In order to understand the Yezidis you have to throw out any Christeo-Islamic notions about Shaitan. According to the Yezidi credo, Shaitan did indeed fall from the grace of God, but unlike in our religions he was restored to favour. And, once elevated, he became and remains God's right-hand angel. I've heard that contrary to popular belief they are very peaceful and do not make human sacrifice, but quite how they do worship I don't know. But I'm aware of the fact that they are misunderstood, persecuted and that they sometimes go to great lengths to conceal their true identities.'

'I know they have dietary laws,' İkmen said. 'Is it true they don't eat chicken?'

Zelfa Halman made a wry face. 'Not entirely. They refrain from eating the cock bird out of respect for the peacock angel.'

'The peacock angel?'

'It's what they call Shaitan. I have no idea why.

They have a thing about beans, lettuce and the colour blue for similar reasons. They prefer to avoid them.'

'Mmm.' İkmen's face achieved a new gravity as he spoke. 'And so this avoiding cock flesh, would they go to some lengths to prevent, say, their children from eating it? Would they perhaps risk disclosure in order to do so?'

'They might. If they were very religious.'

'Mmm.'

Zelfa Halman leaned back in her chair and looked hard at İkmen. 'You intimated that this might have some sort of connection to Suleyman's case. And knowing that Erol Urfa and Tansu Hanım are both Kurdish . . .'

'I wouldn't even start that particular theoretical journey if I were you,' İkmen said sternly. 'We are, as I trust you can appreciate, not having this conversation.'

She shrugged. 'OK.'

The noise of bickering children floated through from the living room. İkmen banged hard on the window before continuing.

'So do you know anything else about these people?'

'As you are probably aware, those unwise enough to declare themselves Yezidi receive an X in the space where their religion should be stated on their ID cards. Consequently I don't suppose your lot see many of them.'

'I don't think I ever have,' İkmen said.

Zelfa smiled knowingly. 'Precisely,' she said. 'Not

that so many of them live here in the city. They come from the east, as you probably know. The headquarters of the religion is actually in Iraq.'

'Oh?'

'Yes. Some shrine which is guarded, apparently, by a eunuch.' She smiled. 'How exotic can you get, eh?'

But İkmen did not immediately answer her. His mind, which had until now been filled with the images of small children refusing chicken was now flooded with the words that İsak Çöktin had uttered to him only a few hours before. Words about eunuchs – words the young Kurd appeared to have quickly regretted. Despite the heat of the evening, İkmen started to experience a cold feeling in his guts. Whether all of this Yezidi stuff had any direct bearing upon Ruya Urfa's death, he didn't know. But little things, like Erol's fear that his daughter might be exposed to chicken, like the rather timely departure of one of his friends in the wake of an identity card request, like Çöktin's reported concern for Urfa, did seem to be at least pointing towards some sort of concealment. But was it, especially in light of the fact that Cengiz Temiz was still very much on the scene, pertinent? To open up such a contentious issue without pertinence was surely an act of madness. And anyway, hadn't Suleyman been totally satisfied with what was written on Urfa's ID card?

Perhaps prompted to movement by İkmen's frozen position, Zelfa Halman stood up.

'There is one thing you can be sure about though,

İkmen,' she said as she retrieved her bag from the back of the chair.

Surfacing from his reverie, he said, 'What?'

'If Erol Urfa is a Yezidi, then so was Ruya. They don't marry out.'

'So Tansu . . .'

'The only way he could marry her, although for the love of God I can't imagine why he would want to, is if she is one of them too. Assuming, of course,' she added as she moved towards the door, 'that he gives a damn about it.'

İkmen stood up to see his guest out. 'You won't tell Suleyman that, er . . .'

'And why should I do that?' she answered challengingly.

'Well . . .'

'I think you assume that I will be seeing the inspector, Inspector,' she laughed, 'which might not necessarily be so.'

İkmen sighed. 'You know you shouldn't be too hard on him, Zelfa. Although he seems to have so much, in many ways he's very adrift in this world.'

'Aren't we all,' she replied with some bitterness.

'Yes, but . . .' Not knowing how much she knew about his colleague's past finally put paid to any further discussion of this topic apart from İkmen adding, 'He must succeed with this case, you know.'

She smiled. 'Why? Because you like him? Or because you say so?'

'Because he deserves to,' he said a little sternly. 'And because whoever killed Ruya Urfa should be locked away before they can do any more harm.'

'İnşallah that will happen,' she said with more than a little irony in her voice.

İkmen simply lifted his eyes to heaven.

'So what are you going to do now then?' she asked as he opened the door to the living room.

The onslaught of light, colour, noise and odour was stunning as children, adolescents and adults all vied for attention, television time or food and drink.

'I think,' İkmen said, eyeing the scene before him with weary familiarity, 'that I might find a quiet place in which to listen to some Arabesk.'

For many and various reasons, sleep was not easily found by any of the actors in the Urfa saga that night. Admittedly, Cohen did, as was his custom, manage unconsciousness although the restless sounds that the wakeful Mehmet Suleyman heard from that quarter indicated that he was nowhere near peaceful. Perhaps, the younger man mused as he wandered out onto the Cohens' darkened balcony, his old friend was wondering why a once beautiful Greek had saddled herself with and then murdered a relic of the old harem system, her eunuch husband. As to why Kleopatra might have married such a person Suleyman, a relic himself he sometimes felt, could only guess at. Eunuchs, it was said, could please women in ways other men could not. But what forces may have driven her to kill, probably no one would be able to discover. No doubt the thought that passion or jealousy may have inspired this act puzzled Cohen in a most disturbing fashion.

But Suleyman's own thoughts were upon more contemporary events. Tansu Hanım had been in a very distressed state when he had arrived at her home earlier. Why this was, he didn't know. That she had shown him all her coats, including two blonde minks, willingly had been encouraging. She had even allowed him to remove fibres which seemed to indicate a lack of fear vis-à-vis complicity in Ruya Urfa's murder. And to be fair, she didn't really, despite her obvious unpleasantness, exhibit any overt similarity to the woman Cengiz Temiz had described. Not that Cengiz described her very well, but he had failed to identify Tansu from a photograph and so that had, surely, to be significant.

Suleyman wiped a thick swathe of sweat from his brow and looked down into the darkened street. There was not much to see out there. The occasional prostitute walking with difficulty across the deeply rutted road – a woman, or perhaps in this part of town a man in inappropriately high-heeled shoes, swinging a large, spangly handbag. Then, even rarer, the appearance of a strangely lonely, almost lost-looking man. Perhaps a simple migrant, or a confused tourist – perhaps even a man pounding out his resentment in the hot midnight street. A man, Suleyman thought, perhaps not unlike İsak Çöktin, that strange, even to İsak himself, contradiction in terms – the Kurdish policeman. In bed probably by now, Çöktin, Suleyman thought, was perhaps dreaming dreams that were livid with the redness of the blood they always mourned, which spilled, so the Kurds said, so liberally upon the ground of the far eastern provinces. Whether or not Çöktin had actually ever been to the east, Suleyman didn't know. If he hadn't then perhaps the fact that Erol Urfa came from there had been the root of the attraction they obviously had for each other. Perhaps the singer had told Çöktin yet more lurid and detailed stories of the hardship and suffering they all seemed to value so highly. Not of course that an Ottoman could even begin to understand such a thing. Suleyman closed his eyes and leaned back in his chair as he contemplated the depth of his own, idiosyncratic, resentments.

But thoughts being, as they often are, quite different to facts, Suleyman was wrong about Çöktin. Far from being home alone in his bed, he was in fact over at the surprisingly modest apartment İbrahim Aksoy had procured for Erol Urfa in Şişli. With the baby Merih now asleep, both men sat companionably in front of the open patio doors, talking, drinking tea and, occasionally, laughing softly at each other's quietly spoken words. Not once did the name Tansu pass either of their lips. That every light in the house of that lady burned fiercely that night was unknown to either of them.

Less comforting than any of these, admittedly rest-less, scenes was the one that was currently assailing the tranquillised eyes of Cengiz Temiz. Although still incarcerated in a police cell, it was not the unpleas-antness of his surroundings, or even particularly the heat, that was causing his drug-fuddled brain to remain awake. In his mind, devils and djinn lurked in corners where, in the daylight hours, housewives went about their domestic cleaning business. Red in the mouth and covered with thick white hair, the demons screamed at him with the faces of murderous women. And although they made him quiet, the drugs the woman who now wept alone in her sterile bed had given him did not expunge the hated, fearful images from his mind. Perhaps his precious love, Mina, could have done that had she been with him. But Cengiz had no idea where she might be now. Poor Mina with her frightening English boyfriend and her ruined womb.

In contrast to all this soporific restlessness, there were some whose thoughts were rather more focused. Tansu's ex-servant was one of these. As she sat alone waiting for the arrival of the laboriously slow Doğu Ekspresi to take her, via Ankara, back to her parents' home in Sivas, her thoughts were not of her rela-tives. To be dismissed by one's employer for what amounted to no good reason was bad enough, but to be shunned by a woman she had once idolised was intolerable. There had been a time when Belkis would have cheerfully died for her mistress – foolish,

231

foolish girl! The woman obviously loathed the sight of her and, in sharp contrast to one of Belkis's more extravagant dreams which involved being on stage and singing with Tansu, the woman had both abused her and rendered her unemployed. Had Miss Latife not given her a little money just before she left, Belkis wouldn't have even had enough cash to buy her ticket home. But then Miss Latife did most things that Tansu didn't want to or couldn't. She even lied for her. Yes, she did, didn't she . . . Slowly at first, but then with increasing power, Belkis's heart started to thump as something extremely interesting came back to her. Something perhaps even those investigating Erol's wife's death might find useful. As the train pulled into the station, Belkis worked hard to remember the name of the policeman she had seen that afternoon, just before she was asked to leave. But search her mind as she did, for the moment she couldn't recall it. When the train stopped and the passengers got out, Belkis looked up at the station clock. Ten minutes to go. Ten minutes to remember the tall, good-looking inspector's name. Ten minutes that would decide where she went and for what reason.

Tansu was very much in Çetin İkmen's thoughts too at that moment. Once again he had been listening to both her songs and those of Erol Urfa. And though it had to be said that in the case of the latter, there was nothing unusual in the lyrics, those supposedly written by Tansu were another matter. He looked down at the pad upon which he had jotted the words and frowned. Surely these references to the beloved object as 'my peacock', 'hated, adored peacock', 'peacock of my heart' and 'resplendent bird of blue and green' could not be coincidental? Loving, killing, dying for the peacock . . . Excessive, like her overblown affection for Erol, but at the same time, if Erol or even Tansu were of the Yezidi faith, surely unwise also. As Dr Halman had said, people just didn't understand them and, as the X in the space for religion on their identity cards proved, things people did not understand they frequently chose to both fear and despise. Not that Erol, or even the strangely knowledgeable Çöktin, had Xs on their cards. But then perhaps İkmen was just seeing devil worshippers everywhere now in the early, lonely watches of the night. It would not be the first time he had seen the shadow of something that did not, conventionally, exist. İkmen smiled at the thought and then put his pad down on the floor, the word 'conventional' resounding loudly in his brain.

'Conventionally' all this musing on songs and slightly off-key occurrences was a total waste of time. There was no evidence for any of this and besides, even if Erol Urfa did belong to some sort of odd sect, that didn't necessarily have any bearing upon his wife's death. No. However, just the inkling that there might be a secret of some sort here bothered İkmen. He didn't like secrets. Secrets could cause damage or even, in his own case, an unhealthy curiosity now over forty years old. But were the unknown circumstances surrounding his mother's death on the same level as wondering whether people might or might not belong to a minority religion? Yes and no.

If someone, as yet unknown, had killed because of it then it was even more important than his own personal demons.

As the night ravelled up around them, black and thick with closed-in heat, those who saw, in their waking or sleeping dreams, the body of Ruya Urfa lying small and alone in the mortuary stopped for a pause where real sleep should be. All waiting for the unrefreshing and already exhausting dawn.

Chapter 11

When Suleyman entered his office the following morning, he found Arto Sarkissian's full report on the corpse of Ruya Urfa on his desk. Although not personally wounding as Zelfa Halman's statement regarding the treatment of Cengiz Temiz had been, it did, nevertheless, make grim reading. Poisoned, as they already knew, by cyanide, Ruya Urfa had been in the early stages of pregnancy when she died. Although her husband was certainly unaware of this, whether Ruya herself knew of her condition could only be guessed at. Her husband, Suleyman recognised, would have to be made aware of this fact. He also knew that he would have to be the one to tell him. He put the report to one side with a sigh just as Çöktin first knocked and then entered his office.

'Good morning, sir,' the younger man said as he slipped lightly into the chair in front of Suleyman's desk

'The report on Ruya Urfa,' Suleyman said as he retrieved the paper and then pushed it across at his deputy. 'Some would say,' he continued as he watched a grave-faced Çöktin begin to read, 'that our perpetrator has the blood of two people on their hands.'

A minute or so of silence followed as Çöktin took in what was intelligible to him from the report. Suleyman, for his part, stared out of the window and smoked. The pregnancy aside, Arto Sarkissian's report had brought to his attention something that, amid his involvement with all the people around this crime, had all but slipped his attention. What had actually killed Ruya Urfa had been poison. Cyanide. Not something that, thankfully, one came across every day. He knew that it had industrial uses, although he didn't know what, but there had to be a limited number of places from which it could be purchased or stolen. And, given Çöktin's forcefully expressed opinions regarding the supposed innocence of Erol Urfa, it was probably not a bad a idea to give him the task of looking into this aspect. Besides, the disappearance of Urfa's only alibi for the night of the murder, Ali Mardin, had rather thrown the investigative emphasis back upon the singer. After all, there had to be more to Ali's absence than just simply an identity card violation. But, until the circulation of Mardin's description bore fruit there was no real way of telling.

'Mr Urfa will have to be told about this,' Çöktin said as he put the report back down onto Suleyman's desk. 'Do you want me to—'

'No. No, that's my job,' Suleyman answered with a sigh.

'Not pleasant.'

'No. Although I suppose he will have Mr Aksoy to help him through.'

'Oh, er,' Çöktin stumbled, 'um, he's not actually at Aksoy's any more actually, sir.'

Suleyman frowned. 'Oh?'

'No, he's, er, rented another apartment in the same block. I think it's number 1/3.'

Suleyman leaned across his desk and eyed his colleague narrowly. 'And how do you know this, Çöktin?'

'Well, he phoned me actually.'

'I trust that was through the switchboard here,' Suleyman said sternly.

Çöktin laughed, nervously. 'Oh, but yes, of course!'

'I mean I would hate to think that you were giving out your mobile and private numbers.'

'No!'

'After all, with Ali Mardin no longer available for comment, Mr Urfa has effectively lost his alibi for the time being.'

'Yes, but—'

'And research does suggest that the person most likely to have committed a homicide is frequently also the person who "discovers" the body. As I keep on telling you, Çöktin, Mr Urfa is still a suspect and is therefore not a suitable person for you to be seen consorting with.' He eyed Çöktin sharply. 'You will cease all contact with him from now on.'

'But, sir—'

Suleyman held up one silencing hand. 'This is not open to discussion!' Then with a sigh, he settled back into his chair once again. 'Besides, I have an important task for you right now.'

Çöktin did not answer but rather just looked up to indicate that he was paying attention.

'I would like you to go over to the Forensic Institute and gather some information for me about cyanide. With regard to people, we seem to be running around in circles to no good effect. Perhaps if we look at the substance used to kill Ruya Urfa we may have more luck. Perhaps the substance, or an individual's potential access to it, may help us to identify that person or people we really need to concentrate upon.'

Çöktin, somewhat calmer in demeanour now, took out his notebook and pen. 'Very well sir.'

'I know that cyanide is employed for industrial purposes, but I don't know what. That is point one. Point two, I need to know where it might be purchased, and point three, it would be useful to know whether it has any domestic uses. For instance, some poisons may be routinely employed to kill pests in the home. Some may even be used medicinally. I believe there is a type of rat poison that is also used as a blood-thinning agent.'

Çöktin dutifully wrote all of this down and then looked up. 'So do you want me to go over now then, sir?'

'The sooner the better,' Suleyman said as he retrieved his jacket from the back of his chair. 'You might also see if they've made any progress with those mink fibre samples from Tansu's coat. It might be a bit early yet, but . . .'

'All right.' Çöktin put his notebook and pen back into his pocket and stood up. 'So what are we doing with regard to Cengiz Temiz, sir?'

'I'm still hanging on to him, just,' Suleyman said. He picked his car keys up from his desk. 'Although Mr Avedykian is moving to bring him before a judge as soon as possible.'

'Right.'

'And if the judge decides that the evidence against Mr Temiz is outweighed by his lack of capacity then he will walk.' Suleyman shrugged. 'But the law must take its course.'

'Not everybody thinks like you, you know,' Çöktin said. 'I mean you could just beat whatever it is Temiz knows out of him. People do.'

'Yes, I know.' Suleyman looked down at the floor. 'And I almost did that once. But Inspector İkmen stopped me, luckily. Had I done so all the reasons why I joined the force would have disappeared.'

'Yes, but with so many others—'

'We can only influence our own practice and try to

lead by example!' He ground his cigarette out in the ashtray and then, nervously, lit another. 'I can't do anything about what may or may not happen when other officers arrest a person. I can't do anything about our anti-terrorism measures.' He lowered his voice. 'All I know is that if people sigh with relief when I arrest them, like they do when İkmen puts his hands on their necks, I am getting somewhere, if slowly. And I know that you being who and what you are, share the same goals. Policing in this country has changed and is changing for the better. I know that!'

'Yes, sir.'

Suleyman walked towards the door. 'I will extend your condolences to Mr Urfa,' he said. 'I will do so in Turkish. Do I make myself clear?'

Çöktin sighed and then smiled weakly. 'Yes, sir. Thank you, sir.'

The two men walked out together into the hubbub of the busy corridor.

İkmen replaced the telephone receiver on its cradle and then walked into the kitchen. Fatma, who had just fin- ished doing the washing up with the help of fourteen- year-old Hulya, was taking her apron off as her hus- band entered the room. Hulya, upon seeing her father, rolled her eyes heavenwards and left without a word.

'What's the matter with her?' İkmen said, watching the youngster stomp out of the kitchen.

'She's part of Bulent's gang.' Fatma lowered herself

gently down beside her husband. 'When you've got as many children as we have, they take sides.' Seeing the crestfallen look on İkmen's face she rubbed her fingers affectionately in his hair. 'Don't worry, she hates Sınan and Çiçek, too.'

'Oh, well, that's comforting!'

'Basically it works out that the teenagers are against the rest of us,' Fatma said.

'Or rather their hormones are,' İkmen answered grimly.

Fatma stood up and walked across the room to put the kettle on the stove. 'Well, you know what I've always said about that, don't you, Çetin?'

İkmen pulled an unpleasant face. 'If we married them off like good Muslim boys and girls . . .'

'But you just wouldn't have it, would you! No!' In her stride now, Fatma flung one exasperated hand up in the air. 'No, you had to fill their heads with ideas! You—'

'This is so hypocritical, it makes me want to vomit!' It wasn't often that he really yelled, but whenever he did, it brought her up short. Not that Fatma was afraid of her husband. Not once in the thirty years of their marriage had he so much as raised a hand to her. It was just that certain subjects, she knew, could set him off on long diatribes that, while they lasted, seemed to have no end. She also knew that he was far from well and that the last thing he needed right now was a fight.

'Çetin . . .'

'We married for no other reason than that we were in love! No religious involvement, no family pressure like poor Suleyman had to endure! Love, Fatma!' He looked her hard in the eyes until, eventually, she turned away. 'And if you want to deny our children the choice of real love then go ahead, but you won't get my support! Not even against Bulent!'

Strangely, she thought, for him, İkmen stopped there and just looked down furiously at the table. It wasn't until she saw that one of his hands was clutching at his stomach that she realised that he was in pain. As a veteran of these scenes and of his pain Fatma knew that to comfort him now would only attract a furious rebuff. And so as he fought to disguise the sound of his laboured breathing, she stood over the kettle and changed the subject.

'So who called on the telephone then, Çetin?'

He didn't answer immediately, pausing first to light a cigarette.

'It was Father Yiannis,' he gasped, 'from the Aya Triyada Kilisesi. He's invited me to Madame Kleopatra's funeral.'

'Will you go?'

'Yes. She was good to my mother. I owe her respect.'

Fatma watched as the kettle started to steam very lightly. 'And the other body?' she asked. 'Murad Ağa? What of him?'

İkmen sighed. 'I don't know,' he said. 'What's left of him is still at the lab. Who's to know?'

Still gently rubbing his stomach, İkmen got up from his chair and walked across the kitchen to open the window. As he walked back to his chair he muttered, 'Too hot,' by way of explanation.

Fatma took two tulip glasses out of one of her cupboards and retrieved a box of apple tea granules from another. 'You came to bed very late last night, Çetin,' she said. 'Was something bothering you?'

'I was thinking about those songs of Tansu Hanım's, the bitter ones. Do you know how many times she refers to the beloved as a peacock in those?'

'No.' Fatma spooned granules into each glass.

'Sixteen. And considering that that type of song doesn't represent the bulk of her output, that is a lot.'

'Yes. But then peacocks are beautiful birds. The male being far more lovely than the female.' Fatma poured boiling water onto the granules and then stirred the mixture. 'And as a symbol for Tansu and Erol it's quite good really. I mean he is quite stunningly attractive and she is, well . . .' She smiled. 'Anyway, why are you thinking about this, Çetin?'

'Well, Ruya Urfa's murderer is still at large—'

'Which is, I believe, Mehmet's case and not yours,' Fatma said as she placed the two glasses down on the table and then sat beside İkmen.

'Yes . . .'

'Yes.' She pursed her lips in a half smile and took one of his hands in hers. 'I know you're bored, but . . .'

'I don't want him to miss anything, Fatma,' İkmen said, suddenly becoming excited. 'I want him to succeed! He's a good man. We don't have that many. He deserves to succeed!'

'Yes, of course he does, but that is not for you to decide, Çetin. If Allah is merciful, then Mehmet will succeed, if not . . .' She shrugged. 'But you must let him go and meet his own fate.'

'Mmm.'

'And anyway,' she continued, 'quite how you think this peacock business might help Mehmet, I really don't know.'

İkmen took a sip from his glass. 'Fatma,' he said, 'have you ever heard of the Yezidis?'

İkmen watched with horror as his wife's eyes hardened. 'They that dance in the dark and then couple with each other? The sons and daughters of Shaitan?' She spat, admittedly in the direction of the sink, İkmen noted, though she missed it. 'İnşallah we will never meet their like in this city.'

'Oh? Why is that?'

'Because, as I just said, they worship Shaitan! Even for someone like you, surely the dangers of actually worshipping evil must be clear!'

'There are some who think they are simply mis-understood, that the Ye—'

'Do not say that name in my house again!' Fatma roared as she clutched her blue boncuk to her neck. 'As if I haven't suffered enough with your addiction to malevolent characters! Soothsayers, beggars, weavers of wicked tales – and you make it quite plain that you still live with the ghost of your witch mother!'

'Fatma . . .'

But she was up now and across the other side of the room from him, wiping dishes that were already spotlessly clean.

'No,' she said, 'I don't want to talk about this any more!'

İkmen sighed. Although horrified by even the slightest hint of anything supernatural, Fatma was deeply superstitious in that particularly vehement way that only religious ladies were. Like the time he had, foolishly, told her about how his mother had always smiled at the new moon to ensure good fortune for the month to come, she was now once again on her guard against the forces of evil. Soon, he knew, she would revert to calling him 'witch's child' again and he would become weary of her ignorance. Not that Fatma was stupid, quite the reverse. She was an intelligent woman – except in this one respect.

But no matter. He had other things to do and, when he returned, she would, as ever, have cooled down again. He knew he would never convince her of Dr Halman's and possibly his own view of these people as merely misunderstood. But if he kept quiet about it when he came home again Fatma would be herself with him.

Not that he could resist just one last comment before he left. 'So I won't bring any Yezidis home for a meal then?' he said as he moved quickly out of his seat and over to the door.

'Get out!' Fatma said as she attempted to both shout and spit at the same time.

Sevan Avedykian took in another deep breath and then started again. 'Look, Cengiz,' he said, 'it's like this. Tomorrow you and I will go to see the judge who will make a decision about whether or not the police can keep you here.'

'I didn't kill Mrs Ruya! Not me!'

'Yes, Cengiz, I know that.'

'The devil woman killed her, she did!'

'The devil woman you have, as yet, failed to identify,' Avedykian said as he lit up one of his large cigars. And by God he needed it! So far, although it was evident to everyone concerned that Cengiz could not in any way have plotted to murder Ruya Urfa, the circumstances surrounding his abduction of the baby Merih were still confused. According to Cengiz, when he had walked out of his apartment and into the hall, the door to the Urfa's apartment had been ajar. Thinking that perhaps his friends were coming out of the apartment, Cengiz had pushed the door open, which was when he had seen this supposedly 'devilish' blonde woman wearing a fur coat. Probably shocked at seeing him there she had then, in Cengiz's words, snarled at him, before disappearing out of the apartment and down the stairs. It was only then, when Cengiz went into the Urfas' kitchen, that he discovered the body of Ruya on the floor. He had not seen the devil woman with the body at any time. After trying in vain to revive Ruya, Cengiz then apparently heard the baby cry and went to her in her room. Still traumatised by the sight of the devil woman, Cengiz decided to take the baby to a place of safety, which to him was not a police station or a hospital but the arms of a prostitute with whom he was infatuated.

A fantastic story and one which, Sevan Avedykian would argue, someone like Cengiz could not have made up. However, there were still significant problems, not the least of which were Cengiz's fingerprints all over the body and the whole question of whether the devil woman actually existed. And even if she did, Avedykian could not help thinking, she had to be most profoundly stupid to leave a front door open while she was committing a murder. Giving little Merih Urfa over to a woman who, by Cengiz's own admission, lived with a drug addict did Avedykian's client no favours either. It was just a mercy that whoever had killed Ruya had not interfered with her sexually. With Cengiz's admittedly very old conviction for indecent behaviour, that would have been evidence which could, potentially, have buried him.

As Cengiz sat slumped, apparently looking at spots on the floor, Sevan Avedykian turned to Dr Halman's psychiatric evaluation document. As he reached for this he purposefully pushed to one side her letter of complaint regarding Cengiz's treatment in custody. Although well-written and almost certainly true, it did flag up the Irish woman's lack of knowledge of the more subtle workings of the judiciary. To antagonise the police at this stage would not be a good idea. That could be addressed later when or if his client's innocence was proven. For now the psychiatric assessment was much more pertinent. With a mental age of just seven, Cengiz would, according to Dr Halman, see the world as fundamentally concrete and absolute and would be influenced less by inference, as in the adult world, and more by how things looked or seemed. In addition he would only be able to classify objects or people with a single attribute at a time. This meant, Avedykian deduced, that asking Cengiz for more details about the devil woman, beyond those already supplied, would be a waste of time. So discovering whether she was young or old, short or tall was going to be difficult. Unless the right question were asked, whatever that might be, or the right photograph shown, no progress could be made. Add to this the idea that Cengiz was also what Halman called egocentric and the picture clouded still further. Basically, Cengiz could see the world only in his own terms. If his concept of a devilish person did not concord with that of the rest of humanity, then tough. So the police could, in theory, be looking for Cengiz's individual concept of this woman and not a real person at all – if Avedykian understood this correctly.

With a sigh he put the document down and looked at his client again. Defending this man was not going to be easy. But then Mr and Mrs Temiz had not signed over vast swathes of their fortune to him to make his life easy. And besides, as he attempted to catch Cengiz's sad eyes with his own, he had to admit that he did feel pity for the man. Damaged and frightened, Cengiz had already experienced more ill fortune in his relatively young life than most. Although very different to his own son, the amount of misery in Cengiz's life was not dissimilar to that in poor Avram's. Like Cengiz, Avram had lived much of his short life in a state of fear and he, too, had been misunderstood on so many levels.

Avedykian patted his client's hand and told him to have courage. Cengiz just stared back, his eyes glassy, his mouth drooling.

'Look, Suleyman,' İkmen said, reverting in his agitation to his old form of address, 'all I'm saying is that I don't want you to miss anything!'

'Which involves my having to believe that we are surrounded by devil worshippers?' Suleyman threw himself petulantly down into his chair. 'I wasn't aware that I'd suddenly stumbled into a scene from *The Exorcist*!'

İkmen pulled a chair up towards Suleyman's desk and sat down. 'Just look at the facts, OK? Fact one,' he banged his fist down on the desk to emphasise his point, 'Urfa specifically appeals to Merih's abductors not to give her chicken or beans.'

'She has an allergy.'

'Yes, she may, I accept that. But no doctor can, at her age, really make a judgement on that. The child would be fed almost exclusively on milk at her age. How would Urfa, or anyone else for that matter, know?'

'Yes, but—'

'Then,' İkmen banged the desk once again, 'there is the disappearance of that man you tried to ID. He didn't want you to see his card.'

'Or he just wanted to get out of the way so he wouldn't crack under interrogation. I mean if Urfa wasn't with him—'

'And then there are the peacocks.'

'Ah.' They had been over this subject before and Suleyman was still not convinced. 'What you're asking me to believe,' he said, 'is that the whole lot of them belong to this sect and, further, that one of my officers may also!'

'Well, you must admit that Çöktin's sudden advocacy of Urfa's cause is a little odd. He's met Kurdish criminals before and he's never been like this. And besides, his knowing about eunuchs in other countries is a bit specialised, isn't it? Dr Halman has made a study of this sort of thing and—'

'But even if you are right, what bearing could this possibly have on Ruya Urfa's death?'

'I don't know!' İkmen paused briefly in order to swallow hard and gather his thoughts. 'All I know is that I distrust secrets and if these people have them then they need exposing!'

A knock at the door brought their discussion to a halt.

'Come in,' Suleyman said with a heavy sigh.

Orhan Tepe smiled aimably into the room.

'Well?' Suleyman asked wearily.

'There's a young lady to see you, sir. She says she's a servant at Tansu Hanım's house.'

İkmen and Suleyman exchanged a look before the latter said, 'Well, bring her up then.'

'Yes, sir.'

As Tepe closed the door behind him, İkmen said, 'I wonder what she wants.'

'I have no idea although I doubt very much that it's about strange sects.'

Ignoring this jibe, İkmen said, 'So where is Çöktin at the moment?'

'At the Forensic Institute, looking at the uses and origins of cyanide.'

'So you're keeping him away from Urfa.'

'That was my intention, yes.'

A moment of silence passed during which Suleyman wrestled with his tongue to make it instruct İkmen to leave. He knew he had the right and the old man's interference was beginning to get on his nerves. But for some reason he just couldn't do it and so when a small, almost child-like figure was escorted into his office, he introduced İkmen as if he were a currently serving officer involved in the Urfa case.

In a voice so small and soft as to be barely audible, the girl announced herself as Belkis Kasaba. She had been, she said, until the previous day, a maid at Tansu Hanım's house in Yeniköy. As she spoke she knitted her fingers nervously, a habit which only abated when she looked up briefly at İkmen who smiled back warmly at her.

'So what have you come to tell me then, Belkis?' Suleyman asked, attempting without success to look her in the eye.

Belkis licked her dry lips before answering. 'I do want you to know that I have always loved Tansu Hanım, sir. I have loved her music and her all of my life.' Then looking across at İkmen who, presumably, she saw as more of a father figure, she said, 'And even though she has wronged me, I still want to be like her one day. I can sing and dance and everything and İnşallah, I will be an Arabesk myself one day.'

'I'm sure you shall,' İkmen said kindly, 'but for the moment, Belkis, you say that Tansu has wronged you. How did she do this?'

'Madame dismissed me just before Inspector Suleyman arrived yesterday.' She threw a short, shy glance at the younger man. 'She thought that Inspector Suleyman might be Mr Erol come back to her and when that wasn't so, she told me to go.'

'That seems particularly unfair,' Suleyman commented, 'Does no one else in her party object to this?'

'Miss Latife, Madame's sister, did, so I had hopes that she might change her mind. Miss Latife does so much for Madame that sometimes even in her rages she can make her do things.'

'But not on this occasion?'

Belkis started to snivel. 'No,' she said, 'Madame was too furious for that. Although Miss Latife did give me money to get home to Sivas with.' Then bursting into full-blown tears, she said, 'Not even Mr Yılmaz, Madame's brother, said goodbye and . . .'

Suleyman took his handkerchief out of his top pocket and handed it across to Belkis.

'Thank you, sir. Thank you.'

After a brief pause during which the girl attempted to get hold of her emotions, Suleyman said, 'Well, that's very bad indeed, Belkis, but I don't think that you came here, instead of presumably going back to your parents, just to tell me this sad story, did you?'

She looked at İkmen, who smiled yet again, before answering. 'No, sir.'

'And so . . .'

'Well . . . Look, I'm not saying all this because I am angry at Madame, you understand. I mean she is still the best star in all the world . . .'

'But?'

'But . . . But I know that Madame lied when she said that she was in the house on the night of Mrs Urfa's murder.'

İkmen gave Suleyman a look which spoke volumes about the value of the serving classes. Suleyman ignored this and went on with his questioning.

'So how do you know this, Belkis?'

The girl breathed in hard before launching into her tale. 'Miss Latife went to bed at about seven,' she said. 'She'd been out all day tending the plants with the gardening man. She likes the plants. She says it comes of being the daughter of a country girl.' She smiled. 'But anyway, that left Madame alone downstairs, sitting out on the veranda. Mr Galip was at that football match and Mr Yılmaz, well, he was upstairs too by then . . .'

'So what happened then?'

'Well, after making sure that everything was ready for the morning, I went out to Madame and asked her if she wanted anything else. She said that she didn't and that I could go to my room now if I wanted. She was quite pleasant to me.' Belkis suddenly seemed very nervous again, presumably because she was getting to the nub of the matter now. 'I, er . . .'

'Go on, Belkis,' İkmen said encouragingly, 'you're doing very well.'

'Yes, but I should have told you this before, should—'

'That's not important now,' Suleyman said earnestly. 'So you did what?'

'I went upstairs.'

'To your room.'

'No,' she said, lifting her tear-stained face just a little, 'to Mr Yılmaz's room. We, um . . .' The tears, silent this time, started flowing once again and Belkis buried her eyes in Suleyman's handkerchief. 'Oh, sirs, what must you think of me!'

Even though he knew he strictly shouldn't, İkmen placed a fatherly hand on the girl's shoulder. She couldn't be much more than seventeen, if that, and sadly he could easily imagine what Mr Yılmaz might have said to get this little one into his bed.

'Did Mr Yılmaz say he would help you with your career if you slept with him?' İkmen asked.

'I only had to take my shirt off at first,' the girl said sadly, 'but then he said that wasn't enough and he'd only really be able to help me if I, I, oh . . .'

'He took advantage of you, Belkis,' Suleyman said with a sigh, 'which was very wrong.'

'Yes.' Feeling, quite correctly, that the inspector wanted her to get to the point of the story, Belkis pulled herself together once again and carried on.

'But you don't want to know that,' she said. 'What you need to know is about Madame.'

Suleyman nodded encouragingly.

'When I went to Mr Yılmaz's room, he had just got out of the shower and was sitting on the end of his bed drying himself with a towel.' She gulped nervously at the memory of this. 'So I sat down next to him, and we, well, I don't want to say, but a little later I heard a car start. It wasn't Mr Galıp coming back, it was definitely someone going somewhere. And Mr Yılmaz, who was recently given a new Ferrari by Madame, which he loves, ran over to the window to make sure that no one who shouldn't was driving his car. Madame and Miss Latife have both driven it and he doesn't like it.'

'So what was there when Mr Yılmaz looked out of the window?' İkmen asked. 'And did you go over there with him?'

'Yes, I did go and I did see.'

'What did you see, Belkis?' Suleyman asked, his heart now beating faster with excitement.

'I saw Madame dressed in one of her big white furs driving off in the silver Mercedes.'

'And did you see her return again?'

'No, I went up to my room soon after that. Then I went to sleep.'

'What about in the morning?' İkmen asked. 'Did you see her then?'

'Yes, I did, and she was crying. I heard her say

to Miss Latife that she thought something bad might have happened to Mr Erol. Miss Latife had to give her tranquillisers to calm her down.' Then as if suddenly aware of what she had said, Belkis clapped her hand across her mouth. 'I won't have to speak about Mr Yılmaz in the court, will I?'

Chapter 12

The pigeon is dead
And so is my heart
His feathers are black as the night
I killed you my soul
For the love you won't share
My hatred puts daytime to flight

'. . . and on and on and on,' Tansu said as she rocked miserably about on the sofa in front of the television screen. Then, laughing, but without mirth, she threw what was left of her champagne down her throat and poured another draft half into her glass and half across the surface of the table. She wasn't bothered. As soon as she had a decent amount in her glass she drank it and then flopped back to look at the TV screen again.

She didn't hear her sister walk across the room towards her.

'Watching one of your old movies, Tansu?'

The star turned to face what looked like a smarter, more sober version of herself. 'Yes,' she slurred. 'I like to look at myself when I was a beautiful girl.'

Latife took a few moments to view the film before saying, 'You were thirty-five in this one.'

Leaning forward with an almost demonic leer on her face, Tansu said, 'You wouldn't say that to me if I was sober!'

'No I wouldn't. But seeing as you won't remember any of this in a few hours' time, I can say what I like.' She sat down beside her sister on the sofa, making sure that she was just far enough away to be out of danger.

'I've given you and our brothers everything,' Tansu murmured as she watched her younger self run fearfully from a big man with a sword. 'Not that I resent that. I would do it all again.'

'Thank you.' It was said automatically, expressing acceptance rather than gratitude.

'Yılmaz is angry that I got rid of his little girl, but I said you can fuck anything you like, you're my brother.'

'What if he wanted his freedom?'

Tansu frowned. 'What do you mean?'

Latife sighed. It was a lot like trying to explain things to a child when Tansu was like this. 'What if Yılmaz wanted to leave this house? Would you give him that?'

'But Yılmaz doesn't want to go. He hasn't got anywhere to go.'

'Yes, but what if he did have somewhere? Would you let him leave?' She looked hard into her sister's face, just at the moment when Tansu's soft eyes turned hard. 'Well?'

The voice when it came was more like something animal than human. 'I'd throw his ungrateful carcass out without a kuruş!'

'Nobody uses kuruş any more, Tansu, they're worth nothing.'

'Well, how should I know that?' She leaned forward, wobbling slightly at the waist. 'I have people to do the money thing, don't I?'

'You have people to do everything except have sex, drink and take drugs.'

Tansu laughed, but not out of good humour, a fact made evident by her words. 'I'll kill you for that tomorrow,' she said, 'my dear, bright little sister.'

With an accepting shrug, Latife pushed herself up against the back of the sofa and was about to close her eyes when Galıp and Yılmaz entered the room. As they walked somewhat shakily across the floor, Latife thought at first that the two men were as drunk as her sister. It was not until she felt a familiar sickening flip in her stomach that she realised that they were quite sober. Another small earth tremor to add to all the others that had been occurring of late. Not, as born and bred İstanbulıs were wont to say, that it meant anything. The earth moved, it sometimes did a bit of damage, it shuffled back again and everything was the same once again. Inşallah it would always be so.

As the tremor subsided, so Galıp and Yılmaz regained their equilibrium.

'If this carries on, I'm going to get out and go down south,' Galıp said as he picked up Tansu's almost empty bottle of champagne.

'A-a-and m-me,' Yılmaz echoed, 'I w-will t-too.'

Tansu observed her brothers with a lizard-like eye. 'You'll go south soon anyway,' she said contemptuously, 'so you can spend my money on beer and foreign women.'

Galıp just laughed, but Yılmaz was genuinely stung by her words. 'I-I'm going to m-my room.'

'To think about poor little Belkis?' Tansu taunted.

'Y-you t-take away everything w-we w-want!' he said, suddenly furiously angry. 'Y-you just give us w-what y-you tthink w-we should w-want!'

'Oh, is that s-so, Y-yilmaz?' Tansu hissed in obvious and hurtful imitation of her brother's impediment.

'Y-you, a-are—'

'Come along,' Latife said and stood up. She took hold of her brother's arm. 'We've all had a very upsetting time lately, perhaps it might be better if—'

'But s-she—'

'Yılmaz! Come along!' And with that Latife pulled her brother bodily from the room.

'I was born a slave, but I will die free!' a much younger version of Tansu wailed from the television set.

The older Tansu threw what was left of her champagne at the image, laughing bitterly as the flowing liquid distorted the rosy-hued skin on the screen.

It isn't easy to concentrate on anything when one's mind is tortured by anxiety. Even the most simple task may be rendered virtually impossible. When, however, that which has to be attended to is both unfamiliar and complex, the task becomes doubly difficult. This was a lesson that İsak Çöktin was learning as he attempted to make some sort of sense out of what Miss Göle, the laboratory technician, was attempting to tell him.

'The principal industrial use of cyanide is in the manufacture of steel. It's used to pickle it. A byproduct of this process is a substance called hydrocyanic acid,' then as if suddenly noticing the glazed look on Çöktin's face for the first time, she said, 'Do you follow, detective?'

'Yes,' Çöktin smiled in that particular way people do when they haven't a clue what is actually happening.

Holding up a fragile glass bottle filled with an amber-coloured liquid, Miss Göle then announced, 'And this is what it looks like.'

'Oh.' Çöktin reached out to take it from her, but Miss Göle stopped him with her free hand.

'No, I don't think so, detective,' she said sternly. 'Your mind is far too distant for you to be trusted with something so delicate and at the same time so deadly.'

How right she was. And yet, try as he might, Çöktin just could not drag his mind away from the subject of Erol Urfa – or the invidious position his relationship with that man might have placed him in. Inspector Suleyman was not happy about what he perceived as partisan behaviour. He was quite correct in his assumption that that was what was happening and he was probably also quite correct in still having his suspicions about Erol. Not, of course, that Çöktin could agree with that. The whole point about followers of the Peacock Angel was that they were not wicked or profane or violent. If only he could explain that to Suleyman – but then that was as impossible as it was ridiculous. It would also be professional suicide – if, of course, he had not already committed that act.

'Cyanide may be created by distilling the stones of either the plum or the cherry. Anyone who has access to distillation equipment may produce it. We here at the institute, for instance,' Miss Göle said with a smile, 'could manufacture cyanide with ease.'

'I see.' Had he been listening with full attention, Çöktin would have been chilled by her words, but instead his responses were as half-hearted as his questions. 'So can cyanide be used domestically?'

'You mean in the home?'

Çöktin shrugged. 'Yes.' Suleyman had used the words 'domestic uses', which he assumed meant within people's houses and apartments. Oh, if only he could just give up on Erol and let the legal process take its course like it had for every other suspect he'd ever come into contact with!

'Well, not really,' Miss Göle said as she shifted her spectacles up onto the bridge of her nose, 'although I have come across several instances where it has been used to kill pests. Rats, mice, wasps – you know.'

He wrote it all down, his pen making notes almost without thought from him.

'Usually, though,' Miss Göle continued, 'when it is used domestically, those employing it generally have some sort of connection with industry. They bring a little home from their place of work.' She smiled. 'A sort of perk, I suppose you'd say.'

'Right.'

She looked down at her watch and then pursed her lips. 'Well, if that is all . . .'

'You've been most helpful,' Çöktin, said taking her hand in his and shaking it firmly. 'Thank you.'

'It's nothing,' and with that she made her way back to the door of the laboratory and then held it open for Çöktin to pass through. 'Goodbye, detective.'

'Goodbye, madam.'

Once back out in the reception area, Çöktin looked briefly over his notes. Sketchy and half-hearted, they were no more or less than he had expected. But then with his mind so alarmingly distracted, what more could he have hoped for? There was no logical reason why he should have become so involved with Erol. After all, the singer didn't actually need to have him as an ally. It was just that as soon as Çöktin knew what he did about Erol, he felt duty bound to help. After all, did he not understand the pressures himself?

In order to assure himself that really he did not, Çöktin took out his identity card and looked at the word that was written beside religion. The bitterness which gave the lie to that word rose up within him immediately. So no assurance here, then?

No. He put the card back inside his wallet and tried to forget about it.

Although famous enough to appear regularly in most of the national newspapers herself, Tansu Hanım's family were almost totally unknown to the average man in the street. It was an ignorance that extended even to the fact of her surname which, İkmen and Suleyman discovered from the singer's brother, Yılmaz, was Emin.

Although considerably younger than his famous sister – Yılmaz claimed he was forty – he had neither her confidence nor her challenging demeanour. And under the sort of pressure Suleyman was exerting, İkmen felt that Yılmaz must soon crack.

But İkmen was wrong. Whenever Suleyman asked him what he was doing on the night of the murder and whether or not he saw his sister leave the house, Yılmaz just said that he was in his room alone all evening and that Tansu, as far as he knew, had stayed in also. He did not mention the servant Belkis, which was clever, or perhaps lucky, İkmen thought, because it meant that Suleyman was being manoeuvred into a position where he would have to mention her. Soon Yılmaz would want to know why this questioning was necessary, and the reason, as both İkmen and Suleyman knew, was only hearsay.

However, recalling the rather impressive set of security measures, both human and electronic, that had greeted the two policeman at the entrance to Tansu's seraglio, İkmen decided to take one of his famous unconventional leaps of faith.

As Suleyman impatiently wracked his brains to think of another approach he might take to his interrogation, İkmen said, 'I expect you're wondering why we're asking you these questions, aren't you, Mr Emin?'

'Y-yes, I w-was. I mean you c-come here—'

'Well, the fact of the matter is,' İkmen said as he looked out into the garden and then beyond at the rushing waters of the Bosphorus, 'the video tape from your sister's security system shows that she did leave this house in a Mercedes car on the night of Mrs Urfa's murder.'

'Oh.' As Yılmaz looked down at the floor, his eyes visibly filled with panic, Suleyman mouthed some very furious if unintelligible words at İkmen.

This had no effect upon the older man, who continued, 'And so you see, Mr Emin, if you did observe your sister leaving this house on that occasion, it would be pointless, maybe even criminal, to keep it from us. Withholding information from the police—'

'B-but I didn't, I s-swear.'

'If we had just the video evidence or just the testimony of little Belkis,' İkmen paused here for effect and watched Yılmaz's face whiten, 'then there might be room for doubt. But we have both, Mr Emin. We have Belkis looking with you out of your bedroom window at your sister driving out of this estate and we have video of Tansu passing through the gates.'

Suleyman cleared his throat in a very obvious manner.

İkmen deliberately did not look at him. 'And so, Mr Emin?' he asked softly.

'W-with the g-girl I d-didn't do anything b-bad.'

'What you may or may not have done with your adult maid is not for us to judge, Mr Emin.'

'I . . .'

'Think carefully before you answer, Mr Emin,' İkmen said with a smile. 'I know how difficult these things can be when family are involved. But just take a moment to consider your own position.' He got up from his chair and walked over to Suleyman who all through İkmen's conversation with Yılmaz had continued to mug furiously at his old boss.

'If I had known you were going to lie to him, I would never have brought you along!' Suleyman hissed.

Holding up one hand to silence his colleague, İkmen kept his eyes firmly on the back of Yılmaz Emin's slumped head. 'Sshh!'

'What may or may not be on those security cameras—'

'We may well soon discover,' İkmen said and then added, his eyes twinkling in what to Suleyman was a maddening fashion, 'or not.'

'I—'

But before Suleyman could continue, Yılmaz turned to face his tormentors.

'I-I did s-see my s-sister leave that night. S-she drove out in the—'

The door which gave out onto the main hallway of the house sprang open with a loud bang as something that looked like a cross between a madwoman and a wild animal threw itself into the room.

'Yılmaz, you stupid, fucking fool!' Tansu raved as she ran, sharp fingernails raised, towards her brother. 'There is no tape in those cameras, there never has been!' And then she was on him, clawing at his face, her rank alcohol-soaked breath filling his nose.

As İkmen and Suleyman wrestled to remove the singer from her brother before she killed him, Latife watched from the doorway, visibly shaking.

In spite of the fact that the voice coming out of the radio was that of his beloved Tansu, Erol Urfa turned the volume down. It was one of those songs, those bitter, almost violent numbers that he really disliked. Songs which also contained references to things he preferred to brush aside. Not that Tansu knew. How could she?

He had, until Merih went missing, always been very careful about what he said and did, as had Ruya. And besides, it wasn't as if Tansu were educated or knew much about anything. But still she persisted with her 'peacocks', both dead and alive, and still she talked of the colour blue 'blinding her eyes'. He had once, some time back now, asked her why she used the symbol of those birds so frequently in her songs. At first she had just looked confused but then she had simply shrugged and said, 'I just do' in such an innocent way as to preclude further discussion. Anyway, with Merih sleeping contentedly at his side he had other more pressing considerations now. And besides, if Tansu loved him, as she undoubtedly did, even if she knew she wouldn't want to hurt him. Would she?

As the car in front of Erol's shuffled forward, he flipped his sunglasses down over his eyes. There were two teenage girls in the back of the vehicle in front who might recognise him. He couldn't take the risk. Fragile in spirit since leaving Tansu's home, all he wanted now was to get a little time out in the open alone with Merih. He looked across at the baby and smiled. Now that Ruya and what he now knew would have been his second child were dead she was, apart from Ali Mardin, the only connection he had with his old life in this horrible city. Sometimes, like now, he wanted to go home very badly. For all the problems and hardship that attended his life back there, the mountains and the plains more than made up for all that. And to be able to perform the morning and evening devotions outside and without fear of discovery, ah, that was something. In the meantime, he and Merih would just have to make do with Yıldız Park. With luck and on a hot afternoon, there would be more couples with children than clandestine lovers. Not that he was part of any sort of 'couple' himself; he never really had been. Poor Ruya had been far more Merih's mother than his wife. That 'honour' had gone to Tansu, his love, the woman who inflamed his flesh.

'What a weak and disgusting man you are!' he murmured to himself as he touched the accelerator pedal gently. Blinded by fame and money and sex. And although he was indeed suffering now, he had not suffered for his sins in the way that Ruya had. She, still alone and disregarded in the mortuary, had in the end paid the ultimate price for his vaulting ambition, his unnatural lusts. Some vile creature, he couldn't even imagine who, had come into their lives and taken her away for reasons that were still cloaked from him. According to İbrahim, word in the bazaars was that Tansu had done it. But he couldn't or wouldn't accept this. The police still had that strange drooling neighbour in custody and although Erol knew nothing about Cengiz Temiz or his supposed friendship with Ruya, he hoped that this man was responsible. He hoped it would all end. If he had spent more time at the apartment, he might have been able to give the police more information about Temiz, but as it was he could do nothing to move the case forward.

The mobile telephone which was lying on the seat beside his sleeping daughter started to ring. Erol, keeping one eye on the traffic, picked it up quickly lest it wake Merih. She just muttered briefly before descending again into her carbon-monoxide-drenched dreams.

'Hello,' Erol said as he placed the thing to his ear.

'Erol, it's İbrahim, where are you?'

'I'm in the car taking Merih to the park,' he told his rather anxious-sounding manager. 'What's the matter, İbrahim?'

'You'd better turn round and come back,' Aksoy said. 'I'll meet you at your apartment.'

A slight twinge of panic started inside Erol's chest. 'Is there a problem, İbrahim? Speak to me, brother!'

'There might be, but . . . Look, meet me back at the apartment and I'll tell you all about it then.'

'Why not tell me now?' Erol said as he felt his heart begin to race in panic. 'İbrahim!'

'Just get back to the apartment and I'll tell you then,' Aksoy snapped sharply.

'But—'

'As soon as you can, Erol,' and there was a click as Aksoy put his telephone down.

In spite of the thick heat around him, Erol suddenly felt very cold. Something had obviously happened. Maybe his manager had somehow found out what he shouldn't about the family Urfa. Although quite how he would find conclusive proof, Erol couldn't imagine, and surely that was not something that had to be dealt with urgently. No, it was something else, something far more immediate and serious.

Perhaps at last the police had actually arrested somebody for his wife's murder. But if that were so, İbrahim would not, surely, have said that it could be a problem. If the Temiz man were found guilty, that would not be a problem, that would be a relief, unless . . . Well, the strange neighbour was not the only suspect, was he? As far as the police were concerned, everyone connected with Ruya basically fitted into that category – even Erol himself. As he felt his throat dry up and his eyes bulge with the pressure of fear he switched the radio over to one of the news stations. Not that there would be anything on there yet, but it gave him something to do. And caught in one of İstanbul's legendary gridlocks, there wasn't much that he could do except listen to the radio, sweat and begin to become irrational about his own position in this drama. After all, had he not, alone, found Ruya's body in the apartment? But surely if İsmail's problem were Erol himself, the police would have come for him by now, wouldn't they? With a slightly shaking hand Erol turned the radio down once again, to listen for sirens.

Chapter 13

By the time she arrived at the threshold of the tar- and nicotine-stained cell that was Interview Room 5, Tansu Emin Hanım was completely sober. Dressed in a plain white shift she was, as ever, heavily made up – Inspector Suleyman had allowed her the dignity of cleaning up and primping before they left for the station. Travelling as always with a retinue, Tansu was accompanied by her brother Yılmaz and sister, her manager Ferhat Göktepe, and a very sharply dressed young man who, it soon transpired, was her lawyer. The still weeping, and bleeding, Yılmaz Emin was quickly taken to another interview room while the others were told to wait outside. Only Tansu and her lawyer, Adnan Öz, entered Interview Room 5 with İkmen and Suleyman.

Not wishing to give Mr Öz any opportunity to encourage his client to dissemble, Suleyman launched immediately into the attack. 'Now, Miss Emin,' he said as he sat down beside İkmen and then looked Tansu hard in the eyes, 'you are in a considerable amount of trouble here. Both you and your family lied to us about your whereabouts on the night of Mrs Urfa's murder. I now want to know the truth from you about that night.'

Tansu looked briefly across at her lawyer before replying. 'I'd rather not say,' she said. 'It's personal.'

'I'm not really giving you a choice, Miss Emin,' Suleyman retorted. 'As I've said, you're in a lot of—'

'Had I been allowed to consult with my client,' Adnan Öz put in, 'I might have been able to advise her of her options.'

'Miss Emin was out of her house on the night of the murder, a fact she and her family covered up until this afternoon, Mr Öz,' Suleyman said and then added sharply. 'I don't think she has too many options, do you?'

But Adnan Öz only smiled. 'I am not unduly concerned about what, in reality, constitutes no more than circumstantial evidence,' he said. 'With forensics now presumably complete, had you gleaned any evidence linking my client with the crime from that quarter, you would not be questioning my client now.'

'Ah, but you don't know that we don't possess such evidence,' İkmen said with a smile. 'That is only an assumption on your part.'

'A blonde, fur-coated woman was seen at the scene of the crime,' Suleyman said. 'We have a witness.'

'A retarded man, an idiot,' Tansu said to her lawyer

and then turning to the policemen she added, 'Erol told me.'

'Did he indeed.'

As if suddenly galvanised to action, Tansu sprang from her seat. 'You can't keep me here anyway!' she cried. 'I'm a star! I'm bigger than all of you put together! Turkey's sweetheart!'

'Will you please exercise some control over your client!' Suleyman said to a bemused Adnan Öz.

With a shaking hand, the lawyer took hold of Tansu's arm and with some gentle shooshing noises carefully eased her back down into her chair. She wasn't happy about being there but, her small outburst over, she did appear to be calm once again.

'Now I need some answers,' Suleyman said, 'and I need them now. Why did you go out on the night of the murder and why did you lie about it to us?'

Tansu sighed and then looked up towards the ceiling in a despairing fashion. 'As I've told you,' she said, 'I went out on personal business which you would not understand.'

'Make me!'

Once again, Tansu turned to look at her lawyer who, in response, simply shrugged his shoulders.

Sensing a slight fissure in the singer's psychological armour, Suleyman pressed his advantage. 'I should remind you that were you to be convicted of the murder of Mrs Urfa, you would spend the rest of your life in prison.' Then leaning in towards a now cringing Tansu, he added, 'And you and I both know what those places are like, don't we?'

'My client has committed no crime, she has nothing to fear.'

'If that is the case,' İkmen said with a smile, 'she can tell us what she was doing on the night of the murder, can't she?'

'All right! All right!' Tansu said, her hands raised above her head in a gesture of frustration. 'I'll tell you, but . . .' She looked at the three men around her, each in turn, her eyes nervously shifting from one to the other.

İkmen raised his eyebrows. 'But?'

Tansu took a long white cigarette from inside her handbag and lit up. Her fingers were shaking. 'But I don't want Erol to know.' Her eyes filled with tears and she added, 'You know?'

'I take it,' İkmen said with as much gravity as he could muster, 'that what we are talking about here is something of a, er, romantic nature?'

'Well . . .' Again the eyes were shifty. Adnan Öz, for his part, took to close observation of the floor.

Patience not being one of Suleyman's strong points, he moved into the silence that had overwhelmed Tansu's last remark and said, 'So, Miss Emin, are we talking about another man here?'

'I don't want Erol to know,' she reiterated urgently. 'You won't tell him, will you?'

'Whether or not this information becomes public

depends largely upon what bearing it has upon Mrs Urfa's murder. Now, Miss Emin, are we going to work together or not?'

Tansu's shoulders heaved upwards in a resigned little shrug. Her silicone-filled breasts, İkmen silently observed, stayed exactly where they were.

'Erol and I had argued,' the singer began, 'in the afternoon.'

'What about?'

She sighed. 'About him going off to his friends to see the football and then spending all of the next day with her.'

'With his wife.'

'Yes. I'll be honest, I hated Ruya Urfa and I wasn't sorry when she died, but,' she looked up at the policemen with what could have been a straight and honest face, 'I didn't kill her. After I argued with Erol, I had a little too much to drink and in that state I started to think about . . .' she suddenly looked away, her face a little red now, 'about myself and my life and, well, I decided as the evening went on that what I should do is go out.' She looked up at them again. 'And so I did.'

'Where did you go?' Suleyman asked.

'I drove around. I thought a lot about what I had given to Erol and I felt bitter.'

Suleyman looked at İkmen who refrained from catching his colleague's eye. If Tansu had given so much to Erol, it certainly wasn't on one-way traffic.

Tansu straightened her shoulders. 'And then, Allah

forgive me, I parked up by İstiklal Caddesi, had a few more drinks and found a boy.'

Adnan Öz frowned down at the floor and then cleared his throat.

'And who was this boy?' İkmen asked as he attempted to wrest his eyes from the livid colour of Mr Öz's cheeks.

The singer laughed, a rough, smoke-scarred rattle. 'How should I know!' she said. 'Such meetings don't involve an exchange of personal details. Besides, I'd had a few drinks as I said and so even if he did tell me his name, I wouldn't remember.'

'Do you know what he looked like? Was he in uniform or . . .'

'He was twenty something, I suppose, and pretty. What more can I say? We shared a few drinks, he put his arm around me . . .'

'Did he know who you were?' Ikmen asked. 'If you can remember, that is? I mean your face is not exactly unknown, is it?'

She laughed again but this time with even less good humour than before. 'Oh, come on!' she said as she pointed with both hands at her face. 'Does this look like the photographs in the newspapers or what?'

'Well, er . . .'

'I know you all think that I'm some dreadful plastic doll sort of woman, and I admit I am.' Her facial expression turned from bitter to grave. 'Even I know

I am not like that air-brushed odalisque in the magazines. No amount of surgery can possibly take away all the lines and creases. I always wear dark glasses . . .'

'Were you wearing your fur coat?' Suleyman asked.

'One of them. But I left it in the car.'

'Where did you meet this boy?'

'In a bar. I don't remember which. Some place off İstiklal.' She looked straight at both of the policemen, 'And yes, I know I must have been close to Erol's apartment, but . . . Anyway, the boy and I eventually left and . . .' She hung her head in what looked like shame.

'Did you take him home or did you go back to his place?' Ikmen inquired. 'It's important we know.'

A moment of stony silence passed during which Adnan Öz looked around the squalid room for something upon which to pin his attention.

'He took me down a side street to a shop doorway,' Tansu said softly. 'I pulled up my skirt . . .'

'You had sex in the street.'

She shrugged. 'It's not something that I do every day but when I first came to this city I did things like it from time to time, to survive.' She smiled. 'For just a moment it was almost like being young again.'

Suleyman sighed. 'And afterwards?'

The smile still on her lips, she said, 'Afterwards he left as men always do and I went home. I drove with a lot of alcohol in my body, I freely admit, but I did nothing else. I didn't murder anyone.'

İkmen nodded gravely as he looked at Suleyman and a few moments of silence passed as everyone in the room absorbed Tansu's story. Then picking up his pen from the table, Suleyman jotted down a few notes on the piece of paper in front of him. 'So,' he said, 'you're saying you went to an unnamed bar where you met a boy whose name you don't know.'

'Yes.'

'Did you tell any member of your family you were going to go and do this?'

She threw him a distinctly acid look. 'What do you think? I told my sister afterwards, in the morning. I felt so guilty that I had betrayed Erol, I had to tell someone.'

'Your story is not going to be easy to substantiate, Miss Emin,' Suleyman said gravely.

'Ah, but I am sure that with a little research . . .' Adnan Öz began.

'Assuming Miss Emin is telling the truth.'

'I fucking am!'

The re-emergence of this rather more familiar incarnation of Tansu Hanım made İkmen, at least, smile. The part she had been playing of the softly contrite, damaged woman had suddenly slipped and although he accepted that this was not in itself a sign of guilt, it was far more a part of her real character than any other facet she had shown them here. But what of her story? Although all of Tansu's movements and associations on that fateful night were effectively, and some would say conveniently, anonymous, she might well be telling the truth. She was, after all, a very unhappy middle-aged woman who was besotted by a much younger, married man. Why shouldn't she have a quick fuck up against a wall if she could get one? The only real connection that could be made between Tansu and the scene of the crime was a few stray strands of fur – not an uncommon item in the wardrobes of İstanbul ladies (excepting Fatma, of course). And Cengiz Temiz had not managed to identify her from her photograph. But then . . .

Ah. İkmen smiled still more broadly. Yes, now that was a thought, wasn't it? And most especially it was a thought that Tansu herself had inspired.

'May I have a word with you outside, please, Inspector?' he said to Suleyman.

Two uniformed officers sat with Tansu and her lawyer while İkmen and Suleyman repaired to another room which appeared to be empty but in fact contained a rather heavily smoking İsak Çöktin. Standing as his superiors entered, Çöktin looked unusually tense, leading Suleyman to wonder whether he had been overly severe with him. Not, of course, that he said as much.

'Ah, Çöktin,' he said. 'How did you get on at the Forensic Institute?'

'I found out that cyanide is used in the steel industry.' He took his notebook out of his pocket and read,

'Hydrocyanic acid, it's called. You can also distil cyanide from the stone of some fruits, but you do need special equipment.'

'I presume laboratory equipment or that used in the production of liquor,' Suleyman said as he gave İkmen a cigarette and lit up himself.

'Yes.' Çöktin perused his book for a little longer and then said, 'Domestically it's used to kill pests mainly. Rats and wasps, things like that.'

'Mmm.' Suleyman looked up at İkmen. 'Belkis said that the Emin family have a gardener, didn't she?'

'Yes. Why?'

'I seem to recall something about wasps. Anyway, you wanted to talk to me, Çetin?'

İkmen looked first, briefly, at Çöktin and then back at Suleyman.

'Ah,' Suleyman said, understanding immediately, 'yes. Çöktin, could you write me a full report on your researches at the institute, please? It may prove useful in time. Oh, and you might like to ask Miss Latife Emin the name of her gardener too. You'll find her outside with Tansu Hanım's manager and, I think, her brother.'

'Yes, sir.'

He left in the same manner as they had found him, miserably contemplating something other than the task at hand. İkmen and Suleyman, with some concern, watched him go.

When Çöktin had shut the door behind him, İkmen observed, 'He's very unhappy, isn't he?'

'Yes.' Suleyman sighed. 'My little speech about not getting too close to Urfa did not go down very well.'

'Mmm.'

'Anyway, I don't suppose Çöktin was what you wanted to talk to me about, was it? Unless you're still chasing peacocks . . .'

'Do not mock!' İkmen said and held one warning finger aloft. 'They are still foremost in my mind, as I imagine gardeners are in yours. But no, that was not why I needed to speak to you.'

'So?'

İkmen sat down on one of the less greasy-looking chairs. 'It was Tansu herself who gave me the idea. She admitted she doesn't look much like her photographs. And in view of the fact that Cengiz Temiz has only ever seen a photograph of her and not the woman in the flesh . . .'

Suleyman's eyes shone. 'You thought . . .'

'Exactly. If we could engineer a sighting for him – I assume he's still somewhere in the building.'

'Yes. Yes he is.' Suleyman joined İkmen on the chairs. 'And of course you're right.'

'I can see no other way of quickly either proving or disproving Tansu's story about a drunken fuck up against a wall.'

Suleyman smiled. In spite of all his bluster, İkmen was about the most solid family man he knew. And although he had over the years dealt with much that was either distasteful or bizarre in the sexual arena, he still disapproved of both unfaithfulness and deception.

'I was thinking,' İkmen said, 'of something along the lines of escorting Tansu out of the building via the back entrance.'

'Past the cells.'

'Yes.' He smiled. 'And we could move Mr Temiz to rather more sanitary accommodation at the same time.'

'Yes.' Suleyman bit down thoughtfully on his lower lip. 'And if he doesn't ID her?'

'Then she must have been fucking instead of killing,' İkmen said with a shrug. 'But let us meet that eventuality if it arises.'

'All right.' With a sudden rush of energy, Suleyman got to his feet. 'Come on, then,' he said, 'let's get on with it.'

'You go ahead.' İkmen nodded towards the door. 'I'd better phone home and tell Fatma what I'm doing.'

'Oh, yes,' Suleyman said. He reached the door and turned. 'You really should be there, shouldn't you?'

'Yes,' İkmen replied tartly, 'but I'm not, and so there it is.'

Quickly, before he lost his nerve, İkmen punched his home number into the telephone and then waited for that familiar, angry voice.

Erol Urfa paced restlessly back and forth across the floor of his living room. Just looking at him made

İbrahim Aksoy, who had taken refuge in a large bottle of raki some hours before, feel dizzy.

'I don't know why you don't just settle for a bit,' the manager said from inside his anise-tinged haze. 'Ferhat Göktepe said that he'd call as soon as there was any news.'

'I should be there with her,' Erol said vehemently. 'I should go now!'

'Oh, and take Merih into a stinking police station, that's a good idea!' Aksoy said acidly.

'If you would look after her . . .'

'Now, you know I can't do that, Erol,' Aksoy said as he poured himself yet another draught of the oily, transparent liquid. 'I can't possibly do all that stuff with the feeding and then the, er, the toilet business. And anyway, I'm really quite drunk. You know I'd gladly lay down my life for you but . . .'

'İbrahim, she didn't do it!' Erol raked one shaking hand through the thickness of his hair. 'Tansu did not kill my wife!'

'You don't know that, Erol.'

'I do!'

'Oh, so who did kill her then?' Aksoy's face, though drunk, was full of challenge.

Erol flung both arms into the air in a gesture of hopelessness. 'I don't know!' he said.

'Right,' Aksoy replied. 'You don't know, so it could be anybody, including Tansu. I mean, with Ruya out of the way, she probably thought that you might marry her.' Then under his breath he muttered, 'Silly old . . .'

'But if that is the case, it is I who have brought Tansu to this trouble and it is also I who, indirectly, have killed my own wife and unborn child!'

'Nonsense!'

Erol put his hands up to his face and then sat down beside his manager. Although it was hot, he knew that the palms of his hands were sweating far more than they usually did. He also knew, or rather felt, that perhaps now was the time to confess to those most close to him – in this case, İbrahim Aksoy.

'İbrahim,' he began and then faltered. 'İbrahim, much as I may wish to marry Tansu, that can never be.'

'Well, of course not, she's old enough to be your mother!'

'Yes, but that is not the reason why I cannot marry her.'

Aksoy peered out from deep inside his alcoholic mist and leered. 'Oh, is there another—'

'No!' Erol put his head down and stared at the rug on the floor. He would need to look at something while he said this, something other than İbrahim's face. Since coming to the city, there was only one other person he had told his secret to and that was because that person had known – it was a secret they shared.

'İbrahim,' he said slowly, 'I am not the man you

think I am.' Then looking up sharply into that raki-sodden face, he added, 'Everything you think you know about me is a complete and utter lie.'

Sergeant Orhan Tepe was given the task of moving Cengiz Temiz from his current abode to another cell a few metres away. Why Inspector Suleyman wanted this done, he didn't know; in all likelihood Temiz would be released within twenty-four hours and so, to Tepe, it all seemed a bit pointless. However, something had to be up on account of the fact that the inspector had told him to watch Temiz very closely during the next few minutes. He didn't know what he was supposed to be looking for or why, although he did gain an inkling when he saw the inspector, Tansu Hanım, someone who could be one of her brothers, and her lawyer, Mr Öz, walking down the corridor towards Temiz and himself. Behind, at some distance, he could just make out the slight form of old Inspector İkmen.

'Well, Cengiz,' Tepe said into Temiz's large, red-tinged ear, 'here is a little present for you. A real life superstar.' In order to direct Cengiz's eyes to the star, he waved one hand in Tansu's direction. 'Look, there.'

The first indication that something was seriously amiss came in the form of a sharp intake of breath. Cengiz gasped and then, looking up at Tepe, the officer immediately noticed the fear that had suddenly settled in his eyes.

'Cengiz . . .'

Still fixated on Tepe's face, Cengiz Temiz simply whimpered.

'It's only a lady, Cengiz,' and then physically turning the man's head to watch the progress of the party toward them, Tepe said, 'Nothing to be frightened of.'

With small but obviously terrified noises of protest, Cengiz tried to resist Tepe's hand, but without success. For a moment he simply stood looking at Tansu with an expression of frozen horror on his face. At this point, Tepe observed, Suleyman turned round and looked at İkmen.

But then suddenly there was a change. At first Tepe felt this rather than saw it for it came in the form of a slackening that shot through the whole of Cengiz's body like an arrow. Initially, imagining that his charge was about to faint, Tepe moved closer to him in order to offer some sort of support. When Cengiz didn't fall, he turned to look at him again. What he found was a very winning, if child-like, smile upon his face. And as Tansu, Suleyman and party passed by without a word or a look, Cengiz made several small grunts and gestures of approval.

'Cengiz . . .'

'I thought it was her, but it isn't,' he said and giggled with what might have been mirth or relief or both.

'It isn't who, Cengiz?'

'The demon who killed Mrs Ruya,' he said in a voice

that boomed towards the rafters with glee. 'That lady isn't her!'

'You thought it might have been?'

The party heading for the back entrance had stopped now. Slowly, her eyes full of a furious malevolence, Tansu Hanım was turning to face Suleyman.

'You . . .' she began.

'I had to see whether or not he would identify you,' Suleyman said, adding quickly, 'and he has not.'

'That man is—' But then she stopped and for just one frozen, monstrous moment she watched as Cengiz Temiz did what, at first sight, could have been an ungainly dance.

'The demon walked like this, you see,' Cengiz said as he tottered backwards and forwards on Tepe's arm, with what looked like a very pronounced limp. 'White hair like the lady but,' he teetered back and forth once again, giggling, 'like this!'

'Allah!' Although said under her breath, Tansu's exhortation to divine intervention, coupled with the whitness of her face and the shakiness of her hands, caused İkmen to look at her sharply. She gave every appearance, he thought, of one who has just woken from a beautiful dream only to discover reality. It was one of those moments when a person involuntarily gives others fleeting access to the raw core of his or her being. But, as ever with things psychological, unless one could interpret such a moment, its true meaning could not be ascertained. And as the door to

Tansu's soul closed and she regained her composure, İkmen realised that he hadn't a clue about what he had just seen.

'Get me out of this stinking pit, will you, Adnan?' she said as she took hold of her lawyer's arm and began to walk forwards. 'I want to see my manager and my sister.'

'They're waiting with your car,' the lawyer soothed, 'ready to take you home, away from all this hideousness.'

'We had to do this, madam,' Suleyman began.

'You will be hearing from me in due course,' Adnan Öz said with a slight bow. 'You can't trick people like Tansu Hanım and expect to get away with it.'

Suleyman indicated that Tepe should put Cengiz Temiz, who now appeared to be disturbed by what was going on, into his new cell. Then turning once again to Adnan Öz he said, 'I look forward to hearing from you, sir.'

Dutifully holding the door open for Tansu, her lawyer and Yılmaz Emin to pass through, İkmen bowed to them politely as they left. The fact that Tansu averted her eyes when he looked at her could just have been bad manners, but it could also have been because she didn't want him to know that she was crying.

Once they had gone, İkmen shut the door and looked across at Suleyman who was now slumped against the wall with his head in his hands. Tepe, for his part, had settled Cengiz Temiz into his cell and had just come back out into the corridor when İkmen said, 'Don't lock up yet, Tepe. I need a moment with Mr Temiz.'

'Oh, right.' Tepe stood to one side while İkmen entered the cell. Suleyman, who had come back to himself somewhat as İkmen spoke, was right behind him.

The overweight, unwashed heap on the edge of what passed for a bed in that terrible place rolled his eyes as İkmen approached him.

'You had a bit of a fright there, didn't you?' İkmen said with a smile.

'Who are you? Have you got a cigarette?'

'My name is Çetin,' İkmen said as he took a cigarette out of his packet and handed it to Cengiz.

'Can I have a light too?'

'Yes.'

İkmen handed over his lighter and Cengiz lit up. For a few moments he puffed contentedly before saying, 'Mr Avedykian said I don't have to talk to him any more.'

'Who?' İkmen asked.

Cengiz pointed rudely towards Suleyman.

'Oh.'

Suleyman duly turned away and walked towards the far corner of the cell.

İkmen smiled. 'But you can talk to me though, can't you?'

Cengiz didn't answer, seemingly absorbed in his cigarette.

'Cengiz?'

'What?'

İkmen held out his almost full packet of cigarettes to Cengiz and smiled. 'Listen, Cengiz,' he said, 'if I give you this packet of cigarettes, will you answer just one question for me?'

For a few moments Cengiz looked from the packet of cigarettes to İkmen's face and then back again. He licked his lips as if just the look of the cigarettes was making him drool with anticipation.

'You can keep the lighter too,' İkmen offered.

A small grunt-like noise seemed to indicate that Cengiz had consented to this. It was enough for İkmen.

'OK, Cengiz,' he said, 'why didn't you tell Inspector Suleyman that the devil woman, or whatever you call her, walked with a limp? Can you tell me that?'

Cengiz's eyes narrowed and he put his hand out for the cigarettes.

'Not until you answer my question,' İkmen said, putting the pack back into his pocket. 'Well?'

Cengiz, pouting a little now, shrugged. 'He never asked me.'

'He never asked you what, Cengiz?'

'Whether the lady had one leg smaller than the other leg.'

İkmen took the cigarettes back out of his pocket again and held them up close to his face. 'But she did, is that what you are saying, Cengiz?'

'Yes.' He made a quick grab for the cigarettes which İkmen foiled.

'Ah, not yet!' he said. 'Not yet. So what you're saying is that the woman you saw just now looked like the woman who killed Mrs Ruya except that that woman had one leg which was shorter than the other. Is that right?'

'Yes.'

'Are you certain?'

'Yes!'

İkmen handed the cigarettes over and then leaned back to watch as Cengiz Temiz secreted his precious haul within the considerable folds of his clothes. Turning to face Suleyman, İkmen said, 'Latife Emin does look remarkably like her sister, don't you think?'

Chapter 14

'Latife Emin does not limp, nor does she have one leg noticeably shorter than the other!'

'Ah, but have you really looked at her legs, Suleyman?' İkmen said. 'No, you have not!'

'Well, of course I haven't!' Suleyman cried as he flung himself wearily down behind his desk. 'I have paid Latife Emin very little heed during the course of this affair. I mean, what would have been her motive?'

'I don't know.' He sat down in front of Suleyman's desk and lit a cigarette. As he did so, his ulcer made small twinges of protest. 'But that surely is something we must now find out.'

'Oh, so I just drag Latife Emin back in here and parade her before Cengiz Temiz!'

'No.' İkmen sighed. 'Both you and I know that given the status of these people, we can't do that. If they were nobody, then we could, but it is in the nature of all societies to have those on top and those on the bottom, and those on top get treated more gently.'

'So what do you suggest then?' Suleyman asked

angrily. 'I pass this over to MIT on the pretext that because all the protagonists involved are Kurdish it might be political?'

'You wouldn't do that.'

Suleyman looked down at his hands and groaned. 'No, you're right.'

'Let us try, if we can, to think laterally,' İkmen said in a slow, considered voice. 'Why don't you get the file out and let us review the evidence in the light of what happened today.'

Suleyman took the folder out of a drawer and laid it on his desk. 'Of course, you don't actually have to be here at all,' he said as he rubbed his tired eyes with his fingers.

'No, but I am and so . . . OK, Mrs Urfa was killed by the ingestion of cyanide-laced halva. What other forensic evidence do we have?'

Suleyman consulted the various documents in front of him with a grave expression on his face. 'We have Cengiz Temiz's prints all over the body, plus some footprints that match his footwear . . .' He perused the information, frowning. 'Erol's prints on the table, the child's, Ruya's on kitchen equipment and her pen . . .' He looked up, frowning even more. 'Except that . . .'

'What?'

'Erol said that his wife didn't read or write and so why would she have a pen?'

'She could have used it for drawing,' İkmen opined,

'but I take your point. Write that down, just in case.'

Suleyman took a sheet of paper from his desk and scribbled this seeming anomaly at the top of the page.

'So, as I understand it,' İkmen continued, 'Cengiz Temiz basically walked in on the murder scene.'

'According to Cengiz the door to the Urfas' apartment was open, he went in, saw both the devil woman and Ruya Urfa's body.'

'The devil woman ran when she saw him . . .'

'With, what we now know, was an unsteady gait.'

'But why was the door open?' İkmen asked. 'I mean, the idea that the woman murdered Ruya with the door open, notwithstanding the fact that the world was currently watching football, is absurd.'

'Unless,' Suleyman said, 'she had gone back to get something she had forgotten.'

'True. But what?'

'Who knows?'

'How possible do you think it is that Cengiz Temiz murdered Ruya in order to procure a baby for Mina Arda? Really?' asked İkmen.

Suleyman smiled a little sadly. 'Even if one takes into account the fact that Cengiz has a previous conviction for immoral behaviour, I don't think he'd have the cognitive skills to kill in this way. That his "theft" of the baby was both opportunistic and philanthropic seems to me beyond doubt. I am quite in accord with Dr Halman there.'

'Right.' İkmen paused for a few moments before carrying on, as if absorbing what had already been said. 'So let us assume that the devil woman does indeed exist.'

'Right.'

'She looks like Tansu Hanım, wears clothes like her, and Tansu, let's face it, has a very good motive.'

'Yes,' Suleyman said, 'except that Erol told me that even with Ruya dead, he would not and could not marry Tansu. He will, he says, marry another woman from his village. He wants more children.'

İkmen's eyes narrowed a little. 'Mmm. Indeed. Not one he is betrothed to, though. Must be quite some tight little community he comes from. Any idea where?'

'Out east,' Suleyman replied. 'I could find out, I suppose.'

'Yes, that might be a good idea.'

İkmen knew full well that Suleyman was far from convinced with regard to his theories about Erol Urfa's beliefs but this piece of information, which seemed to point towards a very closed and old-fashioned community life, only served to heighten his own interest. But if Tansu knew about Erol – which, given the content of her songs, seemed to be so – she would also know that murdering Ruya Urfa would do her personally no good at all. 'Unless of course,' he said out loud, 'it is not Tansu who writes her songs but another member of her entourage.'

Suleyman, who had not been privy to İkmen's thoughts, looked confused. 'What do you mean?'

'I mean that if Tansu did write her own bitter songs, it indicates that she knows that Erol is a Yezidi.'

'Oh, not this again!'

İkmen held up a hand. 'No, hear me out,' he said, 'please. If Tansu wrote those songs, it could be that she knew he was a member of the sect, which would mean she would know she could never marry him. Motive gone. But if, as I feel, she is not a very literate woman, she could have got someone else to write her songs for her. Someone who, possibly, got to know about Erol's origins.'

'Or someone who just has a particular liking for peacocks,' Suleyman said acidly.

'Well, yes, but—'

'What you're saying is,' Suleyman interrupted, 'if someone else wrote those songs, Tansu's motive still stands. But without a positive ID from Cengiz Temiz . . .'

'We arrive back at her oh so similar sister yet again.'

'Who has no obvious limp and no coherent motive that I can see,' Suleyman reminded him.

'Unless it was to free Erol for her sister. They are all awfully close, aren't they, the Emins? I mean, Tansu keeps them all in some style, doesn't she?'

'Yes. But if we assume that Latife did kill Ruya in order to free Erol for her sister, then she, at least, could not, following your reasoning, have written Tansu's songs. Assuming of course, as I do not, that this Yezidi thing means anything at all.'

İkmen smiled. 'You know what this case is like, don't you, Mehmet?'

'A nightmare?' He shrugged. 'The one where I fail spectacularly and have to take a taxi-driving job?'

'No,' İkmen said as he removed a cigarette from his packet and placed it in his mouth. 'It is an arabesque.'

'Well, it's about those involved in Arabesk, yes.'

'No, not the music Arabesk, but the form,' İkmen said with a decided twinkle in his eye. 'Arabesque as in a complicated pattern of either form or calligraphy designed by the Arabs and then refined by our ancestors. Art without the human or animal form which, as we know, only Allah may create or destroy. You must know what I mean, surely!'

'Well, yes,' Suleyman said, 'although the connection did not occur to me until you mentioned it. Some arabesques are positively maze-like, aren't they?'

'It is said that the rooftops of Saa'na in the Yemen almost seem to move with the proliferation of fiendishly complex mazes.' A moment of silence passed between them and then he said, 'So what are you going to do about your maze then, Mehmet?'

But before Suleyman could answer, there was a knock at the door.

The familiar features of İsak Çöktin appeared within

the office. 'I've written that report you wanted about the cyanide, sir,' he said as he placed a sheaf of papers onto Suleyman's desk.

'Thank you.'

'I did also ask Miss Latife Emin about their gardener,' Çöktin continued.

'Oh?' Suleyman said, looking up now with interest. 'And?'

'Well, he's called Reşat, he does quite a few of the big gardens in and around Yeniköy.'

Suleyman smiled. 'Including, I think we will find, that of a Mr and Mrs Ertürk,' he said with some satisfaction. 'For if this Reşat is indeed the same as Ertürk's man, then I know for a fact that he uses cyanide to kill their rats.'

'How do you know all this, Mehmet?' İkmen asked, really quite amazed at the younger man's sudden insights.

'It is a long story involving two deranged young women.'

'Oh?'

'Which I really don't have time to go into now.' As he spoke he shuffled once again through the file on his desk until he eventually found a small scrap of paper. He handed it to Çöktin. 'This is the telephone number of a Mr Kemal Ertürk,' he said, 'which I would like you to call in order to get hold of some details about where this Reşat lives. I think we may need to speak to him very soon.'

'Yes, sir.' Çöktin took the paper over to his desk and dialled the number on his telephone extension.

Until somebody answered Çöktin, neither İkmen nor Suleyman spoke. As soon as he got through, all that changed.

Lowering his voice in order not to disturb Çöktin's conversation, İkmen said to Suleyman, 'I have the feeling, or rather I gained the distinct impression downstairs, that Tansu Hanım knows who the culprit might be. She realised when she saw Cengiz do his limping impression.'

Suleyman sat and digested this until the click of a replaced telephone signalled the end of Çöktin's conversation.

'Reşat lives in Beşiktaş 22/3 Mısır Bahçe,' he said, looking at the piece of paper in his hand. 'Do you want me to go out there, sir?'

'No.' Suleyman leaned back in his chair and lit a cigarette. 'I would like you and Tepe to perform some discreet observations regarding the comings and goings to and from Tansu Hanım's house.'

'Oh, but I thought that she—'

'Yes, Mickey Çöktin,' İkmen said with a smile, 'Tansu and all her retinue have indeed departed from this place, but we still have some doubts and so it would be as well for you and Tepe to remain vigilant.'

'And I want to know everything,' Suleyman added sternly, 'including when Erol makes an appearance.'

'Oh, but that's not likely to happen now, sir,' Çöktin said before he had really thought his words through.

Suleyman frowned. 'Oh? And why not?'

Çöktin knew that his face was bright red. He also knew that he had to say something fast in order to save himself. If Suleyman suspected that he'd been talking to Erol, well, it didn't bear thinking about. 'Well, er, I thought it was common knowledge,' he said falteringly.

'Oh?' Suleyman reiterated suspiciously. 'And this knowledge comes from?'

'Oh, gossip in the bazaars, you know,' Çöktin said with a nervous laugh. 'Shall I go and get Tepe and—'

'If I find that you have been talking to Erol, you know that disciplinary procedure will follow, don't you?' Suleyman said gravely.

'Yes.'

Suleyman looked Çöktin deep in the eyes for just a second and then said, 'Off you go then.'

'Right.' And with that he left.

When İkmen could be certain that Çöktin was out of earshot he said, 'Do you believe him?'

'Not in the slightest.'

İkmen shook his head. 'It's a shame, he's a good man.'

'Who has changed considerably since being in contact with Erol Urfa.'

'Well, it could well be as I said,' İkmen expounded.

'They could well be brothers in religion. He's never been like this about any other Kurdish suspect.'

'Yes, well,' Suleyman rose to his feet and put his cigarette out in the ashtray. 'But now I must go out and speak to this Reşat.'

'About his work and his cyanide?'

Suleyman smiled. 'Yes,' he said, 'and also about wasps. The Emins had a problem with wasps a little while back, I believe.'

'Mmm. And with Miss Latife, as Belkis told us, being so keen on gardening . . .'

'Oh, yes,' Suleyman said as he picked his car keys off his desk and put them in his pocket, 'she did say that, didn't she? Makes you wonder whether her interests extended to disposing of pests, doesn't it?'

Strangely, for Tansu, she had been very quiet during the journey back to Yeniköy. Yılmaz had thought that even with the lawyer in the car she might still rail at him. But she did not. Perhaps she had come to terms now with the fact that Erol had deserted her – or maybe her interview with the police had been so horrendous it had robbed her of speech. He still felt bad about having been the cause of her ordeal in the police station. The Emins had always been staunch and faithful to each other – until now – and he had no doubt that at some point recriminations would follow. But for the moment he just sat back and enjoyed the fading of the fierce sunlight and the coming of the slightly cooler evening breezes. The Bosphorus was, he thought, probably at its most beautiful at this time of day, when its blues and whites were just touched by the gentle coppery tones of sunset. If only he still had little Belkis to share such moments with, but there.

Latife and Ferhat Göktepe strode into the hall to meet a tense-looking Galıp.

Still silent, Tansu then entered the house, followed by Yılmaz and, until the singer dismissed him, Adnan Öz.

'You can go back to your office now, Adnan,' she said as she mounted the steps to her front door. 'I need to be alone with my family.'

'Ah, but—'

'I will call you when I need you!' she said commandingly and turned on her heel and entered the house.

Yılmaz shrugged at the rather taken aback lawyer and followed his sister who, now in the hall, was saying something very similar to Ferhat Göktepe.

'But Tansu, my darling,' the manager was saying, 'if you do need anything, anything at all, you must call me.'

'Yes, yes.' Distractedly, or so it seemed to Yılmaz, she patted her manager on the arm and gave him a small smile. 'But please go now, Ferhat, I need to be alone to . . .'

'Yes, of course, my soul,' he said as he kissed both her hands several times over. 'I do understand, I—'

'Ferhat, please!'

'I'm going! I'm going!' Which he did, blowing kisses to his most lucrative star as he went.

Tansu, followed by Yılmaz, walked into the large, pale living room where Galıp and Latife were waiting for them.

Tansu crossed the room in order to get herself a drink, then moved back to the door which she slammed on the outside world with some vigour.

Although Suleyman hadn't formally dismissed İkmen, he had not asked him to accompany him to Beşiktaş. So, try as he might, it was difficult for İkmen to carve a role for himself in the current round of activity. And besides, there was still Fatma to contend with; she would be furious at his breaking doctors' orders. There was also Madame Kleopatra Polycarpou's funeral tomorrow morning. Somehow he would have to try and persuade his angry wife or even one of his moody daughters to press his best suit for the occasion. Unlike Cohen, who was also due to attend, he did not have the luxury of still being in uniform.

As he made his way down to the reception area, İkmen once again pondered why Madame might have killed her husband, the eunuch. Sexual jealousy, surely, could not have come into it, and marital violence, another favourite when it came to homicide, was unlikely. Murad Ağa, to his recollection, had always seemed to be completely under Madame's control. He always looked as if he adored her. Perhaps the motive was monetary. It was a thought, seeing as people always said that the hamam did in fact belong originally to Madame's husband who they now knew was none other than Murad Ağa. Still, with all the protagonists in that little saga now well and truly dead, İkmen's thoughts upon this were more along the lines of interested speculation rather than active inquiry. And anyway, more pressing concerns were afoot now. His other cigarette packet, which he hadn't given to Cengiz Temiz, was completely empty – a situation that needed urgent attention.

At the front desk, however, something much more interesting from the point of view of the current case confronted İkmen. Erol Urfa, complete with baby Merih in a car seat plus someone who looked like an attendant drunk, was talking anxiously to the duty officer who was, in this case, Kaya.

'So how long is Inspector Suleyman likely to be?' Erol was asking as İkmen approached the scene.

'I have no idea, sir,' Kaya replied. 'Perhaps you would like to wait.'

With the aid of a slightly disgusted sniff at the swathes of cigarette smoke that were emanating from a cloth-capped individual who was also waiting for somebody or other, Erol said, 'Well, I'd rather not really. Not with the baby . . .'

'Quite right,' the drunk at his shoulder agreed

somewhat volubly. 'Not one of your better ideas, my dear Erol.'

'I'd really rather you were quiet now, İbrahim,' the singer said, turning, rather sharply on his companion.

As he drew level with the party, İkmen briefly made eye contact with Kaya before he said, 'Is there anything I can do for you, sir?'

For a moment, Erol Urfa looked at İkmen with a puzzled expression on his face. It made the inspector feel as if he were some strange type of fauna the singer had not previously encountered.

At length, Erol said, 'Who are you?'

'My name is Inspector İkmen. I work with Inspector Suleyman.' İkmen smiled. 'You are, of course, Erol Urfa, are you not?'

'Yes.'

İkmen offered his hand which Erol took.

'Is there anything I can help you with?'

'Well, I was really hoping to speak to Inspector Suleyman,' Erol said as he looked down at the baby who appeared to be stirring.

İkmen sighed. 'Well, he's likely to be some time. You are welcome to wait in my office if you wish.'

'Oh, I don't think we want to do that, do we, Erol?' the drunk said unsteadily. 'I mean . . .'

'Well, you don't have to stay if you don't want to, İbrahim,' Erol said, turning to the man with a taut expression on his face. 'But I would rather—'

'You know you're committing fucking professional suicide, don't you!' the man said loudly. 'In my—'

'And I think that you've had far too much to drink to be in a place like this,' İkmen said as he took hold of the man's arm and started to move him towards the door.

'Hey! Erol is my—'

'Erol and the baby will be quite safe with me,' İkmen said to him firmly as he propelled him forwards. 'You just go and sleep it off somewhere, yes?'

'I'll wait for you in the car, Erol!' he said over İkmen's shoulder. 'Don't say anything stupid, will you?'

'I'm sure he won't,' İkmen said with a smile.

The man, now out in the street, wobbled off in several different directions before finally settling upon a chosen course.

As İkmen returned from the doorway, Erol said, 'He means well.'

'I'm sure he does.' İkmen said, bent down to smile at the waking baby. 'Come on, let's get you to my office.'

He led the way across the reception area and up the two flights of stairs to the offices. As they mounted the second flight the sound of İkmen's coughing was augmented by small whimpers from Merih.

'I think she probably needs a feed,' Erol said.

'Uh,' İkmen replied, the grunt being the only noise his congested lungs could manage at this point.

At the top of the second flight, while İkmen gasped painfully for air, Dr İrfan Akkale closed the door to the corridor behind him and made to descend the stairs. Until he saw İkmen. Peering closely into the inspector's greenish-white face, he said, 'What are you doing here, İkmen? If you have a coronary here when you should be at home, I take no responsibility.'

'Yes, Dr . . .' İkmen gasped.

'You're a very silly man!' And then with a brief 'Good evening' to Erol Urfa, Akkale descended the stairs.

When they finally arrived at İkmen's office, Erol asked, 'So are you sick then, Inspector?'

İkmen breathed in deeply and replied on this exhalation, 'I have a stomach ulcer, but it doesn't really bother me.'

Erol placed Merih's seat on one of the chairs in front of İkmen's desk and then riffled in the bag on his shoulder until he located a bottle of milk. Merih took the drink he offered to her greedily.

'You didn't look terribly well just now,' Erol said, feeding the child while looking at İkmen. 'If you will forgive me saying so.'

İkmen smiled. 'I just have a few problems with stairs sometimes,' he said as he shuffled various large piles of paper around on his filthy, beloved desk. He had missed all of this sorely – the disorder, the smell, the thrill of the chase . . .

With a sigh of contentment, he flung himself

down into the depths of his battered leather chair and watched the young man feed the baby across the top of a mountain of files. It wasn't that he suddenly came to the realisation that the combination of children and work constituted his own personal paradise, the sights and smells around him were just a reaffirmation of what he personally was about. And that felt good. Now if he just had a cigarette or two . . .

'So, was there anything in particular you wanted to see Inspector Suleyman about?' İkmen said as he threw his feet up onto his desk.

Erol sighed. 'Yes. But . . .'

'Oh, you don't have to tell me,' İkmen said in tones of one who really couldn't care less. 'I was just, as you can imagine, a bit curious about the statement that man who was with you made.'

'You mean İbrahim, my manager?'

'If that was the rather inebriated gentleman . . .'

'Yes.'

İkmen shrugged. 'It was what he said about professional suicide. Sort of piqued my interest. But no matter.'

They sat in silence for a while, the gentle sound of the baby's feeding interrupted only by the distant strains of Arabesk music from the street below. But there was a tension around Erol Urfa that İkmen felt signalled both a reluctance and at the same time an urgent desire to talk. At length, the policeman felt that the time had come to break the silence.

'So, if you don't mind my asking,' İkmen said, 'did your late wife and Tansu Hanım ever meet?'

'Yes, once, at a party.'

'Oh?'

'It was about a year ago,' he said, looking, İkmen felt, very sadly at his now motherless child, 'although to be honest they hardly spoke. But then they wouldn't would they?'

İkmen smiled. 'I suppose not.'

'Although Latife, Tansu's sister, was very kind to Ruya, I must say. She sat and talked to her for quite some time. Ruya was very . . . very awkward in company.' He smiled once again at his child and made small cooing noises to her.

'Did Tansu or her sister ever see your wife again?'

'No. From then on Ruya was alone except when I was with her.'

That was the country way, İkmen thought, recalling all those little towns he had visited as a young man, towns out east that were, to all intents and purposes, entirely populated by men drinking tea and smoking cigarettes. Which reminded him . . .

Both the personal appearance and home of Mr Reşat Soylu came as no surprise to Suleyman. At around fifty, Soylu was a flat-capped, heavy-smoking brown nut of a peasant. And although he would probably have liked a little more material wealth out of life, the three-room apartment he shared with his veiled wife and severe-looking daughter was both clean and comfortable. Indeed, with the exception of the vast array of plants growing in old oil cans on the balcony and the hugely ornate chandelier in the living room, it was not unlike Cohen's place.

Once the preliminaries of assuring Mr Soylu that he was not actually in any kind of trouble were over, the peasant called for tea and sat Suleyman down upon the only proper chair in the room. This was directly underneath the chandelier which, the gardener told the policeman with some pride, had come all the way from Munich. When the tea arrived and Mrs Soylu had once again made herself scarce, Suleyman started to question her husband.

'I understand you garden for quite a few families in Yeniköy,' he said, 'including Mr and Mrs Ertürk and the Emins.'

'I do have that honour, yes,' the peasant replied. 'Allah, in his goodness, has always favoured my poor hands with sufficient work.'

A little embarrassed by this effusive outpouring of religious largesse, Suleyman took a sip from his tea glass and said, 'Good.'

Mr Soylu, pleased that Suleyman appeared to approve of him, did what a lot of peasant men do and sank back into a state of contented, straight-faced silence. With a small string of plastic worry beads in his hands, he could just as easily have been sitting beneath a tree in Cyprus or in the corner of a coffee house in distant Erzurum.

'I understand,' Suleyman eventually offered as he sought to penetrate the clamorous stillness around his host, 'that you poisoned some rats for Mr and Mrs Ertürk. Is that correct?'

'Yes.'

The wife, all knotted and draped scarves, put in a brief appearance until the slow lizard-like gaze of her husband caused her to flee to another part of the property.

'Could you tell me then, Mr Soylu,' Suleyman persisted, 'what sort of poison you used for this purpose?'

'Cyanide.'

He might just as well have been talking about tea, ayran or some other totally innocuous substance for all the emotion that showed, or rather failed to show, on Reşat Soylu's flat, brown face.

'And you obtained this very dangerous substance from where?'

For the first time the peasant smiled, large fissures appearing around his eyes and down his cheeks, like those great, dry cracks left behind by earthquakes. 'From my brother in Germany,' he said and then, amazingly, elaborated, 'like my chandelier. Germany is a great bazaar of all good things. I have never been, but my brother has lived there for ten years now.' Shaking his head against the sheer wonder of the thing, he added, 'He drives a BMW and has a German wife. Not that her people will speak to my brother.'

'Indeed.' For Suleyman, a one-word answer seemed the safest course of action at this point. Turks had been going to work in Germany for many years, and for many years had consequently come home with quality consumer goods and, occasionally, blonde-haired wives or husbands. These Europeans, although they did not always look down on their Turkish spouses themselves, usually possessed families who did that for them – people who found the Turks both primitive and backward. Suleyman's argument that the Ottomans were taking baths and writing courtly poetry when the ancestors of so many 'Hermans' and 'Dieters' were mere excrement-encrusted vassals of the Holy Roman Empire was far too vehement for the current situation, not to mention totally inaccessible to the likes of Mr Soylu.

'And your brother obtained the substance from where?' Suleyman asked, hoping to rouse Mr Soylu from his Bavarian ecstasy.

'He works at a steel plant,' Soylu said, adding proudly, 'in the Ruhr Valley. He brought it back with him because I asked him to. German cyanide kills far more pests than ours.'

'Right.' Not wishing to continue with this theme of German superiority, Suleyman said, 'So does it work for other pests too?'

'I've used it for wasps, to kill their nests.'

'Was it you who killed the nest at the Emin property?'

Soylu smiled. 'Yes. That was a huge one. But I got it. Tansu Hanım was very grateful.'

Suleyman took another sip from his tea glass and then placed it on the small table beside him. 'So when you eliminate these pests,' he said, 'do you ever have any poison left over at the end of the process?'

'Yes.'

'What happens to it? Do you bring it back here with you?'

Soylu smiled again and then got up and walked out into his kitchen. During the silence that wafted in in his wake, Suleyman regarded the posters of Rhineland castles that adorned every wall with a jaundiced eye. If these people would only take a little interest in their own noble past, perhaps they might be able to free themselves from, what to him, appeared to be the most awful cultural servitude.

When he returned, Soylu was carrying a large glass container that looked like something in which one might brew beer. It contained a darkish yellow liquid.

'I have all I need here,' he said as he held the vessel aloft for Suleyman to see.

The policeman walked over to the man and, taking the cork out of the top of the bottle, sniffed at the liquid inside. Bitter almonds, unmistakable.

'I take it,' he said as he replaced the stopper firmly

in the neck, 'that you don't carry this with you to and from your various jobs.'

'No. I decant it into smaller bottles. Rakı are the best.'

Suleyman went back to his seat while Mr Soylu put enough cyanide down on the floor to kill most of the inhabitants of that district.

'So when you've killed the rats or wasps' nest or whatever, if there is any poison left over . . .'

'I leave it there,' Soylu said simply. 'All my people have greenhouses. I leave it there.'

'In old rakı bottles.'

'Yes.'

Suleyman rolled his eyes to heaven in disbelief. 'Doesn't it worry you that someone might mistake it for drink?'

Soylu shrugged. 'I hide it well and at the Emin house it is clearly marked what it is.'

A frown creased Suleyman's brow. 'Only at the Emin house? Why only there?'

Although he was obviously not terribly bothered about what he said next, Soylu exhibited just a little shame when he lowered his eyes briefly to the ground. 'I can't read or write so Miss Emin writes the labels for me. None of my other employers take as much interest in the garden as she does.'

Suleyman felt the hairs on the back of his neck rise as he asked his next question. 'This is, I take it, Miss Latife Emin and not her sister Tansu?'

Soylu grinned. 'Yes,' he said, 'she just loves to tend the plants and trees, you know. A proper country girl.'

Suleyman felt the gravity of expression that overtook his face as he asked, 'And is cyanide at the Emin house now?'

'Oh, yes. Enough to kill another nest if need be. They do have a lot of problems with wasps and so that's quite possible.' He lit a cigarette and then threw the dead match down beside the bottle of cyanide. 'Just not worth bringing it back here when I've got all this lot anyway, is it?' he said as he patted the side of the sinister receptacle.

Suleyman watched, fascinated, as the gnarled peasant stroked his gently lapping personal lake of death.

Orhan Tepe, whilst not having anything against his colleague, İsak Çöktin, was not exactly his best friend either. And although the man was pleasant enough to pass the time of day with, being incarcerated in a hot car with him was not easy. As the sun began to set over the distant fortress of Rumeli Kavağı and both men started to contemplate a long night together, conversation finally came to a standstill.

It was impossible to deduce from Çöktin's fixed, blank expression anything of what he was thinking but Tepe's far more mobile face eloquently illustrated the strains and boredom inherent in long stretches of observation. Quite often such work would, once those being observed began to move, involve some sort of action on the part of the officers looking on. Pursuit of those moving on was quite common, as was the investigation of the property recently vacated. But not this time. The task at hand was merely to watch, take note and call in any outside activity or unusual occurrence within the property. To say that it was dull was an understatement. After all, a person can only look at an old Ottoman gateway and ugly house beyond for so long.

'So what's Tansu Hanım actually like, then?' Tepe asked, for want of anything more interesting to say.

Çöktin, his eyes still fixed on the gateway, shrugged. 'I don't know.'

'Well, you met her, didn't you?'

'Yes.'

A little aggravated by his partner's short and uninterested answers, Tepe said, somewhat aggressively, 'And so?'

Turning briefly to look at the dark, annoyed man at his side, Çöktin replied, 'So she's a middle-aged woman who has a young lover, what do you want me to say?'

'It's said she's got a bad temper, that she's controlling.'

'I met her only briefly,' Çöktin said. 'What would I know?'

Çöktin's tone, which was decidedly sulky, finally got to Tepe, who raised his voice. 'I don't know why you're so hostile about it!'

'I'm not hostile!' Çöktin said as he turned a very hostile face on his colleague. 'I'm as tired and bored as you are! Plus, considering the fact we've allowed Tansu Hanım to go because we have no reason to detain her, I don't actually see the point of all this.'

'But if Suleyman ordered it—'

'He ordered it under the direction of İkmen and we all know,' he said, his face resolving into a scowl, 'what he's like.'

Tepe frowned. 'What do you mean?'

'I mean he goes off onto his own private missions.'

'Which frequently prove to be very valuable. And if I do eventually get to work with him I will feel very honoured.' Tepe eyed Çöktin closely. 'Anyway, I thought you liked him, I thought you got on well.'

'I do like him.' He lit a cigarette and then puffed hard on it for a few moments. 'I just don't always understand what he's thinking.'

Tepe laughed. 'That's the whole point,' he said. 'He's an enigma. He likes it that way, it's part of his legend.'

'I find it unnerving,' Çöktin said with an almost visible shudder.

'If you have something to hide then it probably is,' Tepe replied, unwittingly bringing to a close any discussion of that particular topic.

Çöktin cleared his throat as he watched several lights come on at the front of the Emin house. It had been a long day for all of the residents and he wondered, in view of recent events, whether Erol had now rushed to Tansu's side. That he loved her was evident. But whether or not he would now break his vow to keep some distance between them was not clear. Çöktin could not see Erol's car, though it might be parked at the back of the property.

'So do you have any ideas about who might have killed the Urfa woman?' Tepe said as he turned the air conditioning up a notch.

'No. Do you?'

Tepe shrugged. 'I'd still put money on Tansu.'

Çöktin turned to look at his colleague. 'Why?'

'Female rivalry. In my opinion, most women will content themselves with just one man.' He smiled. 'They're not like us. I mean men lived very happily with harems for centuries. It was the women who fought and plotted against each other. They don't like sharing and they don't, usually, have the wit to look elsewhere.'

'If they do we call them sluts.'

'Which they are.' He stopped speaking to peer closely at the long driveway that led to Tansu's house. 'Is that some movement down by that garage or . . .'

Çöktin, too, looked in the direction indicated and then tipped his head slightly backwards to signify his assent. 'Yes.'

'You can't see who it is, can you?'

At the distance they were from the scene it was almost impossible to identify people as anything more than just blobs. 'No. Except that there are two of them.'

'The car looks like a . . .' Tepe considered just what exactly the low-slung, bright red sports model might be for a few seconds before he said, 'a Ferrari, I think.'

'Mmm.'

As the two officers watched, someone switched the car lights on and, moments later, the vehicle started moving forward.

'Well, someone's going somewhere,' Tepe said as he put his own lights on and turned the key in the ignition.

Çöktin, who was watching the approaching vehicle intently now, observed that even for a high-performance model, the Ferrari was being driven by someone who was obviously in a hurry. Even with the motor of their own car ticking over beneath them, both the officers could clearly hear the loud roar of its highly tuned engine. By the expression on his face, Tepe, at least, showed that he was very impressed.

The vehicle pulled up, very sharply, in front of the large main gates. Leaving the engine running and the door open, a figure emerged from the driver's side. It was quite clearly a woman.

'Tansu,' Tepe said in response to the sight of white-blonde hair and a voluminous fur coat. It was not an assessment Çöktin could easily argue with.

Frantically, as if pressed for time to an almost unbearable extent, the woman fumbled with the padlock on the gates until she managed to free it from the wrought iron that surrounded it. Then, pushing the gates open just enough to allow the car to pass through, she ran back to the Ferrari, taking the padlock with her. A terrible gunning sound was heard as she revved the engine hard. And as the brake was released the vehicle shot forward towards the road.

'You'll have to really move to keep up with that thing,' Çöktin said to Tepe as the latter put the car into gear and took the handbrake off.

'I hope that wasn't a criticism of my driving.'

'I wouldn't dare!' Çöktin said, acknowledging the intimate relationship that exists between the Turkish male and his car.

Tepe's foot had just pushed down hard onto the accelerator pedal when the sickening crunch that brought the Ferrari's progress to a halt occurred. The vehicle it appeared to have just rammed was a lorry, the driver of which was already out of his cab and yelling loudly.

However, there was as yet no sign of life from inside the buckled Ferrari.

İkmen smoked three cigarettes one after the other on

his way back to his office from the cigarette kiosk. Some people, like Erol, didn't much like a lot of smoke around their small infants and so he had to make sure he had a big hit before going back in with him. He also felt that he needed to fortify himself a little too. There were some questions, or rather points, he wanted to put to young Urfa that were not going to prove easy, especially if Suleyman, whom Erol seemed now to trust on some level, had not yet returned.

When İkmen re-entered the station it was evident that Suleyman was still absent. He went into his office and saw that the child was asleep and the man was standing at the window, apparently watching the sun set. The sinuous strains of the evening call to prayer started to spin their slim tendrils towards the station and its occupants.

İkmen sat down at his desk and watched as the younger man looked at the descending crescent of the setting sun.

'I take it you're not a religious man, Mr Urfa,' İkmen said.

'No.' He neither moved nor acknowledged in any other way that he was paying anything more than cursory attention to what İkmen was saying.

'Like me,' the policeman said with a smile. 'It may indeed say Muslim against religion on my identity card but that is only for the sake of form.'

Slowly, Erol Urfa turned just a little so that he was at an oblique angle to the policeman. İkmen noted with interest that although he could now talk more easily to him, he could still not see Urfa's eyes.

'So what are you then, really, Inspector?' the singer asked.

'Oh, I'm absolutely nothing with regard to religion,' İkmen said. 'But I do accept that others have beliefs and I don't much care what they are provided they don't commit offences in the name of their faith. You can worship Allah or a tree or even a large bird with very bright tail feathers, it's all the same to me.'

Whether Erol Urfa experienced fear or relief or shock during the frozen moment that then passed between the two men, İkmen would never know. Outwardly impassive, it was only his words that gave any indication that he had both heard and understood the meaning of what had just been said to him.

'How did you know?' he asked, still looking out of the window, still seemingly listening to the exhortations of the numerous muezzins of the countless imperial and other mosques of old Stambul.

'Chicken and beans are such unusual things for such a young child to be noticeably allergic to,' İkmen said. 'I suppose that for a man of faith like yourself, you had to take the risk. But then you were coming to commit "professional suicide", to use your manager's words, with Inspector Suleyman, weren't you?'

'Yes. When I heard that Tansu was no longer here I did briefly reconsider, but . . .'

'What bearing does Miss Emin have upon this?' İkmen said with a frown.

He just managed to make out a sad smile on Erol Urfa's lips. 'I only married Ruya because of the needs of my religion. We never marry outside. And so if Tansu did kill her I am partly to blame for that. I wanted two women and that is wrong.'

'Did Tansu know about your religion?'

Erol shrugged. 'I don't know. I never told her myself.'

'And yet the words of some of her songs . . .'

'Yes,' he turned now to face İkmen who noticed that his eyes were wet with tears. 'The peacocks, the bitterness towards them . . . I have asked her about that, albeit obliquely. She's always said she liked that image. That's all.'

'Did she actually write those songs?' İkmen asked.

'She says she did. She is credited with them.'

'And yet if she did, and deduced the reason for your concern, then surely she would have enough knowledge to realise that you could never marry any woman who is not Yezidi – assuming of course that she is not.'

'No. She is Kurdish, but not . . .' He bit his bottom lip thoughtfully and then moved across the room towards İkmen's desk.

İkmen sighed. 'So who else, apart from your manager, knows about your religion? Here in the city, that is.'

Erol sat down in the chair opposite İkmen's desk. 'I only told İbrahim today,' he said. 'But there is also my friend Ali Mardin and . . .' The curtailment of his speech was quite sudden, but also quite deliberate.

İkmen rubbed his chin and considered carefully before he spoke next. 'İsak Çöktin,' he looked across at Erol at this point, 'risked his career by continuing to see you when Inspector Suleyman had specifically instructed him not to, which might lead me to certain conclusions.'

'I have nothing to say on that matter.'

Although İkmen did think about pressing this point, he decided in the end that it probably wasn't worth the aggravation. After all, Erol's refusal to discuss Çöktin told him everything he needed to know about the matter.

'Anyway,' he said at length, 'interesting though your revelation has been, you do know that if Tansu Hanım is guilty of murder, it will not make the slightest difference to her fate.'

'She is still under suspicion then? Even though you have let her go?'

'Yes. We still have doubts which, I imagine, you share.' İkmen smiled. 'Otherwise why would you have so wanted to tell Inspector Suleyman your secret? A secret you know could damage you and little Merih in so many ways.'

Erol bowed his head, as if he were bending under the weight of some awful, crushing presence. He took a deep breath and then let it out on a sigh. 'You will, of course, report the falsified information on my identity card.'

'Oh, I only deal with homicide, sir,' İkmen said and attempted to ape normality by shuffling papers across his desk. 'Anything political is quite beyond me.'

'But you will report this to others who . . .'

İkmen smiled. 'I tend not to take too much notice of information I receive that doesn't actually impact upon the case I am working on. I am reliably informed that, contrary to popular belief, your people don't actually dance naked around the bodies of Muslim virgins, so I have no problem with you. In a sense you are no different from me. I've got Muslim on my ID card and that is a blatant lie. So there's little to choose between us, is there?'

'You know, where I come from policemen are not like you.'

'Are they not?' İkmen said. 'Some would say that was a good thing.'

'Not me,' the singer said with an intense look at the policeman. 'I would say that you are one of the most decent men I have ever had the good fortune to meet.'

Although İkmen was not one to be easily embarrassed, he did now feel more than a little awkward and so he just grunted his thanks while turning his attention, and his eyes, to the mess on his desk once again. Before Erol could become any more effusive in his praise, there was a knock at the office door.

'Come!'

The door opened to reveal Suleyman with a rather excited light in his eyes. Somewhat incongruously, to İkmen's way of thinking, he was holding a large jar of dark yellow liquid.

'Oh, Çetin, I saw the light on and, er,' as his eyes lit upon Erol Urfa, he looked surprised. 'Oh, Mr Urfa, I . . .'

'Mr Urfa came to give you some information he thinks might be pertinent,' İkmen said as he spared a brief thought for the pleasure he was going to get out of telling Suleyman that he had been right about the singer.

'Ah . . .'

'I have actually spoken to Inspector İkmen,' Erol said, then turning to İkmen he asked, 'Do I have to go through it all again with Inspector Suleyman?'

'No,' İkmen replied. 'I will tell him and as I've said, if this proves to have no bearing on the case . . .'

Suleyman's mobile telephone started playing the latest tune he had chosen for it, the beginning of Beethoven's Fifth. Still in the dark about what had been happening between İkmen and Erol Urfa, Suleyman put the jar down on the floor and turned aside to answer his phone.

After a brief glance at the sleeping Merih, Erol rose from his seat. 'I had better get my child home now,' he said, 'if that's all right with you, Inspector İkmen.'

'I have no problem with that,' İkmen said with a smile even though his attention was now distracted by the sound of what appeared to be an urgent conversation between Suleyman and somebody.

Erol picked the baby up and prepared to leave.

'All right,' Suleyman said into the telephone, 'I'll meet you there. Let me know as soon as you know. Yes. Yes.'

As Erol moved towards the door, Suleyman held up one hand to stop him.

'Right,' he said into the phone and then, 'OK.' He pressed the end button and put the telephone back into his pocket.

'What's the problem?' İkmen asked as he looked at Suleyman gravely considering the face of Erol Urfa.

'While there is no need to panic,' Suleyman said, 'I do have to tell you that Tansu Hanım and her sister have been involved in a minor road traffic accident.'

Erol's face lightened serveral shades. İkmen moved quickly forward to take the baby from the singer's arms.

'Neither lady is noticeably injured, but they should both be taken to hospital for observation and treatment for shock.'

'I must go to her.'

'I don't think that would be a particularly good

idea at the moment,' Suleyman said. 'As I told you, Mr Urfa, she is not hurt. The best thing you can do is go home. We can, if you wish, arrange for Miss Emin's family to call you. Do you have your car?'

'Yes, he does,' İkmen put in, remembering the intoxicated manager who said he would wait for Erol in the vehicle, 'although it might be an idea, under the circumstances, if we provide a driver for Mr Urfa.'

Suleyman agreed that, given Erol's state of mind, a police driver might be prudent. And so, after a few telephone calls to significant others, the shaken singer and his child were eventually led out of the office and into the care of a uniformed driver.

As soon as he had gone, Suleyman placed the jar of liquid on his desk and said, 'Reşat's cyanide,' by way of explanation.

İkmen raised one eyebrow and then, changing the subject, said, 'Any idea where Tansu and her sister were going?'

'No.' Suleyman took his car keys out of his pocket and looked up expectantly at İkmen. 'Coming?'

'Why? It's only road traffic—'

'Yes, but with a twist,' Suleyman said as he started to move towards the office door. 'Tepe said that just after the car impacted with the other vehicle, he and Çöktin ran over to help. As they approached, he clearly saw and heard Tansu shout "Run" to her sister.'

'So?'

'Well, Latife Emin tried to do what Tansu told her

333

but, according to Tepe, her limp was too pronounced to allow her to move very quickly.'

İkmen shrugged. 'But if she'd just been injured . . .'

'Oh, I agree entirely,' his colleague assented as he held the office door open for the older man, 'but until we go and check it out we won't know, will we?'

'So which hospital have they been taken to?' İkmen asked.

Suleyman sighed. 'Tepe says that at the moment both women are refusing medical treatment.'

'Indeed. So what can we do?'

'Well, I'm just going to speak to my men.'

'Mmm.' İkmen, motionless beneath the door frame, put his fingers to his lips in a gesture of thoughtfulness. 'But they should have medical attention, really.'

'Oh, yes, I agree, but—'

'No, I mean that they should *really* have medical attention, Mehmet,' İkmen said with a twinkle in his eye. 'As in we should perhaps take it to them.'

Suleyman frowned.

'Look, if we take a doctor with us,' İkmen explained, 'she has the perfect excuse to look at Miss Latife's legs unshod.'

'She?'

'Well, psychiatrists do have to study anatomy before they specialise, don't they?' İkmen moved out into the corridor. 'And anyway, Dr Halman might be very useful should things prove a little bizarre.'

'Yes, but—'

'Just get your phone out and give her a call,' İkmen said gently. 'The number's programmed in so it's not as if you've got to make an effort, is it?'

As İkmen tripped lightly to the top of the stairs, Suleyman pressed a button and then listened for the ringing tone. His face was taut and strained.

Chapter 15

Dr Babur Halman looked across the table at his clever blonde daughter and nodded his head. Forty-six years old and possessed of, to him, a stubborn Irish mind, his girl was not one with whom frail old Turkish men were wont to argue. If nothing else, her kind but firm treatment of her demented patients was strong evidence for this. But she was still his daughter and knowing that she had recently experienced some turmoil with regard to the young man who had telephoned half an hour before, Babur did feel compelled to speak.

'So your going out is on police business, is it?' he asked as he placed his knife and fork down onto his plate.

'Yes.' Her turning away from him at that point, Babur knew was significant.

'So not . . .'

'Father, I do consult for them from time to time as well you know.'

Babur shrugged. 'Yes, well . . .'

She put her hands down on the table and leaned across towards the old man. 'The only thing stopping

me from returning to Dublin is you,' she said vehemently, 'and only you.'

'But I would go if—'

'Oh, yes? And where would we live while I got
myself another job, eh? Unless we sold this house,
which I know you don't want to do, we'd have to
lodge with Uncle Frank at least at first. And you know
what that means, don't you?'

Babur sighed. 'Yes.'

'Nuns in and out all day long, not to mention
parishioners who'd look at you like you were the
devil himself. And that housekeeper of his, well . . .'

Babur smiled. 'The lovely Mrs Reynolds.'

'Cooking up all sorts of horrors,' his daughter raved,
flinging her arms expressively into the air. 'And she's
a stranger to bleach or any other sort of cleaning
material, for that matter!'

'What a colourful turn of phrase you have,' her
father said with genuine appreciation. 'So obvious
that you are of the soil that bore Yeats, Wilde and
Behan.'

It had been said with such admiration and kindness
that Zelfa, for a moment, felt quite deflated. With a sigh
she sat back down at the table. 'And you are an astute
man whom I shouldn't even attempt to dupe. I'd like
nothing better than to go home now . . .'

'But?'

She smiled sadly. 'But as you know there is another
consideration here.'

'A young man.' Babur reached out and took one of her hands in his.

'Too young for me,' she said and lowered her head in order to avoid her father's eyes.

'Maybe. But then we cannot chose who we love, can we? Many people said that I was foolish to marry your mother—'

'Well, you did end up getting divorced,' his daughter interjected.

'True. But at least your mother and I tried. We were in love, we gave our love a chance and,' he shrugged, 'well, it didn't work, but had we not tried we would never have known that and I wouldn't now have you who is such a blessing.'

She leaned forward and kissed her father affectionately on his forehead. 'Oh, Father,' she said, 'how on earth can I be forty-six years old and still behave like a girl of sixteen?'

'You're the psychiatrist,' her father said with a wry grin on his face. 'Perhaps your Catholic guilt made you a late starter in the romantic sphere or—'

A loud knock cut Babur's speech short which, from his daughter's point of view, was probably a good thing. Although completely untroubled by religious affiliations himself, Babur, Zelfa knew, had never been happy about her being educated within the convent system. It had been one of the nails that had sealed up the coffin that became her parents' marriage.

'I've got to go now,' she said. She picked up her

medical bag, already packed with essential supplies, and stood up.

Babur first sighed and then smiled. 'Well, just be careful, won't you?' he said. 'In all sorts of ways.'

'I'm a big girl now,' his daughter replied as she walked out of the room, blowing her father a kiss as she went.

Babur looked down at his plate and muttered, 'No, you're not,' and then with one last glance towards the place his daughter had vacated, took his eating utensils out into the kitchen.

Much as they may have welcomed the kudos that came with treating a major Arabesk star, the staff of the Alman Hospital, which is where Tansu and her sister should have been taken after the accident, were to be disappointed. Neither Tansu nor Latife would agree to any medical intervention. Instead, Tansu screamed at İsak Çöktin to phone his 'friend' Erol Urfa for her.

'But madam,' the officer pleaded as he indicated the large gash on the singer's calf, 'you are bleeding.'

'Yes, and I will only stop bleeding when you get Erol for me!'

Tepe, who was standing behind his colleague, a far less involved expression on his face, added, 'But if you don't attend to it, the cut could become infected.'

'I don't care!'

'I could clean it up myself for the time—'

'If I wanted your dirty hands on me, I'd ask you!'

Tansu snapped as she shuffled herself deep into the corner of her settee.

'As you wish.'

Galıp Emin who had earlier disappeared upstairs with his other sister, Latife, now re-entered the room, his face stern.

'What are they still doing here?' he said as he flicked his disgruntled head in the direction of Çöktin and Tepe.

'Well, unless this one,' Tansu stabbed a finger at Çöktin, 'calls Erol for me, then I really do not know!'

'Why you were outside our house in the first place is a mystery to me,' Galıp said as he drew level with the much taller Tepe. 'As if my family haven't had enough of your incompetence already.' Turning from the stone-faced Tepe to Çöktin, Galıp sneered, 'And as for you, Kurdish brother—'

'So is Miss Latife all right now?' Tepe managed to interject before things took a turn for the worse.

'She'll live,' Galıp answered. His eyes bore relentlessly into Çöktin's.

'I know that you know what Erol's new telephone number is!' Tansu yelled. 'And you call yourself a Kurdish—'

Çöktin suddenly and violently snapped. 'That's good coming from Turkey's only true darling who courts the forces that paint our villages red with our own blood!'

Turning away from Galıp to glare at Tansu, Çöktin,

or so it seemed to the anxious Tepe, briefly held the whole party in a tense silence. As the large antique French clock ticked ponderously in the background, Tepe wondered if he was alone in wondering whether Çöktin's own position within the police was about to be flung at him. It was something that he knew was a possibility even though he was struggling to understand its implications. Until the singer spoke again, Tepe meandered helplessly in what had suddenly, for him, become a foreign country.

'I'd like you to leave my house now,' Tansu said, her voice small and almost strangled by the control she was having to exert over it.

Not taking his eyes from hers for a moment, Çöktin replied, 'But you need medical attention.'

'If I wish to die, that's my choice.'

'But—'

'Your report, should that happen, would make interesting reading, wouldn't it?'

Stung, Çöktin overreacted. 'Don't be so ridiculous! Dying in order to spite me would be—'

'Just perfect!' the woman screamed. And then hurling herself onto the floor in a flood of enraged tears she yelled, 'Without Erol I am dead anyway!'

Galıp and the until now silent Yılmaz raced towards their sister.

'I th-think you'd b-better go now!' Yılmaz man said to the two policemen as he eased Tansu's head out from underneath the coffee table.

'Yes, but—'

'Come on, let's go,' Tepe said and placed one determined hand on Çöktin's shoulder. 'There's no point.'

With a sigh Çöktin turned and then almost as quickly turned back again. 'But—'

'Come *on*!'

Tepe took hold of Çöktin's arm and, despite some reluctance on the Kurd's part, led him out into the large rose and gold-coloured hall beyond. Once out of the Emin family's orbit, Çöktin allowed himself to be taken towards the front door without resistance. And although Tepe was tempted to ask him at this point just what he thought he'd been trying to prove with Tansu and the others, he resisted in favour of a quiet life,

But as he opened the front door of Tansu's house, two things happened to change that. Suleyman, together with two other figures Tepe couldn't quite make out in the gathering darkness, were getting out of the former's distinctive white BMW and Latife Emin stepped out of one of the bathrooms and into the hall.

'Y-you r-really m-must try to be c-calm now, Tansu,' Yılmaz said as he wiped the edge of his handkerchief across his sister's heavily perspiring features.

'Have those dogs gone yet or—'

'Yes, yes yes!' an exasperated Galıp said as he sat down next to Tansu and took her hand.

'They'll be back though, won't they?' the singer said darkly, reaching forward to take a cigarette from one of the boxes on the table. 'I mean why were they out there if they didn't *know*?'

'I have no idea.'

'You never do!' she snapped at the now exhausted figure of her brother. 'You're useless!'

'Yes.' It was said with what, to an outsider, sounded like a practised lack of either resistance or hope.

'W-we d-do t-try, you know, Tansu.' Yılmaz for once seemed to be expressing his true feelings on the matter. 'W-we d-do—'

'If you have to try then you're no fucking use to me, are you!' the singer roared. And then in emulation, as was her custom, of her brother's infirmity, she added, 'If you c-can g-get Erol's t-telephone n-number for me then you won't be q-quite so u-useless, Y-Yilmaz!' And then she laughed at him, which was also her custom.

'The sound of happy laughter,' an unfamiliar voice suddenly said, 'leads me, my dear Tansu Hanım, to hope that perhaps you are not badly injured after all.'

As one, Tansu, Galıp and Yılmaz all turned towards the source of the unknown voice which had, apparently, come from the throat of a small, rather dishevelled-looking individual who was standing over by the recently opened door.

'Such a charming house,' İkmen lied, 'such a wonderful example of the Bauhaus style,' and then moving to one side to admit Suleyman, he said, 'Of course I don't have to introduce Inspector Suleyman, do I?'

'Who *are* you?' Galıp, his eyes narrowed against the appearance of this stranger in their midst, inquired.

İkmen pulled an innocent grin. 'Oh, did I not introduce myself? How remiss of me. I am Inspector İkmen, a colleague of Inspector Suleyman.' He held his hand out to Galıp in a friendly manner. 'And you are?'

'Galıp Em—'

'I thought I made it clear I didn't want any more policemen!' an enraged Tansu cried. 'I've just thrown two of your men out of this house and—'

'Yes,' İkmen said as he moved towards the prone woman on the settee and took her hand in his, 'Sergeants Çöktin and Tepe. I am so sorry if they caused you pain. However, Inspector Suleyman and myself are here to alleviate your agonies, my dear Tansu Hanım.' He kissed her hand, feeling the revulsion that swept through her body as he did so. But her voice was calmer when next she spoke.

'Alleviate my agonies?'

Moving Galıp a little roughly to one side, İkmen sat down. 'Sergeant Tepe informed us that you had refused hospital treatment.'

Tansu eyed him suspiciously. 'Yes?'

'Well, as a responsible organisation, we could hardly countenance Turkey's brightest star taking such a risk,' he smiled. 'And so I have brought you one of our own doctors. As a devotee of everything you have ever done, madam, I could do no less.'

Fearing that perhaps İkmen had gone just slightly over the top, Suleyman nervously cleared his throat.

Tansu's lizard-like gaze clung stonily to İkmen's face for several moments before it started to soften. 'You like my music?'

'I love it,' İkmen said enthusiastically and leaned forward to light the cigarette that still dangled from Tansu's fingers.

'What do you like about my music, then?' the singer asked suspiciously.

'I adore your passion,' İkmen said as he closed his eyes in imitation of one rapt with pleasure.

'My passion?'

'Oh, songs like "I Want None of You", "Hate Is My Only Friend", "The Blue-green Bird Lies Bleeding" – I could go on and on!'

'Could you?'

'Yes.'

'So where's this doctor you say you've brought?'

All eyes now turned towards Galıp who, resentful at having been pushed out of his place on the settee, was eyeing İkmen with some hostility.

'The doctor is washing up in your bathroom,' İkmen answered with a smile.

Galıp's gaze narrowed into one of obvious suspicion. 'How does he know where our bathroom is?'

'Your sister, Miss Latife, actually directed the doctor to it,' Suleyman said and then added, 'Oh, and the doctor is a she, actually, Mr Emin. Dr Halman.'

'We felt that a female doctor was far more appropriate for a lady patient, did we not, Inspector?'

'Oh, yes, absolutely.'

'B-but w-where is the d-doctor?' Yılmaz said, his face panicked.

Turning away briefly from Tansu's tear-ravaged face, İkmen said, smiling, 'As I said, Dr Halman is washing.'

'Have you any idea how clean a doctor's hands have to be before he or she touches a patient?' Suleyman added.

'I do,' Tansu snapped. 'I've had to have a lot of operations for, er, um, problems, pain and bad things and . . . But neither of these,' she said as she loosely indicated her brothers, 'have ever been in hospital in their lives.'

'Yes, but—'

'You are just an ignorant peasant, Galıp!' she shouted harshly. 'Doctors take a long time to prepare. I know, I've suffered, I've lived!'

'Indeed you have,' İkmen said as he mugged the falsest smile of his career, 'and as soon as the doctor has finished washing and has looked briefly at your sister she will attend to you.'

Tansu's face flushed. 'My sister . . .'

'Yes,' İkmen replied, 'she was, after all, also involved in the accident, wasn't she?'

'Yes.'

'Then a doctor is probably the best person for her to

see at this point,' İkmen said with a smile. 'Nothing to worry about, I'm sure.'

Just as Tansu turned to look at her brothers the door to the room opened and then closed on a small, plump woman with blonde hair. Everyone looked up in her direction. İkmen and Suleyman both rose to their feet.

'Ah, Doctor!' the former said with enthusiasm, and then indicating Tansu, he added, 'Your exalted patient.'

'Ah.'

The two men walked towards the doctor who, as İkmen passed her, murmured something into his ear. Although none of the Emins could hear it, they eyed each other warily as they observed this exchange.

İkmen's face broke out into a broad smile.

'Shall we go, gentlemen?' Suleyman said, looking pointedly at the rather nervous pair of brothers.

'Well, it's only her leg,' Galıp began.

'You think,' Dr Halman said as she moved in a very business-like fashion towards her patient, 'but I will have to check Miss Emin for internal trauma too and that,' she said pointedly, 'will necessitate her having to remove her clothes.'

Galıp looked at Yılmaz and mouthed, 'I don't like this.' But his brother only shrugged as he rose slowly to his feet.

With a smile, Suleyman said again, 'Gentlemen?'

Yılmaz walked slowly across the room, followed at an even slower pace by his brother.

'Now,' Dr Halman said as she sat down next to her patient, 'let me have a look at this leg.'

Chapter 16

She was standing in the hallway as the party emerged from the drawing room, her eyes fixed upon the expressions on the faces of Sergeants Çöktin and Tepe at the bottom of the staircase. Not that İkmen was looking at the eyes of Latife Emin. His gaze was firmly fixed upon her shoes which, he saw, were sturdy and 'sensible'. Given what Dr Halman had just told him, he could clearly see that the left shoe had a thicker sole than the right.' Yılmaz, who was standing, seemingly dumbstruck, to İkmen's right, gave a short gasp of surprise – or fear.

'I thought they had gone . . .' his more voluble brother exclaimed.

'Sergeants Çöktin and Tepe will take care of you for the time being,' İkmen said as he turned and smiled at the white-faced brothers.

'No!' Galıp began, until Suleyman took hold of his arm and then wound it painfully up behind his back.

'Oh, I think yes,' he said with some force.

'I suggest you find a nice comfortable room to share with these gentlemen,' İkmen said to the two sergeants who had now, in the face of Galıp's outburst, made it quite plain to all concerned that they were armed. 'If of course you can find anything remotely pleasant in this ghastly pile of crap,' he added with a smile.

Suleyman pushed the two brothers in front of him and handed them over to the two younger men.

'Sir.'

And then İkmen turned to look at Latife Emin. Her face was as white as the thin linen of her blouse.

'You know you really shouldn't be wearing such heavy shoes on a lovely parquet floor like this,' İkmen said taking her arm gently between his fingers. 'You could be doing it terrible damage. Why don't you take them off?'

Latife Emin moved the biography of Marilyn Monroe, which was her current entertainment when she was seated on the veranda, from her chair onto the table.

'Mmm,' İkmen said as he watched her lower herself into her seat. 'Like Marilyn do you?'

'Yes.'

'A woman unrecognised for her true talents.' İkmen picked the book up and turned it over. 'So you read English, do you, Miss Emin?'

'I manage,' she said as she motioned for the two men to sit down.

İkmen, as ever observant with regard to smoking requisites, viewed the numerous ashtrays with approval. 'I take it you don't mind if we smoke?'

he said as he offered Suleyman a cigarette from his packet.

'No, that's all right,' the woman replied, absently brushing a stray platinum hair out of her eyes.

The two men sat down and then lit up simultaneously. A few moments of silence, broken only by the barking of a distant dog, passed.

'So why did you murder Ruya Urfa?' İkmen asked when, in his estimation, enough time had elapsed.

'I didn't.' It was quite bald, a statement of fact.

İkmen smiled. 'Oh? Did you not?'

'No.'

'So why did your sister shout at you to run after the car accident?' Suleyman asked, trying but without success to catch Latife Emin's elusive eyes.

'Because she thought that the petrol tank might be about to explode.' She looked up, questioningly, as if seeking approval for this perfectly sensible reason.

'Yes, quite right,' İkmen said, 'very wise. And your leg?'

She frowned. 'What?'

'The leg our doctor assures us is shorter than the other. The left one, if my observation of your shoes—'

'I was born with that defect,' she said, 'but I don't usually limp. I compensate using the ball of my foot. Only since this accident.'

'Oh, come on now, Latife!' İkmen said, a deep chuckle rumbling at the back of his voice. 'I may be only a common İstanbul policeman but please do not insult my intelligence.' He leaned forward and studied Latife's shod feet hard. 'Even a fool can see that this one is built up to accommodate your infirmity,' he said, as indicating the large, if currently rather fashionable left-hand platform sole and wedge heel. 'A very professionally made shoe, Miss Emin, but please . . .'

'I always wear my shoes! Tansu hates people to see me without them! I would never, ever—'

'Did I say that you have ever been without your shoes, Miss Emin?' İkmen asked, his eyes just briefly flicking across to Suleyman's face. 'I don't think so. And even if you have, quite what that would mean I really don't know. Do you?' He sank back slowly into the depths of his chair and concentrated on his cigarette for a few moments. Latife Emin, her eyes still downcast, studied the top of the small occasional table at her side with some intensity.

'Where were you on the night of Ruya Urfa's death?' Suleyman asked.

'I was here in my bed.'

'While your sister was either here with you or out at a bar in the city, depending upon which story you decide to tell.'

İkmen leaned forward towards Latife. 'You see, madam, when you tell us lies we do get awfully confused.'

She looked up, her eyes exhibiting the fear both

policemen knew she must be experiencing. 'I was here,' she said. 'It was Tansu who was out, doing whatever.'

'And can anyone confirm your whereabouts?'

'Apart from, of course, either of your brothers,' İkmen said with a smile.

'No.' Latife cast her eyes down once again at the table.

Again the silence rolled in across the room like a long, thick carpet.

'We could go on like this all night,' İkmen said as he ground his cigarette out in the ashtray and then lit another, 'with us putting points to you and you refuting them, but . . .'

'But?'

'But I think that if Inspector Suleyman here gives you the whole story, that just might move things along a bit.' Then looking across at Suleyman he said, 'What do you think, Inspector?'

'I think that is an excellent idea.' Suleyman turned to look at Latife Emin's profile and smiled. 'Ruya Urfa was poisoned with a piece of cyanide-laced almond halva. Cleverly, the sweet disguised the smell of the poison and, cleverly again, it was performed at a time when the whole of the city was engrossed in a game of football.'

'The only person definitely placed at the scene,' İkmen interjected, 'a middle-aged man with Down's syndrome, could not, I'm sure an intelligent woman like yourself will understand, have possibly planned and executed such a complex crime.'

'Quite,' Suleyman agreed as he observed just the slightest greying of Latife's face. 'This man's prints were, however, found on the body of Mrs Urfa and he did remove the child, Merih Urfa, from the scene.' He leaned forward, again seeking to catch Latife Emin's eye. 'He said he did this because he feared the murderer, a woman answering your description, might return to harm the child at some time.'

'And so the İstanbul police take the word of a congenital idiot.' It was said more as a statement of fact than as a question.

İkmen smiled. 'Although somewhat slow, Mr Temiz is no idiot, madam. He possesses two working eyes and he knows fear when he experiences it.'

'And the description he gave of the woman he saw in the Urfas' apartment was good,' Suleyman said. 'Blonde hair, fur coat, of which we have some fibres.'

'You questioned my sister about this, my sister who was out all night.'

'Yes, we did,' İkmen said, 'which is why you know all about the significance of your unfortunate infirmity and its resultant awkward gait.'

'What gait? What do you mean?'

'The gait Mr Temiz demonstrated in front of your sister.'

'Who,' İkmen said quickly, 'he thought was the

perpetrator until he saw her walk towards him. But then you know that already, don't you?

'But I don't have a gait, as you call it!' Latife cried, her face just a little flushed. 'I told you, if I go barefoot I always compensate using—'

'The ball of your foot. Yes,' İkmen said, 'that I understand. And I expect that under normal circumstances you do just that. In the heat of the moment, however, for instance if you were disturbed—'

'But then if, as you are suggesting, I went to Ruya Urfa's home for some reason that night, why would I go without my shoes? As I've said, I always wear them.'

Suleyman smiled. 'Except,' he said, 'if it would be foolish to do so. And, given the size and heaviness of your shoes they would make rather more noise than I imagine you would want to generate on the marble floors of the İzzet Pasa apartments. The football notwithstanding, someone might have heard you. You couldn't take that risk.'

Latife Emin pushed herself back into her chair and observed the two men harshly. 'But I would look stupid and surely attract attention if I went somewhere without any shoes. And anyway, if my feet are so noisy, why have you not noticed it before?'

'If one is not looking for a certain thing or if something appears irrelevant one does not always notice it,' İkmen said gravely. 'And, if on the night of the murder you were wearing one of your sister's nice long coats— Well, as you've said yourself, you do routinely compensate for your infirmity and so you would look quite normal, wouldn't you?'

Briefly, as the silence of the night moved into the glass-bound room, Latife Emin looked sharply down at her feet before returning her gaze once again to the faces of her interrogators.

'Your doctor is spending a great deal of time with my sister,' Latife Emin said as she tried to make herself more comfortable in her chair.

'Maybe your sister has injuries of which she was previously unaware,' İkmen said calmly, 'or perhaps Dr Halman is administering a sedative.'

'In order to keep her quiet while you interrogate me?' Latife said with a smile. 'I don't have to tell you, I suppose, that all the points you have put to me so far are speculative.'

'So you know law as well as English, do you, Miss Emin?' İkmen said. 'You're a clever lady. I wonder what other skills you possess.'

She turned away, looking out through the glass and into the garden.

'Having spoken to your gardener, Reşat,' Suleyman said, 'we are aware that a bottle of the same poison that was used to kill Mrs Urfa is on the premises.'

'Yes, in the greenhouse,' she replied smoothly. 'Do you want to see it?'

'Not yet.'

'I believe you labelled it for him.'

'Yes, Reşat can neither read nor write.'

'But you like writing for him, don't you?' İkmen said as he lit up another cigarette. 'You like to label things properly and show Reşat that you can do that.'

Latife Emin pushed one hand up into the thickness of her hair and then looked down at her watch. 'You do know,' she said, 'that if this business goes any further your so-called witness will be given a very hard time. Our lawyer can easily confound sane people, but with an idiot—'

'Oh, Mr Temiz is quite sane, I can assure you,' İkmen replied and then frowning he said, 'And besides, why should Mr Öz wish to confound Mr Temiz if, as I believe you are implying, he is not telling the truth? An "idiot", confounded or not, will become very quickly overawed and disorientated by the judicial process anyway. And if Mr Temiz has not been telling us the truth then it will come out at that stage.'

'Although it is, I must confess,' Suleyman said, to İkmen rather than Latife, 'much better if the real facts are known prior to trial.'

'Oh, yes,' his colleague replied, 'it allows the defence to really think about what mitigating circumstances might have been at work and, of course, to prepare the accused for all eventualities.'

Latife Emin laughed, quite a pleasant, trilling sound, devoid, unlike her sister's laugh, of any thickened smoker's cough.

'Oh, good try, gentlemen,' she said, 'but I know that if you had any conclusive forensic evidence I would be at the police station now instead of sitting here comfortably in my own home.' She rose to her feet. 'So, if you will excuse me . . .'

Suleyman looked across at İkmen, his face registering some panic. But İkmen, unmoving, seemed perfectly calm.

'You can of course go, madam,' he said, 'although if you are innocent, as you say, I am sure you won't mind getting dressed and coming with us to see Mr Temiz down at the station.' He smiled. 'Just to clear things up, you know. I mean in light of the fact that Mr Temiz was convinced that your sister was the assailant until he saw how she walked and considering that the two of you do look so very alike . . .'

'You may wear your shoes to travel, but we'd like you to take them off when we arrive,' Suleyman added. 'You do understand, don't you?'

She looked at both men in turn, and for quite some considerable time before answering. 'I'll get ready then,' she said decisively. 'Let's get this cleared up as quickly as possible, shall we?'

As she left the room Suleyman shot İkmen a nervous glance.

'I think I'll go and help Doctor Halman take Tansu Hanım to her room now,' the older man said, to Suleyman's ears, somewhat cryptically.

*   *   *

Tepe, who was now a little more relaxed than he had been during his silent vigil with Çöktin and the Emin brothers, offered to drive his superiors, the doctor and Tansu's sister back to the station. He liked driving Suleyman's car, when pushed it really did go. Not of course that he would be racing the BMW on this occasion. Çöktin, for his part, drove alone in Tepe's car. One didn't have to be a genius to work out that he was unhappy about the events of the evening so far. But then it had all, for him, got rather too personal – especially when the singer and her brother called, somewhat desperately, upon his loyalty as Kurd. As Tepe pulled away and down the drive, he saw two pale faces at one of the downstairs windows. The brothers.

Once on the road, Latife Emin, who was seated between Suleyman and Dr Halman in the back of the car, turned to the psychiatrist and said, 'Will my sister be all right?'

'Yes. She's had a nasty shock, but I've given her something to help her sleep which will also bring her blood pressure down.'

'She has high blood pressure?' There was genuine concern, if not panic, in her voice now.

The doctor shrugged. 'It often accompanies stress. I doubt if it is a permanent condition.'

As the car passed though the picturesque districts of İstinye and Emirgan, both wealthy areas characterised, now that the sun had set, by fashionably dressed people going out to either eat or just enjoy the cooler night air, silence entered the BMW. And although Suleyman did, from time to time, look out at the colourful scenes which flashed by his window, he also occasionally stole a glance at Latife Emin's face which, with the exception of her continually darting eyes, was quite calm. But then, he thought, why should it not be so? She had been correct back at the house. All of the evidence against her, unless Cengiz Temiz identified her was circumstantial. And besides, he couldn't imagine what her motive for killing Ruya Urfa might have been, especially in light of İkmen's belief that Latife probably knew about Erol's religion. OK, Latife had on one occasion, as far as they knew, got closer to Ruya than most people, but whether she found out then that the Urfas were Yezidis was unknown. And anyway, if Latife were as clever as İkmen seemed to think, then she would not have killed Ruya in order to free Erol for her sister. She would have known that he would never marry Tansu. So if Latife had killed Ruya, there would have to be some other motive, wouldn't there?

Heading south underneath the great supporting struts of the Fatih Bridge, the car was making rapid but safe progress towards its destination. Glancing up at the mirror İkmen, who was seated beside Tepe, looked at the reflection of Latife Emin's pale face with interest. Not a flicker. Her nerve, he had to confess, was quite remarkable. He wondered how long it would last, especially when she was confronted with Cengiz Temiz. After all, the man had nearly collapsed when he saw Tansu – a fact which, surely, Latife knew.

Half an hour later, after the car pulled into the station car park, İkmen got his answer.

Quite when İstanbulis developed the overwhelming anxiety so many of them exhibit when brought into contact with the police or the army is difficult to say. The troubled times of the 1970s when politics became both dangerous and polarised, or in the more settled eighties when the country, though quiet, lived under the yoke of martial law? Perhaps although İkmen felt personally that this phenomenon went back far further, back to the days when every man and woman lived in fear of what he or she might inadvertently say, back to the time of the despotic Sultan Abdul Hamid.

Had Abdul Hamid never reigned, it is difficult now to say just when the republic would have come about. Perhaps it would have still come into being in 1923, but living under a despotic regime for so long had certainly added impetus, the nation had been aching for change. Abdul Hamid, it is said, possessed more spies, who pandered to his paranoid fears, than any other modern monarch. There were thousands of them and he read every one of their reports. On a daily basis.

Latife Emin got out of the car quite calmly and willingly. She even, without assistance, walked purposefully over to the back entrance.

'You will be required to remove your shoes and then walk up and down in front of Mr Temiz,' İkmen said as he placed the large carrier bag he had just taken from the car boot in front of her. 'And, of course, you will have to wear this,' he added.

But it was the smell that finally did it.

When Suleyman opened the door onto that long, cell-lined corridor illuminated by the weak yellow light of night-time incarceration, a hot waft of reeking air escaped into the night. The scent of miserable unwashed bodies. Or perhaps it was the actual sight of the long blonde coat inside the bag. Latife Emin placed both her hands on the door posts and braced herself rigid inside the entrance. From the back she looked like a figure, so it occurred to İkmen, of Christ crucified.

She said just one word, 'No.'

'Having come this far, we must go on,' İkmen said as he placed one hand gently on her shoulder. 'Mr Temiz has already been prepared for your visit.'

'No!'

'Miss Emin . . .'

'And if he identifies me?'

İkmen looked at Suleyman and then back at what appeared, in the shadows, to be the deep blackness of her eyes.

'Then we will have to ask you some more questions, madam.'

Her face contorted in a way that, had İkmen been

a less well-informed individual, he could easily have mistaken for the mask of a female devil.

Gently, but with some insistence, Dr Halman took hold of Latife Emin around the waist in an attempt to steer her into the building. 'Come along,' she said, 'this needs to be—'

'No! No, I can't!'

'But then why did you—'

'I'll tell you, all right?' she cried as great, misery-fattened tears streaked down her face. 'Just take me somewhere civilised and I'll tell you anything you want to know! And here,' she kicked the bag containing the coat violently away from her, 'take that thing away from me! Take it now.'

Chapter 17

Unusually, Inspector İkmen asked that Interview Room 3 be thoroughly cleaned before he and Inspector Suleyman took the small, platinum-blonde woman into it. Quite why, the two young constables charged with this task didn't know. But then İkmen could be very odd at times, and even though they knew that officially he was not supposed to be at work, the constables did as he instructed, albeit slowly. It was not, they knew, a good idea to do otherwise.

Once Latife Emin had settled herself into her chair she spoke her name and age clearly for the purposes of the tape. She was, she claimed, fifty-two, which provoked a small flurry of speculation on İkmen's part as to the real age of her older sister, Tansu.

Suleyman, sitting directly opposite Latife, began the interrogation immediately. 'When did you first meet Ruya Urfa, Miss Emin?'

'A year ago, maybe a little more,' she replied. 'She was pregnant at the time. Sweet girl.'

'Did you talk to her?'

'Yes. My sister was pointedly ignoring her. I felt sorry for her.'

'What did you talk about?' İkmen asked as he removed his jacket in the face of the growing heat within that room. 'Can the sister of Erol's lover and his wife have anything to talk about?'

Latife smiled. 'We talked about education actually,' she said. 'Ruya was worried in case she let both Erol and her unborn child down.'

'Why? Why should she let them down?'

'She was illiterate.'

Suleyman looked knowingly at İkmen and then said, 'Did you meet her again?'

Latife Emin shrugged. 'She said that she wanted to learn to read and write and I said that I'd help her. It was her idea to keep our lessons a secret from Erol. She wanted to surprise him. He was rarely at home with her and so sometimes we would meet at her apartment and sometimes in a park or pastane.'

'You liked her?' İkmen bit his lip and then frowned.

She replied very simply, 'Yes.'

'And so when,' Suleyman said as he took a packet of cigarettes out of his pocket and then lit one, 'did your liking of Ruya Urfa turn into something more malignant?'

'Never. I always liked her, she was sweet.'

'And so . . .'

'It was only when I'd put the extra pieces together

to confirm what I had suspected some time before that I decided to, er . . .' She looked down at the floor before composing herself once again. 'I knew that Ruya would be alone on the night of the football game. I suggested we use that time to improve her skills and she agreed. I had access to Reşat's cyanide which I drizzled onto a block of almond halva, knowing that the sweet would disguise the smell.' She looked straight into İkmen's eyes as she spoke. 'She struggled for what seemed like hours even though it can only have been a few moments. I didn't intend for her to suffer.'

It had all been recited so coldly, almost like an exercise in linear thinking, that for a moment İkmen found himself quite lost within the horror of it all. If she had not spoken again almost immediately, neither of the men would have uttered a word for some time.

'When it was over I left,' she said. 'I picked up what remained of the halva, I took off my shoes so I wouldn't make any noise on the stairs and I started to go.'

'But?'

'But just as I was opening the door I remembered Ruya's pen. Anyone who knew Ruya would know that she would never use such a thing and so I went back into the kitchen to get it. If I hadn't heard the idiot man behind me when I was halfway back, I would have got it. But he gave me a fright and so I just ran.'

'Leaving the pen and Cengiz inside the apartment.'

'With Merih, yes.'

'So you must have left the front door open in order for Cengiz to . . .'

'Yes. I thought I had time and that no one was about.' She shrugged. 'I did intend to remain undetected if I could. Fate, maybe.'

'So how,' Suleyman, ever the stickler for detail, asked, 'did you get from your sister's house to İstiklal Caddesi without being seen?'

Latife Emin sighed. 'If you walk out around the back of the house and then make your way through the trees on the left-hand side, no one is going to spot you easily, especially if you wear black and cover your head. The reason I wore the particular coat of Tansu's I did was firstly because it was long and so it covered my feet and secondly because it has a black lining which I made the most of, together with a dark scarf, when I was amongst the trees. I would never normally wear such a thing. As I know you know, our security cameras contain no tape and besides, no one in our household would even think of looking for a person on foot. My siblings barely cross rooms without their cars.'

'But then you are a country girl at heart, are you not, Miss Emin?' İkmen asked wryly.

'Yes,' she smiled. 'I like the garden and the greenhouse. I'm happy to walk from the house to the road to get a taxi into the city.'

'Even with bare feet?' İkmen enquired, wincing at the thought.

'Yes,' she smiled. 'When I was young, Inspector, shoes were a rarity.'

Her smile, seemingly frozen across the mask of her face, for a moment held both men entranced. Whether this hold was benign or malignant or a little of both, neither man would have been able to say. All they knew was that for this small space in time they had shared with Latife Emin the magnetism of her personality, and however warped that might be, it had held them both in far greater thrall than her sister could have hoped to exert in ten lifetimes.

'So,' İkmen said slowly when he did finally rouse himself from his reverie, 'we know you killed Mrs Urfa, but I still don't think I understand why.'

'No,' Suleyman agreed. 'You have yet to tell us that, haven't you, Miss Emin?'

'Yes.'

İkmen shrugged. 'And so?'

'It's complicated.'

'I feel you are rather a complicated person all round,' İkmen said. 'Perhaps you're not unlike the late Marilyn Monroe in that respect, Miss Emin.'

She smiled. 'Like me, Marilyn had talents that went unrecognised, yes.' Then looking down at the floor once again, she murmured, 'We could have learned so much, Marilyn and me. Poor women.'

In an effort to catch her eye and so keep to the subject in hand, Suleyman bent his head towards Latife's, 'Miss Emin?'

'Ah.' The sight of his eyes so close to hers brought Latife to herself once again. She looked up and then leaned back into her chair. 'Ruya. Yes.' She wiped away some sweat that had gathered above her eyebrows and continued, 'In order to understand why I did . . . this, you have to know how it is with my sister. Tansu, though very generous, doesn't take kindly to people doing things she doesn't approve of. Because she thinks it is a good idea, she and I share the same hairdresser, the same couturier and the same plastic surgeon. If one of my brothers wants a car, he can have one provided it is one of which Tansu approves. If any of us forms a relationship of any sort, it is subject to the approval of Tansu and if she doesn't like that person then that person goes.'

Suleyman, his face a picture of disbelief, frowned. 'But why?'

'Because she has control of all the money,' Latife said simply. 'All she has ever wanted to do is make us all happy but, Allah forgive her, she has to do it in ways that she likes and understands. She is, in this, like a man, a father, you know. If one doesn't conform then one is thrown out into the world with nothing. And we were all born to such poverty . . .'

'But if your sister denied you something that you really wanted,' İkmen said, 'then surely killing Ruya Urfa was no punishment for that. Tansu hated the girl.'

'Yes. Like I said, you have to understand my sister and my family in order to understand why this happened. You also have to know just how clever I am. I do hope that you gentlemen have a lot of time to spare.'

'My parents were living in Adana, the biggest village in Turkey, when we were born. My father worked packing fruit. We were very poor – poor Kurds. But then just after Yılmaz was born, when I was twelve, my father died and we became still poorer.

'At the time and in fact for some few years previously, my sister Tansu who was then sixteen had been having singing lessons from an old Armenian woman who lived down by the Ulu Cami. My sister's talent had, so my mother always said, been apparent almost from birth. It is said that, before I was born, an aşik who came to our quarter in order to play and sing the songs of the people heard my sister's voice and predicted a great future for her. So the singing lessons were of great importance even when we were destitute after my father's death. The singing had to go on.

'In order to support this, my mother started working in the fields. It took her two hours to walk to her work and then two hours to come home again. Galıp, who was about eight, left school in order to shine shoes. I left school too. Suddenly my classes in mathematics, Turkish, history and all the other subjects I had come to love stopped while I stayed at home raising my brother Yılmaz. But still the singing lessons continued. At the end of every week Mother, Galıp and Tansu herself, who was now singing occasionally in dubious gazinos, would put all their money into a cup and take out what was needed for various costs. The money for Mrs Nisanyan, the singing teacher, would always come out first.

'But later on that year, my mother's hopes for a glittering career for my sister nearly came to an end. Tansu, who had become fascinated by a married man she met at one of her engagements, became pregnant. You have, I imagine, heard about her son, whom she thought she had paid off years ago. But . . . So then I went off to work in the fields while Mother tended the baby. Tansu went on as before.

'With absolutely no dowry money for either of us, not to mention the loss of my sister's virginity, the idea of either of us marrying was ridiculous. But as Tansu became more and more noted in Adana, and her engagements got bigger and more prestigious, things did start to improve. As the most literate member of our family, I even wrote some lyrics for her, suggesting that she might like to get one of her musician friends to set them to music. But she never did. Of course when she first came to İstanbul in 1970, she was more prostitute than singer. She met her manager, Ferhat Göktepe, in some Karaköy brothel. Not that he didn't know a good thing when he saw it. As soon as he heard her sing he moved his attentions from her body to her throat and from there the Tansu legend was born.

'The following year, when she had made enough

money, Tansu sent for Mother and the rest of us, except for her son, of course. One of my aunts raised him from thereon. Tansu had just a small apartment in Beşiktaş in those days, but it was like a palace to us. She even had a radio on which I used to listen to the BBC. Between that and talking to some of the local children who were having lessons, I became quite good at English. I even thought that perhaps one day I might be able to have private tuition and apply to university somewhere – Tansu had always said that if she ever made a lot of money she would give us all what we wanted. After all, we had all made sacrifices for her.

'But as her career gathered pace, so did her commitments. Records, radio interviews, television, films, tours. We moved to the house in Yeniköy which was a place she rarely came to in those days, what with her engagements and her many lovers. But with regard to us, she paid for everything. If one of my brothers wanted new clothes, she had a tailor come and measure him up and within a few days suits would arrive. Whenever she bought clothes for herself, she would buy an identical set for me. She was very, very generous, we wanted for nothing. So much so, in fact, that for a considerable number of years I held off from asking her about tuition for university. It seemed so ungrateful in view of all she had done.

'And then one day I was thirty. Thirty years old, still interested in everything, like a child. Reading, reading, reading in order to educate myself – painfully aware of my own shortcomings. But with no money of my own, I had no choice but to ask Tansu to help me with my ambitions. I was sure that she would.

'I was wrong.

'"If you go to university at your age, everyone will laugh at you and at me," she said when I put it to her for the first and only time. "And besides, while I keep you, you won't need to know anything, will you?"

'"But Tansu," I said, "I want to do something with my life. I want to achieve . . ."

'"Well, why don't you write some nice new songs for me?" my sister said, as she in effect sent me on my way. "That will give you a great achievement in your life."

'And so I did just that. I both hated and loved my sister because of it and I exacted a small revenge upon her by frequently using words I knew she would not understand. But then her interpretation of words was never very good anyway. The sweetness of her tone and her large breasts are what Tansu Hanım has always been about. The songs were always credited to her anyway.

'So years came and went, and as my sister's career began to fade, so did my chances of finding a man to love. Yılmaz married briefly back in the 1980s, but his wife never did get on with Tansu and so that didn't last. By the time Erol Urfa came into my sister's life, my brothers and I were idle, uneducated and useless. We were like soft, soporific odalisques. Fresh from the countryside, this young man woke me up in ways he could never have imagined.

'I suppose that in retrospect I was a little in love with Erol myself. Perhaps he represented the kind of man I could have had, had things been different. Tansu, of course grateful, treated him like a Sultan sometimes and like her personal slave at others. She would still pick up young boys on the streets on occasion too, like she did the night that Ruya died. Not that she has ever been caught doing this. I, meanwhile, just did sad, spinsterly things like look up where Erol came from on the map – some nowhere place up near the Iraqi border. I have always been interested in my country and its various regions but this area seemed to have little to recommend it. With the exception of the devil worshippers.

'I read so many things, some true and some false, that at times they made my head hurt. Some books accused the Yezidis of human sacrifice, rape, infanticide, while others said that they were simply misunderstood people who worshipped a deity called the Peacock Angel. They were Kurds, like me, but Kurds who would not eat chicken or wear blue or marry anyone other than their own kind; Kurds who lifted up their eyes to pray not to Allah, but to the setting sun. And it was not long after this that I first saw Erol standing in the trees to the side of our house, his arms raised in honour of the great golden ball setting over the Bosphorus.

'I started to think and to watch. And no, Erol didn't eat chicken, he didn't wear blue, but . . . It was only when I started to include references to the peacock as lover in the lyrics that Tansu passed off as her own that I knew. His expression as she innocently and without any trace of intelligent thought sang those words . . . He knew she couldn't know, and her thoughtless words confused and confounded him.

'I, meanwhile, remained silent. While Tansu screamed on about how Erol would marry her in an instant if Ruya were not around, I thought about how much my sister had become like a child – and about how devastating it would be for her should something happen to Ruya and Erol then not marry her. It's not, as we know, good to be known as a devil worshipper and so Erol would, I knew, never tell Tansu why he would have to return to his village and marry another child-woman instead of her. Tansu would just simply be denied what she most wanted, seemingly on the whim of another. Just like I had been. Then she would hurt, just like me. Then she would become that sad, old odalisque that I have been for so many years. Then I would be content, and so I am.'

A few moments of stunned silence passed until İkmen eventually said, 'But didn't your sister, once she knew that you were responsible for Ruya Urfa's death, try to get you out of the city in her car?'

Latife Emin smiled. 'Oh, yes. She loves me. She was prepared to deceive you for me. She thought that

I'd killed Ruya in order to free up Erol for her. She was very grateful.'

'But . . .'

'She's going to be really very badly hurt when she learns the truth.' She smiled again, broadly.

Chapter 18

Neither İkmen nor Suleyman saw the sun rise over the sparkling waters of the Bosphorus that following morning as the older man helped the younger compose his report on the Emin affair. And as the heat of the day started to build, both of them from time to time spared some thought for the bitter woman who now sat somewhere far beneath their offices, down in the cells. A woman who, just like the odalisques of old to whom she frequently referred, was going to spend the rest of her life amongst other impotent, lonely women.

'We're burying Kleopatra Polycarpou today,' İkmen said as he wiped a tired hand across his features.

'Not the nicest thing to have to deal with after what we went through last night,' his equally exhausted colleague observed.

'No. I was going to ask Sınan to accompany me, but now I'm not so sure.' İkmen chewed thoughtfully on his bottom lip. 'In view of what we've learnt about the Emin sisters I'm wondering whether I ought to get Bulent scrubbed up and take him. Show him I know he exists.'

Suleyman smiled. 'Trying to prevent any nastiness between your two boys in the future perhaps?'

'If Zelfa Halman hadn't postulated such an idea some time ago I would have viewed the Emins as a one-off, but she did and it has made me think. Is she still around here somewhere, by the way?'

'Who? Dr Halman?'

'Yes.'

'No. But I'm meeting her for something to eat after I've spoken to Çöktin,' he looked at his watch, 'in about an hour. You're welcome to join us.'

'Thanks, but no,' İkmen said with a sigh. 'I really must wash and then find something to wear for this funeral.'

A knock at the door interrupted their conversation.

'Come,' Suleyman called and the door opened to admit a very dishevelled İsak Çöktin.

Upon seeing the young man, İkmen said, 'Ah, do you want me to—'

Suleyman held up a hand. 'No. Your input could be valuable here.' And then turning towards Çöktin, he said, 'Sit down.'

Çöktin took hold of a chair that had been leaning against the wall, placed it in front of Suleyman's desk and sat down. İkmen, who was sitting at what was usually Çöktin's desk, put his pen down and looked across at the young man.

'The events of last night,' Suleyman began gravely, 'have, as you know, thrown up some very difficult issues for some of the protagonists in this case.'

'Yes, sir.'

'Miss Emin, although she has now confessed to Ruya Urfa's murder, has raised certain points which her defence team will, no doubt, wish to bring to light in order to, to some extent, discredit those she has harmed.'

'Like what?' the white-faced young man asked, not for a moment raising his eyes from the floor.

'Like the fact that Mr Urfa and his late wife are Yezidis,' İkmen said with a bluntness Suleyman probably would not have employed.

Çöktin turned to look at him. 'But why are you speaking to me about this, sir?'

'Oh, come on, Mickey!' İkmen said with a small if exasperated chuckle. 'You've never got as close to anyone as you got to Urfa. I won't even go into how you have knowledge about eunuchs in Arab countries but suffice to say, Dr Halman was the only other person I could find who knew about that and she studies religion for fun. Come on!'

Çöktin lowered his head down even further on his chest and cleared his throat.

Suleyman looked across at İkmen and sighed. 'Listen, Çöktin,' he said, 'unless, somehow, Latife Emin knows about you then what passes between us here will go no further.'

'She knows nothing because there is nothing to know!' Çöktin suddenly became almost violently agitated. Then reaching into the pocket of his jacket he took out his identity card which he held up for both men to see. 'Look here,' he cried. 'Religion: Muslim. Official, on my card. What more do you want?'

'Çöktin—'

'Erol's bears exactly the same words,' İkmen said with a shrug. 'We all know how easy it is—'

'If Mr Urfa says that his is false then that is his business,' Çöktin said, still holding his card up, 'but mine is not. And besides, quite why you would think that one of these devil worshippers would want to be in the police force, I can't imagine. If you worship Shaitan then you're an evil person quite at odds with the law.'

'On the surface, yes,' İkmen agreed, 'but if they are not evil but simply misunderstood . . .' He shrugged again. 'But your protestations are noted even if, as we all know, they are rather too vehement.'

'Believe it or not, we were just looking out for your interests, Çöktin,' Suleyman said.

'I couldn't care less what a man's religion might be,' İkmen added. 'I don't have one myself and so—'

'But most people do care.'

'You have an excellent record,' Suleyman said, looking the younger man in the eye, in so far as he could. 'There is no question of your being disciplined or dismissed. It was simply that if Latife Emin knew—'

'She knows nothing about me, I hardly spoke to her.'

'And Erol? Would he have spoken to her about you?'

Çöktin twisted nervously in his chair, knotting and unknotting his fingers as he moved. 'Well, not about my religion, obviously. Why would he, being what he is, want to speak to a Muslim woman about a Muslim man she barely knows?'

İkmen smiled. 'Well, that's all right then, isn't it?'

'Yes,' Suleyman agreed also with a smile, if forced, upon his face. 'I should, I imagine, let you go home and get some rest now. You must be exhausted.'

'Yes. Thank you, sir.' Çöktin rose quickly to his feet. It was obvious to all concerned that he was anxious to leave.

'I'll see you tomorrow, then,' Suleyman said as he watched Çöktin move towards the door.

'Yes, sir.'

'Goodbye, Mickey Çöktin,' İkmen called out as the young man closed the door behind him.

And then there was silence. İkmen looked across at Suleyman who, although seemingly busy shuffling papers, was actually waiting for his colleague to open up some sort of debate on what had just passed. İkmen obliged.

He wiped the sweat from his brow onto the stained cuff of his shirt and said, 'Do you believe him?'

'I don't know,' Suleyman replied. 'Do you?'

'No. But then in view of the fact that Erol never actually told Latife Emin what he was, it is highly unlikely he would have mentioned Çöktin to her. And anyway, with aged parents and an unmarried sister to support, Mickey Çöktin probably made a rational decision when he came in here and lied to us. I mean, how would you feel if people thought you ran around naked at midnight and ate the flesh of newborn infants?'

Suleyman smiled. 'I wouldn't be very happy about it.'

'Mmm. Especially considering that the more lurid stories about the Yezidis are, in all probability, complete nonsense.'

'But prejudices against them still exist,' Suleyman said, throwing a cigarette across at İkmen and then lighting up himself. 'And I must admit that it does feel odd to actually have one on the force.'

'No stranger than having someone whose mother could see into the future,' İkmen said, wryly smiling at this dig at himself. 'Which reminds me, I must get away from here if I'm to see the last of my mother's clients bid farewell to this world.'

'Any idea how Madame might have killed the eunuch yet?' Suleyman asked.

'Dr Sarkissian thinks he may have been stabbed.' İkmen moved slowly to his feet and then stretched his arms above his head and yawned. 'Although quite why she would want to do such a thing to that poor emasculated creature we shall probably never know.'

'Perhaps the eunuch had some other woman in his sights,' Suleyman said with a smile.

'Well, I can't imagine why *that* would have bothered Kleopatra,' İkmen replied tartly.

Spreading his long fingers out across his desk in what appeared to be an attempt to distract himself from the topic, Suleyman said, 'You know that in the old households it was always said that a eunuch could often satisfy a woman like no normal man?'

'What?' İkmen, his face creased into sharp lines of confusion, attempted but failed to look into his colleagues now shifting gaze. 'What do . . .'

'To say anything more would cause me tremendous embarrassment, Çetin,' the younger man said as he moved uncomfortably in his seat. 'If you think about it for a while I'm sure that the light of truth will eventually dawn.'

'Oh, will it?' İkmen said. And then, as things did indeed come into focus, he reddened just a little and mumbled, 'Ah, yes, but of course, um . . .'

'So shall I see you later?' Suleyman inquired as he watched İkmen remove his jacket somewhat timidly from the back of Çöktin's chair.

'Yes, this afternoon.'

'Good,' Suleyman smiled. 'I couldn't have finished this case without you, you know.'

'Yes, you could,' İkmen said, moving towards the door of his colleague's office. 'It would have taken you longer, but you would have done it.'

And then with a smile he was gone.

*   *   *

The Hippodrome Tea Garden was almost completely full when Zelfa Halman arrived for her, albeit flexible, appointment with Mehmet Suleyman. Dressed in a very eye-catching dress of red and black, the psychiatrist looked, to Orhan Tepe at least, like a woman who had been home and chosen her ensemble very carefully. He did not imagine she could have had very much sleep, and as she came towards him in response to his shout of recognition, he could see that her eyes were heavy with fatigue.

'I hate it when it's as hot as this,' she said as she slumped down opposite Tepe who was seated at a table facing the Hippodrome itself. 'I wonder where it's all going to end – when my blood's going to start to boil in my veins.'

'Miss Emin must be very uncomfortable down in the cells,' Tepe said as he beckoned one of the waiters towards him. 'What would you like to drink, Doctor?'

'Coke would be good.'

He ordered her drink plus another peach tea for himself before launching once again into the subject of Latife Emin. 'So, I mean, er, will you, um, have to see Miss Emin, professionally, Doctor, or . . .' Although he liked her, Tepe's memories of various of his dubious relatives always made him rather uncomfortable around Zelfa Halman.

'No.' She put a cigarette between her lips and lit it. 'Not from what I've seen of her. You don't have to be crazy to perform an act of spite.'

Tepe frowned. 'Yes, but most people don't usually kill innocent people out of spite, do they?'

'No, but I expect some of us would like to,' she said with a smile. 'And besides, I think she showed amazing restraint to have left it so long.'

'What do you mean?'

'I think that I would probably have stabbed the lovely Tansu and then hurled her into the Bosphorus years ago.'

'Oh.' Tepe laughed briefly before becoming grave once again. 'Well, yes, that I could understand. But to kill Ruya Urfa just to get at her sister . . .'

'Latife Emin is a clever woman,' the doctor said. She smiled up at the waiter who had arrived with their drinks. 'Erol is, was, whatever, probably Tansu's last chance with a younger man. So if Latife set her sister's mind against him then that might well have hurt Tansu for the rest of her life. After all, had Latife's crime gone undetected, then Tansu would never have understood why Erol couldn't marry her and that would have really stung.'

'She's still not going to be able to marry him though, is she? I mean,' he leaned forward in order to whisper, 'if he's one of those then . . .'

'No. Yezidis don't marry out. This won't do a lot for Erol's career either.'

Orhan Tepe sniffed. 'Well, if he's one of those he doesn't deserve a career. They do disgusting things, those people.'

'Oh, bollocks,' Zelfa Halman exploded, briefly slipping back into her native tongue. 'Yezidis don't really rape everything in sight and eat their own young, you know! They're not evil or—'

'But they worship Shaitan!'

Zelfa Halman took a long gulp from her glass before she said, 'Their own conception of him, yes. But in their canon Shaitan has been restored to goodness by God and so the idea that they are evil is preposterous. Anyway, we don't *know* that people will hold it against him. I like to think the Turkish public are more intelligent than that.'

'I still don't like it,' Tepe said darkly. 'It makes me feel uncomfortable.'

'Well, that's your problem,' the doctor replied. She leaned back in order to fan her hot face and caught sight of Suleyman. She waved to him.

As he walked towards the table, the tired young inspector smiled. 'I hadn't realised it was quite so hot,' he said fanning his body with the edges of his jacket.

Zelfa Halman passed her glass of Coke over to him with a ghost of a smile.

Tepe who like so many of his fellows possessed more than a sneaking suspicion as to what existed between this pair, started to move up and away from his chair.

'Oh, are you going?' Zelfa asked.

'I'd better,' Tepe said looking across at Suleyman. 'Sir.'

'You don't have to go, Tepe.'

'I think I'd better,' the younger man replied. 'Reports and . . .'

'Well, don't bother to pay when you go,' Zelfa said with a smile. 'I'll pay for your tea.'

'Oh, well, er, thank you, er . . .'

'It's OK.'

As Tepe threaded his way out of the tea garden, Suleyman slipped into what had been his seat. 'Hello,' he said to Zelfa sitting opposite him.

'Hello.'

Although weary, her face was set in an expression not without humour. Suleyman, consequently, smiled.

'I haven't come to beg,' he said, placing her glass carefully back in front of her, 'but if you have decided not to return to Ireland . . .'

Zelfa Halman leaned forward, a quizzical expression crossing her face. 'Yes?'

Suleyman sighed with what appeared to be some effort. 'Well, I would quite like to, sort of, well . . .'

'I'm not going to help you with this, Mehmet,' she said, just the tinge of a twinkle beginning in her eyes. 'If you want something from me, you're going to have to ask for it.'

'Well . . .'

'Yes?'

He leaned forward across the table and took one of her hands in his. She did not resist which, he thought, was a good sign.

'Now that Cengiz Temiz has been returned to his family and—'

With, to Suleyman, quite frightening rapidity, Zelfa's expression changed and she pulled her hand roughly from his. 'If this is about that report—'

'No, no, no! No!' he said, almost desperately, 'this is about, well, it's about you and me and about how now that I, er . . .'

'Mehmet,' she said as she replaced her fingers slowly under his, 'if this is about your wanting to take me out for a meal accompanied by large amounts of alcohol and dancing . . .'

'Yes.'

She smiled, 'Well, I might think about it.'

'Oh.' As the register of his voice dropped, so did his gaze. Suleyman stared at the top of the table with deep and obvious disappointment.

Zelfa Halman viewed him wryly. What a child her dashing young prince could be at times. And how delicious it would be to string out her torture of him for just a little bit longer. But then, possibly because her name was Zelfa and not Latife, she could not allow her spite to have rein over her any longer.

'Oh, OK then, yes,' she said with a dismissive wave of one hand.

His head literally sprang up from his musings. 'You mean it?' he said, looking even more like a little boy than he had before.

She laughed. 'Yes, I mean it, I do!'

He reached over and, despite the crowds all around them, Mehmet Suleyman pulled Zelfa Halman's face towards his and kissed her hard upon the lips. When he did finally release her from his embrace he saw that she was smiling.

'So,' she said, after a somewhat breathless pause.

'To return to Cengiz Temiz . . .'

'Well, he's back with his family again, as I said. But he'll have to give evidence when the case comes to court,' Suleyman replied, a small frown now disrupting his previously ecstatic features. 'After all, he did technically take the Urfa baby unlawfully.'

'But then surely his lack of capacity to reason in the normal way will protect him from actual charges, won't it?' Zelfa asked.

Suleyman sighed. 'It should do, after all he didn't hurt Merih, did he? And with Sevan Avedykian on his side he shouldn't have any trouble. Although, as to whether his parents will ever let him out alone again, I think the future there may be less certain.'

Zelfa looked down at the table and murmured. 'Poor Cengiz. All he ever really wanted was a little love.' She looked up at him and smiled.

Suleyman smiled back. 'Lucky, aren't we?' he said softly.

She took one of his hands and squeezed it tight. 'Are you saying . . .'

'That I love you? Yes,' he said simply. 'Yes, I think I do. And you? What do you feel?'

Zelfa looked briefly at the other people around them before she said, 'Well, I think I've a lot more passion in my soul than any of this lot, don't you?'

'Yes, but that doesn't answer my question, does it, Zelfa?'

'No.'

Frowning now, he asked again, 'And you, your feelings? Well?'

She sighed and then, once again, slowly smiled. 'Oh, I love you right enough, Mehmet,' she said. 'Even though it scares me to death.'

And then, with uncharacteristic urgency, she took a handkerchief from the pocket of her dress and dabbed at the moisture that was collecting at the corners of her eyes.

Although Cohen left the confines of the Aya Triyada Kilisesi as soon as Kleopatra Polycarpou's funeral was at an end, İkmen, who was indeed accompanied by a moodily awkward Bulent, remained behind to talk to the old woman's priest, Father Yiannis.

'Kleopatra was never an easy woman, Mr İkmen,' the cleric said as he walked with the Turk and his son towards the front gate. 'And, in all honesty, I did know that she was having difficulties with Murad Ağa prior to his disappearance all those years ago. Not, of course, that I ever imagined she might have killed him.'

'What sort of difficulties?' İkmen said, as he lit the cigarette that was dangling from his lips.

Father Yiannis sighed. 'Well, apparently, the eunuch or so she told me, was being unfaithful to her. I know that sounds extraordinary but—'

İkmen smiled. 'Not quite as odd as you might think, Father.' And then lowering his voice in order to prevent his son from hearing, he said, 'A friend of mine who comes from an old Ottoman family assures me that some of these creatures were not unskilled, shall we say, in the bedroom.'

'Oh,' the priest reddened. 'Oh, I see, er . . . That would, I suppose, explain, in part—'

'Precisely.'

'Ah, well. But tragic anyway. And what with the poor man being so far from his native lands.' He sighed. 'There will not be a soul to claim his corpse now.'

İkmen frowned. 'But I thought that Murad was Turkish. At least I always took if for granted.

'No, actually,' the priest said gravely, 'he was of your mother's race. An Albanian. When he "left" all those years ago, I assumed it was to return to Albania.' And then he added, slightly bitterly, 'The old empire never emasculated its own, you know. Your Ottoman friend, at least, should know that.'

İkmen shrugged. 'I guess my mother would have known him then.'

'I should imagine so,' Father Yiannis replied. 'But it was all a very long time ago now, Mr İkmen.' Nodding in the direction of Bulent, he added, 'We must look to

395

the future and, especially, to the young.'

Noticing that Bulent was now squinting in the harsh sunlight, İkmen wordlessly passed his sunglasses over to his son who put them on.

'Yes, that's true, Father,' İkmen said, smiling.

'You do know, of course, that the haman has been left to Mrs Arda?'

'Semra?' İkmen shrugged. 'Well, that's good. Whether she sells it or gets it going again, it means that the extra money will enable that daughter of hers to leave the streets.'

The priest frowned. 'I understand that Mina is still in your cells right now though, Mr İkmen?'

'Yes,' İkmen said gravely. 'We cannot overlook attempted abduction charges. I mean she did intend to keep that child even after she discovered her identity. And there are drug charges too, involving her pimp who is a foreign national. It's complicated.'

'When she is released she will however have somewhere to go, though,' the priest said.

'Which is good, yes.' İkmen smiled.

'Yes,' Father Yiannis agreed. Then he shook hands with both İkmen and Bulent and returned to the confines of his church. The İkmens, for their part, walked the short distance back up onto İstiklal Caddesi and then turned left.

'Do you want some tea before we go home?' İkmen asked his son as they walked past a tram that was headed for Taksim Square.

'No, I want to get this suit off,' Bulent replied in his customary mumbling tone.

'It looks good on you. Smart,' his father observed.

'It's Orhan's.'

'Yes. But if you would like one of your own . . .'

'Suits aren't really my style.'

This effectively killed the conversation and the two continued walking in silence, the tall son slouching along in front of his much shorter father. İkmen tried to divert himself from his son's mood by looking into the windows of shops and restaurants as he went but eventually he felt that he had to speak again, he had to try. In spite of the heat and his own lack of fitness, İkmen speeded up until he drew level with Bulent's bowed shoulders.

'What *is* your problem, Bulent?' he asked, attempting but failing to catch his son's eye.

'What do you mean?'

'I mean, why is it that you can behave so well with others, like you did in the church just now, and yet when it comes to myself and your mother and indeed anyone who has authority over you—'

'I don't want to talk about it.'

'No, you never do.'

'Look,' the boy turned to face his father now, an almost violent expression crossing his eyes. 'You're not at work so don't try to come on to me like a policeman, OK?'

'I'm not.'

'You are.'

Resisting, for once, the urge to fly into a rage and then justify it with his authority over his son, tactics which so far had not worked, İkmen took a deep, calming breath before he spoke again.

'So is it my job? Does it bother you that I'm a policeman? Is it that I'm an establishment figure?'

The boy just shrugged.

'I mean that could explain your drinking and—'

'No.'

'Then is it your older brothers and sister?' İkmen asked, now quite desperate for some sort of explanation from his son. 'Are you jealous of their achievements? Do you feel that you have to try and live up to them?'

'What, be a doctor?' Bulent sneered. 'Not likely!'

'Well what than?'

'I don't want to talk about this any more.' Thrusting his hands deep into the pockets of his brother's suit, Bulent walked off rapidly.

'Bulent!'

Once again İkmen found himself chasing, breathlessly, after this miserable boy – a boy who, if he wasn't too careful, was going to cause his father to have a heart attack.

'Bulent!'

The boy stopped and then rounded on his father with an expression of such naked animosity that for a moment İkmen was rendered speechless.

'What?'

'Bulent . . .' And then he saw that a trickle of water was dripping from underneath the sunglasses he had given his son. 'Bulent, are you c—'

'No!' He turned away quickly in order, it was easy for İkmen to see, to wipe the tears from his eyes.

'Oh yes you are,' İkmen said and then quickly changing to a far older strategy, he firmly took hold of his son's arm and steered him into a small and shady side street.

'Now, what's the matter, Bulent?' he said sternly. 'No more games, no more guessing. Just tell me what is going on in your brain and tell me now.'

'I can't.'

'Yes, you *can*!' his father said, watching all the time to check that the small group of headscarfed women opposite did not take too much notice of them.

'Why do you have a problem with authority? Why can't you keep the simplest job? You're not stupid! Why are you drinking?'

'Well, if I'm going to die in the very near future then why not!'

For a moment the world and everything in it came to a halt as İkmen attempted to come to terms with what his son had just said.

'Die?'

'Well, I'm going to the army soon, aren't I?' Bulent spat venomously. 'Same thing!' He dropped his voice. 'And if I don't get killed then I'll go mad like Yusuf

Cohen and that terrifies me. As soon as I heard about him I just lost it, you know. It's not that I'm afraid to fight because I'm not. But I don't want to kill people. Some of my friends' families came from the east. Why should I want to kill them?'

'Bulent, you don't even know where you'll be sent yet. And anyway, it's not for a couple of years. You might not—'

'Dad, I'm not going in as an officer. Boys like me are just gun fodder.'

İkmen put his hand gently on his son's shoulder and led him over to a small table that stood in front of a tiny kebabci. 'Let's have some ayran and cool down a bit,' he said.

After settling Bulent into a seat, İkmen went up to the window and bought the drinks. When he returned, his son was looking disconsolately at the ground.

'Bulent,' İkmen said, sitting down opposite the boy, 'service is, I fear, just part of life. I did it, your brother Sınan has served . . .'

'Sınan went in as an officer.'

'Because he has a university degree, yes.'

Bulent downed his ayran in one gulp. 'Some boys get bought out and I did think of asking Uncle Halil to do that for me but then I thought that was unfair. He's always bankrolling this family. And anyway he would think I was a coward. Others disappear to other countries, but . . . but I couldn't do that because of your job. How would it look if a senior policeman's son ran away from his duty?'

İkmen sighed. So this was it, was it? All this trouble was about Bulent wanting to live a little before he died – if he died. İkmen could not even begin to think about an easy answer to Bulent's conundrum. The boy was right, if he deserted it would look bad for İkmen himself and with all the mouths he had to feed, that was not a prospect he wanted to face. Not that he would express this to his son. And then Bulent's thoughts about the action that was not really a war, that raged year in and year out in the eastern provinces, accorded with İkmen's own opinions. Although he would never have voiced his thoughts in public and despite the fact that İkmen believed that a lot of the PKK fighters were just common murderers, he knew some Kurdish nationals, liked many and was naturally averse to killing anyone or anything. But none of this was any help to his son.

'If it's any comfort,' he said as he placed his half-finished ayran back onto the table, 'I don't think that you're a coward. I think your aversion to killing people is commendable.' He smiled. 'I know I've never been a very good example to you with regard to bad habits, getting you to go and buy alcohol for me and . . . But your mother and I must have done something right to make you think like this. When you kill, even for the security of your country, you have to live with that knowledge for the rest of your life and that's not easy.'

For the first time that day, Bulent smiled. 'Thanks for understanding, Dad.'

'Not that I can help you at all,' İkmen said with a shrug. 'I can't.'

'If I knew I was going to be drafted to Cyprus, I'd be OK,' Bulent said, frowning down at the ground once again.

'As you know, my son, I am not a religious man,' İkmen said, placing a warm hand on his son's shoulder, 'but perhaps just this once we should trust to Allah or whoever or whatever controls the universe. There is nothing we can do but wait and see and, as your mother would say, İnşallah you will go to Cyprus.'

'Yes.' Bulent took his cigarettes out of his pocket and offered one to his father. 'Sman says that as Turks we sit uneasily in this world. We live so much like the Europeans now, well in the city we do anyway, and yet we still need our women to be chaste, we still go out to fight in what Sınan calls a tribal war.'

İkmen, declining on principle his teenage son's cigarettes in favour of his own, lit up and smiled. 'Sınan is right and not so right at the same time. Even in civilised England, they engage in their own tribal war in Northern Ireland. Dr Halman can tell you something about that if you wish. But there are no absolutes anywhere, Bulent, absolutes are impossible.

In this so-called Turkish city of ours we live alongside a lot of anomalies. A so-called enemy can join and care about the forces of law, a Greek can marry a castrated relic of the old Ottoman system.'

'And then kill him.'

'For her own reasons, yes. But the human condition, whether one is Turkish, American, Greek or whatever, is nothing if not entirely idiosyncratic. And when your papers arrive to call you to arms, you and you alone will have to make a decision about that. And you will have to do that without reference to either me or your family or even your country. It's your life, Bulent, and whatever values inform your soul will be all that can and will count. And whatever your decision, I will always love you, just as my father always loved me, even after I joined what he always liked to call the "fucking bastard" police.'

But Bulent didn't speak after that. Just a tiny breeze was blowing up from the Bosphorus now and he had closed his eyes in order to enjoy fully the coolness on his body and face. Responding to that which all humans share, the need for a moment of peace.

'Oh,' Mehmet Suleyman said as he approached his office door and saw the figure of Erol Urfa standing in front of it. 'Tansu Hanım is downstairs, did you come—'

'Tansu is not too interested in seeing me right now,' the singer said with a sad smile.

'Ah. I understand.'

'No, you don't.' Erol shrugged. 'But then why should you.'

Embarrassed by what he now saw as a faux pas on his part, Suleyman opened the door and showed his guest into his office.

'I just came to assure you that as soon as I have buried Ruya, I will come back to the city.' He placed a small piece of paper covered in rather childish writing on Suleyman's desk. 'Here is my address.'

Suleyman took the paper and glanced at it. 'You will have to report to the station in Hakkari. If you can let me know when you are going, I can inform them.'

'Yes.'

The cacophony of honking car horns from outside the window seemed to grow louder as the two men were silent for a few moments, until Erol said, 'When the trial is over I will take Merih, my parents and sisters to Germany.'

Suleyman frowned.

'I am told that Shaitan has a different shape there,' the singer continued. His tone was one of sadness rather than bitterness.

'Will you sing there?'

'I have made more money in three years than most men make in their whole lives and fame, for me, has become . . . difficult.'

'I see.'

'We are all leaving our traditional homes now,

Inspector, whether they're in this country, Iraq or Syria.' He got up and walked thoughtfully towards the window. 'My kind. We need to be where peacocks mean nothing to men, where people worship only money.'

'Do you not fear that you may become something of an oddity in those lands? Don't you think you might be even more misunderstood?'

Erol turned, the light from the window behind him throwing his face into a darkened pit of shadows. 'I live in hope that questions about a man's religion are questions that the Europeans do not ask.'

Suleyman looked doubtful. 'I think that they do, Mr Urfa. I think that despite what you might think you believe about their overt materialism, such fundamental differences do have meaning for them too. It was, after all, the Europeans who devised the Court of the Inquisition.'

Erol frowned 'The what?'

'Many centuries ago,' Suleyman explained, 'the Christians in Europe devised a special type of court to try anyone suspected of consorting with demons. They tortured, burnt and hung tens of thousands of people.'

'But not now. They don't do that now.'

'No.' Suleyman smiled. 'No, they don't. But what I'm saying to you, Mr Urfa, is that they did. They have a history, just like us, of fear and prejudice against that which they do not understand. And just because they do not feel this way now, perhaps, that doesn't mean that they will not do so in the future. Things change.'

'You're saying I will never be safe, wherever I go?'

'With the cultural ground, metaphorically, shifting beneath our feet every minute of the day, who amongst us is safe?' Suleyman smiled. 'My family, Mr Urfa, once commanded vast armies. We were Ottomans, we ruled the rest of you.' He sighed. 'But now I am a Turk just like everybody else and, like a Turk, I must sometimes decide whether I am going to eat today or just simply smoke a few cigarettes. No one is safe from change, Mr Urfa, no one.'

Tansu Hanım stood in silence as Orhan Tepe noted the time, 3.15 p.m. and date, August 16th, of her entrance into the cells.

'Is Latife Hanım prepared?' he asked the duty officer who was, though responsive, almost dozing under the influence of the extreme heat.

'Yes.'

'Right.' And then turning to the white-faced woman at his back he said, 'If you'd like to come this way, madam.'

Wordlessly the woman, who was now clad in a very simple black dress, her face almost devoid of all make-up, followed him. For his part, had Orhan Tepe not known that this visitor was indeed Turkey's own true darling, he would never have guessed. Not only was she dressed much more simply than she had been the previous night, she also looked older, much older.

There were two sets of locks to get through in order to gain entry to the festering concrete box in which Latife Emin was now incarcerated. After checking that his charge was ready for her visit via the observation flap in the door, Tepe opened first the top and then the bottom set of locks.

'I'll be outside,' he said as he ushered the woman in black into the presence of her counterpart in grey.

'That won't be necessary,' the singer said, her eyes fixed hard upon those of her sister.

Tepe closed the door on the two silent, standing women. The crackle of fury in the air was so tangible as to be almost audible. But Tepe left them anyway – stood outside with a cigarette and looked up and down at the grim cell walls.

Ten minutes later when he came to tell Tansu that her time was up, the two women were still standing exactly where they had been when he left them. Silent, stone-like, the only movement between them the monstrously developed feeling of fury that, Tepe felt, would utterly crush and destroy both the women, and him if he didn't leave soon.

Quite what had passed between them neither Tepe nor anyone else would ever know. Or indeed want to know.

Night Mares

Manda Scott

Dr Nina Crawford – driven, dedicated, a survivor – runs Glasgow University's prestigious veterinary hospital. But she's losing her grip – on her operating theatre, on her surgeon's skills, and on her mind. Horses are dying of the highly infectious *E. Coli*, and nothing she can do can control it. Now she is spiralling into the depths that led her, years before, to attempt suicide.

Kellen Stewart is Nina's friend and therapist and when her horse needs emergency surgery she is suddenly part of Nina's tragic dilemma. And soon it becomes clear that it's not only horses' lives that are being threatened . . .

'Even more accomplished than the acclaimed *Hen's Teeth*' *Sunday Telegraph*

'Gripping and topical' *Good Housekeeping*

'A familiar landscape warps into terror . . . something epic in this struggle between horse and human . . . Horses, sex and death create [a] potent cocktail' Helen Dunmore, *The Times*

0 7472 5880 5

HEADLINE

Murmuring the Judges

Quintin Jardine

In Edinburgh's old Parliament House, an armed robbery trial is about to take a macabre turn. While the lawyers tussle over the evidence, the judge suddenly collapses in mortal agony – the victim of an apparent heart attack.

For Deputy Chief Constable Bob Skinner, with his life finally back on track after the near-collapse of his marriage, the last thing he needs is to be faced with the most baffling case of his career. But as the wave of brutal robberies continues, it emerges that Lord Archergait's death may have been murder – and he's not the only judge whose life is in danger.

With a gang of ruthless killers still at large, it's down to Skinner to piece together a puzzle of sinister complexity.

'Deplorably readable' *Guardian*

'Captures Edinburgh beautifully' *Edinburgh Evening News*

'Remarkably assured' *New York Times*

0 7472 5962 3

HEADLINE

Now you can buy any of these other bestselling Headline books from your bookshop or *direct from the publisher.*

FREE P&P AND UK DELIVERY
(Overseas and Ireland £3.50 per book)

A Place of Safety	Caroline Graham	£6.99
Running Scared	Ann Granger	£5.99
Shades of Murder	Ann Granger	£5.99
Biting the Moon	Martha Grimes	£5.99
The Lamorna Wink	Martha Grimes	£5.99
Tip Off	John Francome	£6.99
The Cat Who Robbed a Bank	Lilian Jackson Braun	£5.99
Screen Savers	Quintin Jardine	£5.99
Thursday Legends	Quintin Jardine	£5.99
A Chemical Prison	Barbara Nadel	£5.99
Stronger Than Death	Manda Scott	£5.99
Oxford Shift	Veronica Stallwood	£5.99
Fleeced	Georgina Wroe	£6.99

TO ORDER SIMPLY CALL THIS NUMBER

01235 400 414

or e-mail <u>orders@bookpoint.co.uk</u>

Prices and availability subject to change without notice.